About the

Michele Hauf, who also writes as Michele Renae, lives in Minneapolis and has been writing since the 1990s. A variety of genres keep her happily busy at the keyboard, including historical romance, paranormal romance, action/adventure and fantasy. Visit her Pinterest at toastfaery, Instagram at MicheleHauf, and her website at michelehauf.com. Email Michele at: toastfaery@gmail.com

Bewitched

May 2023
Seduced by the Enemy

June 2023
I Put a Spell on You

June 2023
A Hex Gone Wrong

Bewitched:

I Put a Spell on You

MICHELE HAUF

MILLS & BOON

First Published in Great Britain 2023
by Mills & Boon, an imprint of HarperCollins*Publishers* Ltd,
1 London Bridge Street, London, SE1 9GF

www.harpercollins.co.uk

HarperCollins*Publishers*
Macken House, 39/40 Mayor Street Upper,
Dublin 1, D01 C9W8, Ireland

ISBN: 978-0-263-31936-1

This book is produced from independently certified FSC™ paper to ensure responsible forest management.

For more information visit: www.harpercollins.co.uk/green

Printed and Bound in the UK using 100% Renewable Electricity at CPI Group (UK) Ltd, Croydon, CR0 4YY

AN AMERICAN WITCH IN PARIS

This one is for the witch in me. And it's for the witch in you. Honour your soul for what it has been, is now and will be. Namaste.

Chapter 1

Ethan Pierce stood before a steel-barred cage in the Acquisitions department's clean room. He was the director of the department, which was responsible for hunting, collecting and containing objects of magical nature, dangerous curses and talismans, even volatile creatures that may prove harmful to common humans if left unmonitored in the mortal realm. Ethan sent retrievers out on jobs that canvassed the world, and those adventuring professionals returned with the items.

This latest acquisition, brought in hours earlier by the retriever Bron Everhart, was needed to help locate an even more important item. For what Acquisitions ultimately sought was the blood demon Gazariel, who had stolen the code for the Final Days. If that code was to be activated, all the angels from Above would fall and smother the mortal realm with their smoldering wings. Literally. And the only way to find the demon was with the one thing in this world that wore its sigil.

"A witch," Ethan muttered as he paced before the cage.

Behind the steel bars, which were warded to keep in the subject, yet also wired with electricity to keep her docile and hamper any magic she should attempt to use in defense, stood the witch. She was a head shorter than Ethan, thin and dressed in clingy black leggings, fierce-looking black ankle boots with high heels and a silky black shirt that revealed a toned abdomen. Over it all she wore a heavy coat made of what looked like fake gray fur, which was studded with silver and black spangles. Her long white hair spilled forward, concealing one eye, and fell messily over one shoulder to her waist.

The other eye held him intently. It was a blue eye, the iris circled with black as if someone had drawn those eyes to be colored in. And on her eyelids, black shadow granted plenty Gothic melodrama. All together the look was...

Wicked, Ethan thought.

Hatred was too strong a word to apply to his feelings about witches as a species. Not all witches were evil or malicious. Yet he'd never completely get over his dislike for witches. They'd once held a murderous reign over his species, vampires, when their blood had been poisonous. One dip of the fang into a witch's vein could bring an ugly and permanent death. That was no longer. The Great Protection Spell, which had turned all witches' blood poisonous, had been broken decades earlier.

Rationally, Ethan knew not all witches were dangerous. And besides, it was the twenty-first century.

Things had changed. He worked with a few witches here at Acquisitions and the overseeing department, the Archives. For the most part, witches of the light were safe and trustworthy.

But the dark witches, such as the one standing in the cage before him? A shudder traced Ethan's spine.

The witch didn't move, only held his gaze, as if breaking it might arrest her breathing. And he wasn't about to look away. He must show her his dominance. In order to work with the witch to find the demon, she must be kept under control. Subdued. Yet her magic should remain accessible, which would keep the sigil she supposedly wore somewhere on her body open and ready to lure in the demon Gazariel.

Capturing this specific demon would prove a challenge. All perfunctory means of tracking him through Acquisitions' database had turned up nothing, though intel revealed that he was definitely in Paris.

Upon receiving orders to obtain the missing Final Days code—from a highly unprecedented command— Ethan had considered all the dozens of retrievers he had on staff. Who could do the job? Most were currently on assignment. None were stationed in Paris at the moment. But that wasn't the problem; any retriever was available and on call 24/7, able to move about worldwide.

The problem was that blood magic may be required to hold the demon once found. And the best one to deal with such magic? A vampire. Of which Ethan had been since his birth in the 1500s. Of course, he wasn't willing to give his own blood for this mission, but he didn't expect he would have to. He'd learned once that his blood could have a devastating effect on another being.

He never made the same mistake twice.

It had been decades, maybe even close to a century, since Ethan had gone out on a job. He'd become complacent, sitting behind a desk, clacking away at reports on the laptop and ordering others around. He loved his job. He did it well.

And yet, the call to adventure, to get out and actually participate in life again, was too strong to resist. He'd once stood alongside his fellow warrior vampires in the Blood Wars of the sixteenth century, defeating werewolves and slaying random witches who would deign to assist the nasty wolves. Then, he had been undefeatable, powerful and virile. He still was. The urge to exercise his soul beyond the paperwork and office politics was strong.

So Ethan had assigned this job to himself. His knowledge on the various demon breeds was minimal, yet he knew Paris, and more importantly, had the determination to root out the target. And he was the perfect partner for a witch. He wouldn't fall under her spell or forget for one moment who or what he was dealing with.

A dark witch who wore the demon Gazariel's mark.

The deflecting vibrations coming off the steel bars were strong, electronic in nature, but Tuesday didn't allow that to bother her. Yet. What was more disturbing was how she'd just been sitting in a bar, nursing a pink Panty Dropper cocktail, and then the world had gone black. And now she was standing in a cage.

Had someone roofied her? She always wore protective wards to deflect any silly human trick. And a clasp of the obsidian crystal that hung from a leather cord around her neck and above her breasts confirmed they hadn't removed her grounding and protective wards. That could only mean someone with power greater than hers—and was aware of who and what she was—had been able to drug her, kidnap her and cage her.

And while that realization was humiliating she had to remain calm and focused. She wasn't about to let the vampire see her sweat. *No weakness here, buddy.*

She knew the man was vampire because his red, ashy aura gave him away. Very few witches had the Sight— an ability to see vampire auras. Tuesday found it more of a nuisance. There were so many vampires walking the world. Sometimes the frequency of red glows in large, overcrowded cities annoyed her. Seriously. The biters were everywhere.

Not that there was anything wrong with vamps. Every once in a while, she didn't mind the occasional bite with a side of no-strings sex.

The vampire had been observing her for a few minutes. Hadn't said a word. He'd strode into the large, steel-walled, hexagon-shaped room, which only contained the cage and her, and had turned on the lights, which were blue LEDs along the floors and one blindingly white overhead spotlight.

He shoved his hands in the front pockets of his clean black jeans, which fit well, and were tucked into his combat boots. His shirtsleeves were rolled up to the elbows to display muscled forearms dusted with dark hair to match the slicked and cropped hair on his head. From under the shirt, a glimpse of a gray T-shirt hung over his pants. He looked to be strong, a force. And his carriage screamed of discipline, perhaps even military.

A smartly trimmed beard hugged his jaw and a neat mustache framed his solemn mouth. Sprinkled under his lower lip were gray strands amongst the dark brown. His face was expressionless, yet his gray eyes saw everything.

Her unprofessional assessment said that he looked world-weary. Like he'd been doing this far too long and needed a break. Although, what it was that he'd been doing, exactly, she had no clue.

"I'm Ethan Pierce," he finally said. His voice was deep and not unfriendly, and while he used English, he had a noticeable French accent. Tuesday had known a few Frenchmen in her lifetime. She'd visited France a couple times over the centuries.

"And you are Tuesday Knightsbridge," he stated.

He didn't score points for knowing her name. Unless kidnapping random witches was a thing nowadays.

Maintaining her stance, Tuesday held his gaze. But now he swept his eyes back and forth, and his hands slid out of his pockets to clasp before him. Classic villain hand-twist pose? Check, please!

"Do you know where you are?" he asked.

She wasn't ready to speak. Of course she knew where she was. She stood in a frigging cage.

"Not talking? I can deal with that. For now. You are in a holding cell at Acquisitions. We're a division of the Council's Archives."

The Council? That was a supposedly nonviolent ruling board that oversaw the actions of the world's paranormal nations, and was composed of various species to represent most. But they were watchers; they never interfered.

Guess that was a myth.

"In Paris," he said.

Paris? What the—? She'd been flown across the

ocean, from her current residence of Boston, Massachusetts, to France?

Anger rising, Tuesday lunged forward, gripping the steel bars. Vicious electricity zapped at her fingers, and she released them, taking the brunt of the shocking force through her body. She was violently tossed backward to land on her ass in the center of the cage. Legs splayed, she shook off a shiver. Her fur coat slipped down her shoulders to her wrists. She sucked in a gulp of air.

The man smirked. "By the way, those bars are activated."

Tuesday flicked up the sign of the Devil and growled, "Be taken to Beneath!"

"She speaks. And with a curse, of all things. I would expect nothing less from a dark witch. But the cage is warded. As is this clean room. No magic can get in or out. Nice try, though."

Oh, he wanted a curse? Utterly incensed, Tuesday spread out her fingers and focused a stream of magic at the man's crotch. *"Languidulus!"*

While normally invisible, once her magic hit the cage bars, a shot of violet light bounced off and splintered in dying pink embers onto the cage floor.

"What was that?" The vampire's smirk was annoyingly sexy. "Another curse? Did you try to give me a tail?"

Tuesday smiled nicely and tilted her head. "Actually, I cursed your dick to forever remain limp. And my magic is much stronger than you can imagine. I'd invest in Viagra, if I were you." She winked at him.

The slightest flinch moved the corner of one of his eyes. Bull's-eye. She could get under the man's skin. With mere words. This predicament was going to prove an easy escape. She just had to dig under his outer machismo to access the key.

But Paris? That meant she'd been out, at the very least, for eight or nine hours. And moved around according to this bastard's will. Not cool.

"What the hell is the benevolent Council doing sending someone to kidnap me?" she asked. Standing, her heels clicked on the cage floor. She shook out the alpaca fur coat she wore over black leggings and a comfy shirt. The coat was spangled in warding designs. A Tibetan monk had initially made it for her. A glitter sidhe-witch had sewn on the wards a few years ago. "And who the fuck is Ethan Pierce?"

"I'm the director of Acquisitions. We acquire things that need to be locked away. Behind chains and wards."

"And you think *I* need to be locked away?" She flipped him the bird. Yeah, so it wasn't a hex. Some common gestures were much more to the point.

"Actually, Acquisitions needs you to get to what we really want."

"Which is?"

"The blood demon Gazariel."

Tuesday's hand slapped across her chest, below the obsidian crystal. Though rarely spoken, the sound of that demon's name always provoked such an action. She could feel his sigil burn her skin under the silk shirt.

"We know you wear the demon's sigil," Ethan explained. "Got it in the seventeenth century, if our records are accurate. Will you show it to me?"

She wouldn't give him anything. Not until she heard what weird and strange plans he—they; Acquisitions?—had for her.

"The sigil is some kind of blood curse, yes?" He

paced a few steps to the side then turned back to her. "Doesn't matter how you got it. Or what it does. But I've been told, because of your connection to the demon, it makes you one of the darkest of the dark witches. I don't like dark witches, by the way."

"Would have never guessed. Your hosting skills are severely lacking. And I don't care what the hell you are, Pierce, I don't like you."

"I'm vampire."

"I knew that." She sneered. "A flesh pricker. Who is also a Richard."

"A... Richard?" The man narrowed his eyes and shrugged in question.

"Think about it a bit," she offered. He'd get it, sooner or later. "So you think you have the right to pluck any old witch off the streets and force her to do your bidding?"

"I wouldn't use the word *force*. But you are old, aren't you?"

His self-satisfied smirk did not rile her. Too much. Age was relative when a person had immortality; he should know that. She snapped the rubber band she wore about her wrist. The man would not like to see her dark magic in all its wicked glory.

"You have been brought to Paris to assist us in locating Gazariel."

The sigil she'd worn since the seventeenth century burned over her skin. "Quit saying that name," she insisted. "You only grant the demon more power with each utterance. Do you know that?"

Apparently he did not.

The man hung his head for a few seconds, then looked up at her. "I know my demon lore. Basically.

The saying a name three times thing generally only works with Himself. Demons are much more slippery when it comes to summoning them. Which is why you are here in Paris."

Paris! She could not believe this.

"Now, you'll serve to lure the demon to us—me, since I'm in charge of this mission—and then I will obtain from him what we seek to contain."

"The demon has something you want?"

He nodded. "It's dangerous to all. In the demon's hands, the world could be destroyed."

Tuesday scoffed. Always so dramatic with the end-of-the-world crap. It was never a small portion of the world, but the whole thing. What kind of villain would even think to destroy a world he would like to remain on to rule? The demon couldn't rule anything if he didn't have followers to bow down to him. End of the world, her ass.

But then she considered what she knew about Gaz-ariel. He was a trickster. His title was The Beautiful One. Because he was a pretty bit of charm and allure. Vain and self-serving, as well. And deadly. He liked to take advantage of a person when they were at their lowest, defeated. But most importantly, he was an ass-hole. And she didn't want to get any closer to him than she already was. Wearing his sigil did not make her his bitch—so long as she kept her distance from him.

"So let me get this straight." She walked up to the bars until the shock waves from the wards teased at her skin and lifted the hairs in her pores. Must have been warded by another dark witch with a tech edge. It messed with her personal vibrations, so she took a step back and, with a thought, pulled a white light over herself. All she could manage in this damnable cage was a weak veil, but it gave her some solace. "You want to dangle me before the demon as bait?"

The man tapped a finger against his jaw, then nodded. "Yes, that's about it."

She turned and paced in a half arc, hands to her hips, head down in thought. A glance to the man's face found him stoic, trying to show her he would not back down, no matter what. Tough guy, pushing around a helpless woman. Been there, done that. Never going to let it happen again.

If she should refuse him, he would force her. And enjoy it. Typical male.

But he didn't know Tuesday Knightsbridge at all. Helplessness was not a condition she had ever ascribed to. And that would give her the upper hand.

"Sounds like fun," she said cheerily. "Let's do it."

Chapter 2

Another man entered the clean room and Tuesday immediately felt familiar vibrations flow off of him. Another dark witch. He was tall and lean, and everything about him was black, from his long straight hair and thin mustache to his clothing. Spell tattoos covered his hands and exposed neck. A coil of thin rope was attached to his hip holster à la the Wild West. Weird. Also, he wasn't wearing shoes.

"You've got her in a cage?" he said to the vampire. "What the hell?"

"She's dangerous," Ethan said.

Yeah, and don't forget it, buddy. But Tuesday didn't say that.

Instead she crossed her arms and stood in the cage center, taking in her opponents. The dark one was on alert in his movements as he walked around the cage as if sizing up an animal. Shame threatened to rise up in her. She'd been made to feel like less than dirt many times before. Always by those who claimed witches were foul and evil things, and who would seek to allay their shortcomings and misguided beliefs by harming her. But that had been centuries ago.

Would this world never get a clue and drop the old, ingrained prejudices?

"This is Certainly Jones," Ethan said to her. "He's head of the Archives and our resident dark witch."

"Are you okay? Have you been treated well?" Certainly asked her. A touch of British accented his voice, and his tone felt calming.

"I've been kidnapped. Most likely drugged. I'm hungry. And I have to pee," she offered. "How's tricks with you?"

He stopped before the front of the cage and looked over his shoulder at the militant vampire. "You should feed her. And let her go to the bathroom."

"As soon as we've shackled her, she can do whatever she desires."

"Shackle?" Tuesday closed her eyes, fisting her fingers at her sides. "What the hell is going on?"

"We need you to work for us. You've agreed, saying it would be fun," Ethan said. "But in order to work alongside me you'll have to be out of this cage. And I can't risk you running off or using your magic against me. CJ here has a simple shackle spell that'll keep you subdued."

"You are a—" She lunged, aiming to grasp through the cage bars, but too late, she remembered it was electrified. The jolt sent her flying backward again to land on her back in a sprawl. "I hate you!"

"I don't need you to like me. I just need you to help me find Gazariel."

"Stop saying that bastard's name," she said from her position on the floor. Humiliated and utterly exhausted, she wasn't about to pull herself up until he gave her a good reason to do so.

"Saying the demon's name won't invoke him," Certainly said.

"I know that. I just hate his name. You think the two of us were friends? That's why I'm wearing his sigil?" Letting her head fall back, she flipped them both the bird from the floor.

"She's definitely going to be a handful," Certainly commented. "Open the cage and let me in. I've got this rope bespelled to shackle her."

The dark witch was coming inside with her? Well… she wasn't in the mood to fight him. And he thought to shackle her with a rope spell? That wasn't going to go as successfully for him as he expected. Tuesday decided to play along. Just for giggles.

The bars suddenly flickered with static and then Tuesday felt the electric energy shut off. The cage door swung open with a creak. She remained splayed on the floor as the dark witch stepped up into the cage and padded over and stood above her. The door closed and she heard the vampire twist the lock then tap in a digital code.

"I'm sorry about this," Certainly said. "I know you didn't ask for this, but sometimes things have to be done to ensure worse things don't happen."

"Now you're going to tell me not to blame you and that we can all get along, right? Peace, love and 'Kumbaya'? Get it done with, witch. I do need to use the facilities."

"Will you stand, please?"

Tuesday held up her hand and gestured for him to grab it to help her stand. As he did so, she felt his magic jolt against her own. He was strong, but not as powerful as her. But he was cute, and she had a plan, so she was going to let him off easy. Mostly. And hell, she wasn't sure she could even invoke her magic inside this crazy warded cage. But she wouldn't be Tuesday Knightsbridge if she didn't give it a go.

She slapped her palms to his temples and fixed her gaze onto his intense jade eyes. Before he knew to look away she fixed onto his soul. It was a witch's skill, to hold a soul fix on another witch. She felt his inner struggle, his need to close his eyes and lock her out. But she had been doing this far too long to allow anyone escape from her delving soul gaze.

The witch's soul was dark to the core. Less than two centuries old, he'd walked a free and defiant path. He was...connected closely to another. A twin? Yes, he had a twin brother for whom he held great love and respect. He'd once carried dozens of demons within him after a trip to Daemonia. Some of those demons had made him hurt himself. Others had taught him to care more deeply than he could have fathomed. And...the man loved deeply. Another witch, who was mother to his one-year-old twin sons.

That feeling, the emotion of unconditional love that flooded the man's system, pricked at Tuesday's willpower. She winced, fearing what may happen should she allow herself to linger in his eyes. To fall into the deep and devastating emotion of love.

Tuesday released the man and he stumbled backward, catching himself before he hit the bars.

"What did she do to you?" Ethan asked from outside the cage.

"I'm…fine," Certainly said, catching his hands on his knees and huffing. It took a lot out of a person to have his soul tapped. "She just…"

"I looked into his soul," Tuesday explained to Ethan. "I like this one. He's strong." She pointed at the vampire. "You. I do not like."

"We've already discussed our mutual lack of admiration for one another. *Like* isn't a requirement to work together. You going to be okay, CJ?"

The dark witch nodded. "Yep. Just gathering back my wits." He straightened and snapped the simple rope before him in warning. "You going to behave?"

Tuesday nodded. "I saw your wife. You love her very much."

"I would die for her," Certainly said with an ease that tugged at Tuesday's hardened heart. Because she believed that he would. What a lucky woman.

Romantics and silly sops would have a person believe love was the be-all and end-all. Whatever.

"Get on with it."

She held her hands before her, wrists together, waiting to be bound. The rope wouldn't impact her movement or physical health. It would keep her from performing any sort of magic, hex, spell or charm. But if the rope was damaged after the spell had been cast…

"On second thought," she said, "it'll work better if you drape it across my chest."

"Across your heart," Certainly said. "Good idea. And you will need the use of your hands." He lowered the lariat over her head and rested it on a shoulder, then draped it across her heart to fall between her breasts. "You're going to have to remove the crystal."

"I never take it off."

"The spell won't fix otherwise."

She shook her head and clasped the cool obsidian.

"Do you want to get out of here?" Certainly asked.

"Did they drug me?" she asked quietly. "Just tell me what they used to incapacitate me."

"I don't know for sure. Henbane, possibly?"

Tuesday nodded. Henbane, when mixed with a vile adjuvant, could take out a witch for the better part of a day. Damn it! Her wards should have caught that.

Certainly Jones could prove an ally if she played her cards right. But for now she must submit in order to gain freedom. She pulled the leather cord from around her neck and handed it to him. "That must be returned to me immediately."

"It will. You'll be able to wear it after I've cast the spell." He tucked the crystal in his front pocket, then jumped a little in reaction.

"It's not yours to possess," Tuesday warned. "It will come back to me quickly."

"I get that." He tapped the rope. "This will shackle your magic only against Ethan Pierce. You will still be able to wield magic in all other instances. It may be necessary to protect yourself against the demon."

"I appreciate that. What the hell is that guy?"

Certainly looked over a shoulder. Ethan paced, arms across his chest.

"Vampire."

"I know that. I mean, what's his deal? He's so...angry."

"Really? This coming from the angriest witch I've ever met?"

"You guys *did* kidnap me."

"Point taken. Don't give Pierce such a hard time. He generally works behind the desk telling others what to do. But I think this time it's personal."

"How so?"

Certainly shrugged. "Not sure. And even if I did have a clue? That's for him to give to you, not me. Close your eyes."

Tuesday did so because she was tired and wanted to get out of this stupid cage. Much as shackling her magic against anyone would piss her off, at the very least he wasn't completely disabling her.

The witch chanted a spell that caused the rope to suddenly squeeze about her. She felt the sigil beneath her shirt warm and reach out for the rope. It didn't like being controlled. Which was a good thing. And she counted on its retaliation.

In a matter of moments the witch said, "So mote it be."

And the rope fell slack again, as if an ill-hung necklace. Tuesday let out a breath. Her skin tingled, but otherwise, she didn't feel any different. In the next instant, the obsidian on the cord flew out from the witch's pocket and landed smartly in Tuesday's grasp.

The cage door opened and Ethan asked, "How will we know it worked?"

"It worked." CJ stepped out of the cage. "My magic always works." He winked at Tuesday. "I'm sorry, but the rope is the shackle. You'll have to figure out your own style for that." He turned to Ethan. "You going to take her upstairs for a bit, then…off to adventure?"

The men shared a look that was a few seconds too long for Tuesday not to wonder what had gone unspoken.

"Right," Ethan suddenly said. "I've got some things to finish up in the office. Come on, witch."

"Really? You're going to let your new pet out on a leash?" She flopped the lariat around before her. "Aren't you the kindest master ever."

"Good luck," CJ said and wandered out of the room.

"Get out of the cage, witch."

She stepped up to the threshold. "My name is Tuesday. Treat me well and I will return the kindness."

Ethan nodded. "Lead me to the demon and I'll be more than grateful."

"I'm not going to lead you anywhere without cold hard cash."

"What?"

"You think I'm going to do this for nothing? Slavery went out last century. If you want me to cooperate we need to talk money." She jumped down onto the concrete floor, blessedly relieved to have left the smothering confines of that magic-busting cage. With a shiver and a flip of her hair over her shoulder, she walked up to the man.

He stood a head higher than her, but she was accustomed to looking up to people, mostly men. Her stance spoke louder than her lacking height.

"How much do you want?" he asked, surprising her that he hadn't argued.

"A million. US dollars, not your freaky French euros."

He broke out into throaty laughter that, in any other circumstance, might have grasped her by the lusting heart and teased her to flutter her lashes at him. But this was not any other time. With a flick of her forefinger, Tuesday tossed a beam of pain at the vampire.

The magic burst into a spray of violet sparks just inches from his face and dispersed.

Damn shackle.

"Good to see CJ's spell works," he said. "Tough luck, witch. I'm impervious to your magic now."

Only so long as the shackle stayed in place. And her sigil was so hot that it could burn through pretty much anything right now...

"Half a million then," she said.

"Ten grand."

Tuesday spun and jumped up into the cage opening. "I think I'll stay here then. Apparently, I'm the only one who can do what you need done. I'm worth more than a few bucks. You think about it, then get back to me."

"I've got a budget, witch."

"And I've got all the time in the world. Do you?"

He rubbed his stubble-shadowed jaw. Tuesday rather liked it when a man tickled his stubble over her skin, as his gaze journeyed down her stomach and lower. And his beard was frosted with a touch of grey in the dark brown, which added a delicious seasoning to his appearance. If the man wasn't so obstinate he'd actually be sexy.

"A hundred thousand," he offered. "That's as high as I can go."

"Deal." Tuesday jumped down again and marched past him toward the door. She would have taken the ten grand. "Let's get out of this dungeon. Did you forget I need to pee?"

The witch had gone into the private bathroom attached to the office Ethan occupied in headquarters. There were no windows in the small washroom for her to escape through, so he trusted her to shut the door.

Meanwhile, he checked his email. No new orders waiting for retrieval assignment. And he'd sent details regarding his taking this particular mission to the Council. No reply, so far, was good news.

He glanced to the maple-wood bathroom door. He and CJ had only planned things so far. And that plan hadn't quite come to complete fruition. It would, soon enough. He wasn't sure how he was going to work with the witch.

She was obstinate. A smart-ass. And he hadn't expected her to be gorgeous. Utterly beautiful. In a weird, silver Goth sort of way. Behind her defensive, smart mouth and angry rubber band-snapping machinations he felt sure a sensual goddess inhabited the irresistible curves and gemstone blue eyes.

He raked fingers through his hair and shook his head. What was he thinking? He needed to do this right. He was the boss. And he wasn't about to show weakness or failure to his employees by letting his thoughts stray from the task at hand.

He'd handle the witch with a strong hand and command. He had to stay on guard with her. To set an example for others. But it would prove a challenge, not only because of her odd appeal, but also because it had been so long since he'd actually worked a mission. If she learned that he was questioning his own abilities—and thus had taken the job to prove he wasn't washed up and was physically capable of handling such a mission—he'd never succeed.

They headed out, Tuesday following Ethan's sure gait. It was a confident walk. A sexy walk. After many turns and an elevator ride down four floors, the sight of a door up ahead gave her great glee. Soon.

She pressed her hand over the shackle rope, which she'd been holding snug against the sigil. The rope fibers were hot and smoldering. It was working.

"I don't live far from here. We'll walk," Ethan said.

He'd mentioned they would discuss a plan for capturing the demon. Why they didn't simply do it in his office was beyond her, but she appreciated the opportunity to get out of the building. And away.

He opened a heavy steel door. Bright daylight filtered in, making Tuesday blink. She had lost all concept of time, and even though her muscles were dragging her downward from exhaustion, the crisp winter air, inhaled deeply, worked to lighten her. And keep her focused. Tugging her coat closed, but keeping one hand inside on the shackling rope, she followed the vampire outside.

They exited into a narrow, cobblestone alleyway. Ethan turned left.

Tuesday turned right and started to run. She made it ten feet, pulling away the rope that had burned apart thanks to the demon sigil, and dropped it behind her. But as her speed increased and she began to pump her arms, her body collided with an invisible wall, slamming her backward to land in the arms of Ethan Pierce.

"I expected as much," he said. A flash of his bright smile did not give her any mirth. "So did CJ. The rope was merely a distraction until CJ had time to work up a stronger spell."

"Bastard," she muttered, and collapsed in his arms.

Chapter 3

The steel door through which they'd exited opened and the dark witch swung out with urgency. He lifted his hand, exposing the glowing spell tattoos that covered his palm. As he approached, he asked Ethan, "You sure about this, man?"

"Nope. But someone's got to do it. So do your darkest."

"Oh, no." Not knowing what was coming, but not stupid, either, Tuesday struggled out of Ethan's grasp.

The vampire stretched back an arm toward his approaching cohort while he managed to hold her by the coat with his other hand. She wasn't going to let whatever might happen…happen.

She began to speak a deflection spell, but a slash of Certainly's hand caused Tuesday's words to suddenly jumble and drop in the air. He'd deflected her deflection. He was stronger than she'd anticipated.

With his full body, the vampire crushed her against the brick wall. She kicked, unwilling to be contained. Suddenly, she smelled blood. What the—? The dark witch grabbed her wrist and an icy pain seared the center of her palm. A coppery scent filled the air. He was invoking blood magic?

"No!"

Kicking, Tuesday hit Ethan's gut, but the vampire lunged forward and slapped his hand into hers. Heat from his blood mingled with hers. The dark witch held their hands together and recited a simple incantation that she recognized as a binder.

Tuesday growled, but the exhaustion from what she'd been through since sitting in the bar—back in the United States—had depleted her magic. The blood spell coursed through her system, and she felt it bite at her neck from the inside. Certainly Jones's dark and masterful magic bound her to the vampire. They would not be able to leave one another's side, nor would they be able to harm one another.

"This is the only blood you'll ever get from me," the vampire said on a low, accusing tone.

With a shout for survival, Tuesday pushed away from her captor with a shove of her free hand to his chest. The dark witch stepped away, allowing her to stumble against the wall. She caught her hands flat on the rough brick behind her, cursed, then watched as the knife wound sealed in a glow of violet on her palm.

"Had to be done," Certainly commented.

"How close do we have to stay to one another now?" Ethan asked, as if he'd only been given a simple handshake.

"Not sure. Try it out."

"Try running off," Ethan said to her. "See how far you get."

"Try fucking yourself, vampire."

"Like I said, she's going to be a challenge," Certainly said.

"Challenge accepted. I'll start walking home," Ethan said. "We'll see how far I get before you have no choice but to follow." He slapped a hand into the dark witch's. "Thanks, CJ."

Ethan strolled off down the alley. And Tuesday tugged her coat up and adjusted her hair. She pointed an accusing finger at Certainly. "You, Jones, are on my shit list."

He shrugged. "I honor your power, Tuesday Knightsbridge. You are an old and strong witch. But I can feel your darkness is even greater than mine."

"Yeah? Warlock's looking pretty good right about now." If she grievously harmed another witch the warlock title would be slapped on her. "That would really put you in your place."

"As well, it would put you in a place you don't want to stand. Don't let it overwhelm you, Tuesday. Remember what you once were."

Really? The man was trying the New Age-y bullshit on her? "You know nothing about me."

"No, but I saw into your soul when you were looking into mine." He bowed his head toward her. "I am sorry for the things you have suffered because of what we are."

Yeah, so witches had been a favorite cat's-paw over the centuries. She'd survived, and she would continue to so do thanks to her hardened heart.

Suddenly, Tuesday's body jerked forward. Certainly stepped aside and they both looked down the alley. Ethan stood about fifty yards off. He gave them a thumbs-up.

And when he started walking again, Tuesday was pulled after him.

"Shit list!" she called back to Certainly, who had the decency to place his palms together and bow to her in reverence.

Ethan chuckled to himself as the witch reluctantly followed him down the street to his place in the eleventh arrondissement. He lived in a third-floor loft close to Père Lachaise cemetery, which boasted an excellent view of Sacré Coeur up on the hill.

He left the front door open behind him, not feeling the need to wait on the witch. She'd stand back just to piss him off, surely. He tossed his keys onto the gray granite kitchen counter and kicked off his shoes, then wandered through the living area. With a few words to the electronic house butler—"Stuart, modify for sun"— the electrochromic shades fixed between the double windowpanes that looked out over the city adjusted to a soft white that would allow in light but not the UV rays that gave him the most caution.

The layout of the loft was open—no walls, save the ones enclosing the bathroom. Strolling through the living room, around a corner and through the bedroom, he went into the bathroom but left the door open behind him. "Stuart, warm water." Ethan splashed water on his face, then manually twisted off the faucet and took a few deep breaths.

He opened his palm. The cut CJ had given him had already healed. Sharing blood with the witch hadn't been as horrible as he'd expected. Remnants of fear over the once-poisonous witch blood remained. He'd have to get over it. And fast. If the demon was a blood demon, surely much blood would be spilled in the coming days. The witch's. And the demon's. Ethan wasn't willing to give any more than the few drops he'd provided today.

He liked blood. As sustenance. But he never drank witch's blood, even since the Great Protection Spell had been broken. It couldn't harm him now. And there were even some vampires who liked drinking from witches. If you added in sex and a specific spell for bloodsex-magic, the vampire could steal some of that witch's magic for himself.

He had no desire to own magic. But to taste the witch's blood? He couldn't shake the scent of her blood as it had trickled into the air in the alley outside head-quarters. It had roused him so much in that moment that he'd used violence and had shoved her roughly to hide his burgeoning desires. He hoped she wouldn't bleed near him again.

That would prove a challenge.

"Honey, I'm home!"

He shook his head, but no reflection in the mirror showed his exasperation. CJ had warned she would be a struggle. But that was a challenge he welcomed. Now, to work with the witch.

Tuesday had shucked off her coat and now reclined on the leather sofa that sat against a rough brick wall. She'd kicked off her shoes and waggled her bare toes—the nails were painted bright blue—as she stretched out her arms and yawned. The black shirt had a but-ton below her breasts and was open from there down, revealing abs. And much more skin than he wanted to notice right now.

"Tired?" he asked.

"Unlike vampires, we witches do need a little shut-eye now and then. And after all the torments I've endured?"

"Why don't you take twenty minutes to rest? Stuart, close the shades completely."

As the windows darkened, Tuesday sat up and glanced over a shoulder. "Who the hell is Stuart? A house brownie?"

Ethan chuckled. "A bit similar. That's the name of the electronic house butler. This place is high-tech. If you need something, Stuart can usually get it."

"Stuart, book me a flight back to Boston, STAT," Tuesday said.

As the butler began to confirm, Ethan canceled that request. "And ignore all requests from any voice but my own," he ordered.

"Of course," Stuart replied.

"That's creepy." Tuesday lay back down and crossed her arms over her chest. "And so not fair."

"While you rest I'm going to make a few calls. Plan our first move."

"You don't have a plan?"

"Of course I do," he lied. Sitting before the kitchen counter with his back to her, he pushed aside her spangled coat. A pad of paper and a pen waited near the phone. He was all about the high-tech, but he'd never give up the landline. "You want a blanket or something?"

"Fuck you, Richard." And she turned over on the sofa and snuggled up in a ball.

Again with the Richard? He thought about it a few seconds. Ah. Richard shortened was… All righty then. He shouldn't expect her to think very highly of him after having one of his retrievers kidnap her and fly her across the ocean. And then forcibly bind her to him.

He may have to find a means to cozy up to her in order to get her to trust him or he'd never get anywhere with her. At the very least, he needed her to want to trust him.

Pulling out his cell phone, he scrolled through the contacts. He knew the person he had to speak to first to learn anything about any demon in Paris.

Edamite Thrash was a sort of demon overlord with a penchant for niceness. But Ethan didn't tell anyone that, or Thrash would scratch you with the poison thorns that grew from his knuckles. The man was a corax demon, which meant he could shift into an unkindness of ravens and take to the skies. He also made it his job to oversee the demons of Paris, knowing who was where, and when and why. He kept a loose rein on his species, and enforced punishment only when one of them threatened to expose their kind with their foolish actions.

Ethan knew most of the major players in the paranormal realm who inhabited Paris. That was his job, to know whom he could trust and with whom he had best watch his back. Ed was trustworthy.

The dark feather tattoo on Ed's neck always drew Ethan's eye. He wore many sigils tattooed on his skin, and combined with his standard dark business suit and smartly parted and slicked black hair, he looked dangerous yet disturbingly *GQ* stylish.

He shook the man's hand, noting he always wore

black leather half gloves that exposed his fingers. He needed only cover the thorns on his knuckles to prevent an accident.

"Good to see you, man." Ed nodded over Ethan's shoulder. "Who is this pretty?"

Tuesday, who had followed Ethan into the building at a distance, was acting petulant, yet she strolled forward and offered her hand to shake. "Tuesday Knightsbridge."

Ed clasped her hand. "The witch. I've heard about you."

"You have? From who?"

"My girlfriend, Tamatha Bellerose."

"Bellerose? Oh, yes, her mother is Petrina. I know that witch." And the quickness with which Tuesday pulled her hand from the demon's clasp clued Ethan she probably didn't have a good relationship with the family. "Just in Paris for a visit," she added. "Forced, as it is."

Ed looked to Ethan for explanation.

"Tuesday is helping me to locate a demon. That's why I wanted to check in with you. See if you've any information that may lead us to him."

Ed leaned against the desk behind him and crossed his arms over his chest. "Which demon?"

"The Beautiful One," Tuesday said before Ethan could say the name.

"Ah. Gazariel." Ed winced and rubbed his jaw. "I do know he's in town. But haven't a clue where. He hasn't been making much noise so he's not on my give-a-fuck radar. Why is she helping? You only require a witch when you need to summon a demon from Beneath or Daemonia."

"I'm bait," Tuesday said, tossing out the words at the same time Ethan said, "She's my lure for the demon."

"You two don't get along very well, do you?"

Ethan kept an eye on Tuesday as she walked about the demon's office, looked over the marble conference table and then wandered to the wall where various artifacts were displayed on small individual shelves.

"We had to take her away from her home to get her to work with us," Ethan offered.

"Kidnapped me," Tuesday called over her shoulder as she peered into a glass container that likely held faery dust. The contents sparkled in all colors from the afternoon sun beaming in through the windows.

"Sounds on par for Acquisitions," Ed said. "So, a lure, eh? Why would Gazariel be interested in that witch?"

"She wears his sigil. Or that is the information we have."

Ed stood and now he gave Tuesday his full attention. She turned from her curious seeking and splayed her hands. "Yep, I'm the demon's bitch. I carry his curse. And Einstein here thinks that'll draw him to me. Idiot."

"He'll come to you. We just have to get you close enough he puts up his head and notices," Ethan said. "Give him a sniff of the witch's scent."

"He's not going to be attracted to the one who wears his curse," Ed said. "Why would he? I know a bit about The Beautiful One. He put an unwanted curse in her many centuries ago when he had the opportunity. And now he's done with it. I'm not sure of the nature of the curse, but if the demon wants it gone from him, there's not a thing in this world that would incline him to set one foot near her now. She's useless."

"Hey! I can hear you," Tuesday called. The blue glass sphere she had touched wobbled and rolled off the shelf.

She caught it just before it hit the floor. "Oops. Good save, though, yeah?"

"Don't touch the breakables," Ethan said, chastising the overly curious witch. And to Ed he said, "Are you serious? But we need her to open that curse and hold Gazariel so he will submit."

"Why do you need him to submit?"

"He's got something that Acquisitions wants."

Ed lifted an eyebrow.

"It's a book of angel names and sigils. A muse wrote it. It holds the code for the Final Days."

"Is that thing back in circulation? I thought the angel Raphael had taken it underwing, so to speak?"

"It made a series of exchanges before Raphael secured it from a vampire intent on populating the world with nephilim. Let's just say it's been in so many hands, even the Archives' records are confused as to where it was last seen before landing in the demon's hands. But I have good intel that The Beautiful One currently has it."

"Doesn't sound like a party."

"It's not. The list of angel names, when ordered correctly, holds an ancient coded word, or words, that when spoken, will send all angels plummeting to earth to smother mankind with their multitudes. Their wings will burn human flesh, young and old. Paranormals are not exempt, either. The earth will become an ashy cemetery of the mortal, the paranormal and the divine."

"Whew!" Ed ran a gloved hand through his slick hair. "That's something you want to stop. But your challenge will be getting the demon to come to you, *without* knowing you've got the witch, and then surprising him with her at just the right moment."

Ethan's temples had begun to pulse. He hadn't expected this particular complication. If he would have known before the demon didn't want anything to do with the witch, he wouldn't have bound himself to her until after they'd secured Gazariel. Of course, he needed Tuesday to bring the demon to him. This was a mess. Had she known as much?

Her self-satisfied grin answered that one for him.

"Keep her out of sight until you need her," Ed suggested.

"Too late. I bound myself to her to keep her close and protect myself from any retaliatory magic."

"Then you've got a problem, Pierce."

No need to state that one out loud. Tuesday's soft tsking sounds riled him and Ethan fisted his hands. Yet when he saw her smile beam at sight of his anger, he relented the knuckle-whitening clutch. The witch would not get under his skin. He was smarter than this. And he didn't need to snap a rubber band to remind him of that.

He turned to Ed. "Can you help by telling me where Gazariel might be?"

"I haven't a clue."

"But you keep tabs on all the demons—how can you know he's in the city and not have a location on him?"

"It's a feeling, Pierce, not an exact science or even a map. Believe me, I would help you if I could. The Beautiful One is from Beneath, so you might start at l'Enfer."

The Devil Himself's nightclub. It was frequented by demons, vamps, werewolves and most any sort looking for dark and devious indulgences. Just the place Ethan wanted to visit. Not.

"Hey, how much you want for this?" Tuesday waggled a pearlescent alicorn she'd found on a shelf.

Ed shrugged. "You can take it."

"What? Are you serious?" The witch actually tittered with glee. "You do know how valuable this is?"

"It's…" Ed winced. "I should have never obtained that thing. It was taken from innocence. It's not something I have a right to own. I've been meaning to get rid of it for a while now. You'd be doing me a favor by taking it."

"Nice!" Tuesday stabbed the air with the thing. "I can so use this."

Ethan could but shake his head and wish the day would get better.

"I guess you'll be clubbing then?" Ed offered as he extended his hand to shake.

"Sounds like it." Ethan thanked the man and started out of the room, knowing Tuesday would have to follow. Sooner or later.

As he got on the elevator, the witch entered, twirling the alicorn gaily. "I got a prize," she teased.

"What the hell can you do with that thing?"

"You'll find out soon enough. By the way, I'm going to need some magical supplies. You whisked me away from home and cauldron. I need certain items to work magic, put up wards and generally survive."

"Like what?"

She shrugged and tapped the alicorn against her jaw. "This is a start. There's got to be magic shops in the city. And you'll have to pay, sweetie, since my kidnapper decided against bringing along my purse. And I'll be needing some clothes as well. Can't go clubbing looking like this, can I?"

"You like fine. All black and perfectly witchy? You'll fit right in at l'Enfer." Ethan checked his watch. It was around six in the evening. A few more hours before the club opened.

"Can a chick get pizza in this town?"

Rolling his eyes, he strolled out as the elevator doors opened. The witch had no taste whatsoever.

Chapter 4

At the plain black metal doors to the club l'Enfer, they stopped before the bouncer with red eyes. A sign over his high left shoulder stated, in Latin, what basically translated as "no funny stuff" and "you take your own chances entering." Tuesday boldly met the bouncer's gaze and focused her intent toward him. The demon looked down, chastised by her audacity. Served him right. He was young and needed to learn to show respect for his elders.

Blowing him a kiss laced with pizza sauce and some kind of cheese that had not been mozzarella—the French really liked their weird cheeses—she then glided down the dark hallway. The music thudded in her heart and veins. Not worrying whether Ethan gained access, she picked up the beat and danced as she walked.

She sensed the brooding vampire was behind her, and

felt his hand go to her hip, as if to guide her through the darkness, but he quickly removed it. Tuesday smiled. Had he forgotten himself for a moment? Thought of her as an actual desirable female he might get close to? She could work with that.

Much as she had developed a liking for clubbing over the last several decades, Tuesday preferred less crowded venues, and with more upbeat tunes. L'Enfer had not invested any expense in color. Everything was black, with hematite and silver metallic bits and trim here and there. The lighting was red, and flashed across the inhabitants and dancers, who also wore mostly black.

Tuesday was dressed for the part, right down to her matte black nail polish and eye shadow. Yet she felt naked without some lip gloss; a deep violet would be perfect for this Gothic milieu. As it was, she felt virtually exposed without any magical accoutrements to hand, and bound to a freaking vampire. Yet she wasn't powerless. Her simple mastery over the bouncer had proven that. And she did have the alicorn stuck in her waistband. She felt it tremble. This was not a place for such a thing. The demon hadn't wanted to possess innocence? Interesting.

She wouldn't test the alicorn's power here. The place was owned by the Devil Himself, and the sign on the door had clearly stated no funny stuff. The bouncer should have frisked her for weapons. Idiot.

On the other hand, a place like this probably thrived on the illicit use of weapons and how much damage could be done before a person was kicked out. If that would even happen. Again, the sign mentioned taking one's own chances.

"You see him?" Ethan shouted next to her ear.

Tuesday leaned away from him. "I can hear well enough over the noise, vampire. And I just got here. Let me look around, will you? You want to dance?"

"I'm not a dancer. And I'm on a job."

"Right, all work and no play. Should I call you Jack?"

"Just keep your mind on business."

"Can I at least have a drink? We should try to blend in. Look like we're here to party and not jack up some asshole demon, yeah?"

Ethan sighed then reluctantly nodded. "What do you want?"

"Anything that doesn't contain a live entity. I suspect that's on the menu here. And I prefer vodka."

"Live entities," he muttered. With a frown, he headed toward the long, black quartz bar that was edged with a cut-in of red crystals that seemed to glow like LEDs.

Tuesday allowed her body to inhale the beat. Despite the fact this club was owned by the rather dour Dark Prince, the music wasn't too terribly dirge-like. The Goth singer with a string of spikes embedded down the sides of each bare arm sang about his friends being heathens and suggested she should take it slow. All righty, then.

Tuesday swayed to the beat as a crimson-haired faery with violet eyes matched her with a smile and a shimmy. If she was going to be forced to work for some rogue organization to capture a pompous, yet also vicious demon she had no wish to ever see again, at the very least, she could enjoy herself. Lifting her arms, she spun onto the dance floor.

Below her, the Plexiglas floor flashed red and black and then segued into flames. It was a realistic effect, and she almost fancied to feel the heat. A brush of fur tickled her right hand, and with a spin she eyed the tattooed back of a thin person who moved a little too jerkily not to be demon.

A guitar solo screamed and coaxed the crowd to pump their fists and jump in a pounding stomp of fraternity to whatever dark gods were the current rage. Tuesday preferred Loki. The one portrayed in the movies by the handsome dark-haired actor, most specifically. As she spun, arms swaying above her head and hips shifting, she spied Ethan standing at the edge of the dance floor, holding a red glowing drink. His grim look spoke much louder than the music.

"Spoilsport." She wandered over and took the drink, then tilted back a healthy swallow. Instead of the expected burn, she felt a distinct icy grab at the back of her throat, which then melted into a blaze of heat down her esophagus. And it tasted of cinnamon and chocolate. "Whew! That is some good stuff."

"I thought it would be the drink for you. It's called The Devil's Bitch."

"Oh, Ethan, you can hate me all you need to." She fluttered her lashes at him. "I'm not going to crack under all that loathing. You know your emotions only reflect back onto you? Also makes it easy for a witch to use against you. That is, if the witch could drop some magic on your vampire ass. Ditch the frowny face and let's agree to disagree, and then get on with things, shall we?"

"So you've decided to stop pouting and work with me?"

Yeah, she was being as much of a problem child as he was. And if she didn't get to work now, she'd never be free of the man and his brooding grey eyes. And could his teeth be any whiter? She wanted to see his fangs.

To touch them and feel them pierce her neck…but no. She would not bone up this task by falling all puppy-eyed over the vamp. She was better than that. Because she had no choice.

"We're partners." She held out a hand and he shook it, holding it for a few seconds longer than was proper. She could feel his heartbeats in that hold, and they were sure and confident. Powerful. And, yes, controlling. The man would not relent. "Good then. I'll take a look around. You probably wouldn't recognize the demon if he was choking you, so you just…"

His eyes took in their surroundings. He put off a very militant, I'm-ready vibe. "I'll stay close to you."

"Sure, keep close. I'll protect the big bad vampire from a suggestive side glance or a dance-off. Ha!"

She strolled off into the clove-scented shadows that edged the dance floor, knowing the man would follow. It wasn't as if she could get any farther away from him than fifty yards. Nothing like having a puppy dog on her tail. Of course, she liked puppies. Had once owned one, until the local troll had stolen it and— She tried never to imagine what had become of her sweet Nugget after that. Long time ago. Always avoid trolls, had been the lesson.

Noting every face she passed, Tuesday pulled on her Sherlock cloak. It was easy to tell the demons, as their eyes were generally red, although some demon-possessed humans' eyes gave off a dull blue glow. Most natural demons who did not require a human meat suit could disguise their irises, but when out at the club they apparently let their freak flags fly. Red irises everywhere!

Thinking of freaks…

She strolled toward a tall sliver of a demon who looked like a walking skeleton, yet he wore thin, clear muscle over those bones. A wraith? They were usually dangerous and she was surprised one would put himself in a social situation. But when the creature turned to cast her a violet gaze she realized it was faery. And faeries could be even more vicious than demons.

Propping her palm over the alicorn at her waist, Tuesday detoured from her approach, wisely dismissing the oddity. With a flick of her fingers she could reduce them all to gibbering sycophants. But she would not because she didn't want to call attention to herself.

Finishing off the drink, which still cooled then burned, she set the empty goblet on a table and eyed the flashing red-and-silver staircase leading up to the balcony. She skipped up the steps, edging past a couple who made out carefully, for the woman's spiked bra looked quite deadly. Blood tinted the air. Hmm… Perhaps the bra served the exact purpose its wearer desired.

Tuesday glanced back to see Ethan following and noticed his expression when he neared the couple. He winced and shook his head. The man was discerning. Points for him.

Stepping up into the dark and smoky balcony, Tuesday was immediately surrounded by three tall men, all of them demons. The one before her flashed a silver-toothed grin, punctuated by curved fangs, and his nostrils flared and put out little wisps of black smoke. It wasn't cigarettes or weed producing the smoke, but rather the thickness of demons here above the crowd. "A tasty witch has dared to broach our private balcony?"

"I wasn't aware it was private." She lifted her hand, prepared to repel the demon, when suddenly Ethan gripped her wrist and eased himself around to stand before her.

"She didn't know, gentlemen," he offered. "Demons only up here?"

"You got it, vampire. But if she wants to stay—" Silver Tooth let his gaze creep over Tuesday's skin "—we want to play."

"Oh, yeah?" Tuesday reached around Ethan with her free hand and he turned to clasp both her wrists. "Don't restrain me before them," she said. "I can stand up for myself."

"Hear that, vampire? She can take care of herself. Why don't you leave the tasty little witch to us?"

Now Tuesday did feel a shiver of caution, and the touch of someone's fingers from behind, sliding across her ass, made her jump. Right against Ethan's arm, which slid across her shoulder and directed her back toward the stairs.

"We're leaving," he said more to her than the randy demons. "But before we do…" He cocked a look over his shoulder at the silver-toothed leader. "Any of you familiar with Gazariel?"

"He means The Beautiful One," Tuesday quickly amended. It was not cool to call demons by their names, especially around others.

"Get that witch out of here," Silver Tooth said.

"But the demon I'm looking for—" Ethan began.

"No pretty demons in this club, vampire. And if you don't take your pet witch and leave we'll make sure no one ever calls her pretty, either."

Ethan clasped Tuesday's hand and led her down the stairs. The couple was still making out. Blood beaded in various spots on the man's chest and neck. Ethan quickened their pace.

When they landed on the main floor, he directed her toward a wall, where a private moment could be found behind it, as it was set off from the frenzy of dancers.

"I had no idea that was a demons-only area," she said. "But you don't score points for rescuing me. I was fine."

"I know that. But no funny stuff, remember? And I like to take care of my assets. Make sure they survive the length of the job."

"I'm an asset to you? I don't know if that's a good or a bad thing. I'm guessing not especially good."

"You are valuable. What's so bad about that?"

"My value, as determined by what I can do for you, is a very bad thing. Any man who tries to put a—" she made air quotes "—'value' on a woman is not a man at all."

Feminism was her right, and she would never stop to point out the patriarchy's misguided beliefs and lacking empathy for those who were their equals. She strode off toward the front hallway, where they had entered. "He's not here. Let's blow this joint."

Once outside on the street, she walked swiftly away from the nondescript doors, but abruptly hit an invisible wall and couldn't press onward. Curse that vampire! She cast a glance over her shoulder. Ethan stood a good distance away, unmoving, giving her a sly wave.

"Such a Richard," she muttered. "Well? What are you waiting for?"

"I'm going this way." He pointed over his shoulder, then turned and walked off.

And the pull of the binding dragged Tuesday along after him.

* * *

"It was a stupid thing to do anyway," Tuesday muttered as she followed Ethan down the quiet, dark Parisian street toward wherever he was headed. She hadn't a choice in the matter. "Going to that club? Why would The Beautiful One hang out at that depressing place? Do you even know who you're after? That demon likes to shine. To see and be seen. He's vain and all about pleasure and self-gratification. He thrives on attention. Adoration. Love. He's not for darkness and murk. That's why he pawned off his curse on me."

Ethan cast a glance over his shoulder at her, then resumed his pace.

"What kind of sorry adventuring detective vampire are you?" she called. "Don't you know how to do this stuff? I mean, let's go to the least likely place the dude is going to be and feed the witch to the demons, why don't we?"

She smirked to think about getting hit on by those nasty demons. The one with the silver teeth had to have doused himself in body spray for the young and bepimpled. Ugh. And then Ethan had felt the need to intervene. Like some kind of rescuing hero? She could have taken care of herself. But how often did a man step in to try and help her? So rarely, she couldn't think back that far.

"I'm hungry!" she announced in frustration. "That pizza was terrible. Who sells pizza slices out of a freezer? That's like 7-Eleven stuff. So wrong. I thought Paris was classier? Let's get something to eat. Do you have to walk so fast? It's not as if we're going to find the demon now. I'd guess he's more of a day kind of demon. All the better to allow others to admire his beaming gorgeousness. Are you even listening to me, Pierce? Bueller?"

With that, the vampire swung round, marched up to her, bracketed her face with his hands and…

…kissed her.

For no reason. And with no grace. He planted a firm, seconds-long kiss on her mouth. And for those few seconds Tuesday's heart thundered and a tickle-thrill shimmied up the back of her neck. She didn't mind the kiss. In fact, it proved a scintillating connection. The vibrations between them shivered haphazardly, but then quickly started to harmonize. To actually blend—as if they were meant to come together. How weird was that?

But the kiss ended as quickly as it had landed on her mouth. And she hadn't time to determine why it had felt so right.

Ethan stepped back, hands splaying outward. With a sexy wink, he then said, "I knew that would work."

Tuesday touched her lips, stunned that he'd taken her by surprise, but even more stunned that she wasn't upset about the attack kiss.

"I figured a kiss would get you to shut up," he said. Turning, he marched onward.

Really? He'd employed the kiss to make her stop talking? Of all the nerve! She was not one of his victims he could subdue with persuasion or a plunge of fang into vein. And so what if she had been talking? It wasn't as if he'd shown an eagerness to converse with her. She was alone in a strange, foreign city, being led around by a bossy vampire who held her captive with a magical bond. Damn right she was going to chatter away nervously when the mood struck!

On the other hand, she wasn't about to let some cocky vampire feel he had gotten the upper hand with her.

Tuesday raced up behind Ethan. "You want to use kisses as weapons?" She shoved him and he spun to face her with a questioning gape. "One thing you need to know about me—I'm always cocked and loaded."

Grabbing his coat lapel, she pulled him in and planted a kiss on his mouth. This one was as unwarranted and desperately seeking as his had been. The man stumbled backward and his shoulders hit a brick wall, and it gave her the opportunity to move in and deepen the kiss.

His hand caught at the base of her spine under her coat, and he pressed her closer to his hard abs and hugged hip-to-hip. And Tuesday forgot that she was angry and let the lust and want rise and play out.

The man's mouth was incredible. His lips were warm and firm, and when their tongues danced she couldn't imagine doing such a tango with anyone else. And she had tangoed with many in her lifetime. Cinnamon mingled with his clean taste, brewing a cocktail more heady than any weird concoction served in a demonic dance club.

But she was kissing him to make a point. And she'd hate to let him think she actually *wanted* this kiss. She did not. Mostly. Yes, she did!

But that was not how she intended to play her hand.

Shoving away from him, Tuesday swept her hair over her shoulder and assumed a cocky stance. "I won that one, vampire."

If a smirk could get any sexier, she didn't know. A few fine wrinkles creased the corners of his eyes, and she even noticed glints of gray strands silvering the hair at his temples. So sexy. Urm, in a completely uninteresting way, of course.

"Sounds fine by me," Ethan said. "You can have the win, partner."

"Right. Partner." She wrinkled her nose at that one. She *had* suggested they could be partners, hadn't she? "About that food?"

"Just up the street, there's a cheesy little bar that might still be open. It's owned by a couple of expats. They serve American food."

Intrigued beyond what she wanted to convey, Tuesday muttered, "Lead the way."

An hour later, Tuesday was full from pulled-pork tacos with pickled jalapeños, and a fruity drink that had a lot of alcohol and even more sugar in it. She would not even require magic to fly now. And Ethan had watched her gobble the food with little more than that constant smirk and a gleam in his eyes.

They were pretty gray eyes, and added a touch of niceness to his usual dour expression. While he was a handsome man, she could tell he dared not show too much. He had been honed and hardened over the centuries. Much as she had been. And she well knew it was never wise to let life play out on her face for others to interpret and use to their advantage.

"How long have you been walking this seriously whacked planet?" she asked as she noisily sucked the last bits of the red slushy drink through the straw. She wasn't drunk, but she was feeling fine.

"Conversation now?"

"Yes. I'm finished stuffing my face. I'm feeling relaxed for the first time since my captivity—" She caught his scoff. "I was in a freakin' cage."

"Fine. I'm sorry, okay? It had to be done. But now you're out, so get over it."

It took a snap of the rubber band not to flip him off.

"What did you ask?" he said. "How old am I?" He lifted his feet and propped them on a nearby wicker chair, leaning back against the wall in the stuffy bar that had announced last call ten minutes after they'd arrived. "I was born in…the 1500s."

"Can't remember the exact year?"

He shrugged. "Early part of the century. We weren't known for marking our birth dates back then."

"Yeah. I was born in the 1640s, give or take a few years. Or decades. I remember at the time it was the great Puritan migration. They sailed to the New World by boatloads from England. All kinds of religious rabble, preaching and condemning. Fur traders and fishers, too. I dated a fisherman once. He smelled. So! That makes you the old man and me the sexy young thang."

"Which should grant me wisdom and you…?"

Tuesday shimmied confidently on the chair. "A chick with a whole lot of experience on every single thing you can imagine."

"It is interesting walking through the ages, isn't it?"

"It is." She teased a finger around the rim of her glass. "You ever get tired of it?"

"Not yet. Immortality suits me."

"Save for the part about drinking all that blood?"

"Coming from a witch who must have consumed how many vampire hearts to keep her immortality over the centuries?"

"Five," she said proudly. In order to maintain immortality, a witch had to consume a beating vampire heart once a century. Split the rib cage. Reach in. Feast.

And try not to wretch. "Each one of those bastards deserved to die, too."

"And what qualifies as deserving in your book?"

"Assholes. Murderers. And general idiots."

Ethan quirked an eyebrow. "I shall endeavor not to be an asshole or an idiot. At least, not too often."

Tuesday yawned. "You've had a pitiful showing in the trying department. But I won't hold that against you."

"I thought you intended to hold everything that made you uncomfortable against me?"

"Pretty much. But you're lucky I'm tired now. I only got about two winks on your couch. Can we go back to your place? I need to seriously crash and recharge. If I can get some good sleep then I'll be able to think clearly and maybe even stir up a demon-tracking spell."

"Then here's to a well-rested witch."

The witch nodded off within five minutes. Ethan had offered her his bed. It was around the corner in the loft. None of the rooms had separating walls, save bathroom, and he could see the end of the bed from the kitchen. The city lights beamed in through the floor-to-ceiling windows that lined the bedroom area. He'd bought this place for those windows. The view was incredible. He'd wanted to point out Sacré Coeur to her, but she had literally dropped onto the bed and rolled into a snore.

Now, he wondered what their next move should be. And if more kisses would be required to make her comply with his wishes. She hadn't needed provoking to kiss him back after he'd initially kissed her. A retaliatory kiss? Bring them on.

And in his next thought, he frowned. He'd kissed a witch. And...he'd liked it.

Chapter 5

A shower had never felt more welcome. Tuesday dried off in the steamy room. The floor and walls were grey marble that was deeply streaked with clear quartz. Gorgeous stonework. And she could feel some of the earth's energies remaining in the stone when she pressed a palm to it, though they were weak. The manufacturing process tended to rape natural stone of most of its essence, but if she took her time, and had the inclination, she could restore its vital energy with an earthing spell.

It was a hell of a lot more than Stuart could do, that was for sure.

"Take that, Stuart."

It was weird to think that an inanimate object was listening in, all the time, waiting for a cue to turn on some function in the apartment. Electronic witchcraft was not her thing. But apparently Ethan was one of those spoiled rich bachelors who could afford life's luxuries. But he didn't seem to flaunt it, with million-dollar wristwatches or fancy suits, so he earned credit for that.

The bathroom was attached to the bedroom, which was open to the rest of the loft. A nice setup, and she suspected the view out the picture window was awesome, were the shades not blocking the bright sunlight now. She hadn't realized how dead tired she had been last night. Her face had hit the pillow. Snores had commenced.

Now she didn't hear Ethan puttering about in the kitchen, but then, why should she? The guy was a vampire. He didn't eat food. But she certainly hoped he played the charming host and either ordered in or found something for her to nosh on.

Fingering her black silk shirt, which revealed a nicely toned tummy, she sighed. She'd worn it for two days straight *and* a long flight across the Atlantic Ocean. She needed clean things to wear. And at the very least, some basic magical accoutrements.

Combing out her hair with Ethan's comb, she then snapped her fingers and whispered, "Dry," and a whoosh of air fluffed up and through the wet strands, instantly drying them. Sometimes Latin wasn't necessary to kick in the magic. Keep it Simple, Stupid was a motto she followed with her spellcraft. She wove her thick hair into a loose side plait and left some in the back hanging free.

Without makeup or a toothbrush she felt out of her element. Not quite in top form. She scanned the insides of the medicine cabinet and spied the wood-handled toothbrush. Nah. She wasn't going to use a vampire's toothbrush. She squirted a blob of toothpaste on her finger and scrubbed the old-fashioned way. Centuries ago, this had been her only option to dental health. That, or use a bit of twig or the corner of some rough suede. It worked. But her kingdom for a dash of dark eye shadow and lip gloss.

"Ugh. Nature witch," she muttered to her reflection. "I should concoct a makeup spell." She tapped her finger-nails against the mirror, thinking it odd that a vampire even had one in his home. "Yeah, I'll worry about the lacking glamour later. I've got bigger problems to solve."

Putting the obsidian crystal around her neck, she held it a few moments. Grounding herself. Finding a calm tone for her personal vibration.

Now ready to face whatever adventure the vampire with the attack kisses had in mind for her, she wandered out into the living area. Seated on the leather sofa, Ethan was focused on an iPad, but he nodded over his shoul-der and said, "Ran down to the creperie an hour ago when you were still sleeping. Got you some croissants and *pain au chocolat*. Fresh juice, too."

Points for the vampire. But she wouldn't tell him that.

"You mean Stuart is incapable of such errands? Not sure you got your money's worth with that guy," she said gaily.

Sliding onto a bar stool and tearing into the paper bag, Tuesday bit into a still-warm pastry loaded with gooey chocolate. Crisp, thin layers of pastry engulfing sweet, dark chocolate? By the seven sacred witches, it was amazing.

"What are the plans for today?" she asked around chews.

"Thought you could summon the demon. Witches can do that, right?"

"Right, but I can't summon a demon who has marked me. Just doesn't work that way. I can track him, perhaps even locate him, but he's not going to come when I call like a little bitch."

Ethan's sigh echoed across the room. "I thought you'd be more useful."

"Way to boost a chick's confidence. Besides, Edamite Thrash confirmed The Beautiful One wasn't going to come when I call. So get over it, will you? I know what is first on today's list of adventures."

"What's that?"

"Shopping! I can't wander around in this same getup. I mean, I can work it, but I seriously prefer clean clothes. And I need some lip gloss and eye liner. I feel naked without the black stuff."

"Is that going to help you to locate the demon?"

"It will." She turned and fluttered her lashes at him. "Don't you know a woman's power is all in how she feels about herself? When I look good, I do my best."

"I think you look great."

"You're a guy. Guys always say dismissive things like that."

He shook his head and set aside the iPad. "Shopping it is. And then?"

"And then, I also need to pick up some spell supplies. Outfit myself with a makeshift hex-and-spell armory. Then I should be able to set up a grid to map the city of demons. And hopefully, by incorporating the sigil's power, The Beautiful One will stand out on that map."

"Hopefully? I'm going to need more than that. I require assurance."

Tuesday shrugged and bit off another piece of chocolaty pastry. "You get hope from me for now, vamp. Say, do you mind that I used your comb?"

"As long as you didn't use my toothbrush, I don't care."

"What if I did use your toothbrush?"

"We're stopping at a pharmacy, first thing."

The witch could work the tight black jeans and floaty flowered shirt. Her vibe was definitely bohemian, with her thick white hair braided down one side and the furred spangled coat topping it all off. In the pharmacy, she tore open the makeup packaging and performed a quick makeover on herself, fluttering her newly blackened lashes at him and pursing her deep violet lips.

Ethan nodded approval because the sooner she served her personal needs, the quicker he could be done with this stupid stuff and get on to the important work. But he had to admit the deep color she wore on her lips stirred his desires. The violet lipstick emphasized her plump, heart-shaped mouth. He couldn't take his eyes from them. They might taste like sweet grapes warmed under the Tuscan sun.

Yikes. Ethan checked himself. What was he thinking? He was not attracted to a witch. Yes, he was. And what the fuck was that about?

"Come on!" Tuesday skipped ahead, obviously on some kind of spending high.

Ethan kept his credit card handy. Whatever made the witch happy.

Now, she had managed to find a dusty candle shop that opened to a private room in the back that was filled with all the witchy accoutrements he imagined she'd ever need. And while he suspected the shop owner was one of those kitchen witches who spoke incantations from books she'd bought on the internet and thought she was casting spells, she wasn't a real born witch like Tuesday Knightsbridge. And if she knew that the woman buying smudge sticks and candles from her really did possess natural magic, she would be in awe.

Tuesday popped her head out from the back room with a bag full of goodies and winked at Ethan as she wandered by. "Homeward! Stuart waits for us!"

At the very least, he'd gotten a new toothbrush.

Back at his place, Tuesday dropped her shopping booty on the floor by the sofa, tossed her coat on the chair and beelined to the bathroom while he picked up the mess.

Setting her heeled boots on the rug by the door, he then placed the bags neatly on the kitchen counter. He liked a clean, organized home. Which was probably why his few attempts at living with women over the years had failed. Also, the lack of privacy was jarring. Sharing a home with another person was hard work. And since he could have a relationship without moving in with the woman, he chose to stick with what worked.

Although a few relationships here and there, over the centuries, had worked for him. Most had been so long ago he'd forgotten what it felt like or how it had lasted. That wasn't exactly true. A man never forgot the women who had passed through his life. And the current one was moving through like a hurricane intent on settling and spinning about for a while.

"Stuart, be sure to send the vacuum through when next I leave."

The home butler confirmed with a blip on the wall panel and a solid green light. Ethan had programmed it not to return voice reply unless necessary. It wasn't like he needed to talk to the artificial intelligence to make conversation. He used it merely as the maid he liked to have available at all hours of the day, yet didn't want a human stumbling around in his life discovering that he didn't need to sleep and eat. And he'd bitten a maid once. Early nineteenth century? It was best not to drink from the help.

Tuesday returned, flipping her hair over a shoulder, and stretched out on the sofa. "Where's my stuff?"

"On the kitchen counter. You can't leave a trail of bread crumbs wherever you walk."

"I don't need to. We're attached at the hip. If you should lose sight of me, you'll find me soon enough. Bring me my bags."

"Get them yourself." He settled onto the big leather chair with the wide wooden arms. The wood was worn from decades of use and connection to life. And more than a few frenzied bang sessions. "Dazzle me with your witchy magic and this demon map you said you could conjure."

"I don't dazzle on command." She wandered over to the counter and pulled out things from the bags.

"Then how do I get you to dazzle me?" Ethan asked. "Is there a magic word?"

"*Please* seems to work most of the time."

He pressed his fingers to his forehead. He should have left the witch in the cage.

On the other hand, she couldn't hex him and he did need help with this case. He had absolutely no clue how to lure in the demon otherwise, so he would take her sassy mouth and… Well, he'd kiss her again if need be. Heh. That kiss had set her off-kilter.

But the return kiss had surprised him. And then he'd

accepted it for the retaliation it had been. *Now* a kiss from those grape-stained lips would give him what he wanted from her. Another taste. A teasing test of his abilities to remain completely unaffected by her charms and attraction.

She had some. Somewhere in that scatter of spangles, sass and black eye shadow.

"Black salt and raven's ash." She waggled between them two vials of a dark substance that she'd purchased from the candle shop. "This will do the trick."

She wandered over and pushed the narrow coffee table up against the sofa. The wide dark-stained plank flooring was the original from when the building had once been a millinery factory. Ethan liked it because he'd known a man who had worked here in the 1920s. He'd taken immense pride in the cut of a woman's hat, or even the specific froth of a silk flower adorning a sweeping brim. He'd also asked Ethan for vampirism after learning that the mercury used to cure the felt for his creations was driving him insane. Ethan had convinced him an insane vampire would be worse than a human prematurely dead from bleeding out.

In all his centuries, Ethan had never created another vampire. And he didn't intend to do so anytime soon. It was too much power to simply give away as if a holiday gift. And besides, he was blood-born, not a created vampire. His breed were superior to those who had been transformed in a back alley or at a lover's lusty request. And he wasn't about to tarnish the line. If he ever desired to procreate, he would have a child, who, depending on its mother's lineage and paranormal species, would very likely be born vampire. He preferred to mate with another vampire, but he wasn't rigid in that stance. Love was actually his key requirement to a happy, lasting relationship.

But love was fickle and...well, he'd take it if it came his way, but he wasn't on a quest to track it down.

Ethan leaned forward to rest his elbows on his knees and watched as Tuesday sprinkled black salt in a pattern before her on the floor. He was curious about witchcraft, and knew it was powerful. No man should mess with a witch. But he was feeling cocky with the protective bind against her. So long as it lasted until they found the demon.

Leaning over the scattered salt, which designed a pentagram inside a circle, Tuesday closed her eyes and spread her arms wide. She chanted words that Ethan would never try to decipher. Witch words. Dangerous words. Yet he could feel them forming sentences in his veins, warning that she could take him out if he dropped his guard.

With a snap of her fingers, the salt suddenly illuminated and jittered on the floor, moving, ordering and aligning. The tiny grains jumped and crackled. The scent of salt tinged the air. And when it settled and continued to glow, Tuesday sat back on her heels, hands propped on each thigh.

"A map of Paris," she said with a gesture over the salt. "What do you think?"

Ethan leaned over to inspect the map. It included both the right and left bank, and the Seine and the main island. It even showed faint demarcations for the twenty arrondissements. "You've dazzled me, witch. Now where are all the demons? Or just the one in particular?"

"That requires more intense chanting. And an elemental callout. You stay there. Don't move, because I don't want the bond between us to tug me out of concentration. Deal?"

"I am a captive audience."

She looked at him a moment, and he couldn't decide if she thought she was peering into an idiot's eyes or, in fact, seeing beyond his irises and into his very soul. He'd witnessed it when she'd peered into Certainly Jones's soul. Was it a skill they could only perform on other witches? Or need he worry, too?

"What?" he finally asked.

"There's something about you, Ethan Pierce. Something that keeps me from stabbing you through the heart with this athame." She twirled the knife she'd bought from the store. The hilt looked to be carved from opal. That was why the bill had registered in the hundreds of euros. "I'm not sure what that is, though, so I'm going to keep the blade close."

"Whatever works for you. You couldn't harm me if you tried."

"Probably not. But you are racking up the points against you for when the bond is lifted. Know that."

"I'm not afraid of a witch."

Her head tilted and her gaze narrowed as she said simply, "You should be."

And Ethan realized she was right. But he wouldn't show his anxiety.

Casting her focus over the salt map, she moved up on her knees, spread out her arms and began to chant.

Tuesday felt the presence of every demon inhabiting the city prick at her skin. It wasn't pleasant, but it wasn't painful, either. Rather a sort of vehement and

inner knowing. The elemental spell had been successful. She opened her eyes and looked over the map.

Ethan kneeled on the opposite side of the map and
scanned the results as well. "What are all the glowing
red salt crystals?"

"Demons," she said.

"There's so many. Thousands."

"Are you surprised?"

"No. But how is this going to help our search?"

"Hold your horses, big boy. The real magic comes
next."

Tugging loose the ribbon ties at the bodice of her
new shirt, Tuesday tossed the obsidian crystal over her
shoulder and then pressed her fingers against the sigil
between her breasts. She lowered her other hand over
the map, moving methodically as she silently thought
Gazariel's name. The sigil warmed and she could feel
the tendrils of it creep through her chest and toward her
extremities. It noticed her.

And that was not a good thing.

Wanting to abruptly end the spell, she suddenly noted
the violet glow at one edge of the map. "There! Where
is that?"

Ethan turned his head to assess the map. "Looks
like the Bois de Boulogne. A big, forested park at the
edge of the city. Is that purple spot The Beautiful One?"

"It is. And now I'm cutting the connection before he
catches on."

"Wait!"

Tuesday pulled her fingers from the sigil. The violet
light snuffed out.

"If you would have held on longer, I could have
marked the exact location," Ethan protested. "That

would have made our job easier. Are you helping me or hindering me, witch?"

"What do you think I'm doing? You think I enjoy being your captive? I want this over as quickly as possible. But I will not call the demon directly to me. He could manifest within me. And then what will you do?"

"That can happen?"

"It's likely. But remember what Edamite said. If he's smart he's not going to come near me. And he is."

"Sorry. I, uh… I don't intend to place you in harm's way. I just want to utilize your expertise."

"And this, eh?" She tapped the sigil.

"Can I take a look at that?"

She studied his curious gaze. He wasn't aware that a childlike wonder could overtake his normally serious expression. Nor could he be aware how much that relaxation of his outer shield attracted her. Because it made him everything he probably didn't want to be— soft, kind, accepting.

Tuesday nodded her consent.

Ethan reached over and pressed two fingers to the sigil. It was an intimate touch and her skin warmed. Her breasts hugged his knuckles. He flicked his wondrous gaze onto hers.

"I can feel your fear," he said. "I don't want you to be afraid. I will protect you."

Tuesday wrapped her fingers about his wrist, holding him there at her breast. "There's nothing a vampire can do to protect me that I can't already do myself. You're going to have to make a better plea for my continuing to work with you than that."

"All right. How about this?"

And with that, he slid over the salt map, smearing

the left bank of Paris, and cupped the back of her head as he pulled her in for another sudden kiss.

His mouth warmed against hers and demanded she not ignore him. That she allow him to protect her. And at the same time, it teased her to submit in a way she generally didn't care to with a man. It was the surprise of their connection, their easy manner of locking lips, that excited her, and made her want to not break it.

On her knees, Tuesday scooched closer. He slipped one hand down her hair and clasped his fingers into it, easing her forward, into his arms. Into his interesting acceptance. She'd thought he didn't like witches. So why was he kissing her?

Did it matter? Not in this moment. She wanted to taste every sensual, hot bit of him. Inhale his cool, fresh-air scent, and every breath that he greedily gave and took from her. Moaning into his mouth, she grabbed at his shirt and straddled his legs with hers. They kneeled there on the scattered remains of the city map, a strange fusion of opposites who couldn't resist the pull to experience one another.

And when he put his hand again on the sigil, she moved his fingers to cup her breast. She hugged up against him, giving him permission to touch her, wanting to own the vampire's desire… To control him as he sought to control her.

Ethan broke the kiss and pulled his hand abruptly from her skin. "Uh…"

Appearing befuddled, he probably wasn't sure why he'd kissed her. And had manhandled her boob. So she wouldn't let him consider it too long. Because if she had to use normal skills instead of magic to control him, it was best to keep him unsure and wondering.

"Feel like a walk in the park?" she asked.

"Sure. I um…"

She stood and knotted the ties of her shirt into a bow. "Then let's get to it before I shove you down and have some hex with you."

She'd let him ponder the use of that word for what she really wanted to do to him. The man had ignited something within her. And she had never been a witch to deny herself the pleasures life offered.

Chapter 6

Parked at the curb, Ethan waited for Tuesday while she purchased food from a stand. He didn't use the BMW often because he walked to work even in the winter. Vampires could easily regulate their body temperature. But the trip to the park would prove long on foot, and he didn't want the witch to suffer the cold, especially walking in those high-heeled boots.

Tuesday slid in and closed the door and settled back to chomp on a savory-smelling crepe.

"You want a bite? It's got weird French cheese and ham in it. This is amazing."

"I'd rather suck dead blood," he muttered.

"Oh, yeah? What's wrong with a little taste once in a while? I know vampires can eat small amounts of food."

"I don't have a taste for meat. I get enough of the flavor when I drink blood. And you just dripped fontina onto the leather seat. Would you be careful?"

"Fontina, eh? Don't tell me you don't steal a taste every now and then." She swiped a napkin over the seat and then leaned forward, pointing. "That's the— What is it?"

"The Louvre," he pronounced carefully.

"Louv-ra, with the ra-ra shout at the end," she mocked. "You're not French, are you?"

"I'm English. Born in London, actually, but I didn't stay there more than a decade. I've lived everywhere. Spent some time in the Americas in the 1700s. Right around the time Massachusetts became a state."

"Good times," she said, sitting back. "Puritanical shame, Indian genocide and witch hunts. Go, witch hunters! Not."

Ethan shouldn't have brought that up. If she knew about the travesties he'd committed against witches when he had been a young vampire only set on impressing his tribe leaders? He'd be very thankful for the binding spell that prevented her from using magic against him.

"Have you been in Paris before?" he asked.

"Once or twice. Never for longer than a month or two. And never in a mood to do any touristing. Once I was here looking for a bastard imp who stole my voice. Little creep isn't singing or snickering anymore. What's that?"

"The Luxor Obelisk." Ethan drove by the seventy-five-foot-high yellow granite obelisk placed in the center of the Place de la Concorde at the end of the Tuileries Garden. "Originally located at the Luxor Temple in Egypt—a gift from Muhammad Ali Pasha, the ruler of Egypt at the time."

"You know the city's history."

"I've lived it. Of all my centuries, I've spent the most time in Paris. And up ahead is the Champs-Élysées."

"Oh, I know that's a good shopping street. Should

have waited to get my togs up ahead." She scanned the signs screaming for customers to come in and spend their precious euros. They passed luxury-car dealers and high-end clothing retailers. And... "There's a Mc-Donalds on the classy upscale shopping street?"

"And movie rental stores," Ethan said. "Go figure. It's all a big tourist trap. But then, this street has been ever since Napoleonic times."

"More good times," Tuesday offered. "The Inquisition was still around then. You gotta love a self-righteous maniac intent on destroying that which he does not understand. And if it's a woman, then even more reason to put her in her place."

"Do you remember any good times that were actually good?"

"Oh, sure. I loved the late nineteenth century. So bohemian. We witches really got to shine then. The seventies and the hippies also welcomed us with open arms. What's that? Wait! I know this one."

Ethan stopped the car at a light before he would enter the roundabout before the monument.

"The arch of triumph, right?"

"Right." He wouldn't correct her too harshly. "Napoleon's Arc d'Triomphe, erected to honor those who served in the Revolutionary and Napoleonic wars. There's a tomb of an unknown soldier beneath it. If you go to the top it offers a great view of the whole city."

"Then let's do it. Yeah?"

"After the demon is found you can take all the time you like for sightseeing."

"Because then you'll cut my leash and set me free?"

He didn't like hearing it put that way, but it was the truth. "Exactly."

Ten minutes later they pulled in to the park, which was massive and filled with sports areas, a zoo and playgrounds, housing and entertainment complexes. And yet there was still a preserved forested area, an oasis set at the border of the big, cosmopolitan city. A light dusting of snow clung to the trees, giving the forest a faery-tale touch as sun twinkled on the snow.

Ethan parked in a lot before a hiking trail. He kept the car running because the witch would probably appreciate the heat. He pulled on his blue-lensed sunglasses. He could walk in direct sunlight a few minutes without feeling the burn, and much longer in the winter sun. And these lenses were also charmed to view wards, which served as more than a means to protection from sizzling retinas.

"What's the plan?" Tuesday asked. "Are we going to tromp about the park and call 'Here, demon, come on, demon!'"

"Won't that sigil you wear lead us to him?"

"Right." She touched her chest and closed her eyes. "Or him to me. Not that he'd come running with arms wide open to embrace me."

Ethan sensed she plummeted to some place very low whenever she touched the sigil. He had to ask. "Tell me how you got the sigil? It could be helpful to know what I'm dealing with here."

"*Now* you decide to ask about the stakes? You are so not a romantic, vampire."

"What does romance have to do with anything?"

"Nothing." She crossed her arms over her chest and averted her gaze out the window. "Kisses don't have any place between us, either."

"I beg to differ. They have proven a useful tool for me."

"Again, not a romantic bone in your body, eh?"

"What? Do you require emotion, some feeling next time I kiss you?"

"You think you're going to kiss me again?"

"Probably."

She turned on the seat to look at him. "Why? Do you like kissing me?"

"It was pleasant." He sounded like an asshole, but what was she angling for right now with that teasing question? The woman was a curiously complex mixture of opposites. One minute she was trying to put a hex on him to make his dick limp, the next she wanted to make out. "Do *you* want to kiss me again?"

She sat up, lifting her chin haughtily. "You haven't been kissed by me yet, vampire. When I kiss you properly? You'll know. And you'll never have to wonder if you want another again. Because you will. You'll crave my kiss, my touch. You'll want to hex me every chance you get."

Ethan offered a shrug. "Have to say, that does sound intriguing."

"Damn right it does. So we heading out on the demon quest?"

"First, I need the details." He pushed back his seat and tilted to face her comfortably. Taking off the sunglasses, he asked, "Tell me how you got Gazariel's sigil."

Boston, MA—1680

Finnister McAdams was going blind. He wore a black strip of sack cloth across his eyes now because he had explained to Tuesday how the light bothered him. Made him blink and gave him headaches. 'Twas as if the devil was prodding his eyes with his mighty pitchfork.

Tuesday knew well the Devil Himself did not wield a pitchfork, but to correct him would only put her in danger. She'd prepared Finn an herbal tincture in his morning tea. Rosemary, black salts and feverfew. Had cast a healing spell...without him knowing. Even laid mustard plasters over his eyes. Nothing proved efficacious.

Now she considered calling up a demon to aid in healing her lover's eyes. Such creatures did possess healing powers. At least, a few of them did so. If only the witch summoning them could find a beneficent demon. And that was the challenge.

Tuesday loved her man, Finn. From the moment he'd settled next to her in the lavender field and compared her eyes to the sky, she had loved him desperately. Three months they had been sharing her tiny cabin at the edge of the village with one another. Finn was strong and proud, and very handsome. His hair was copper, his thick beard as well. His skin was ruddy and pale, so he always wore a wide-brimmed hat when outside. He was fashioned of flame and earth. And when he held her in his arms it wasn't tentative or rough. He knew how to hold a woman. And Tuesday's heart fluttered when he kissed her.

But if he knew she was a witch he would be displeased. The man was Puritan. His family had sailed across the Atlantic Ocean from England six months earlier. His father was seeking a congregation to share and spread the word of God. And Finnister, while a godly man, seemed more inclined to craftwork that involved turning wood into beautiful creations. He even fashioned lovely knife hilts, and had skill with a blade.

With the witch trials and all the heinous accusations running rampant of late, Tuesday did not dare reveal her truth to her lover. Because even if he could accept her, she risked the townsfolk putting him on trial for harboring her secret.

But she could no longer bear to see him stumble about the house, seeking wood for the stove and instead stabbing his fingers into the log pile and yelping as slivers cut through his skin. Or to watch him try to piss in the chamber pot and instead spray the stone floor.

She would care for him. Because she loved him.

But she must try one last thing before giving up on his healing. And that required she summon a demon. She wasn't schooled in demons, didn't know which to summon for the healing of sight, but would take whatever beast she could conjure. Surely, even a lowly demon might have some healing skills. And she had a way of winning a man's trust with her gentle confidence and attentive manner.

Shouldn't be so different with demons.

So just before midnight, on a hot summer's eve, she kissed Finn's forehead as he snoozed before the window, and snuck out with her cotton bag of charms and potions under her arm. Her wood-soled clogs took the soft red earth in quick strides and she was thankful for the fast-growing moss that muffled her steps. She would avoid the gatekeepers, and slip into the forest half a mile from the village. It was a haunted forest, or rumors told, so that kept out most villagers.

All except those who knew better. Like her. The forest was a thin place where the realm of Daemonia overlapped this mortal realm. Summoning a demon would be as simple as snapping her fingers. And having the fortitude to do so.

Tuesday had lived nearly forty years, and had honed her magical skills in privacy and under the tutelage of some powerful aunts and good women. She had eaten a vampire's heart to secure immortality and a youthful appearance—at least, for another century—and had cast down the moon and summoned healings and utilized the natural elements to move through life.

She was not like those women who were being accused in the trials. Women who had knowledge of female anatomy and tried to heal and teach others. They were merely humans who sought to educate and save. But the menfolk would not condone a smart woman living in their midst. Females were to submit and serve. And they used them as cat's-paws and accused them of witchery. Anything to subdue and make them submissive.

Of course, Tuesday could be thankful for the distraction of that wayward and unprofessional witchery. It kept most eyes from her, a true witch. And she was wise enough not to share her skills with anyone who had not been vetted to her by a witch elder. Even when Finn slyly questioned if she would ever attempt witchcraft, she laughed and told him he was silly. It was something she imagined most every woman in the village had been asked. Men were suspicious creatures. Their fear of losing control to what they deemed a *mere* woman made them so.

A woman would do well to learn how to control such irresponsible creatures—men. And she was teaching herself that by learning all that she could about herself, her body, nature and the universe. Strength came with wisdom and knowledge.

But tonight she would reach beyond her own capabilities in a quest to save her lover's sight.

Once deep in the forest, she did not light a candle. She didn't wish discovery by hunters. Drawing out a pentagram with black salt on the leaf-crusted forest floor, she spoke the invocation to summon a demon. The surprise she felt when one appeared made her step back and clutch the smoky quartz she wore from a leather strap about her neck for protection. He stood within the circle, but posed gallantly beside a thick oak, elbow propped high to lean against it.

His eyes glowed red, so she knew he was demon. But otherwise he looked a human, dressed in a fine blue silk frock coat, shot through with silver threading, and with lace dripping around his wrists and at his neck. Such finery belonged only to royalty. She had seen Pandora dolls imported from Europe wearing such elaborate silks. And his hair was long and wavy and black as midnight. He smelled...of lilacs. A pretty man—demon—if she was to size him up. And that notion startled her. Should not demons be more creature-like? Horned and possessed of red or black skin with claws? This demon's handsome appearance was disconcerting, to say the least.

"Who are you?" she asked, a bit too timidly for her comfort. So she set back her shoulders and lifted her chin. Courage hummed in her bones. "Have you come from Daemonia?"

"You don't even know who you've summoned? What a sorry witch you are!" The demon tugged out the lace from the end of one sleeve. "Daemonia is the last place

I should ever tread. I am of this realm. And I am Gaz-ariel, The Beautiful One."

Tuesday knew demons often went by monikers, and that one was right on the nose. Beautiful, indeed. And he seemed to believe it himself, judging by his man-nerisms. Primping and preening. Not a wrinkle to the silk, nor a hair out of place. Was that rouge on his pale cheeks?

She tested the binding on the summons and did not feel a weakness in the air. He could not approach her, and if he tried, the circle should keep him in check.

"I need your help," she said. "With a healing."

The demon rolled his eyes and shook his head sadly. "Bother. Always with the sicknesses! And here I thought you might request I attend the next village soiree and impregnate a dozen virgins with my demon babies." He gestured dismissively. "You're boring, witch."

"My lover is going blind. You can kiss his eyes and give him sight."

"Of course I can." He rubbed his fingernails against the embroidery edging his silk lapels. "We demons have such skills. Most of us, anyway. I would not dare to ask a wrath demon for some delicate brain trephination, though, mind you. What is this lover's name?"

"Finnister McAdams. His sight is almost completely gone. He is a kind man. And so young. He is strong and contributes all that he can to the village. If you could see to healing him, I would be ever grateful."

"Release me," the demon said.

Tuesday's spine stiffened. She was no fool. "Not until you give me what I ask."

"I can't go near the man unless you unbind me, now

can I?" He splayed his lace-encircled hand toward the circle on the ground.

That was true. He did need to move about freely. And she could hardly lead Finn here to the forest to receive what healing magic the demon could provide. Such had to be managed with cunning.

"You'll follow me home and attend to him while he sleeps?"

"He doesn't know you're a witch? Of course not. You may be a bore but you are not stupid. Take down the circle. I'll see what I can do. And in turn, I'll ask a favor from you."

"Which is?"

He shrugged and flipped out a hand to display the lace grandly. "I'll decide on that after the task is complete."

A favor to a demon? It was only fair to reciprocate. But she wasn't sure what she could do for him. And she had no intention of having one of his demon babies. Well. She could not. Her womb was barren. She'd known that for decades. A condition she'd been born with, according to a wise witch who had gazed into her soul and seen her birth.

With trepidation, Tuesday slashed a foot through the salt circle. The demon disappeared instantly, leaving her alone in the dark woods. An owl hooted, chastising her with his repeated tones.

"I have been a fool! He will never give me what I want. I should have offered him a gift immediately. Given him reason to want to help me."

And what would the creature demand of her should he serve her wishes? It would never be good, she felt sure.

"It is a sacrifice I am willing to make," she muttered and turned to wander back to the village.

By the time she returned home, she saw the demon standing outside her door. His pale blue frock coat was an unwanted beacon in the darkness, and in a village where the only colors worn were black, brown and gray.

She rushed up to him. "What are you doing here? You can't be seen!"

"Oh, Tuesday Knightsbridge, you sad, pitiful witch." He placed a hand over her chest, right between her breasts, and Tuesday felt a searing pain but she could not step away from the demon. "Your lover lies to you. I came here to find him returning from the forest. He followed you. Watched you and I. He knows. And he is not going blind. His sight is as perfect as yours or mine."

"No, that's—"

"That's a foolish witch for you," the demon said piteously. "And you have fallen in love with a witch hunter. Ha!"

The searing at her chest now burned as if in flames.

Then her front door opened, and Finn spilled out with hell blazing in his eyes. He looked right at her. Saw her for what she was. Finn snarled, "Witch!"

The torture began the next day. The water chair was the one that siphoned all Tuesday's gumption from her. She was tied to a chair on the end of a seesaw and repeatedly dunked into the filthy, muddy river. Each time she was lifted above water, gasping, choking, pleading for Finn to stop, she was commanded to confess to being a witch and consorting with demons.

She would not. She would survive this. Somehow.

Later, the whip that flayed at her skin left deep gashes, and caused Tuesday to pass out more than a few times. Hot pokers to her hips and between her toes almost made her confess. Almost.

After four days of suffering her lover's vicious, hateful punishments, Tuesday was lying on the cold, hard dirt floor on a tiny cell at the edge of the village. No moonlight on this night of the new moon. On the other side of the building, the village pigs snorted and rooted, and filled the air with a nauseating odor that she breathed as if a toxin.

All vitality had been beaten out of her. Even the will to live had been vanquished with a humiliating search of her private body parts in search of devil's marks. Finn had done so before a dozen village elders. All men. All leering. If she'd the strength she would have cast a spell over them all, reducing them to stupid, foul, snorting pigs like those outside her cell. Alas, she'd expelled all her energies with a breathing spell during the dunking.

She would be dead by morning. Her tattered heart told her as much. And she sighed with acceptance.

When the flash of red light flickered in the cell and she scented a brief fragrance of lilacs, she tried to lift her head to look at the demon, but the flay marks along her neck pained her with every subtle movement.

The demon's silk, red-heeled shoes were but inches from her face. "Men are terrible, yes?"

Indeed. And yet, she was not prepared to condemn them all. Her father had been a good man. And the village baker, who she knew was married to a witch whom he protected, was also kind. "Not all of them."

"You're right. It is love that is so vile. Can't be trusted. Merely a means to trick and use innocence. And you have been thoroughly used, my witch."

Indeed. Why had the demon returned? To rub her failures into her open wounds? Or did he still require she serve him something in return? He hadn't healed Finn, for the man hadn't required any healing.

The demon bowed low and the tickle of his hair across her cheek smelled sweet and too luxurious. "I can give you something that you'll find most useful."

"Leave me to die, demon."

"Do not address me so. It is vulgar. I am The Beautiful One."

She could but close her eyes tightly and wish death would quicken its pace.

"I carry a curse," Gazariel continued. "But I don't need it. Or want it. And you can have it if you'll willingly accept it."

A curse? Why ever would she ask for a curse?

By some means, Tuesday managed to roll to her back. The red light surrounding him illuminated her cell. Her tormentor looked down over her. Pity from a demon? She'd thought being held under the river waters for long minutes had been her lowest. Gazariel's pouting mouth reduced her to less than that low.

"If I am dead," she whispered, "curse or not, it will not matter."

"Oh, you're going to live, witch. I will make sure of that. The question is, do you want to walk this earth a wise, smart, powerful witch who will never again be defeated by love?"

The demon placed his palm between her breasts. And Tuesday felt a darkness tickle into her heart.

"What is the curse?" she asked.

He leaned in and whispered in her ear, and his voice was melodious and warming. "You will never know true love again. Your soul will repel it, and even should it occur, the moment your lover realizes he loves you he will suddenly hate you. Perhaps even suffer a cruel malady or some such," he added offhandedly.

Such a curse actually sounded sweet and tempting. She was lying here, near death, because of love. Fickle, cruel love. And she wanted the demon to save her. No one ever wanted to die. And she wasn't singular for wishing it so. Even for the sacrifice of accepting such a deal. To never again know love? To feel the pain of what love could do to her?

To live so that she could walk away from the bastard Finnister McAdams and all those men who had wounded her soul deep?

With a nod, she said, "I'll take the curse."

The demon lifted her under the chin, dragging her body to sit up. With a forceful shove, Tuesday's back hit the cell wall and she screamed at the pain as the sigil seared into her skin.

Gazariel apported out of the tiny cell. And she did not see him ever again.

Chapter 7

That was a heavy past to carry in one's baggage. Ethan rubbed his jaw and shook his head. "I'm sorry."

A smirk to send away the horrible remembrance of the pain she had endured at her lover's hand was all Tuesday could manage. "Don't be. I took the curse willingly."

"To never have love?"

She shrugged. "It was a means to escape the torture and to live."

"But you can't still want such a thing?"

She shrugged and looked aside. Ethan's heart shivered as it had when she'd described the awful torture she'd endured at the hands of a witch hunter, a man she had loved.

He knew what it felt like to wield the whip. Never against a witch, of course. Their blood could have killed him back in the days when such violence had been acceptable, a means to survival. As a young vampire in his tribe, he'd been tested, asked to prove his alliances, most especially during the Blood Wars that had seen his tribe fighting the werewolves. Never had he regretted those acts more than now. Yet to mention it would not win any trust from the witch.

Could his actions since she'd arrived in Paris be construed as a subtle torture, a form of control? Surely. Hell, he didn't want to think about this too much. It would only stifle the mission. He had to focus on the task at hand. Her tale was sad, but she had survived, and seemed the stronger for it.

She'd been punished for caring about another man. By a seemingly selfish and narcissistic demon, who had cursed her only because he could. And yet, she had willingly taken his dark curse in a moment of such weakness she could not have known the impact it would have on her. No one would wish to never know love. Even he, who was jaded by love, would take it if the time was right and his heart leaped.

"We can't wander about the forest calling out for the demon," she said as a means to indicate she was finished talking about her history.

The demon had taken advantage of her.

Now more than ever Ethan wanted to find that bastard, and once he gave up the book with the code, then Ethan would banish him to Daemonia, never to return. Was there a possibility he could have Gazariel take back the curse from Tuesday? With the forced expulsion to Daemonia, all curses, hexes and otherwise foul doings would be erased in the demon's wake. She could be freed if he found the demon and kicked him the hell out of the mortal realm.

"You're right about wandering around without a clear direction." He started the engine and the car heater roared up again. "Tell me what to do."

With a heavy sigh, she pointed behind her. "I think he's probably living in one of those fancy apartments we passed. I mean, he's not living in a tree. The man can obviously walk and live amongst the mortals without suspicion, like all the other demons that showed up on my map. They hold jobs, they live and love, they pass for human."

"As we all do."

"Exactly. So, I need to cast a GPS spell and that should lead us in the right direction."

"A GPS spell? Like the map you cast at my place?"

"This one is more advanced. A witch has got to evolve with the technology, yeah?"

A witch, a vampire and every other paranormal species. The mortal realm was not designed for their sort. At least regarding being out and vocal about who and what they were. His species did what they had to do to survive.

"What do you need to cast such a spell?"

"Your cell phone, and the demon's sigil. And a couple drops of blood."

About to ask why they couldn't use *her* phone, Ethan remembered she'd been taken from a bar in Massachusetts, with little more than her clothes and shoes. She probably didn't have a phone.

He tugged the phone from his pocket and before he handed it to her, he asked, "Is this going to brick my phone?"

"Nah." She grabbed it and tapped the home button. "Maybe? No. I don't know. I've never tried it before. I'm only just learning tech spells. But you're rich. You can afford another."

"What makes you think I'm rich?"

"You're driving a Bimmer. And that apartment with the stunning view had to set you back a couple million."

So he was well off. That happened when a vampire took care to invest over the centuries and kept a healthy portfolio across various international markets and banks. Tech stocks were a gold mine. His accountant was a vampiress who lived near the Eiffel Tower, and she was a gem.

"Just don't set it on fire," he said.

"I won't. I think. Maybe?" She winked at him. "I do have water magic in case of emergency."

Her mood had lifted since she'd told him her tale, and he was grateful for that. Though he'd never discount anyone's suffering. There had been occasions he'd been hunted over the centuries—by slayers and werewolves—but nothing could compare to being caught and tortured. And to live to tell about it.

Tuesday set the phone on the raised center console between them and opened up her coat to tug free the ribbons at her shirt front. Those full breasts were a sweet tease, and Ethan had to remind himself he was on a mission. His attention swerved from her breasts to her lips, and back again.

Hell yes, he'd kiss her again. But thinking that made him wince as he sensed a swift boner could give him up. And the last thing he wanted to do with this witch was prove to her that he was the Richard she'd accused him of being.

"Got a knife?" she asked and extended her forefinger toward him. "I left my athame at your place."

Ethan stared at the finger and all lusty thoughts were replaced by sudden horror. Maybe that limp-dick spell had a delay set on it because he was no longer hard. Because what she asked...

She needed blood for the magic. Blood magic was wicked and he'd known a lot of it might be needed on this adventure. He knew better than to challenge it, or try to interfere with it. But what should he expect from a dark witch?

"No knife," he said.

"Then take a bite, yeah?" She waggled her finger before him. "I just need a couple drops."

"Take a bite?" Aghast at her moxie, he shook his head in bewilderment. "What the hell?"

"Seriously, vampire? Just prick my finger with one of your fangs. Come on, you want to find this demon or not?"

Tonguing the insides of his upper teeth, he met her assessing stare, which wasn't so much aggressive as impatient. She was trying to cast a spell with the tools she had to work with. Yet a taste of blood could do *things* to him. Things that would bring up his erection again. He shouldn't make a big deal out of it.

Fuck, this woman challenged him on so many levels. He'd not expected this mission to become fraught with...emotion and utter mental challenge.

But he would not reveal his consternation. If he'd learned anything about Tuesday Knightsbridge, seeing him in a quandary would make her too happy.

Fangs lowering, he grabbed her wrist and pierced her finger with the pin-sharp tip of one of them. Blood scent curled into his nostrils. It was more alluring than the usual quick bite's coppery, chemical-laced blood. This blood was deep, thick and steeped with the centuries.

He quickly shoved her hand away so the temptation would not drip onto his tongue.

Tuesday squeezed a couple drops onto the iPhone screen. She glanced at him. "You okay, vamp? Not going to attack me in a raging blood hunger?"

"I am perfectly capable of being around blood without turning into a monster." Turning into a horny flesh-pricker, on the other hand? When had he last smelled such…tempting blood?

"Good for you." She stuck her finger in her mouth and sucked at it. "Holster those fangs then, will you? Makes me nervous."

"Really?" He leaned forward, brandishing his fangs boldly. "You scared I'll attack?"

"No, I just like the bite too much."

Startled by that reply, he sat back. Was she a fang junkie? He'd thought only humans succumbed to such base lust for the bite. It was the orgasmic sensations the bite delivered. Such highs could become a drug. Some humans could not get enough.

She winked at him. Ethan willed his fangs to rise to their normal positions.

"Hey, it's as good for the bite-ee as it is for the biter," she said. "You know that. So! Let's get this spell going, yeah?"

Sure. But it was difficult now *not* to think about clasping her long white hair in his hand as he breathed against her neck, dripping with blood. It would taste like the world and all he had lived through. And such memories were both sweet and sour.

Tuesday drew the demon's S-shaped sigil on the phone screen with the blood. A line was drawn through that, connecting both curves. The GPS app was open, he noticed, and now he found it easier to turn his attention to what she was doing instead of slipping into a lusty fantasy of slurping at her neck and making her come with nothing more than the bite.

Pressing her bloodied finger to the sigil between her breasts, Tuesday bowed her head and began to chant. The air in the car grew throat-clutchingly humid, and then it took on an icy chill that hardened his sinuses before returning to normal. Ethan coughed. The phone jittered. The blood purled and rose in droplets, reaching for the hand Tuesday held but inches from the phone. And the scent swarmed Ethan's senses and pushed him headfirst into the unavoidable fantasy.

She would taste old and ancient, laced with centuries of experience. He could sup at her, drain her of her magic… A vampire could steal a witch's power by enacting bloodsexmagic. It required having sex with the witch while drinking her blood and enacting a spell. He'd never thought to do something so wicked. Until now.

A snap of fingers stirred Ethan back to the now. "What?"

"Where were you, vampire?"

In a heated embrace with a witch who could give him so much more than he'd ever dreamed to have.

"Sorry, got lost for a minute there."

"Oh, yeah? Are you aroused?"

He tilted his head, sneering. "You think a few drops of blood is enough to get me horny?"

She shrugged. "I do. Truth be told, I'm feeling it. I mean, like I said, fangs do it for me. Seriously."

Ethan ran his tongue under the tip of one fang. Oh, the serious action he could show her. But he wasn't a fool. And he was a man on a mission. "Did it work?"

"I got a hit." She tapped the phone. "Looks like he's north about a quarter of a mile."

The twosome got out of the car. Ethan scanned their surroundings. Beyond a copse of ancient oak trees rose a gated community that likely sheltered old money and self-made tech millionaires.

"You ever break and enter?" he asked.

"I don't think I should answer that one." Tuesday shrugged up her coat and then shook her hands out at her sides as if preparing for a gunfight. "But whatever fun you're planning? I'm in!"

Attempting to enter a gated community in full daylight was probably not the wisest move, but Tuesday was in it to win it. Besides, she wanted to see if Ethan had a plan. He didn't have a plan. She knew it. But she'd give him the benefit of the doubt. Until he failed, and she'd have an argument for her release and could be done with him.

Telling him about her past hadn't been a problem. She held no emotion for the stupid witch she'd once been. Smarter, wiser, she now did better because she knew better. And she hadn't been looking for sympathy from the vampire, though she'd felt it rise off him in the car. Whatever.

She'd revealed her curse, but she would never tell him the ridiculous means to break that curse. That was a secret she'd take to her grave. Besides, knowing it would keep it from ever happening.

They'd parked a block down from the black wrought-iron gates and now strolled casually along the hornbeam hedgerow that grew eight feet high. Hands shoved in his coat pockets, the vampire kept a keen eye from behind the sexy blue sunglasses. Not many were out walking because the day was chilly.

One small reason to be thankful—when she'd been kidnapped she'd been wearing her alpaca coat. She loved this thing, and it was warm.

The vampire looked…cold. His coat was short, stopping below his waist, and revealed a nice tight ass that was emphasized perfectly by the dark jeans. If the fangs in the car hadn't started her engine, that view certainly revved it to a wanting purr.

To do the guy or not? Everything about his controlling authority screamed *no, run away!* And everything else, from the fangs to the sexy smile, begged her to give him a chance. One more kiss. One good fuck. A no-strings hex-fest of nudity, fangs and orgasms unending.

Tuesday suddenly bumped right in to Ethan, who had stopped walking for some odd reason.

"Really?" he murmured. "I thought witches had a built-in sixth-sense kind of thing. Were you walking with your eyes closed?"

"My sixth sense isn't tuned to idiots," she responded. Good save. She'd been thinking about his fangs in her neck and how strong of an orgasm that would give her. If her tale of taking the curse wasn't enough to remind her what a fool she could be for a handsome smile then…whew!

The entry gate was twenty feet ahead. Time to pull on her stern witch and focus. "What's the plan?"

"I don't have a plan."

"I knew it."

"Why not just stroll in?" Ethan asked.

"Awesome. The direct approach, it is. Let's see you work your skills, vampire."

"I've got skills." And with that he strode toward the small, freestanding office situated next to the entry gate. He cast her a smirk over his shoulder.

And Tuesday was all in with the tease. She hastened her steps, following him like a witch to the lying witch hunter.

Inside the outhouse-sized office situated before the gate, a man pushing ninety lifted his chin and eyed their approach. He shook his head, obviously not recognizing Ethan, and said, "We don't allow solicitors, monsieur. Move along."

Ethan slid his hand through the small space beneath the protective Plexiglas window and smiled charmingly. "This won't take long."

The old man shoved at Ethan's hand, but then all of a sudden his fingers shook and he dropped them onto Ethan's palm. The vampire clasped his fingers and said calmly, "We're here to visit friends. Won't be long. You won't remember us, nor will you consider anything out of the ordinary. Open the gates, please."

Dropping the old man's hand and stepping back to stand next to Tuesday, Ethan waited while the gates swung inward.

"Nice." She marched forward, giving the gatekeeper a thumbs-up as she did. "Persuasion?"

"I can convince a man to jump into flames," he said

as he passed her by and wandered along the edge of the curbed and curved drive.

The road was bare of snow and Tuesday assumed it had heat coils beneath, for she could sense the electric vibrations as she walked it. Ethan's steps moved faster and all of a sudden she was tugged along against her will.

"Damn binding spell." She picked up her pace.

There had to be a way to crack the bond open. For as intriguing as it was to follow Mr. Tight Pants, she could not abide this humiliation for much longer. This was one curse she had not asked for.

Ethan paused before the garage entrance. To each side of the underground lot stood a massive four-story complex that stretched longer than a football field in each direction.

"Now what?" she asked.

"What's your tracker say?"

She checked the GPS on his phone. One tiny blood drop moved over the screen as they had walked. "He's to the left."

And her heart dropped as she realized she could be so close to the one demon she'd tried to avoid and had done so successfully for centuries. Why was she walking into a grand old reunion now?

"Wait, Ethan."

He turned and waited for her to speak.

"Maybe you can take it from here," she said, hating her sudden rise of worry and weakness. She stood up to demons all the time. She was witch! Hear her cackle!

But Gazariel?

The image of the demon's silk shoes with painted red

heels standing but inches from her face was the most heart-wrenching memory.

"You think he's going to hurt you?" Ethan asked. "I don't know why he would. It sounds like you took the one thing from him he least wanted. He should welcome you with open arms."

"Yeah? I don't think so. He probably thinks I can return the curse back to him."

"Can you?"

"No! The only way to break the curse is…" Yeah, that part about a true love willing to die for her? Ethan didn't need to know about that. "Like it or not, we are connected. He probably knows I'm close right now."

"Which means we should hurry. Whether he's happy or angry to see you, we'll find out soon enough."

She grabbed him by the coat. "Give me a plan, yeah? I mean, when we do find him, what then? Are you going to slap a pair of handcuffs on him and hope the steel doesn't instantly melt, and in turn, the demon melts us?"

He took the phone from her. "I've got a containment crew on speed dial. They'll be here five minutes after my call. Can I, uh…use this now?"

"Yes, sure." She wiped off her blood from the screen and he started to scroll. "But what are we going to do while we wait out those very long and most likely painful five minutes in the demon's presence?"

"Certainly Jones gave me a demon manacle." He patted his pocket. "It'll contain the subject."

"Let me see it."

"Don't you trust me? Do you think I'd walk in on a demon ill-prepared? I've done this before."

"Have you?" She wasn't feeling it. He hadn't seemed

to have a plan yet. Why all of a sudden should he be prepared?

"Don't worry, Tuesday. I've got this one."

She sighed and dropped her shoulders. Wasn't as if she had a right to argue. She was merely the lure. And she did want to get this show on the road. The sooner they found Gazariel, the quicker she would be freed.

Ethan talked to someone on the line, confirming arrival in five minutes.

Time to let the guy show her he was the man and that he had everything under control? In her experience that never seemed to go quite as spectacularly as the man thought it would. And she was always left to sweep up the bloody pieces.

He smiled at her as he conferred with whomever he was talking to.

Why she should let Ethan take the alpha route was beyond her, but she submitted because…that ridiculous charming smile did possess a magic of its own.

As did the wanting, needy witch who had been willing to summon a demon to save her fickle lover's eyesight.

"Let's do this then," she said as Ethan hung up. "But don't say I didn't warn you in advance. This is not going to go well."

Chapter 8

Ethan did not appreciate that the witch had no trust in him. Before taking the cozy seat of director of Acquisitions, he'd been a retriever for a century. He knew this job and had chased every artifact, magical spell and creature in existence. Demons were easy enough to subdue if a man had the proper bind. And CJ had promised the manacle he'd given him would work.

He checked his pocket for the small iron pod, which he need only toss at the demon to bind him. And at his wrist he'd drawn a demon protection spell with a felt-tip marker before leaving his loft. He would be able to approach Gazariel, but it should deflect any demonic magic until the subject was securely bound.

Proceeding onward, he strode toward the elevator in the building lobby. Tuesday followed. He probably didn't need her from this point on. The phone GPS spell had taken them as far as it could. The demon was somewhere in the building. But the fact she wore the demon's sigil, and was feeling the demon's presence now, could not be overlooked.

And as long as she was with him, he could protect her from Gazariel. "Up and to the left," Tuesday reported as they stepped onto the elevator and the doors closed behind them. Barry Manilow's "Mandy" hummed out of the speakers while they slowly rose two floors.

"You're tracking now from a...feeling?" Ethan asked.

"It's the sigil. It senses the demon. As I'm sure he feels me. And that is not a pleasant feeling, let me tell you."

"You can wait outside."

"Don't think so, vampire. I'm not a pussy. I'm in it to win it. Besides, how do you intend to enter a private residence?"

Vampires could not enter a private residence unless invited. It was something that didn't ever cause Ethan concern because he'd developed ways to get around that detour over the years. "I'll call out the demon."

"Not going to happen. He's too smart. You'll have to follow me inside." She looked upward, then closed her eyes. "Must be the top floor. Yep." The doors dinged and she strolled out, heading left down the hallway. "You should probably call in your containment crew right now."

"They should already be on the grounds." Ethan took out his phone. He dialed and gave the team leader directions to the building and floor. Estimated arrival time was less than five minutes.

"I feel like it's...just ahead," Tuesday said as she

pressed her fingers between her breasts. "Must be that door at the end of the hallway."

"Must be?"

The witch stopped and tugged apart her blousy shirt to reveal the glowing sigil. It was faint but glowed red, as if it burned. Definitely working.

Ethan nodded. "All right. It's that suite. I suppose if a demon is going to live it up in the ritzy part of town he should go for the best. Let me take the lead."

"Why? You got magic to keep back the demon?"

"I've got the manacle and demonic wards."

"That's sweet." She stopped before him, hands to her hips. "But what are you going to do when the bastard charges us and then smokes out of sight? You can't manacle smoke. We need to catch him unawares. Which I'm guessing is going to be impossible thanks to your bait."

She suddenly hissed and swore, pressing her hand to her chest. Actual smoke tendriled between her fingers.

"He's close. I gotta ward myself." She stretched out her arms over her head, then swung them down along her body to her feet. A whoosh of cool air prickled across Ethan's skin. "You want in?"

Ethan didn't have to consider it. "Hell yes."

She slapped her hands to the top of his head, then dragged both down along his shoulders and his length to his feet, drawing around him with what he felt as a tightening tingle that briefly squeezed his skin. He'd never submitted to witchcraft before, but this adventure was offering up a slew of new challenges.

"What will this do?" he asked.

"Hopefully, keep the demon from peeling our skin off too terribly quickly." She noticed his gape. "I don't know. Maybe he's not the skin-peeling type."

"I thought you knew this demon?"

"I do, but it's not like we had coffee and got to know one another. Last time I saw him was in the seventeenth century. And he placed his hand on my heart and filled me full of yuck."

"A yuck that you asked for."

"Stating facts isn't going to win you points."

"I know. You were near death. Anyone would have taken what he offered just to stay alive."

"Right, I wasn't thinking with all my faculties. And hey, I'm still alive, so I guess I should be thankful. Now. You take the lead. Knock on his door, why don't you?"

Ethan stepped up and took a moment to consider what he was doing. Casually knocking on a demon's door? Perhaps a team fully armed with semiautomatics and full assault gear? His days of knocking down the door to a werewolf pack's lair with a battering ram were long gone, but he never lost the skill or the caution.

Of course, the witch was right. If entry was required, he'd need to follow her in.

Ethan knocked on the door. The containment crew would be armed to the extent that they could hold the demon and some powerful spells. Where were they?

Tuesday hissed and clutched her chest. The demon had to know she was near. If they didn't act now they might lose him. She stood beside him. And he strangely felt like they were two door-to-door salesmen, hawking their mundane and ridiculous goods to complete strangers. Tuesday winked at him.

Her winks always made him feel a twinge of promise. The job did have some high points, after all.

"He's gone," she said with a gasp.

"What?"

"I don't feel him anymore. The sigil has gone cold. Look."

Indeed, the mark between her breasts was now merely dark gray, as if a faded tattoo.

Ethan reacted. He stepped back and lunged a kick at the door right beside the lock mechanism. The door swung inward and slammed against the wall. Tuesday walked over the threshold and said, "I invite you to enter, vampire."

Didn't matter who offered it, the invite was the key to breeching that nuisance vampire deterrent.

Ethan strode into the apartment, which opened into a vast room, gaudily furnished with a leopard-print sofa and chairs. The entire opposite wall sported floor-to-ceiling windows that looked out over the snow-dusted forest below. He had the option to go left or right. Right was a kitchen, so he turned left and raced down the hallway.

Tuesday stayed behind and began to chant some witchy incantation. It tightened the ward about his skin. *Good call, witch.*

The bedroom was empty, though the bedclothes were rumpled and the sheets pushed to the end. He held a hand over the mattress but didn't sense any warmth. In the bathroom the gleam of silver fixtures advertising ridiculous wealth blinded him, but no one hid in there. He rushed back out to the kitchen, where Tuesday stood surrounded by a glowing violet light.

"What are you doing?"

"He's coming," she said from within the violet aura, and turned toward the kicked-open front door.

Charging down the hallway strode a tall, dark-haired

man—demon—with fire in his eyes and wicked curved blades in each of his hands.

Tuesday felt her violet protective ward crack and fall away as the demon crossed the threshold into his own home. She was the intruder, and she felt a wicked tug at her energies because of it. As well, her initial white light began to shiver. It wouldn't hold for long. Nor would Ethan's.

Yet at the same time her chest lifted, her hands reached as if to caress, and her body wanted to walk toward the man. Demon. The one who had cursed her. Who had tricked her and set her on the path toward a loveless life. But as much as she embraced her choice to take that curse—at the time it had been her only option to survive—she did not want to embrace Gazariel. She had too much fight in her to succumb to anything else he should wish to put upon her.

But did Ethan? The vampire stood before the demon, shoulders back and in a defensive stance. He held the manacle bind in one hand, but had yet to toss it at the demon. Because he could not. The demon's power filled the room.

Gazariel clanked the curved blades together before him. Brilliant sparks scattered to the floor. He then splayed out his arms, not quite ready for battle, more a show of power. "So my curse taker has returned for more? Long time, no see, witch."

His voice was liquid and compelling. And indeed, the man was beautiful beyond compare. Dark hair spilled like diamonds past his shoulders. His face was perfectly symmetrical and his eyes glistened like blue gemstones.

A mouth that any woman would dream to kiss curled in wicked satisfaction.

"Idiot," Tuesday admonished herself as she shook herself out of the stare. That was exactly what the demon wanted. Her adoration. "I didn't return of my free will," she said to Gazariel. "I would never purposely seek you again. Never."

"And yet you have." Gazariel glanced at Ethan. "Vampire. Can't release the manacle?" The demon blew him a kiss. "What do you want from me that you would enter my home without permission?"

"You have the book of angel names and sigils written by the muse. Give it to me and we'll leave without incident."

Gazariel's laughter echoed like dulcet chimes throughout the room, but ended on a deafening snarl that coiled in Tuesday's lungs and tightened her breaths. Her white light wisped away, leaving her vulnerable. And the wanting rose. He was so attractive. And his voice...

"I don't know what you're talking about." The demon strolled casually toward the windows. With a flick of each hand the curved blades apported away from him and disappeared.

Taking his chance, Ethan flung the manacle toward the demon. Gazariel put up a hand, stopping the manacle in midair.

Startled out of the ridiculous pining, Tuesday snapped back into focus. She threw her own magic into the mix and asked the bind to find its victim. The small black hexagon manacle shuddered in midair, struggling against the demon's magic and her own. It cracked, emitting a beam of green light, and then dropped to the floor and shattered.

Ethan spoke into his phone. "Now!"

"The cavalry?" Gazariel glanced out the opened doorway. He shook his shoulders and spread out his arms, great black wings suddenly emerging behind him, wide enough to stretch the width of the room. "I don't think so."

With a bend of his fingers, Gazariel tugged Tuesday across the room, her feet dragging on the marble floor and toes tilting backward. She couldn't stop the movement. And when she landed in the demon's arms, he turned her back against his chest and clamped a hand up under her jaw. The icy prick of his fingernails to her skin pushed her back four centuries to that dreaded night he had touched her heart. And had taken love from her life ever after.

A forward sweep of his wing glanced across her face. It burned yet smelled sweet, as if flowers mingled with the most delectable treats. Lilacs. Oh… He was a wicked beauty.

The sigil on her chest burned brightly and she cried out at the pain of it. And at that moment Gazariel cried out, too, releasing her and shoving her to the floor.

"Damn it!" Wings folding down and dusting the floor, he shook out the hand that must have touched the sigil. "I forget we are inexplicably bound. And that was a curse I did not want to ever feel again. You, witch, are an imposition."

"And you are an asshole. But nothing has changed in four centuries, eh?"

"The containment team is on their way up," Ethan

announced. "Hand over the code now and we won't have to use force."

"Force?" The demon laughed. As his wings assumed full, shiny display behind him, he lifted his head regally. "You don't know what you're dealing with, do you, vampire? You, who would ally yourself with a powerful dark witch, yet are completely unaware of how her connection to me is forged. I might have put the curse inside her, but it will forever be rooted in my bones. It is why I have chosen to avoid Miss Knightsbridge for all this time. I can feel that bedamned curse. It wants back inside me." He clutched the fingers of one hand before him. "And know that for as long as she wears my curse, whatever I feel she will feel when we are in proximity."

Ethan glanced to Tuesday, who pushed up from the floor and backed away from the demon. She wasn't about to use any more magic when she knew it would be ineffective. Expelling such would only drain her.

"I think that means that if you hurt him, you hurt me," she said. "Peachy." Especially since she knew the retrieval of the book probably meant much more to Ethan than protecting her.

"She may carry the one thing I least want in this realm," the demon said. With a discerning tilt of his head, he appeared to sniff the air, perhaps take her in a bit more deeply. "But I must admit, it is attractive the longer I stand in its presence. Love can be so…heart-wrenching." He pursed his lips at them. "Oh. Sorry. You don't know that, do you, my witch? Or at least, you don't know anymore."

"If you're having relationship issues, then take it back," Tuesday said. "The curse is yours for the taking. I've had enough of it."

"Is that so? Does the pitiful witch now desire love? Perhaps you wish to fall head over heels with another witch hunter. You wore the gashes in your skin so beautifully." Gazariel chuckled and shook his head. "I will never have enough of the mortal pleasures I am able to enjoy thanks to not being shackled by that curse. Love and adoration are my oxygen! And I have tired of the two of you."

Out in the hallway a crew of three appeared, approaching cautiously.

Gazariel shook his head. "Too little. Too late." With a jaunty tilt of his head, he winked at Tuesday. "Let's have a little fun."

Spreading his arms out wide, Gazariel recited a demonic incantation. His wings closed about him, circling him, yet still kept a border of four feet around him. His own summoning circle, Tuesday guessed. From within the circle it began to glow blue, and a flurry of blue light wavered and then shot out to disperse into the ceiling, walls and floor.

Suddenly the building began to shudder. Tuesday had never experienced an earthquake but this must be what it felt like. Her body jittered. The floor tremored beneath her feet. A lamp toppled and Ethan stepped before her, as if to protect.

The demon smiled wickedly. In his hand he held a glowing blue light. "I will bring this building down if you do not take your minions and leave, vampire."

"He's serious," Tuesday said through a tight jaw. She could feel the demon's intrusion into her very being. He was using her magic, the darkness that coiled in the sigil, to enhance his own magic and spread it out as wide as the building. "Get out of here!"

"I'm not leaving you." But when Ethan tugged her arm, she felt as if she was planted on the floor. Her legs were leaden. She could not move.

The walls began to crack.

"I can't move. You've got to get everyone out of the building. Save them! Now!"

The containment crew shouted to Ethan for orders. Ethan commanded them to evacuate the building— knock on all doors to get everyone out. He caught Tuesday's gaze and didn't ask her anything, but she understood. He would protect innocent lives first and foremost.

"I'll be fine," she said. "If this bastard takes me out, he might take himself out, too. He won't let that happen. Just hurry. Get the people out of this building!"

Ethan dashed off.

And Tuesday growled at Gazariel. "You dare play with the lives of innocents?"

The demon chuffed. He tossed the blue ball of light through the open doorway and down the hall. "Always."

A painting fell off the wall and the window shattered behind him. Tuesday tried to conjure up the shards and send them back at the demon, but she couldn't focus beyond merely standing upright and not screaming. She felt as if he touched her heart. Again. And then a sudden tug at her entire body, similar to when she'd walked too far away from Ethan, briefly knocked her off balance.

Had the bond been severed? Ethan wouldn't be able to run through the building otherwise.

The demon winked at her. "I did that. You're welcome."

She acknowledged the sudden release, a freedom she'd desired since arriving in Paris. That was a good thing. For more than her. It would allow Ethan to clear out the innocents and escape the shaking building.

"Don't harm anyone," she pleaded. "Please, Gazariel."

"You surprise me, witch. With all the darkness I can feel within you, such an incredible lack of love, and still you plead for the lives of innocents. Something wrong with that. You're but one step away from warlock. Why not let it happen?"

"Is that what you want? Wouldn't that then give me power over you?"

Speaking it made her realize suddenly that maybe it could be so. If she went warlock could she control Gazariel? She'd never had a reason to do so—for centuries—until Ethan had gotten her involved in chasing the demon down. Warlocks were witches who had gone against their own, and often committed terrible acts against humanity. But they were so powerful.

Was it worth the sacrifice of her last remnants of light to subdue this threat? Gazariel held a book that could destroy so many innocents.

All of a sudden Gazariel fisted a hand before him and Tuesday was pulled across the room toward him. She slammed against his chest and he spun, gripping her against his body. The final window smashed out and he soared through it and over the nearby treetops, landing her on the snowy ground with a spine-crimping thump.

Tuesday lay on her back with Gazariel kneeling over her. His wings coved them in a private embrace. The demon pressed a palm over her chest. "You have been such a good girl, keeping this wicked curse from me. But the vampire has drawn up your naughtiness. And... do I sense you really *do* seek love? Poor, pitiful witch."

"I get the feeling you are having love troubles your-self. Did someone jilt you? Why not take back the curse so you won't be bothered by such foolish human emo-tions? If only for a little while?" Desperation did not suit her, but she'd not been able to stop speaking her hopes.

A curl of his fingers felt as if he was gripping her very heart. Tuesday moaned at the pain.

"Ethan just wants the code," she blurted out. "Give him the book and we'll leave you alone. Why do you want to destroy the world when you're having so much fun in it?"

"The book isn't for me. It's a gift for…a woman."

"What? Did you give it to someone else? Someone you love? No. You're trying to win someone's love? Is that it?"

"Enough talk about a stupid book."

She'd guessed right. "So not everyone loves you, eh?"

The demon was not having it now.

"You, witch, are going to leave me alone. Because I promise…" He bent forward, his hair dusting her face. A dark wanting desire melted over her skin as he whis-pered against her ear, "If you follow me, I will take out your loveless heart and devour it."

With that, a force whisked Gazariel away from her in a beating of wings and a swirl of snowflakes from the ground.

Gasping and panting, Tuesday rolled to her side and coiled up into a ball on the cold, snowy earth. He'd touched her heart again. And each time it left behind a mark that she would never feel heal over.

The demon had plans to give the code book to a woman? Why? And who was this woman? Had to be a lover, someone he was trying to win, as she had guessed. It made little sense. She couldn't imagine Gazariel stooping so low. Couldn't he have love with but a flutter of his thick, black lashes? And he was not a demon who could condone the ending of the world. Who, then, would remain alive to worship and adore him?

Through the wide-spaced tree trunks Tuesday saw a man's legs running toward her. Ethan plunged to the snow-littered ground and leaned over to embrace her. He'd left her alone with the demon.

She shoved him away. "Don't touch me!"

Ethan reared back and put up his palms. "I'm sorry. Everyone is out of the building. The shaking has stopped. I've called in the fire department and the police. Where's the demon?"

"Gone." For good, if she would only stay away from him. Which, at the moment, felt like the safest and smartest thing to do.

"Let me help you up. Get you to the car so you can warm up. Did he hurt you?"

Only for centuries. And so deeply, even she could not have foreseen the depth of such wounds. Something Ethan could never understand.

Tuesday pushed up and stood, backing away from the vampire. She put up a hand and focused her repulsive energies toward him. She was tattered and weak, but she did manage to topple him backward a few feet.

"The binding between us has been broken," she said. "Time for you to let me go."

"We haven't gotten what we want."

"It's what *you* want, not what I want." She sighed and winced. This whole mess was because some demon who had an abundance of love wanted even more? What the hell? "Just let me go, Ethan. Gazariel is…too strong. I need to be away from…this."

"I still need your help."

"As your prisoner?"

He inhaled through his nose and splayed his hands before him. "I'm sorry, Tuesday. You're right. I've gone about this wrong. You should… Yes, you're free to go. I still need your help, but I won't force you. If you feel the desire to stop Gazariel from harming so many, you know where to find me." He stepped back, but then stopped. "Let me at least get you a ride. A place to stay."

"Leave me," she said. A shiver of cold traced over her skin. A hug would feel welcome. She didn't know how to ask for it, though.

Ethan nodded, then turned to stride off. It was too easy for the vampire to walk away from her.

And Tuesday exhaled and held her breath as she watched him slip between the trees and back into the commotion surrounding the evacuation. Police cars had arrived. Red and blue lights flashed. The building had not collapsed, but she suspected it was so structurally damaged it would have to be condemned.

He was needed there in the midst of that chaos. The man had chosen the correct fight, instead of staying and holding her. Because…she did need someone to hold her right now. Her body felt ready to tumble onto the ground and melt into the snow. To surrender.

The demon had taken so much from her today.

She cast a look up into the sky. She did not know where Gazariel had gone. And she didn't want to know.

Chapter 9

Ethan had paced the loft for hours. He'd not been able to get leaving Tuesday alone in the woods out of his mind. Now as he strode the halls of headquarters, destined for the Archives, he wished he would have tried harder. To make her understand that he needed her help and that she could trust him.

And beyond that, to let her know that his initial feelings for her had changed. They'd shared much in the past few days and he'd developed a real understanding for the witch. He genuinely cared for her.

The binding CJ had conjured between Ethan and Tuesday had been a mistake. It hadn't given her a reason to trust him. And she had been a good sport, going along with every request he made of her.

But he'd felt her terror when they'd stood in the apartment and Gazariel had begun to make the walls shake. The demon had connected with Tuesday. In a terrible and painful way. And then to find her lying in the snow outside, looking so defeated and frail, his heart had cringed.

The witch had been cursed to never know love. What sort of hollow, empty life had she lived? He couldn't fathom such a lack of love.

Yet she deserved more protection and respect than he could give her. So he'd let her go. He'd find another way to track Gazariel. He now knew the demon was in the city. And if he had been in Paris for this long, then what reason had he to leave now? Unless they'd spooked him.

Ethan needed to learn as much as he could about the demon. The knowledge could only enhance his search efforts.

The vast Archives was located many stories below ground. It was a repository of all things, from books and ancient artifacts, to histories of the various paranormal species, and related ephemera. It basically housed all the information about the paranormal nations that could be contained. There were also catalogued weapons, shackled magics, volatile items placed in containment and even a few creatures that were much better off—for the humans' sake—locked up than out running loose in the mortal realm.

As director of Acquisitions, Ethan had seen to placing a good majority of the contents of the Archives there. Acquisitions was often referred to as the Archives' dirty little secret, for their methods were brutal and unforgiving. And if the Archives needed to contain an ancient evil—or merely wanted it to study—they asked Ethan to deploy a retriever.

As well, if a mysterious stranger showed up in his office with information that a certain book of angel sigils and names had gone missing, Ethan was charged to react appropriately. At all costs, the mortal realm must be protected from discovering there were creatures and magics that existed beyond myth and fable.

Secrets. It was always about keeping secrets. He knew too many of them. And some days he wished he could erase them all from memory and start anew. Other days, it was good to know exactly what the world could—and did—deal him.

Entering the Archives' office, Ethan spied Certainly Jones sitting behind an ancient wood desk, his feet propped up on the desk as he sipped tea. The man rarely wore shoes, which always startled Ethan. He liked to maintain a certain business decorum at the office. But the Archives was not his domain. And CJ possessed mysterious ways and a manner that was ever polite but also secretive. However, the man was trustworthy, and that was what mattered most to Ethan.

"How'd the containment go this afternoon?" CJ asked, not bothering to sit up from his relaxed posture.

"Do you have a new demon behind bars?"

"Nope."

"Then you know how it went. I need your help, Jones."

"Where's Tuesday Knightsbridge?"

Ethan gestured with a vague sweep over his shoulder. "I let her go. She'd served her purpose."

"Uh-huh." CJ sat up, giving Ethan that I-know-you-better-than-you-know-yourself look. Witches and their looks. A man had to be cautious around them.

"The demon broke the binding between us," Ethan

said. "It didn't feel right to make her stay unless she wanted to actually help."

"And she did not. Makes sense. You did kidnap her."

"I did not—" Ethan knew an argument over semantics was senseless.

The witch stood. "What help can I offer? I can provide knowledge, but as for hands-on, you know I'm not much for taking on demons. Not anymore, you understand."

CJ had once gone into Daemonia, purposely, and had returned from that despicable, demon-infested realm. Actually, his return had been an orchestrated rescue by his twin brother, Thoroughly Jones. The trip there had changed CJ, made him miserable and dark and... he'd come near to death. But another witch—a pretty red-haired woman named Viktorie Saint-Charles— had helped him to escape the psychological torments of those demonic hosts and now he avoided demons like the proverbial plague.

"I need all the information you have on Gazariel," Ethan said. "Specifically, what you can tell me about the curse he had. The one he gave to Tuesday. And if there's a way to break it."

Because if they could break the curse then he need not fear that Tuesday would be harmed when finally he did capture Gazariel.

"I'll have to search the records." CJ gestured toward the silver service by the wall behind Ethan. "Tea?"

Tuesday sipped the thick hot chocolate and tugged the alpaca coat snugly around her shoulders. She was still cold even though she could feel the heat blast through the nearby vent that was level with her ankles. She sat before the front second-floor window of Angelina, having been drawn to the chic yet touristy café because she'd once heard they served the best hot chocolate ever.

Truth. But it was also rich and so sweet she was already flying high on a sugar rush. Good thing she'd foregone checking out the decadent pastries. With but a clasp of her waitress's hand, she'd assured the bill was paid and that no one would remember her sitting here for two hours, staring out over the snow-frothed horse-chestnut trees that edged the Tuileries Garden across the street. And wondering.

What to do now?

Ethan had released her from duty. Well, she would have walked away from him no matter if he'd given her leave or not. Wasn't as if she'd volunteered for the mission. She'd had no choice. It hadn't been duty, but forced servitude.

But now that she did have a choice, she wasn't sure what came next. Her intention was to hop a flight back home. That was the logical decision. Maybe do a little touristing before hopping on that flight? That option was a little less safe and she risked the vampire deciding he needed her again and finding her.

Or she could walk back into the fray and put up her fists and show the demon her teeth.

All her life she had stood up for her beliefs, ever since she'd been given a renewed chance at life thanks to the dreadful curse the demon had put inside her. But if she couldn't know love then she'd be damned to sit around and pout about it. She had not once felt regretful for her decision made in that dark cell outside the pigpen.

And yet, she wasn't feeling so strong or powerful

at the moment. Her chest ached from Gazariel's touch. He had touched her heart. And should they meet again he wouldn't pause to rip it out. That was a truth she inexplicably knew.

Back in the seventeenth century, the demon hadn't wanted the curse he'd put inside her. But this afternoon, she'd seen the glitter of desire in his eyes as he had recognized the tease of lacking love. He'd wanted it. And he had not.

Something was up with Gazariel and his love life. He'd not been able to hide his reaction to her guessing at that. Of course, it was possible not everyone would love him. Yes? Maybe? Tuesday couldn't fathom being loved by everyone she met. Was The Beautiful One growing weary of unending love and devotion? It did sound tiresome.

And yet, a small taste of love seemed too delicious to Tuesday right now.

Yes, she'd been near death, wishing to die, when she'd accepted the curse. Over the centuries, she'd made it her own, embracing the utter lack of love. How easy it was to never have to worry about love and all its ridiculous predicaments.

And she'd been fine with fleeting romantic relationships over the years. Just when the man started to get all doe-eyed and she suspected he was falling in love, he'd suddenly notice something about her he hated, or he'd simply leave. She had expected those reactions, so they hadn't bothered her. Too much.

But now she wasn't so sure. Gazariel's touch had given the curse new life. Had strengthened it. Ethan had walked away from her with ease. And that was because of the curse, surely.

Suddenly the thought of not having love in her life was

tangible and real. A hole in her heart. And she couldn't be a strong powerful woman if part of her had a hole in it.

Did she want to shuck off the curse and allow love into her life? Could she be so brave? It wasn't as if she was in love with Ethan Pierce or he with her. But she wanted that option. She really did.

"Just leave Paris," she whispered over the cup of chocolate. "You know it's the right choice. The vampire has no interest in you beyond what you can do for him."

And what she could do for him might bring back the demon. And that would see her bloody heart dangling from Gazariel's fingers. One way or another, she would not survive if she didn't leave the city today.

She snapped the rubber band.

Yeah, it was the only choice.

Pulling out the cell phone she'd slipped from Ethan's pocket while lying on the snowy ground, she downloaded an airline app and checked the schedule for flights leaving for the US. There were four this evening. And each one still had remaining seats.

The Archives had a room for virtually every species of paranormal that inhabited the mortal realm. The room on witches was the largest. The unicorn room was the smallest due to a lack of information. But Tuesday did wield an alicorn, Ethan thought, as they passed by that room. Just what sort of trouble could a witch get into with that thing? He wanted to know.

He really did.

As Ethan followed CJ into the demon room, he felt a cool chill fall over his skin and he adopted a militant need to scan the room and look over his shoulder. Nothing followed him down the aisles of dark, dusty bookshelves, nor did he see anything flying above near the two-story-high ceiling. But he was not mistaken that pairs of red eyes seemed to flicker here and there from within the books and haphazardly stacked artifacts.

"Tamatha has been rearranging," CJ said. "It's a bit of a clutter right now. The inner chamber is neater."

CJ pushed open a heavy steel door. It looked like something that should front a bank vault. The dark witch's casual manner relaxed Ethan's tensions. He followed him inside the massive annex room, taking in the musty odor and the many aisles that boasted boxes or small cages with creatures inside. Books papered an entire wall that stretched the length of the chamber.

"Ignore the blaggert," CJ offered as they filed past a small glass-barred cage, secured with electronic locks. Inside, a diminutive red creature with tufted ears bent and waggled his bare ass at them as they passed.

"The *Bibliodaemon* is up on that dais," CJ said. "As with most species, there is a book, or bible, that describes them all, and is constantly updated."

"Like the *Book of All Spells*."

Ethan knew that book was like a living archive of any and all spells created by witches. If a witch was speaking a new spell right now, it was magically being written into that book. There was another for vampires, *The Vampire Codex*, though he'd never been curious about it. Weird, to think that now. Of course, he lived the vampire's life; no need to have it explained to him in text.

"Yes, like that book." CJ skipped up two steps to a steel dais, where a table displayed a huge book that was about three feet high and two feet wide. It sat open to some pages that looked like time-stained parchment. With a sweep of his hand and a mutter of Latin, followed by the demon Gazariel's name, CJ sent the pages fluttering. "It'll take a few minutes to bring up the records. Kind of like the internet but slower and more interesting, eh?"

"Your job must never see a dull day," Ethan commented as he pulled up a stool to sit and watch the book pages move rapidly in search.

"It's a kick, that's for sure. But we could use more help. I've only got Tamatha as my assistant. She's off in the harpie room today. Maybe? I don't know. It's quite the labyrinth down here. A couple more hands would be helpful. We've such a backload of stuff from your retrievers."

"You mean it hasn't all been catalogued?"

"Who has the time? I have a holding room that's warded to the nines. Tamatha and I are working as fast as we can to keep up with the acquisitions."

"You should put in a requisition to the Council. I'm sure they'd approve you hiring more help."

CJ nodded. "Thing is, I'm very particular about who I work with. And I don't have time to vet someone new. So I guess I either lighten up or shut up, eh?"

"Seems to be the case."

The pages stopped moving and CJ leaned over the book and read. "'Gazariel, master angel of the First Void, Creator of Vanity, fallen to Beneath where he became known as The Beautiful One, and was cast out by the Devil Himself.'"

"That demon was once an angel?"

"Many demons were originally angels," CJ said. "When they Fell, those who landed in Beneath assumed demonic form. Others became the Sinistari, who now hunt the Fallen."

"I thought the majority of demons were from Dae-monia?"

"They are. Yet you'll not find a former Fallen One who is now demon who would ever set foot in Daemo-nia. While Daemonia has its own version of royalty, the Fallen Ones deem themselves highest of all demons since they originated in Above. Daemonia is, literally, beneath them. Looks like your guy has a reason for being called The Beautiful One. Creator of Vanity, eh?"

The demon had been primping when he'd stood be-fore them in the apartment complex. It was as if he couldn't *not* flaunt his beauty.

"Does it say why Himself cast him out of Beneath?" Ethan asked. "Isn't that odd? I thought The Old Lad was always looking for more minions."

CJ leaned over the book and read silently for a while. "Himself was jealous."

"Why, because Gazariel is pretty?"

"Exactly. So he cursed Gazariel with an evil that would not allow him to own love and cast him out to the mortal realm."

"To own it," Ethan repeated, thinking, trying to work this out. "But not necessarily to never know it?"

CJ shrugged. "I suppose. But I assume if a person would have fallen in love with the demon, while he still wore the curse, something terrible would have happened to that person to make them stop loving him."

"Yet Gazariel himself could actually love still." Which would mean that Tuesday could still love. Maybe.

"So the curse came from the devil…" Ethan did not repeat Himself's name. Say the name three times in a row? You've invited the devil for a visit. Not some-thing he ever intended to do. "And obviously Gazariel didn't want that hanging on him, so he pawned it off on a witch."

"Interesting that he was able to so easily give it away."

"Tuesday said she asked for it."

CJ lifted an eyebrow.

"She had been beaten and tortured by a witch hunter, whom she loved, and was very near death."

"Then some demon offers to take love, which hurt her, from her life?"

"Exactly."

"Poor thing." CJ propped his arms akimbo. "Tuesday is dark but she doesn't strike me as evil incarnate."

"If the curse is designed to keep away love, maybe that's all it can get out of her? If she is innately good?"

"Possible. But how is learning this going to help you get a hand on the demon? If he's slipped through your hands once already?"

"I'm trying to gather as much information as I can. And whatever happens I don't want Tuesday getting hurt. She and Gazariel are tied together. He told us if we hurt him she will feel it."

"That makes things difficult. But if she's left the city? She could be at a safe distance."

"But how to know what that safe distance is?"

"Why is Gazariel in Paris?" CJ asked. "If he's got the Final Days code, why not use it? Or is he holding it for someone? Waiting to hand it off? Or has he already done so? There's a reason he's not running far."

"Right. And now that he knows I want what he has…"

"Then he'll make himself scarce."

"Or will he? I'm not sure." Ethan crossed his arms, considering what he'd learned. "There is the connection between him and Tuesday. She is key to calling the demon forth. And there was a moment when I'm sure I saw the desire for the curse in the demon's eyes. When he touched Tuesday, he could feel that darkness calling to him. He said something about love not being what it was cracked up to be. I think he would take the curse back if given the right conditions."

"Which are?"

"I don't know. A bad love affair? Can you perform a tracking spell like Tuesday did? I need to know where Gazariel is right now."

"I'm sure she was using the sigil as a direct conduit. Do you have something from Tuesday that I might use to call up the demon?"

"I…no. Maybe? She was at my place for a bit. I'll have to go see if she left anything behind."

"If you could find some hair strands that would be optimal. That still won't guarantee I can get a fix on the demon. I'll give it a shot, though."

Ethan slapped a hand into CJ's. "Thanks, man."

"Have you considered calling in a reckoner for when you do find Gazariel? Perhaps as a threat?"

A reckoner consigned demons to Daemonia. To threaten Gazariel with going to that place, which he must fear as most mortals feared Hell, could provide some leverage, perhaps even get him to confess about where the book was.

"Good call. I'll have to look up Savin Thorne."

"He's living in the fourteenth. Bit of a hermit. But yes, I'd recommend the man."

"Thanks. I'm heading home to see if I can find traces of the witch. Can I get a copy of that page?" He pointed to the oversized book.

"Why do you people think I'm some kind of a copy machine?"

Ethan shrugged. "You're not?" Then he chuckled. "Have your assistant send me a digital file of it, yes?"

"I can have it to you in a few hours."

"Thanks." Ethan patted his jacket pocket. No phone. Had he lost it in the scuffle at the Bois de Boulogne? Damn. "Send it to my office email," he said. "I seem to have misplaced my phone. Er, will you show me the way out of here? We took so many turns I don't want to end up in the werewolf room."

"Why? Not keen on the dogs?"

"Not so much that as not in the mood to relive some rather sketchy history."

"Blood Wars?" CJ asked.

Ethan nodded.

"I completely understand. Just being in this room creeps me out. Too many memories of an experimental magic excursion to Daemonia gone awry. Let's go."

Tuesday stood in line behind a family of six, who waited with shoes in hand to pass through security at Charles de Gaulle airport. The flight took off in an hour, and she was ready for the eight-hour sleep she would sink into as soon as her butt landed on the narrow seat.

But for perhaps the fifth time, she glanced over her shoulder and gazed out the windows at the stream of cabs letting off travelers or picking them up. Was she really ready to write off this adventure and mark it as defeat? That wasn't like her. She reveled in a good challenge. And if it involved getting down and dirty with some bastard demon? Bring it on. She could stand up to the most powerful of them and win. Every time.

Yes, even the one demon who wanted to rip out her heart.

And there was a certain sexy vampire who had sparked her interest. Was she simply going to walk away from the man without having gotten more than a few kisses? Didn't feel right. Even if she returned, fucked him and left, at least she'd have had that pleasure.

To leave or not?

She knew Gazariel would rely on her fear, on not wanting to lose her heart. And the idea of shivering before the demon did not sit well with her. She was stronger than this. And the demon was messing with her. He wanted to end the world because of…unrequited love? Sounded like a bad romance to her.

It was time to seriously consider transferring this curse back to Gazariel. If he wore the curse, he'd fall out of love and lose the desire to hand off a dangerous gift to goddess knew what kind of malicious entity.

Love? Tuesday clutched her shoes tightly against her chest. Yes, she was ready to welcome it into her life. She wanted it. And if that wasn't reason enough to turn and aim for the exit door, she wasn't about to let that ridiculous fop of a demon tell her what to do. It was time to stand up and show it her teeth.

"Mademoiselle?"

She turned to find the security guard waiting for her to remove her coat then step forward through the X-ray machine. She'd never liked those machines. Something wrong with peering inside a person and seeing their very bones.

"Right." She took one step forward, and then…one step back.

Chapter 10

Ethan opened his apartment door to discover a yawning witch waiting outside in the hallway.

She snapped her mouth shut and put up one finger. "I've got one more idea for a tracking spell on that bastard demon."

"Okay."

"But first, I need a shower." Tuesday strode inside, passing him by, and rummaged through her bag. She tugged out his phone and dropped it on the couch. "Yeah?"

He gestured toward the bedroom, which led to the bathroom. "You know where it is."

She didn't say another word. Didn't explain why she'd returned, or for how long. And he felt it best to let things play out and see what she'd offer him. Because he hadn't found anything of hers to give to CJ for a summoning spell, not even a single strand of hair.

He needed her. In more ways than he was willing to admit to himself.

But this time around, he'd play things closer to the vest. Not go all director-in-charge on her by forcing her to comply. This time, he'd follow the witch's lead. It felt right. It felt as though his heart demanded it.

After a shower, Tuesday pulled on a T-shirt that hung to her thighs, then looked in the mirror. Emblazoned across the shirt were the words, Surely Not Everybody Was Kung Fu Fighting. She'd found it in a vintage store while shopping with Ethan. Ha! And yes, there had been occasions in the nightclubs during the 1970s disco frenzy when everyone had been kung fu fighting. In dance mode, of course. Good times.

She was ready to pull out all her moves against Gazariel. She had no clue how to give the curse back to him, but she would not relent until it happened. If he was in love, maybe she could use that against him. She had to find out who his lover was. And how much she meant to him. Apparently enough to give her a trinket that could end the world.

Tuesday did a few kung fu moves in front of the mirror, then gave it her best fighter's face. That demon wanted to threaten her?

"Let's see what he does when love is taken away from him." And she delivered a knockout kick to her absent opponent.

Grabbing her bag, which she'd filled with a few more magical accoutrements thanks to her rushing around on a hot-chocolate high earlier, she wandered out through the bedroom and set down the bag in the corner between the bed and the living area. An old wood vanity held a record player and a neat stack of albums sat beside it. And on the other half of the vanity a crystal decanter with dark alcohol in it sat surrounded by three wide-bowled glasses.

Ethan sat on the sofa, legs up on the coffee table, bare feet tilted outward. He gazed idly at her.

"Let's do this spell before I fall asleep from utter exhaustion," she said, taking a few items out of her bag. "Get me something to write with. Like a felt-tip marker. Take off your shirt. And lie down in this big ol' salt circle I'm about to make."

She began to pour the bag of ordinary table salt she'd bought at a local market onto the wide plank flooring before the vanity.

Ethan, meanwhile, got a pen from the kitchen and tugged off his shirt. She did notice those washboard abs, and at that moment her circle took a distinct swerve inward.

Shaking off the alluring sight, Tuesday redirected the salt and closed up the circle. It was big enough to contain a very sizable vampire and his nekkid abs that screamed for some hella licking. She gestured toward it. "Lie down."

Ethan scratched his head, then pressed his thumb and forefinger close together. "Just a teeny bit of info first?"

She propped her hands on her hips. Fine. The man was cute enough that he could command that of her. "We want to catch The Beautiful One, yeah?"

"Agreed."

"I am the one who alerts the demon we're near. Not cool. So you need to become the bait or lure or even the GPS. With this spell, I'm going to make you into a tracker. You should be able to turn it on or off when needed. It'll be like you borrowing some of my magic but without having to perform bloodsexmagic."

He shrugged, then stepped inside the circle. "This doesn't require blood?"

"It does, but yours this time."

He put up a hand. "I'm a vampire."

Tuesday gave him a droll look. "I got that. First try, even."

"I don't give blood," he said. "I only take it."

"Get over your bad self."

He crossed his arms. "I refuse to give blood."

Tuesday inhaled through her nose and met the vampire eye-to-eye. All seriousness in those pretty gray irises. For all that she had given thus far, a few drops of blood shouldn't be a hardship for him. And yet, she looked down his face, to his neck, which was tight with tension, and along his arms, that ended in fists. Something was bothering him. And it had to do with the blood.

"It's not going to hurt. Promise," she lied. "And besides, you did give blood for the binding between the two of us."

"That was different. You were a mere…witch. And I was desperate."

"And you're not now?" Though she had caught the vitriol in the way he'd said *witch*. He had not liked her very much when she'd first arrived. A mutual feeling. But her feelings had changed. And she'd thought he was starting to come around as well.

"Why can't we use your blood?" he asked.

"Because you'd get turned on and toss me on the end of the bed before I could finish the spell."

He smirked and shook his head. Not the reaction

she'd been hoping for with the gibe, either. "We've been through this, witch. I don't go from calm to horny with the sniff of a few drops of blood."

"You were aroused by my blood in the car."

He closed his eyes. And Tuesday had to keep herself from leaning forward, moving in to smell his fresh outdoors scent. She wanted to kiss him. Damn her, the stupidest witch of all time. He had a certain allure, not unlike Gazariel's strange pull. But with Ethan it felt honest and even promising.

"The last time I gave blood I killed a woman," he stated plainly.

Tuesday leaned back and met the man's gaze. Stoic and calm, as he had been that first time she'd woken up in the cage to look upon her captor.

"You...killed. You're a vampire—"

"We don't all kill to survive," he interrupted. "I've never killed merely for blood. It is beneath me. It is unnecessary."

"But you have killed before. Many," she said, knowing it to be the truth. For she had walked through the same centuries as he had. No one lived that long and got out of it untouched by foulness or evil.

"I fought in the Blood Wars," he said. "Of course I've killed. It was kill or be killed then. But what I'm talking about is the voluntary giving of blood that results in loss of life. I can't do it. I won't."

"Ethan." She grabbed his hand and held it with both of hers. "Help me to understand. You killed someone by giving them blood? Were you...trying to transform them?"

He made to tug out of her grasp, so she pulled his hand closer and held it firmly. "Talk to me. I shared my ugly stuff with you. I've done desperate things at desperate times. Tell me why donating a few drops of blood is such a big no-no for you."

"A few drops? That's all you need?"

She shrugged. "Yeah?"

He lifted an eyebrow.

"It's not going to be a lot. I need it to trace the spell on you. I'm not going to take it into my veins, if that's got you worried. I don't intend to die today. Swear it by the seven sacred witches."

He studied her, and as he did she suspected he wasn't going to explain to her the whole deal behind his killing someone with a blood transfusion. She wanted to know about that wackiness. But really, this spell did not require a surgical operation or large amounts of the red stuff.

"There's no such thing as the seven sacred witches," he finally said.

Tuesday shrugged. "You got me. Now can we do this? Just a tiny donation is all I ask of you." She pinched her fingers together before him. "I won't even need an athame. Just…" She spun and leaned over to shuffle around in her bag, pulling out the alicorn. "This will be perfect. Yeah?"

"Just a small amount?" Ethan asked. And when she nodded, he sighed and sat down.

"All the way down," she directed, and the vampire lay on his back. "This won't hurt a bit. Maybe a little. You're a big boy. You got this."

But what she wouldn't give to have heard about the person he'd killed. It bothered him enough to freak him out over a little blood ritual. She would learn about it. Soon enough.

With Ethan prone in the circle, Tuesday remained outside the line of salt, and took a moment to admire his physique. What was it about vampires and how they didn't need to work out, yet they all seemed to have the abs and pecs of a bodybuilder? Wasn't easy to disregard. But she would.

For now.

Kneeling, she leaned in and placed a palm to his chest. "Just go with it, okay?"

"I do owe you this much. Thanks, by the way."

"For what?"

"For coming back. You had every right to leave."

"Yeah, well I'm not going to let that asshole demon shove me around and make me feel like the weak one. If he's have relationship issues, ending the world is not the way to resolve them."

"Relationship issues?"

"Yeah. I think the demon wants to give the book to some chick to win her love. Or maybe he already has. He wasn't clear. I just knew with certainty that whoever the woman was, she wasn't in love with him."

"I thought everyone adored him?"

"Do you?"

"He was kind of handsome."

Tuesday couldn't stop some head-shaking laughter. "Right? I mean, it's crazy, but I thought the same."

"That's what makes him so dangerous," Ethan said.

"And why we need to be vigilant. We're strong. We can do this. Together…" She uncapped the red marker he'd found and checked the writing on the plastic tube. Water soluble. Good for him. He'd be able to wash this off later. "We make a pretty decent team. Now I'm going to draw a tracking grid on you."

Ethan put his hands behind his head and closed his eyes as she drew a circle on his chest, and within it, a pentagram. She marked the four compass directions. A copy of the sigil she wore was placed at the spirit peak of the pentagram. Gliding the marker under his pec, she couldn't help but slow down and study the rigid nipple and the sudden goose-bumping of his skin. He was aware she was studying him.

The man would jump if she dashed out her tongue and licked his skin. He wasn't overly hot. Vampires never were too hot, but weren't cold, either, as one might expect. The flesh and muscles beneath her hands were solid and hard. And oh, so delectable. And as the red line journeyed over one abdominal ridge and then the next, she pressed her lips together.

Didn't want to start drooling on the guy. That would be so not cool.

"Are you thinking what I'm thinking?" Ethan asked softly.

She finished her line work with three short dashes above his navel and set aside the marker, but remained leaning over the salt circle and close to his body. "What's that?"

He nudged up a shoulder. "That I like you touching me."

Tuesday lifted an eyebrow. He still had his eyes closed. And from her vantage point, so close to his ribs and looking up over that hard pectoral landscape, she thought she saw his smile grow.

"I am thinking the same thing," she answered truthfully. "You make for a nice drawing board."

"Your breath on my skin is making me uncomfortable."

She glanced down toward his jeans and…oh, yes, he

was growing hard. Well, she didn't need him aroused for this spell—nor did she want to spend too much time considering his arousal because that would only do the same to her—so she gave his stomach a quick smack with her fingers and sat back.

"What the hell?" He lifted his head to seek her.

"Had to be done. We've got to focus. No silly stuff."

"If that's the way you want to play it." He put his head down and closed his eyes again. "But I wouldn't call what I was thinking of doing to you silly."

Mercy. Had he really needed to say that? Because now Tuesday wanted to know what had been running through his thoughts. And how not-silly it might have been. Surely it had involved lots of skin-on-skin contact. And more of his devastating kisses. And if they were forced to do it inside the salt circle without upsetting the perimeter, they might have to get into all sorts of weird yet tight positions.

Hell, she must be overtired if she was slipping into random moments of sex fantasy. What the hex? She shook her head and grabbed the alicorn. The quicker she finished the spell, the sooner she could find out the answer regarding the silly stuff.

Waving the alicorn above the man's chest, she told him to be quiet.

"When will you need my blood?" he asked.

"Oh, uh, soon." She didn't want to freak him out and have him running away before she even got this going. "I'll use this." She waggled the alicorn. "Now. Silence. Just focus on the tone of my voice and drawing in the vibrations that I send to you, yeah?"

He nodded and closed his eyes again. Moonlight gleamed through the big windows to their sides, and fell across his face as if lighting a Hollywood vampire in the big redemption scene. Oh, what a pretty man.

She'd returned from the airport for more than one reason, and she would not forget that.

Soon enough.

Standing, Tuesday first walked the circle widdershins, enclosing it in a permeable violet light that would allow her access to the inside, but wouldn't include her as part of the spell. Stepping inside, she straddled Ethan's legs. She wore only the long T-shirt, but his eyes were closed and she—she had to keep it together and rein in her lusty thoughts. Just for a while longer.

Holding the alicorn in one hand, she spread the fingers of her other hand and leaned forward, focusing her energies toward the sigils drawn on his chest. The words to the spell came by rote and she chanted them over and over, changing her tone to a deeper resonance after a few successions.

The red marker began to glow white and appeared as if it opened Ethan's skin, though it did not. It was a deep and luminous glow. It allowed in her magic. Pointing the alicorn in each direction—north, east, south, then west—she then drew a line down to the center of the pentagram.

Then, with a forceful stab of the alicorn's point, she punctured Ethan's chest.

Chapter 11

Something ice-cold pierced his chest. Ethan gasped, winced. Slapped a hand to his chest, but the witch pushed it away immediately. She'd...staked him?

"Just go with it," she said calmly. "It's only in a quarter of an inch. I need blood, remember?"

She...needed blood? Fuck. Just...what the fuck?

As he felt blood drool from the puncture, Tuesday quickly used the tip of the alicorn to draw with his blood, tracing the sigil over his chest. She'd freaking staked him with a unicorn's horn!

Closing his eyes and letting his head fall back to the floor, Ethan then smirked and snorted. What the hell kind of whacked adventure had he tumbled into? He'd let a witch stake him and...he'd survived. He was still here. Not ash. And she was speaking her witchy voodoo words and humming above him.

When she'd asked for him to give blood, memories of the time he'd killed another with a blood transfusion had almost stopped him from doing this. That had been a different time. A completely different century. Medicine had advanced greatly. And…he hadn't wanted to give her details. To expose his broken heart to her. So he'd dropped his nervous worries and succumbed to Tuesday's wishes.

The witch didn't need to see into that soft and weak part of him. Because apparently she was more into stabbing a man than sympathizing with him. Bloody hell.

Opening his left eye, Ethan spied Tuesday as she kissed the blood-tipped alicorn. Then, kneeling and still straddling him, she bowed to blow across the wet blood. Her magic stirred up a violet fog and with her hands she coaxed it into a malleable cloud over his body, stretching it to encompass him from head to toe. And with a single clap of her palms, the fog dropped over his body and permeated his skin with a sizzle that made him hiss.

Tuesday stood, looking over her work. "That was it. You're such a big boy," she cooed as if he was a child. "That wasn't so bad, was it?"

He would not reply to her mocking tone. Even if he sensed she was teasing him. But it was difficult not to admire the view from where he lay. The woman wore but a T-shirt that was long enough to cover everything, but short enough to make him want to lift his head and take a closer look.

She just staked you, idiot. Right. Ethan pushed up to his elbows and looked over his bloody chest.

Fool that he was, he'd had the thought while in the Archives earlier that he'd like to see what she was capable of when wielding the alicorn. And now he knew.

Twirling the bloodied alicorn, the witch waggled an eyebrow. "Remember when you shoved me against the wall in the alleyway before the dark witch bonded us? You said that was the only blood I'd ever get from you." She shrugged. "Guess you were wrong, eh?"

"I'm doing this to help the mission. Unlike you, who seem to merely want to gloat about taking advantage of a man's kindness. You fucking staked me, witch!"

"And now you can tell everyone you've survived being staked. You don't have to mention it was with a unicorn horn and resulted in you looking like a glitter-bombed clubber."

Her giggle was enough to make Ethan mentally snap a rubber band at his wrist. But he wouldn't get angry at her. He was doing this to help the mission. And if he had gained some sort of magic out of the deal? So be it.

"Now you should have a sixth sense about the demon's location," she said. "You just have to learn to tap in to it. Focus inwardly, keeping the demon's name fore and your intent to find him as the guide. Shouldn't be too difficult for a vampire who has used persuasion on humans. Yeah?"

He had mastered enthralling humans centuries ago. He'd been born innately knowing how to control others with but a tweak to their thoughts, a subtle whisper after the bite, or even a gentle caress that would send a shiver of compliance through their system along with memory loss or even altered thoughts.

"Sounds good to me." Ethan touched the blood on his chest. It sparkled with violet. Was that a condition of using the alicorn? Interesting, and yet a bit too night-club-glitter for him.

"You can get up. But it'll take a bit for it all to soak

in, to really get a fix in you. What would be helpful is…" Tapping a finger to her bottom lip, she stepped out of the circle and gripped the obsidian crystal that hung about her neck from the leather cord.

"Is…?" He stood behind her, and brushed some of the violet dust off his jeans.

"Is what?" she asked.

"You were about to say something would be helpful?" He dismissed the query. "Whatever. Can I wash this off?"

"No, leave it on. The marker, anyway. It'll disappear when the spell has set. But you can wash off the blood that dribbled down the side of your ribs. You got a broom?"

"Stuart, vacuum the living area," he said and wandered into the bathroom.

Tuesday stood aside and watched as the Roomba vacuum cleaner appeared from out of a closet and scurried over to sweep up the salt and random drops of Ethan's blood. Skipping to avoid being attacked by the tenacious thing, she sat on the chair to stay out of the way.

A glance to the bathroom door made her smile. She had freaked the fuck out of the vampire by stabbing him with the alicorn. He might have thought she'd been staking him. Ha!

She shouldn't gloat over that sneaky triumph, but— Yes, she would. She'd caught him unawares, and yet, he hadn't overreacted or tried to push her away. He'd complied and had allowed her to finish the spell. He earned points for that. Not many vamps would do the same, she felt sure. Especially the ones with a bossy, controlling complex.

Yet, he had been not so eager to order her around since she'd returned from her near escape from the country. More points to the vampire for that restraint. Was it a new tactic to get her to ultimately work with him? Probably. Yet he'd given her a clue that there was more between them than mere spellcraft and demon chasing.

He wanted her.

And she was the witch to let the vampire have what he wanted.

When he returned to the room with a blood-free chest, but a few sparkles still in his hair and on his back, he wandered over to the vanity by the wall and poured himself a snifter of brandy. The city lights gleamed against a gray sky, highlighting his physique with a golden glow. He wore nothing but jeans, which he must have unbuttoned to clean off the blood—and he'd forgotten to rebutton them—and tufts of dark hair were visible.

Comfortable? Check.

Sexy? Mercy, could a witch get a break?

"You want some?" he asked as the vacuum rolled off to its closet and shut down.

Hell yes, she wanted some. "Uh…" Turning on the leather chair and pulling up her legs, Tuesday asked, "Oh, you mean brandy?"

"Yes."

"Ugh. That stuff makes me gag."

"Then you haven't tried the good stuff." He held up the goblet and strode over to the window, which was parallel to the bed. An outside light flashed crimson in the glass, winking at them. "A man can drink worlds in brandy. I've tasted Greece and Armenia, Turkey and

Chile. Stravecchio is one of my favorites. It's distilled in copper pots."

"I may have once dated a winemaker," Tuesday said.

"A vintner?"

"Yeah, that's what he called himself. Maybe *date* is too technical a term. More like fucked once or twice. Or a dozen times."

It was either that, or she'd dated a dozen different vintners and fucked them once or twice. Details. He didn't need to know everything about her life.

Ethan leaned back against the brick wall, where the window frame began; the massive pane was but inches from his left shoulder. The moonlight mixed with city lights gave his face a stark quality that Tuesday admired. While vampires as old as he could often look as young as teenagers or twentysomethings, Ethan had a certain seasoning to him that appealed to her centuries-gained sensibilities. He was not young and the years had imprinted on his face. In the line that cut down between his eyebrows when he flashed her the serious look, and in the silver hairs that dashed through his brown hair and beard stubble. A wise toughness deepened his gray irises to a cunning yet knowing stare.

He would be called classically handsome by those who cast Hollywood movies, and probably pigeonholed into the widowed or divorced single-father-with-an-edge role. The man was solid. Physically aware. And comfortable in his skin, muscles and bones that wrapped and formed him into a startlingly exquisite physique.

Washboard abs? Check.

"So, you fucked a lot of men over the centuries?" he asked, as he stared off through the window.

Now he was getting to the interesting conversation. Of course, she had mentioned the vintner.

"A dozen or hundreds. I don't record notches. You?"

"Fuck men?" He shrugged. "Not as often as you, I'm sure."

That nugget of info swirled a deep, hot thrill right between her legs. She could entirely see the man swinging for either women or men. That was sexy to her. A man who was not afraid of his sexuality and who lived his life the way he chose.

"I know the world is vast and coincidence rare," she said, "but if I ever learn we've fucked the same man that would so rock my world."

He chuckled and sipped the brandy. "I never kiss and tell."

And now she really wanted to delve into his love life. The fantasy of him bedding another man put a tight pull at the base of her throat and heated her breasts. And... oh, yes. She shifted on the chair, squeezing her thighs together to catch the flutter of want in her pussy.

"Sex becomes different the longer you live, yes?" he asked.

She nodded. Because it had. In ways no mere mortal could ever imagine.

"It's not so much about the romance and roses," he continued. His gaze was fixed on some point out the window. His rugged profile teased Tuesday's sense of control. "Nothing like what you see in the movies or read in those romance novels."

"Have you ever read a romance novel?"

"No."

"Then don't knock them. I even like the ones about the vampires and werewolves, despite the authors getting their paranormal attributes wildly wrong most of the time. But you're right. As the years, decades and centuries glide by, sex becomes less about the physical. And yet, at the same time, the meaning of it becomes more."

"Exactly," he said with a tilt of the brandy snifter toward her. "It's less about an emotional bond and more about..." He gave it some consideration. "It's about finding yourself in someone else, yet not getting lost there. Knowing that you both are a part of something much bigger. And also, surrendering to the moment, and being able to focus completely on that other person and yourself. Love has nothing to do with sex. It's too messy, and too much thinking is involved."

"I agree. Though—" Now that she'd decided she might welcome love into her life, Tuesday wasn't one-hundred-percent certain anymore what, exactly, sex did mean to her. Though she did know one thing. "It's definitely a soul thing."

"Yes. It's...well, it's worlds." He tipped the glass to his lips for a swallow. "So are we going to avoid the obvious?"

"Which is?"

"That we need to discuss what is going on with us moving forward."

"Honestly? I wish we would avoid it. For now. I'm tired." She pushed her hands through her hair and let the heavy tresses drop over her shoulders. She was aware it was a sensual move, and took all the leisure in drawing her hair back over a shoulder for him to watch. "I just want to sit here and watch you drink your brandy."

He shrugged, then took another sip. That the conversation had turned to sex only spurred her on. She had been thinking the man needed to have sex to make the spell sink in, and had almost said as much earlier, but had wisely stopped herself. And she was very willing to volunteer to assist in the said process of spell-sinking-in.

"Worlds, eh?" she asked.

"Yes, indeed."

"Worlds in the brandy and in sex." She leaned forward, a hand to her knee. Lowering her lashes, she looked up through them. "I bet you've seen worlds unending."

"That I have." He turned to face her. The sleek line of his body stretching his long torso, down his hips and the length of his legs to bare feet screamed out "sex" to Tuesday. "Do something for me?"

She shrugged. "Anything. As long as it's interesting."

He crossed the arm he held the drink in over his chest and eyed her for a moment. That gaze could strip a woman bare. And Tuesday felt it move over her skin as a warm breath that tickled and tightened her nipples. It traced along her side and shivered down the length of each of her legs. And there at her core, it teased her to open herself, to want what she'd been cursed to never have.

Finally, Ethan said, "Show me your world."

Chapter 12

Tuesday lifted an eyebrow. Show him her world?

Now that request was interesting enough to make her want to comply. She had been waiting for this moment. It was time the two of them, indeed, peeked into one another's worlds. Or even went for a running dive.

Yeah, she favored a good splash that would land her all in.

She settled back against the cushy leather seat that she imagined Ethan must have lived in, sat in, perhaps even fucked in for decades. It was so comfortable. And she felt at ease sitting before his soft gaze.

Drawing up her knees, she let them drop apart and to the sides, exposing herself to him. The T-shirt inched above her trimmed patch of pubic hairs, teasing him with the view.

His attention was easy and yet focused. As he tilted

a hip forward, she noticed his erection bulged beneath the dark jeans. He'd been hard for much longer than the few seconds she'd taken to get comfy. It was a good thing for him her limp-dick spell had not succeeded that first day when he'd held her captive in the cage. Good for her, too.

Tapping a finger against her lips, she eyed him teasingly, yet the promise was true. She licked a fingertip and kissed it. Gliding her fingers down between her legs, she watched Ethan as she slid that wetted fingertip along her heated folds. Slowly, deeply, she traced up a slick wetness and skated across her clit, which now hummed with a greedy need for attention. A delicious, erotic thrill shivered in her core and loosened her shoulder muscles.

This was her world, as Ethan had put it. A woman who knew how to gratify herself. She knew what made her squirm, what strokes could make her hum with pleasure, what pressure, speed and the length of time to gauge each touch. And knowing that about herself made her strong and wise. It was a knowledge she had tried to teach those women she had healed over the centuries. The body was theirs to understand. Treat it well, and they would be well. And that included self-care. Which meant jilling off.

Because really, what woman could ever teach a man what she did not first know herself from experience and practice?

Ethan watched without a lusty gape or a smirk. It was his calm, gleaming gaze that made the tease more exciting for her. Everything about him called to her on a sensual song. The relaxed curl of his fingers cupping the brandy snifter. The liquid flame scent of the golden brown liquor. And the tilt of his head that caught the moonlight in the silver strands near his temples. Mmm...

Tuesday moaned appreciatively. The man was something to admire. She didn't need to see fangs to get off on his sexy. Her finger stroked faster and firmer, focusing where she was most sensitive. Wet, swollen and tingling, her body stepped forward to sing its alluring wisdom.

She could do this quickly or draw it out, and prolonging it won the vote.

Ethan tilted his head, turning to study her with more intensity. His upper teeth eased over his lower lip in a tense but wanting slip. The man's abs, still marked with the tracking grid, flexed. And a wince signaled her he was feeling the intensity of the moment in the tightening of his erection. It strained against his jeans. And his fingers curled about the brandy glass more possessively.

Her motions quickened. Tuesday closed her eyes briefly, falling into the sensations, the tightening in her core, the promising jitter of release that seemed to reside at every place within her body at once. And yet... she slowed, easing up on the pressure so that the high began to simmer. Too fast. Never too slow.

"Is this a world you want to learn more about?" she said in breathy gasps. "Ethan?"

"Fuck yes."

"I'm so close." She moaned sweetly. But she wouldn't get herself off. Yet. Not until he joined in on the fun. "Take your cock out. Let me see your world, vampire."

He unzipped and his cock, granted release, sprang up against his tight belly. Still holding the glass, the fingers of his other hand curled about his sizeable hard-on and squeezed, then stroked.

"Turn and face the window," Tuesday directed. "I want to see you from that angle."

He did so, setting the glass up on a jut of wood that was part of the design along the brick wall to his side. He placed the heel of his palm up high on the window, and with his other hand he stroked up and down, slowly, measured, and tightened then loosened his grip. He knew exactly what worked for him. He also knew his body, and so she paid attention to his motions, the pace and the intensity.

"I can't watch you when I'm facing this way," he said.

"You've seen me. It's my turn to watch. Your cock has an inward curve. That's sexy."

He glanced aside at her, smiling briefly, but then his jaw tightened and Tuesday knew he had hit a sweet spot with his pumping motions. She sucked in her lower lip, biting it lightly. Her own motions synched with his, moving faster, more firmly.

"Come over here," he said. "I need your wet pussy to slick my strokes."

She obliged with a teasingly slow stroll over to the window. Leaning her shoulders against a thin connecting steel column, she eyed him from his shuttered eyelids, to his pulsing hard abs, down to his cock. The head of it was red and swollen. Angry and virile. The color of his want and of her desire.

"Take off that shirt," he said.

The T-shirt was abandoned as she flung it to the bed. Ethan moved his gaze over her body, and Tuesday leaned her shoulders back against the cool windowpane, the action lifting her breasts. The nipples were so tight and her pussy demanded touch. Yet she could stand there and soak up his adoration for however long he would give it to her.

Ethan gestured his stroking hand toward her mons. "May I?"

Strangely pleased by his polite request to enter her wanting heat, she nodded and tilted her hips forward. Keeping his gaze pinned to hers, Ethan slid his fingers into her folds. He groaned, and slid them within her moistness. The tease of it, of his welcome invasion into her, was enough to make her gasp.

A glint in his gray irises stole something from her. She gave it willingly.

His didn't remain within her long enough to give her more than a heart-pounding tingle and a wish for him to move deeper. The man returned to the task literally at hand; her wetness gleamed on his length as his strokes about his erection increased velocity.

Sex without the commitment or relationship expectations was exactly the way she preferred it. And it seemed Ethan was completely on board with that. This night was going to be a hell of a lot more interesting than an eight-hour flight to the States.

Slipping her fingers between her folds, Tuesday matched Ethan's rhythm. They held eye contact, mouths slightly parted, gasps punctuating the brandy-tinted air. A dare was volleyed between them with the curl of a lip, or the lift of an eyebrow. Then of a sudden his strokes slowed. His grin revealed bright whites. And in his eyes a question alighted.

Tuesday turned toward him and tapped her finger on his lips. He lashed out his tongue to taste her salty sweetness. She glided it in deeper, skating his tongue, then slipping it under each of his pointed fangs. They were not lowered, but that didn't matter. She knew touching a vampire's fangs was an erotic act. Like touching his cock, it produced the same titillating sensations throughout his system.

He grasped her hand and sucked in her finger, slow, hard… He dashed his tongue firmly at the base, where it met her palm. An exhale heated her skin and she felt the prick of his fang—but he didn't break skin.

"Taste me," she dared. "You know you want to."

He shook his head. "That's not how we're doing this."

"Oh? Is there a guidebook I wasn't allowed to read?"

"There might be."

He kissed her finger and placed her hand about his cock. He moved his fingers to squeeze over hers and show her the speed he liked for her strokes. Tuesday was a fast learner and she took over immediately.

The man cupped her jaw and slid his palm over her cheek. His thumb rubbed her lower lip. With a lash of her tongue she tasted his musky flavor twined with hers. She pulled him closer by his hard-on and touched the head of him to her pinnacle, where she was achingly wet and slick. Leaning into him and lifting one leg to hook at his hip, she hinted at allowing him entrance.

Ethan bowed his head to meet foreheads with her. "Tease me, witch. Don't make this easy."

She gripped his rod tightly, pushing him away from her. Then she lifted her mouth toward his but didn't quite connect, save for with a wink. She liked the tease, too. It was filled with heartbeats and breaths, and silent pleadings that were so loud she felt them racing in her blood. Heated sighs mingled. Skin, moist with desire, slid against skin. And their worlds opened wide, coaxing one another to explore. To learn. To know.

"Kneel," she boldly commanded.

The vampire kissed her lips. A smirk formed behind that kiss, curling on her mouth. A secret he wouldn't allow her to do more than taste. Then he began to lower. His lips brushed her chin, his tongue dashed the pulse on her neck. He held there, scenting her heat, drawing her in, content to indulge himself in her. She wanted to force him lower, but instead she closed her eyes and took in the frustratingly delicious shiver of Ethan taking his time.

Finally, he kissed lower, slowly, and lingered over her breasts, breathing across them—*hush, hush, hush*—but not touching for more than a second. And on his path he veered toward her heart chakra, the center of her being, and kissed the sigil, which didn't glow or pain her in any way. His tongue traced the *S* shape of it, then followed the straight line that dashed from curl to curl. The tickle of his beard on her breasts tightened her nipples. Another *hush*.

The man's journey took him down her stomach. Hot breaths circled her navel. He kneeled and looked up to her, his mouth but inches from her pussy.

Tuesday ran her fingers through his short, spiky hair, reveling in the luxurious softness of it. Yet it looked rough, stalwart. Manly. He begged her permission with his gray eyes. And with a tilt of her hips, she invited him closer.

The first stroke of his tongue to her clit roused a chuckle of affirmation from her. Oh, yeah, the man was on a mission. And his focus did not veer. It required but a few more careful and firm strokes to lift her from the denial she'd been forcing herself to maintain and set her free.

Tuesday came with a throaty growl and a slap of her palms against the window glass behind her. "Yes!" She clasped her fingers tightly against Ethan's scalp. "Oh, you perfect, nasty vampire."

The moon highlighted their naked antics, and she realized that the neighbors were probably getting a good show.

Let them watch.

She bowed forward over her lover as the shivering effects of the orgasm tickled through her system and made everything so much brighter, crisper and fan-freakin'-tastic.

"You taste like many worlds," Ethan whispered against her wetness. "And you come like no world will ever contain you. Powerful witch."

He kissed her there, and there, and then he slid his fingers inside her and groaned with pleasure. "Fuck." He tilted his head against her belly, lashing out his tongue across her skin, then looked up to her. Another request for permission gleamed in his eyes.

"I want this—" she toed his cock "—inside me." She lifted his chin with her fingers. "Now."

He moved backward toward the bed. Tuesday followed, her fingers still under his chin. With a lift, she directed him up and onto the inviting soft bedding. She then straddled him and crawled forward to position herself as if upon the siege perilous. She may not find the Holy Grail, but she would invade Ethan's world tonight.

The man spread his arms across the bed and closed his eyes, giving her the control, the freedom to explore his world. He would take what she would give him.

Ethan slid his palms up her arms and then around to cup her breasts. He thumbed her nipples and pinched them gently, then not so gently. That erotic twinge pulled her forward and hastened her need to feel him within her. Gripping the control stick, Tuesday mounted his thick cock and slid onto him slowly, inch by hot inch, taking him into her feminine power and granting him that secret.

The vampire groaned and squeezed her breasts, but without any purpose, for he was falling into her. Filling her. Being owned by her as she squeezed her inner muscles to hug him tightly. His hips rocked. He swore and insisted she go faster, but she kept her pace slow, lingering, enjoying every hot, thick measure of him.

Bending her knees she settled completely onto him and leaned back, catching her palms beside his thighs. He tilted his hips forward, deepening their connection. She may have opened her world to him, but right now the world slipped away. Only they two existed. Rocking, engaged and finding a harmonious rhythm. Such luxury to feel so full and powerful.

Yet the power was shared. And Tuesday didn't mind that at all.

As the moon slowly glided across the inky night sky, together they rose to a climax that made their bodies shudder. Ethan's chest muscles and biceps flexed into steely ropes. His abdomen clenched. His hips tremored as he spilled inside her.

Shivering with exquisite orgasm, Tuesday flung forward to hug her lover. Nestled in his panting embrace, she smiled with satisfaction.

Tonight she had entered the vampire's world.

Chapter 13

Tuesday rose with the sun, or rather what she expected was early morning. The window shades had drawn down while she had been slumbering. Good ol' Stuart. She could get used to a home butler like that.

"No, never," she muttered. There was something creepy about a robot tending the household duties. She'd seen the movies. It never ended well.

Shaking her head, she wandered into Ethan's kitchen to pour some orange juice. On the kitchen counter, she found one stale croissant in a brown patisserie box so she gnawed on that, thinking to leave the vampire to sleep.

Settling onto the sofa and pulling the bag of supplies she'd purchased onto her lap, she again eyed the bed for movement. That had been some good sex last night. But she didn't intend to sew any strings of attachment between the two of them. It had just been sex. Leave it at that.

Because she didn't belong in Paris, and she most certainly was not in the frame of mind to begin an affair with a sexy vampire who knew how to touch her in all the right places in all the right ways.

Even if she had decided getting rid of the love curse was most important.

She blew out a breath and shook her head.

She wasn't a romantic. Romance had gotten stale for her somewhere around the mid-eighteenth century. Hell, it had been earlier than that. The four days and nights Finnister had tortured her relentlessly had pretty much banished all her idiotic desires for love and romance.

Sex was as she and Ethan had discussed. More than romance, it was a world. And if a person went into a relationship expecting it to fulfill and complete them and make them happy, then they were doing it wrong. Happiness could only come from within. And recognizing that Ethan made her happy—but wasn't the source of that feeling—was key.

However, there was nothing wrong in reveling in the afterglow of a night having been well-fucked.

Pulling out items from the bag, she decided the Tibetan quartz points might come in handy for a summoning spell. She really needed some shungite, something powerful to shield her from the demon's awareness, but the shop had been out. The obsidian she wore was strong and attuned to her body, but it tended to shiver when attacked.

The tracking magic she'd given to Ethan with last night's spell might work. And it might not. Surely, the sex had settled that magic into his very bones. Now, it was all in how he worked with such power. And much as she felt he was a smart guy who could handle this mission on his own, she didn't want to be left standing on the side. Seriously. She liked to participate. And she owed the demon a smackdown that would make his heart crumble and fall from his chest. He'd gotten all the love over these centuries. It was time to tilt the scales in her favor.

"Time to let the witch reign," she murmured, and sipped the orange juice.

Another glance to the bed found the sheets pushed away and the mattress absent of a slumbering vampire. He must have slipped into the bathroom. And she hadn't even noticed. Vampires were shifty like that.

She could only smile at the thought.

Ten minutes later the shower stopped and Ethan wandered through the bedroom with a towel wrapped about his hips. Water droplets glinted on his chest and shoulders, and he scrubbed his hair with a smaller towel until it stood up all over. A slick of his fingers over each side of his head left it styled perfectly. He noticed her watching him and winked at her.

Tuesday experienced a sudden desire to kneel before him and give him whatever he may ask of her.

But she didn't. That would be pushing it. Was she all of a sudden so wishy-washy simply because she'd been considering romance? Silly witch.

"You're an early riser. For a vampire," she commented as he padded into the living area and stood before her.

Tossing the towel he'd used on his hair back to land on the end of the bed, he shrugged. "Never need much sleep. And it's supposed to rain today around noon. I'm getting ready to go out."

"Yeah? You got a date?"

His smile was quick and easy. And it held all the answers to the secrets she'd given him last night. "I'm going to test out this tracking magic you gave me." He splayed a palm down his chest and abs. The red marker was gone, washed away in the shower. The sex had quickened the spell sinking in. The man was now a walking demon compass. "Can't sit around hoping the demon will come knocking on my door, can I?"

"Does that mean I have to stay here?"

"You do know the danger of coming along."

"It's not so much a danger as me being the plague the demon wants to avoid. Do you have your crew ready to go this time?"

"I will." He sat on the sofa next to her, and the towel parted to reveal his muscular, dark-haired thighs and a tease of penis. "Can I kiss you this morning and tell you how beautiful you are? Or are we not doing that lovey-dovey kind of stuff?"

"I'll take a kiss and a compliment any day."

"Good." He leaned in and kissed her, taking his time as he opened her mouth with his and slipped his tongue against hers. Instant recall of his tongue tasting her pussy filled Tuesday's chest with a deep and wanting moan. The vampire ended the kiss with a slip of his thumb over her bottom lip. "You're beautiful, witch."

"You're pretty sexy yourself. Want to have hex?"

"I hope that means what I want it to mean."

"Oh, it does." Tuesday plunged her hand under the towel and claimed his semi-erect cock with a firm grip. "I get a head start."

As she bowed to tug away his towel and lick up his quickly hardening length, Ethan commented, "I think

I'm the one with the head start, if you know what I mean. Oh, yes, this is a good way to begin the day."

Ethan slipped on his Ray-Bans and exited the building. He vacillated on whether or not to drive on his quest to find the demon, then decided against it. On foot he could maneuver quicker and into tighter situations. As vampire he had the ability to traverse the entire city in a swift dash, leaving those he passed only wondering if it was a sudden wind that had brushed their hair across their skin. But he'd start slow as he learned to work with this magic Tuesday had given him.

The training session had been all of a few minutes as she'd explained he had to focus inwardly on his sense of direction and need to stand before the demon Gazariel, while also dividing that focus outward to pick up on signals that indicated he was moving toward that goal. Elementals would work with him, she had explained. He knew elementals were tiny creatures, like sprites, but also not. They were of the elements—earth, air, water and fire—and could resemble their namesakes or not. And they could either choose to be seen or not. A mysterious species that Tuesday had said he should trust would guide him.

So he did.

The forecasted rain was more like a mist, but the sky was clouded and that was all that mattered to a vampire. Still, he kept on the sunglasses so as to notice any wards he should avoid.

Leaving his coat open, and his shirt unbuttoned, he needed to access the invisible sigil on his chest that Tuesday had drawn. Before he'd left, she had taken his hand and placed his forefingers to each of the compass points, between his nipples, above his navel and under his ribs on each side. He had to focus on the demon's name and his intent, so he murmured, "Take me to Gazariel, The Beautiful One."

With a touch to the north direction on his chest, he felt nothing. He slid his fingers down to the south and an inexplicable tug turned him toward the Seine. Had that been the elementals?

"Trust them," Ethan muttered, and he began to walk, following the minute but definite sensation that seemed to keep his feet on track and his eyes on the prize.

If tracking a demon was this easy, he should consider staffing a dark witch to train his retrievers. On the other hand, none in his employ seemed to have too much trouble locating a mission target. It was the adventure and the hunt that fueled a retriever, and he was feeling that old yet invigorating thrill again. He wondered why he'd ever thought settling behind a desk was for him, and now challenged his idea of where, exactly, he wanted his future to go. Perhaps he should participate in fieldwork more often?

When he reached the river and crossed the busy street to lean over the stone balustrade and peer into the inky waters, he touched his chest again and turned his attention inward to divine his next move. This time he was drawn across the Pont de Sully and into the fifth arrondissement to pass before the Arab World Institute. It was a favorite building of his. The facade was paneled with metal squares that were light-sensitive and could regulate the amount of light that entered the building. They mimicked an element of Arabic architecture, the *mashrabiya*. It was gorgeous, plain and simple.

Pulled now with more urgency, he walked swiftly

down a curving street, and turned this way and that until he'd broached the depths of the fifth and the traffic slowed and the number of pedestrians decreased. He dodged to avoid a cyclist on the sidewalk, then abruptly turned to the right.

He stood before a three-story white stucco building hugged by a small patio area with outdoor dining tables capped by red-and white-striped umbrellas. The aroma of roasting meat appealed to him, and he also picked up the delicious caraway scent of baked rye bread. A four-star restaurant?

He supposed demons did have to eat. And the place was large and spacious, so Ethan could enter without being noticed. But also, it was filled with humans. He couldn't risk taking the demon into captivity here. He'd have to get him outside.

He buttoned up his shirt so he wouldn't stand out in such a tony place. At the hostess station, Ethan explained he was looking for a friend and wanted to take a look around. The receptionist with emerald eyes and too much red lipstick started to explain that wasn't the policy and that the place was reservations-only. So Ethan touched her hand and traced his finger along her wrist right above the vein, making sure she felt his persuasion.

She suddenly nodded and gestured him to walk inside. With a sigh, she then turned back to her black leather book of names and tables, instantly forgetting Ethan had been there.

The main room, which hummed with low conversation, was vast and spacious and walled completely in windows, such as in a Victorian conservatory. Massive plants grew up along the walls and hung from the ceiling, and were positioned to give privacy to most tables. It smelled like summer, too. Ethan wouldn't be surprised to see a parrot or even a snake gliding amongst the greenery, but he quickly reined in his wonder and scanned the room from his discreet position beside a tall, bushy ficus.

The pull he felt in his chest was unmistakable. Tuesday's magic had worked. The demon had to be in here.

Methodically, he scanned over every table until he spied a head of dark hair sitting before the far window. A man was talking animatedly to a woman whom Ethan couldn't quite see, for a frond of greenery obscured the view. Didn't matter. He'd found Gazariel. Dressed in an elegant business suit that gleamed when he moved. Like hematite catching the sun, his wavy dark hair looked styled and ready for a magazine photo shoot. Indeed, he was beautiful, and Ethan could admit that.

Now, how to get him out of the restaurant and in position for capture?

He tugged out his phone and texted the containment team leader his location. Five minutes and they'd be outside near the hornbeam shrubbery that demarcated the edge of the property.

Whoever the woman was that the demon spoke to could be a girlfriend or lover. The one he had given the book to? Or had he yet to give her the gift? What sort of gift was a book of angel names and sigils? The woman had to be paranormal. Ethan didn't see the point in a human wanting something like that. Or knowing the value of such a gift.

On the other hand, there were many humans who genuinely Believed, and those sorts could be the most dangerous to his species, to all species.

A waiter neared Ethan and cast him a curious look so Ethan sent out some more persuasive vibes. He needed to remain unremarkable to those around him.

On the other side of the room, the demon clasped the woman's hand from across the table and she leaned forward, a spill of coal-black hair falling over her cheek and veiling her face. Dark lipstick emphasized her narrow mouth as she spoke. Yet when she stroked her hair back with a hand, curling it over an ear, Ethan saw clearly what she looked like.

And he recognized her.

"Holy—what the hell?"

He knew the woman's name. Anyx. She was not human, but rather vampire.

And she was his ex-wife.

Chapter 14

Outside the restaurant, Ethan stalked over to the containment crew waiting for action and told the leader the grab had been called off.

"Not today," he said at the crew leader's inquiry. "There's been…a glitch. Sorry. Thanks for being prompt. But we can't take the demon in hand just yet."

The crew left, and Ethan ran his fingers back through his hair, hoping he'd made the right call. Gripping and ungripping his fingers into fists, he paced before the shrubbery.

Why was Anyx with Gazariel? And how did that change things? He could have taken Gazariel. But without knowing whether or not the demon had given her the book—or Gazariel may have given the book to someone entirely different—Ethan had decided not to move in. Because what if they grabbed the demon and the vampiress got away?

He could take them both into custody. The vicious yet vain demon with a flair for taking down buildings by stealing a witch's magic, and a vampiress whom Ethan had once shared his bed with for decades. Their marriage had lasted sixty years.

Punching the air in frustration, Ethan strode off toward the street, then paused and turned back to the restaurant. This was not how the director of a black ops team that collected dangerous objects from across the world must react in the face of adversity. If he intended to continue with fieldwork he must get this right. Stand up to the challenge. As strange and perplexing as that new challenge had become.

He would wait and track them both. He had to know what connection Gazariel and Anyx had and then he would decide how to deal with this.

Of all the women in the world the demon could be having a relationship with, why did it have to be that particular vampiress?

Tuesday was listening to one of the jazz albums Ethan owned. Having never been interested in the musical style before, she warmed to it now. Swaying to the saxophone's mournful cry, she wrapped her arms across her chest and closed her eyes. She'd dated a musician once. More than once. A handful of musicians over the centuries. But the one she remembered with a self-indulgent smile had been an '80s hair-band drummer. Those guys could keep a steady rhythm going. For a long time.

Smirking, she turned to find Ethan standing before her, smiling widely to have caught her in a personal moment.

She stopped swaying. "I didn't hear you come in."

"The music is on."

"You don't mind? I'm starting to like this stuff."

He tossed his coat aside to the couch and approached, taking her hands in his as if to dance. And then he did start to dance with her, slowly, turning her and finding the beat.

"Billie Holiday is one of my favorites," he said. "I never missed a concert when she performed in Europe."

"Really? You were a fanboy?"

"I suppose. I dated a musician or two."

She chuckled. "I was thinking the same. Two or three, or maybe a dozen. It was all good."

"That it was. We who have lived so long have time on our hands. Time that needs to be filled. So I adventure. Try new things. Keep an open mind about what I encounter. And fuck a musician every once in a while."

"Good life goals, if you ask me. Yeah, settling down in one place, or with one person, only stays interesting for so long. I move around a lot." She tilted her head onto his shoulder because it felt a natural thing to do. He smelled like the cool outdoors. "Just returned to Boston a few months ago after some world traveling."

"You have a permanent residence there?"

"I've owned the place for about forty years. I was thinking I'd open up a New Age shop and sell candles and crystals. Maybe. It sounds…kitchen witch. Yet it gives me something to do, you know? I've lived in the city off and on over the centuries. I always gravitate back to home."

"Never had a hankering to settle in Paris?"

She shrugged and hugged up against him and their footsteps slowed as they swayed. "Too cosmopolitan for me. I like slow-paced and homey. I live in a little suburb at the edge of the city that hugs a forest. We witches do need nature to survive."

He bowed his head and nuzzled his nose beside her ear. The tickle and his warm breath sent a shiver across her skin. A good shiver. But as she looked up at him, she remembered where he'd been and what for.

"How did it go? You're in a good mood, so…?"

"I, uh…" Ethan broke their clutch and walked to the window, his back to her. The shades had risen completely to let in the clouded light. He raked his fingers through his hair. "I didn't apprehend The Beautiful One today. There was an issue."

"But you found him?" Tuesday plucked the needle off the vinyl and set the arm aside, then turned off the record player. "Where did you find him?"

"I tracked him to a four-star restaurant in the fifth. He was lunching with…a woman."

"A lover? I wonder if that's the one he told me he was going to give the book to."

"Do you think he's already given it to her?"

"I don't know. I got the impression he had or would soon. And if he knows we're after it, then he probably wants it out of his hands. What happened? Why didn't you capture him? Did they see you? Was your containment crew late again? Ethan?"

"Tuesday, just—" He turned and took her hands.

And suddenly, heart dropping to her gut, Tuesday felt as if he was going to lay some great confession on her and, whatever it was, she wouldn't like it. "What's going on? You could have had him."

"I made a judgment call. Didn't think the time was right. I want to learn more about the demon's connection to the woman. She's, uh… Tuesday, I recognized the woman Gazariel was with. Her name is Anyx. She's vampire. An old and powerful vampire."

"Yeah? What kept you from taking the demon in hand? You afraid of a vampiress? Didn't want to hurt her feelings by capturing her lover?"

He bracketed her face with his hands and said, "Anyx is my ex-wife."

Tuesday shoved out of his reach. His ex-wife? But that meant he'd once been married. Which—okay, after five hundred years the guy could have been married a time or two. Or even four or a dozen. Shouldn't bother her. Some paranormals who lived a long time had a tendency to collect spouses. And yet…

"Tuesday? I know that's some freaky information to out with, but what's this about?" He gestured toward her stiff posture and open jaw. "Are you…angry? I've lived a long life. There's a lot you don't know about me."

"I know that." She put up a palm as if that could block all the feelings from streaming into her soul. Feelings of betrayal, rejection and downright jealousy. What was up with that? She had no right. And really, she'd decided this was just a fling with the guy. She didn't care what he did, or *who* he did, or when he had done it. Maybe? "You took me by surprise."

"You're upset."

"No, I'm not."

"You—"

He grabbed her by the shoulders and shoved her against the wall. Pinning her with his hips and hands, he kissed her soundly. It wasn't sweet or tender, nor lingering or heady. The man was kissing her in punishment. And as quickly as it started he ended it.

"You don't get to do this," he said. "You have a past, too, witch. Don't go all raging, jealous lover on me. It's beneath you."

He shoved away from her and walked in a half circle, shoving his fingers through his hair. A side glance delivered her a stern reprimand.

Tuesday exhaled. His words were not wrong. But. Just…but.

"Will you let me explain?" he asked. "Or are you going to start calling me Richard again?"

Well, it had been a dick move to slam that one on her.

And yet. Fuck. What *was* up with her? The man had done nothing wrong. Except let the demon get away. Because of his ex-wife.

"Yeah, you'd better explain things to me," she finally said. "I'm having a hard time figuring why some chick could keep you from capturing the one demon you've been jonesing for these past few days. End of the world, remember? That's kind of important."

"I know!" he shouted.

Tuesday toned down her accusatory voice. "Did she see you? Recognize you? Why did you two break up? Ah, shit. I'm sorry, I don't have a right to those answers."

"Yes, you do. And I'll give you those answers. Sit down. I'll get you something to drink."

She could use the whole bottle of brandy right now. Even if it did taste nasty to her. Instead, Ethan returned with a glass of orange juice. She pressed the cool glass against her cheek. When Ethan sat next to her on the sofa, she shifted and pulled up her legs to face him. And also to put some distance between them.

With a nod, he accepted the defensive move. "Fine.

The witch is mad at me. But you haven't managed to bespell my dick limp yet, so... I can deal."

"I would never. I mean, I *can*, but I won't. Promise?"

"You're not so sure about that one. But I'll deal with that challenge if and when it comes my way. And no, Anyx didn't see me, nor did Gazariel."

"Quit saying his name. And hers, for that matter."

Ethan sighed. "Are you really going to do this?"

Ready to swing up and punch him, Tuesday stopped her fingers from curling into a fist by wrapping them around the glass of juice. She reasoned with her shivering inner self that had wanted to believe in the man. To believe that they had started something. She'd wanted love, but maybe this was the universe telling her to back off. Keep the curse. Her heart was safer that way.

When had she begun to think in such a way? Really? She was asking to be let down.

"I was married to Anyx in the sixteenth century," Ethan said. "Right out of my parents' home. The marriage was arranged. We were both vampire. My tribe wanted to form an alliance with another tribe. It was a mutual decision, though. I knew her and had my eye on her before the proposal was even suggested."

Tuesday sighed heavily. She didn't want to hear all this romantic bullshit. Or did she? By the seven sacred witches, she'd listen. He did deserve that much from her.

"We were married for sixty years before we decided to part ways. A couple can only remain together so long before they grow apart and develop different interests. Interests that may oppose one another. And the indifference that grows slowly yet deeply—it's a strong divide. The institution of marriage is not something that lends well to monogamy. We'd both discovered that. We parted amicably."

"Then why the sudden horror at seeing her today? It's been four hundred years. You seem to be over her. Why didn't you march up and take Gazariel out of there?"

"First, because it was in a public place. I required a means to lure him out, and with Anyx there...well. And also, I'm not sure what's going on between Anyx and the demon. And I think learning about that connection may be important. One of the main reasons we parted ways was because she developed a dark obsession with death."

"Coming from a vampire? That doesn't surprise me."

He flicked her a stabbing look. "Really? Is that what you think of me?"

She shrugged. "You're not like that."

"But all the rest of the vampires are walking purveyors of death? You sound worse than I do when I was initially cursing you a witch."

He was right. And she was giving this vampire bitch too much power by hating her for merely having been in Ethan's life. As his wife. For sixty freakin' years. But they'd been apart four and a half centuries. And that did mean something.

"Sorry." Tuesday clasped one of Ethan's hands. "All vamps are not like that. I know you don't kill to survive. It's a stupid myth only made stronger by movies and fiction. I shouldn't buy in to the hive mind's vampiric beliefs. And I don't. It's just a shocker to hear all this. You know?" Bowing her head, she winced and looked up through her lashes. "I gotta know, though... Was she your only wife?"

"Yes." He kissed her forehead, and she lifted her

face up to meet his small smile with one of her own. "I soured on the whole institution of marriage after we parted ways. It falls in the same category as sex with regard to what it should mean and what it really means. A piece of paper uniting two people until death parts them is nothing but trouble waiting to happen."

"So I've heard." She set the empty glass on the floor beside the couch.

"What about you? Any exes I should know about?"

"I've never put on a ring." She waggled her bare fingers. "Never will."

"A ring means so little. A man or woman can have a lover, for years, decades, and it can be a stronger relationship than some marriage certificate could ever forge."

"We are in agreement on that. But love, well…"

"I'm sorry. It must be hard for you if you've never known love."

"Maybe. I don't know. How can one know to miss something they've never had?" She swallowed. That was a lie. "Well, I did have it once. At least, I thought I did. Asshole witch hunter."

And yet, her soul sighed and uttered a longing cry for such an experience. Love?

Best not to think about it right now.

"Okay, I learned something new about you today and I didn't fall apart because of it," she said. "Not yet, at least. I guess I would be stunned if you'd *not* been married. You're quite the catch."

"Why, thank you. But it was a political thing, as I've said. The tribes eventually went back to warring against one another, even though Anyx and I remained man and wife. We did love each other, though. In our own ways."

"What tribe are you in?"

"Right now? I am unaligned. Then? I was in tribe Nava. They are still together to this day, but they've spread across Europe from our humble Parisian beginnings."

"What tribe was your ex-wife with?"

"Sarax," he said. "They disbanded last century. They'd gotten into some really dark shit. I'm pretty sure she was still with them then."

"What did you mean about her having an obsession with death?"

Ethan stood and paced toward the window, arms akimbo. He looked over his shoulder at her. "Anyx began collecting ephemera related to death spells and memento mori. She never used any of the spells—at least, not to my knowledge—but she liked to know what the spell or object could do. After she acquired a plague curse I called it quits. Yet her interest in such dangerous objects may have been what led me to the work I do today. In fact, I know it is."

"A plague curse? Sounds like the kind of chick who would be interested in a book that, when the code is deciphered, could end the world."

"Yes. No. I don't know. I mean, Anyx loved life when I knew her. She was not a vampire who would ever kill indiscriminately. I can't imagine her wanting to destroy the world."

"People change."

"Yes, and she probably has."

"Tell me this. Do you still love her?"

"I did. As I said, in my own way. It was appreciation and admiration. And we were physically attracted to one another. And then the love faded. I don't hate her, but I'm indifferent to her. She would be like a stranger to me now." He placed a hand over his heart. "She's just another vampiress to me."

Tuesday nodded. The hand over his heart had been an unconscious move. He might think that was what he believed, but if she meant nothing to him then why hadn't he walked up to Gazariel and grabbed him? It shouldn't have mattered what the woman meant to him.

"So what's the plan now?" she asked.

"I followed them out of the restaurant. The demon dropped Anyx off on the rue de Rivoli. I then followed him to a parking garage and he joined her in shopping. It looked to be a long day of retail adventure that I wasn't up for. I'll go out again. And next time, I'll take the demon in hand, no matter what. But I'll have to take measures to contain Anyx as well."

"You need me."

"I don't see how that will work if your sigil tips off the demon we're after him."

"I'll figure this one out." She pressed a hand between her breasts. "But admit you might need an uninvolved party to keep you on point."

"Uninvolved?" He leaned forward, close enough to kiss her. "I thought we were involved?"

"You know what I mean." She tapped his mouth. "I have no ties to the vampiress. You need me to keep you steady."

"You do have a manner about you that challenges me, yet also, stills me. Not sure what that is, but I don't mind it. In fact, I might even say you make me better."

"I'll take that. And I'll raise you with this."

She kissed his chin, nipping the stubble and then rubbing her lips over the rough hair. The brush of it tickled across her skin delightfully. So she played at a few more nips to his chin, along his jaw, and then landed on his lower lip and tugged it with a gentle, biting hold.

"You're feisty this afternoon," he said, and pulled her tight against his body. He still wore the coolness from outside on him, and it shivered into her being and ruched her nipples. "Mmm, I like that." He thumbed one of her nipples through the T-shirt, then pinched it, but not as softly as she had been with the nips.

Tuesday squirmed, yet arched her back to lift her breasts, and he took the hint. Bowing to her, he pushed up her blousy shirt and sucked in a nipple. His mouth was hot and his tongue firmly traced and lashed and teased her to a whimpering, clutching, wanting witch.

She shoved at his shirt, but realized it was a button-up. Wasn't going to come off without some pause to make it happen. And she needed to press her bare breasts against his hard pecs.

"Take this off," she pouted, and tugged at the shirt.

"We're going to do this right now?" he asked, plucking slowly at each button down the front of the shirt. He stepped back and pulled it off, exposing a feast to her eyes.

"Oh, yeah." Tuesday veered toward the bed, but Ethan grabbed her wrist and spun her around. She almost walked into the leather chair in the process, and suddenly, he spun her to face away from him, and pushed her forward.

She caught her hands on the back of the chair, and with a grin, leaned forward onto her elbows. A wiggle of her ass received a hard smack from his palm. He pulled down her leggings and gave her another smack that stung yet made her instantly wet.

Behind her she heard him unzip, and seconds later his heavy cock fell against her buttocks. Ethan grinded against her, fitting himself between her legs. She reached down and gripped the head of him, squeezing the length between her thighs.

"Fuck yes," he said tightly, as he cupped a hand over her breast and leaned down to kiss her nape. His hot breath caused erotic sensations that traveled her skin from neck to toe, and danced everywhere in between with the giddy madness of frenzied desire. Turning his head, his cheek hugged her spine. He clutched her breast as an inhale drew in her scent. "Put me inside you." He rocked his hips, pleading for entrance.

Tuesday guided him inside, and he slid in forcefully, pushing her stomach against the back of the chair and pulling her shoulders against him with a hand across her breasts. He kissed her hard again on her nape and bit, but not with his fangs. Just a soft, clinging, feral bite.

He rapidly thrust in and out of her, seeking his pleasure. Yet when his hand slid around to finger her clit, she cried out at the surprising attention. He pushed into her hard while she rocked forward, meeting his finger to adjust the pressure there. Inside her and outside, the man fit her perfectly and knew how to play her to the edge.

"Now," she gasped, hoping he was close to climax. Because she was. And then she decided she didn't need to wait. So she slapped a hand over his finger, moving it a bit to the left, and that was what released her to orgasm. She shouted and gripped the leather.

And behind her Ethan swore again and hilted himself as her orgasm tightened her about him, and with a few more thrusts, he came, too.

Chapter 15

"That was good." Tuesday sat up on the bed and looked over Ethan's bare chest. The soft beige sheet barely covered his cock, yet exposed those gorgeous muscles that pointed to all the action. The window shades had darkened by half to subdue the setting sunlight, and a hazy pale light softened the air.

"Good?" Ethan whistled lowly. "What does it take to rate a great?"

"Are you competing for a better grade?"

"No. Just not sure I can live with a mere good."

"Well…" She trailed a finger along the muscle that led to his crotch.

The sex had been amazing, and it had given her an idea. Together, they could do wondrous things. And if he thought she made him better now, he might be blown away at what a little bloodsexmagic could do for them. She'd already given him some of her magic. With the bite, he could become that much more capable of utilizing that magic. But...

"What would take this to *great* might offend you."

"There's nothing you can do that would offend me. Of course, I wouldn't mind you trying. Over and over." He winked at her.

"Very well. I'm going to ask for something. Something I've never done before but have been curious about."

"Ask away. If it leads to *great* I don't know how I can say no."

She crawled on top of him and stroked the dark hairs that trailed up from his cock to his belly button. Leaning down to kiss his chest, Tuesday lingered there and licked his skin, which had cooled considerably. Sculpted from steel, he was a new plaything that she wanted to learn more about. And she would. In every way possible.

She pushed her hair over one shoulder. "Bite me," she said. "Drink my soul, vampire. And in turn, let me feel yours in the thunder of your heartbeats as we climax together."

Ethan pushed up onto his elbows. His eyes, colored like a rainy sky, held her gaze, searing into her irises so she could feel his thoughts. No fear, yet something made him pause.

"I thought we'd already discussed my nixing the blood-giving stuff."

"I don't need your blood. Heck, I don't want it. Unless it's for a spell. But now that you bring it up, you never did tell me what was up with that. You stopped talking after saying you killed someone. What happened that you're such a freak about giving blood?"

"I'm not a freak." He laid his head back on the pillow and closed his eyes. Still, he winced. "I killed someone I loved, Tuesday, by giving her a blood transfusion. And I won't ever be responsible for another innocent's death by doing the same. No blood from these veins for any reason. Ever."

It was a heavy confession, and she wanted to honor it. Even if a few drops would never harm anyone. But who was she to judge him for something that obviously had hurt him deeply?

She stroked a fingertip over the faint spot below his left pec where she'd stabbed him with the alicorn. No scar, only a slight discoloration in the skin remained.

"This blood transfusion," she said quietly. "I thought you said you weren't trying to transform her?"

"I wasn't. I will never make another vampire. Not unless it is my own child. The woman—she was human. I loved her, but…" He sighed and stroked a hand down her hair. Still, he kept his eyes closed. "It was in the nineteenth century in a little seaside village in Scotland. We were on holiday there, and she'd gone out for a walk in the sunlight, knowing that I was back at the inn buried under the covers, still sleeping. It had rained through the night and the grass was wet and slippery. She fell down a cliff and landed on the boulders fronting the sea. It was hours before I found her and was able to get her to the hospital. So many broken bones. And she'd lost so much blood. And yet, I'd read about blood transfusions, and the medical science behind the operation. I knew there was a possibility of saving her, so I offered my blood."

"Was she your blood type?" Tuesday asked with surprise.

Ethan shook his head. "At that time, the doctors and surgeons weren't aware of blood types. They performed the operation unknowing that the type of blood was important. Unfortunately, we were not a match, and after pumping four pints of my blood into her, she seized and went into a coma. She died an hour later."

Oh, the poor man. "I'm sorry, Ethan."

"I'd been with her for a year. We never fooled ourselves that we'd marry and have children. She knew I was vampire. Had no desire for the lifestyle, either. I did have a moment of thinking I could save her if only I transformed her. But I did not. I respected her choice not to become vampire. And yet, I killed her by giving her my blood."

"That wasn't your fault. Medical science wasn't advanced enough at the time. You could never have known."

"I never should have offered in the first place. I should have let her be. She may have recovered."

"You don't know that. She'd fallen off a cliff? And you said she'd broken bones. It sounds like she would have died no matter what."

"Do we have to talk about this?"

"Of course not. But I have one more question."

"Shoot."

"Did you love her like you loved your wife?"

He wobbled his head. "Love comes in many different forms. You know?"

"Not really."

"Right. Sorry. There are many kinds of love. At least, from my perspective. I loved Anyx because it was something we learned and it grew between us over the years. A certain respect, and yes, sexual desire developed the love between us. But I would never call what we experienced a soul love."

"Even after sixty years?"

"Even after. As for the woman who died, I did love her passionately, but again, it wasn't soul-deep. And I'm okay with that. Whether we are human or creature or other, we love. It's what we do. And I wish you could know love."

"Well, I can love. I just can't receive love. Not for long, anyway. And always to the detriment of the guy who might think he loves me." She shrugged. "I'm fine."

"I don't think you are."

"Do we have to talk about this?" she said, repeating his question.

"Not right now, no."

"Good. And I'm glad you trust me to tell me about the blood thing." She kissed his collarbone and laid her head on his shoulder. "I won't ever ask you for blood. Promise. But…"

"You know when a person tosses in a *but* that means disregard everything I said before that word and only pay attention to what follows?"

Tuesday propped herself up over him. "There's nothing stopping you from biting me. And it could enhance the magic I've already given you. Bloodsexmagic, you know."

"I thought that was what vampires used to steal a witch's magic?"

"It is, but if given freely, and if I control the hex…"

"I don't want to get hexed."

"You've already been thoroughly hexed by me, lover."

He snickered. "Your use of the word has too many meanings to keep straight. I do like hexing you. But I'm not keen on bloodsexmagic."

"Fine. I can deal. But that doesn't mean you still can't

bite me. You know you want a taste. You've thought about it. Don't deny it."

"I have." He stroked the hair along her cheek, and traced her neck where her carotid pumped in anticipation, but then dashed downward to tickle the ends of her hair across her breast.

"I dare you," she whispered, unwilling to back down from the challenge.

Because it was a challenge between the two of them. She'd mentioned to him that fangs got her off, but he had initially been offended by her being a witch. It was an old and innate vampire hang-up. He'd lived through the Great Protection Spell when one drop of witch's blood could destroy a vampire.

"I'm not poisonous," she whispered. "Promise."

"I know that. But you have to know I've never bitten a witch."

"Understandable. But you don't strike me as the type who would carry a centuries-old fear within you."

"I don't fear your blood. But I do think you're a fang junkie."

That was a term vamps reserved for humans desperate for more of the fang. But Tuesday didn't take it as an offense. She shrugged. "Not quite a junkie, but I do love the bite. The orgasm is incredible. Much better than good."

He smirked and humor danced in his eyes. He might buckle…

"You are cute," he said.

She nodded, agreeing.

"And your blood smells different than most."

"How so?"

"Old. Luxurious. Aged, like a fine wine."

"You are not winning points by calling me old, buddy."

"It's the aged vintages that are always best."

Ethan parted his lips and she watched as his fangs lowered. Beautiful weapons. Pearly white. Sharper than most animal incisors. Made for piercing. She tapped one, and then stroked it until the man's hips rocked beneath her thighs. It was a unique way to jack him off.

"Taste me, vampire. Dive deeper into my world."

Ethan dashed out his tongue to lick her finger and she leaned forward, putting her breasts level with his mouth. Offering herself, waiting…wishing for the ultimate connection between the two of them. Because, she'd had it all thus far in life. Sex with so many different species. Bites, blood-sharing and even magic-sharing. But never had she had the bite at the same time as sex. It was a sacred act, and could actually enhance her blood bond with another.

He licked her nipple. And even after making love and having him touch and taste her for hours, she felt it as a new and exciting tingle that shivered through her system. She arched her back, then lifted her breast, putting it in his mouth.

And then the painful pierce of his fangs entered her body. Tuesday gasped at the sharp and intense intrusion. But she didn't flinch or pull away as his tongue lashed after the blood that spilled over the curve of her breast and toward her nipple.

Cleaning it off, he then suckled at the twin pierce marks, drawing out her blood. The sensation was sweet, and wicked. Delicious and deadly. And when his fangs grazed her skin they raised shiver bumps in the wake of his formidable weapons.

"The other," he whispered, and she shifted on her hands, tilting her chest so he could get a firm hold on her other breast.

The second piercing felt as painfully exquisite, and she shuddered, and put a hand to the back of his head to hold him there as he fed from her. Sensation soared through her body, coiling at her pussy and making her instantly wet again. He had penetrated her in a different way, but the feeling was beyond that of simple insert-tab-A-into-slot-B intercourse.

All of a sudden he flipped her onto her back. His strong hand clutched behind her head and lifted her neck to his fangs. With an animal fierceness, Ethan growled and sank his fangs into her carotid. One hand clutched at her breast while he fed ravenously from her pumping life. She could bleed out if he let the blood flow too long, and he might tease at that, but the vampire's saliva was healing and wouldn't allow such to happen.

"Oh, Ethan..." She twined a leg around one of his and let her head fall back, unsupported as he followed her down. "Fuck me now. With your teeth and your cock."

As he shoved into her with his hard-on, Tuesday gasped because she felt that sensation as if...she was the one entering him. Ethan's pleasurable groan ceased his sucking at her neck only momentarily as their gazes met. "You feel that?" he asked.

"I feel...what you feel?"

"Yeah, and...damn." He slapped his chest. "That's amazing."

"We're sharing the blood pleasures. Don't stop. More!"

He dropped his mouth to her neck again and the tug at the wound ached as he touched a fang to it and allowed the blood to flow. And as he greedily took from her, he pumped his hips against hers, gliding in and out. One hand thumbed her nipple, pinching, squeezing, demanding.

Everything was different, and the same, and new, and familiar. The intense squeeze of her insides about his cock…she could feel that as if his steely hard rod was her own. The taste of her blood in his mouth—she experienced that sweet delicacy trickle at the back of her throat. And the coil of orgasm that mastered her core seemed to triple in intensity as it enveloped them together.

"I can feel what you feel," he gasped. "Tuesday… This is… I've never known this before." He hilted himself inside her and then reached down to thumb her clit. "Oh, Christ, that's…wow."

"Invoking a Christian deity's name? You're telling me." She held him at her neck, and rocked her hips upward, meeting his thumb strokes with exacting movements to keep him right where she wanted him. "Give it all to me, Ethan. With my blood you've entered me. And I have entered you."

"Is this witchcraft?" he said on a gasp.

"Call it bloodcraft. A kind of bonding that goes beyond the external. Our souls are touching."

"Yes, that's exactly how I feel it. Some kind of soul bond."

And she didn't want it to stop. But it really was too much. Her mind flew. And her body shuddered uncontrollably. Ethan's teeth had left her neck, his tongue losing its pace lapping her blood. Together they had ceased to rock into one another for they'd become bound in an inner embrace that sparkled and held them at the edge of life and death.

Ethan's jaw tensed. He growled, gasping then searching for the release. And with a flick of his finger across her clit, he surrendered and Tuesday fell into the strange but marvelous experience as her body released. Ethan bucked against her. She took it all in as the world moved through her veins and to her every nerve ending.

They froze together in that penultimate moment catching one another's gaze and peering deep into their reflections. And in that moment the twosome had never known another being so intimately.

Tuesday slid out of bed and padded into the kitchen, where she pulled the orange juice from the fridge. She poured a glass then drank it.

"Tuesday…"

She turned toward the bedroom, but shook her head. She hadn't heard Ethan call out to her audibly. Had she…?

"The bed is growing cold on your side. Come back to me."

Touching her ear, she realized she'd heard him say that to her…in her thoughts. Like a dream, but only it was happening now while she was wide awake.

Let me finish my juice, she thought.

And then she heard him chuckle. Again, not audibly. She felt Ethan's mirth warm her chest and it was almost as if she'd laughed herself. What was that about?

She set down the glass and teased the ends of her hair as she stared off toward the bedroom. They'd been so close in those moments when he'd been drinking her blood and fucking her at the same time. Truly, they had delved into some kind of blood bond.

Walking fast, she entered the bedroom and glided

onto the bed beside Ethan. He patted the cooling side of the sheets, indicating where he wanted her.

"Did you just talk to me in my head?" she asked.

"I did."

"Vampire persuasion?"

"No. I mean, I don't think so. It was a thought that I sent to you, hoping you'd hear. I heard you reply when you were drinking juice."

"We can communicate silently now?" She snuggled up next to him, fitting one leg between both of his as she nudged up her breasts to hug his chest.

He pushed the hair from her neck and studied where he'd bitten her. "It must be residual effects from what we just did."

"Yes. I've never tried it before," she said.

"Really, Miss Fang Junkie?"

"It was either the bite or sex. Never at the same time."

"Wow, you do have a discerning bone."

"Richard."

"That was deserved. But you did say this would bond us and make us stronger together."

"I did say that, didn't I? It was a lark. I've heard it could work, but I was thinking more toward making us a powerful duo tracking the demon. I'm not sure how feeling one another's pleasure is going to help that. Did you feel it all? When I did this…" She reached down and fluttered his forefinger over her folds and then pressed at the peak of them, igniting a twinge of pleasure at her clit.

Ethan sucked in a hiss. "Just the right amount of pressure and, ah, witch, you really fly."

"Yeah? Well, I never knew what it could feel like to do this." She gripped his cock and squeezed, and in reaction she felt her stomach tense and her loins sing. "That is so not bad. Do you think we bonded? I mean, I've heard that vamps can bond with others by sharing blood. I didn't take your blood. And I've been with other vampires before. This never happened."

"I don't have an answer for you. It's weird, but cool. Probably it was a soul thing."

"Would that be okay with you? I mean, you said you've never felt soul-deep toward a woman."

"It's all right by me for now." He clasped her hand and leaned in to kiss her neck, which sent a shiver down her spine. He breathed on her skin, which tickled as well. "Who knows how long it'll last. Let's go with it for as long as we have it, yes?"

"No arguments from this witch."

She settled next to him, both of them staring up at the ceiling. Moonlight shone across a nearby rooftop and glinted copper outside the window.

"Tell me why you pulled a three-sixty from flying back to the States?" Ethan asked. "Was it just to fuck me?"

"That was one reason. But another was that this witch never backs down from a challenge."

"Even if that challenge threatened to end you?"

"Oh, yeah. I could feel that bastard hold my heart, Ethan. He promised to rip it out should I go after him again. But bring it on. This witch is not about to run with her tail between her heels because some pretty demon wants to play piñata with my heart."

"It's dangerous for you to go near him. I've learned more about the demon's curse. I stopped into the Archives while you must have been at the airport. CJ and I looked up Gazariel. I had no idea the curse originated with—"

"Himself." Tuesday felt a catch in her throat speaking that name. "It's something I've always known. Felt. But never articulated. Didn't want to put it into words because I didn't want to believe I was in any way connected to that asshole."

"The grand high asshole of all assholes."

"Exactly. A super Richard." She lifted her head to find his gaze. "Just because I'm primed for the challenge doesn't mean I'm not also freaked the hell out. I can't do this alone. And I know you can't do it without me."

"But now you've made me into some kind of magical tracking device. So maybe I can?"

"True." She smoothed her hand over his abs, where she'd drawn the spell and gifted him her magic. "Of course you can, but... Can we do this together?"

"You've no reason to seek the demon, Tuesday. It means nothing to you to get back the Final Days code. You're free to leave Paris. I mean that. I don't want you involved if the expense means your life."

"Seriously? It means everything to me if the result of having the code enacted means I'll be smothered by angels when they fall. I *am* affected by this, Ethan. This is kind of a world-saving venture, and I do live in the world."

"You've got a point."

"I don't understand why Gazariel would give such a devious weapon to the vampiress. He seems to thrive living amongst the mortals. And without them, he would be left with the angels and...Himself. The very last being I imagine he'd want to associate with. There's something we're missing."

Ethan rolled to his side and absently stroked his fingers along her hip and up her stomach. "So you're in?"

"All the way up to my tits."

"They are nice tits." He squeezed one of them then gasped. "Man, that feels ten times better than when you pinch mine. Yours are so sensitive." He leaned forward and sucked one into his mouth, groaning with the shared pleasure.

And Tuesday closed her eyes, wondering when she'd lost her way. This man was only supposed to be a quick fuck and then she had planned to dash back to the States. Yet every part of her wanted to stay near him, to not lose contact with him. It was as if, with the bite and the sex, they had again bound themselves to one another with a stronger bond than even her magic could manage.

And the word *love* kept bouncing against her brain cells. Well, she didn't have to worry about that. The man couldn't love her. He could, but then it would explode and he'd leave or call her a bitch and hate her forever. True love was the key to breaking the curse? Never happen in her lifetime.

"I have a sort of plan," he said, rolling to his back again.

Missing his heat at her nipple, Tuesday laid her palm over the wet peak. "Tell me."

"First we need to capture the demon. Even if Anyx is with him. I have to add measures to contain her as well. If she's been gifted the book she could be attempting to decipher the code right now."

"So we need them both."

"We do."

"And then what?"

"Then we twist the screws to his thumbs."

"Literally? You know, I've seen people tortured with thumbscrews. It is so not pretty."

"I've seen it too. Metaphorically, we'll twist the screws by threatening to send Gazariel to Daemonia."

"Really? He would not like that place very much. They'd chew up a fallen angel and regurgitate him over and over. And over."

"You knew he was a Fallen One?"

"He told me. Creator of Vanity, remember? Just like the curse has always been inside me, and I've sensed it was birthed from the Big Bad Dude, I also felt the demon's ethereal ties before he cursed me. But how would you put him in Daemonia?"

"I know a reckoner."

"Good to have one of those guys on your contacts list."

"Exactly. So our first step is to track the demon again."

"All right, but I'm hungry, and I probably need another shower after all that sex. Want to share the water?"

"Go get it warmed up for me."

"Aha! Yeah, I don't think so, vampire. Why don't you go warm it up for me?"

Ethan sat up and gave her a mock bow. "Your beck is my command."

"Damn right it is. About time I get to tell you what to do."

"Stuart, start the shower."

And as her lover wandered into the bathroom, Tuesday decided that indeed, it was her turn at command. His plan to capture the demon hadn't worked. He was emotionally stalled by the vampiress and he didn't realize that weakness.

Now it was time for the witch to take control.

Chapter 16

Ethan followed Tuesday up the narrow, spiraling stair-case to the fifth floor, where Savin Thorne lived in an apartment building in the fourteenth arrondissement. He'd texted Thorne an hour earlier, asking if he could stop by, and had gotten a return text that he was always welcome. It was evening, but not so late that the streets weren't packed with tourists and the locals were finish-ing an evening meal.

On occasion, Acquisitions employed reckoners in whatever locale they were needed. Sometimes demons who had broken mortal realm laws, or who were volatile and impossible to contain, required deportation back to Daemonia. That was a reckoner's job. And while Ac-quisitions wasn't in the business of capturing demons, sometimes that was a necessary by-blow of a job. Nasty demon attached to a toxic or volatile artifact? The retriever may be forced to take both. A helpful demon who refused to leave after the job was done? So long, Sunshine. Or a demon who had stolen a book that could end the world? The threat of Daemonia may be the only thing that could get him to cough it up.

Daemonia was The Place of All Demons. Not exactly *all* demons. But it was where the majority lived and existed. It wasn't Beneath or the hell the humans made up to balance out their religious beliefs. It was simply another realm where demons lived. Much like Faery housed faeries. It wasn't a good place. A mortal, or nondemon, would not care to go there, even for a brief visit. The dark witch Certainly Jones had gone there and returned without too much physical harm. It was the mental damage that could never be completely assessed. Or healed.

Ethan had personally called in Savin Thorne to send demons back to Daemonia on two occasions. Reckoners had a particular tie to Daemonia, yet they were not generally demons. Thorne was mortal, to an extent. Ethan wasn't sure what to call him, exactly. And he didn't want to get caught up in labels. He knew the man was trustworthy, smart, a loner, and could drink him under the table any day. And that was saying a lot, considering vampires generally didn't get drunk unless they literally swam in alcohol.

The sway of Tuesday's coat focused his attention on the reveal of her ass beneath the long alpaca fur. So tight and…he could feel it in his hands.

Using the silent mind communication they'd gained from their sexual encounter, Ethan put out a thought. *You distract me, witch.*

Right back atcha, vampire was her silent response.

She arrived at the only door on the fifth floor and turned to eye him, with a wink. Teasing her tongue along her lips, she lowered her gaze to his crotch. Where a healthy hard-on threatened to make walking difficult if he didn't steer his mind away from Tuesday's sexy curves and stunning kisses to focus on the task at hand.

Ethan leaned in to brush her cheek with his kiss. "Save it for later," he muttered, then rapped on the door.

Just now noticing the strains of bluesy guitar music filtering behind the door, Ethan smiled. The man did like to settle in with a whiskey and his guitar. He collected guitars, and even played the diddley bow, which was a one-stringed guitarlike instrument.

The music stopped and the door swung open five seconds later to reveal a big, hulking man with dark hair, an imposing beard and narrowed eyes, yet a smile that was so overwhelmingly honest he could tease even the most wicked demon to step forward and risk their chances with his unique skill.

"Ethan Pierce! Good to see you, man. Come on in. And let the little lady through first."

"Savin Thorne, this is Tuesday Knightsbridge. Tuesday, Savin."

They shook hands, and Savin enclosed Tuesday's hand with both of his and bowed to her. "Namaste, dark witch. Enter my home with no ill intent and I open my wards to you," he offered.

"Agreed," Tuesday said.

And Ethan felt a tug at his skin as, with a sweep of his hand before them, Savin released whatever wards he had up.

"That one pinched," Tuesday offered. "You're fully warded."

"Not wise to live any other way." Savin gestured for them to follow him through an industrial-style kitchen and beyond to the living area. Dark beams supported the ceiling and bare brickwork fashioned the walls. Steel shelves and wood furniture with faded and cracked leather cushions revealed the place to be the ultimate man cave. Add to that the wall of guitars behind the sofa, and the amps spread out along one wall, and Ethan decided the man could probably get lost in his music and not give a care for the world that bustled outside.

"Can I get you something to drink?" Savin asked. "I know it's still early but I've got an awesome whiskey aged to perfection. You want to try it, don't you, Ethan?"

"Hell yes."

"I'll give it a go," Tuesday said as she sat on the sofa, crossed her legs and shrugged off her coat. A battered electric guitar lay on the cushion next to her and she stroked her fingers down the strings and along the wooden body. "I can feel the power in this one. You practice musicomancy."

Savin returned with two glasses, handing one to Ethan, who stood by a thick beam that resembled a railroad tie, and the other to Tuesday. "I do. Or I'm learning it. Still don't have much control over it. You could feel it in the guitar?"

"Of course." She took her fingers away from the instrument. "Keep working on it. The guitar is infused with your efforts."

"Thanks. I will. So." Savin turned to Ethan, shoving his hands in his back pockets. "What's up? Generally if you need a demon reckoned you shoot me a call and tell me where to be."

"I don't have the demon under control yet," Ethan

said. "But I wanted to put you on call, if that's possible." He tilted back a swallow of the whiskey and winced. "Fuck, this is tight."

"Secret recipe." He tapped his temple. "Got it from somewhere I don't even want to question too much. What demon are you dealing with?"

"Gazariel, The Beautiful One."

Savin crimped an eyebrow. "Not sure I've heard of that one."

"He's a Fallen One," Tuesday offered. "Not originally from Daemonia. But you can still send him there?"

"Of course. But those Fallen bastards are a bitch to deal with. How do you plan on containing him long enough for me to get there and send him off?"

"That's still in the planning phase," Ethan said. "I was hoping you might have some suggestions. I need all the help I can get with this one."

"What's the demon done?"

"It's what he's got. And I may not need you to send him to Daemonia, but rather, offer the real threat of such a thing happening."

"A Fallen One would not want to go to Daemonia. I've reckoned one of them and it was a bitch. They put up quite the fight. But The Beautiful One? What are we dealing with here? A preening poseur?"

"Something like that." Ethan took another swig and still couldn't stop a wince at the burn. But it was a good burn. "The demon has the code for the Final Days. We need to get that from him and lock it away nice and safe."

"Yeah, I'd agree with that. Not much for being smothered by gajillions of angels. You want more?" Savin asked Tuesday.

"No, thanks. This is some powerful stuff."

"Brewed by Scottish trolls."

Ethan raised an eyebrow at that one. The man did have a habit of making stuff up. Just for shits and giggles.

"It's true," Savin defended, noticing Ethan's doubt. "Just ask the mermaid who sold it to me." With that, he laughed heartily, and Ethan joined him. "You want me to stand by for the call should you manage to wrangle this demon? I can get anywhere in the city in about twenty minutes, depending on how traffic cooperates. I assume you'll probably hold him at headquarters?"

"Yes, in the eleventh."

"And what's the witch helping you with? If you don't mind my asking? Or…is she your girl? Tagging along for the fun?"

"She's the operator to my compass," Ethan offered. "She wears his sigil from a curse the demon put inside her centuries ago. They are connected. She gave me some magic that will lead us to him. We've twice already encountered the demon, but… I wasn't prepared for the containment."

"No containment crew?"

"Yes, but…eh, it doesn't matter. I'm preparing for the third time. He won't slip away again."

"Most definitely. I always tell hunters demons are wily. They'll take advantage of everything you hadn't thought they could. So you two are connected?" He looked to Tuesday.

She nodded. "In a working relationship. And while I'm not looking forward to seeing Gazariel again anytime soon, I want to help Ethan get this weapon out of his hands."

"Noble, especially for a dark witch."

"We're not all bitches," Tuesday said.

"No, but the majority of you can't be trusted." He spread out a hand in placation. "Just my call. Take all the offense you like."

"I take no offense. I know what I am, and I don't make excuses for it. So you're on our team now. Great. What information do you need from us to get ready for your gig?"

"As much as you can give me. Though knowing he's Fallen is enough. But…you said you and the demon are connected?" Savin approached Tuesday and nodded, indicating she should stand. "Do you wear the demon's sigil?"

"I do."

"Can I take a look at it?"

With a hefty sigh, Tuesday rose and lifted her T-shirt. "Everybody wants to touch the witch. Just make sure your hands aren't cold."

Savin bent to study the dark sigil drawn between Tuesday's breasts. And with a brisk rub of his palms together, and a questioning gesture, he was given permission to touch. He put his finger on the sigil and traced the lines, then suddenly snapped back and stepped away, shaking the hand that had touched her.

"Yep, you two are connected. That's a nasty one. No wonder you're dark. That curse originated from the Big Guy."

"You know that?" Ethan asked.

Savin shrugged. "Some shit I just know. Like it or not. I wouldn't call her master The Beautiful One, but rather the Dark Prince."

"No." Tuesday pulled down her shirt. "I've never

been attached to Himself. Never felt that pull or such control."

"Whatever. It's what I feel. But, uh…" Savin glanced to Ethan. "You do know if I send the demon to Daemonia, she's going with it?"

Ethan caught Tuesday's gaping look and in his mind he heard her say, *What the fuck?*

"I didn't know that," Ethan offered. "We have to disconnect them before the reckoning?"

"Either that, or bye-bye, witch." Savin shrugged. "Unless she can ward herself to the nines. Not sure it's even possible with a sigil connected to the Dark One."

"Great. Ever since Ethan kidnapped me this whole ride has been one big party of suck."

"Kidnapped?"

Ethan shook his head at Savin's inquiring glance. "A retriever brought her in from the States. She's the only one with a connection to the demon."

"Since when does Acquisitions force others to do their dirty work?" Savin asked.

Ethan raised an eyebrow. The man knew the answer to that one, and he wasn't sure why he was being so openly obstinate.

"Yeah, I get it. Right." Savin sighed heavily. "You give me a call when you've got the demon contained. But I won't hold my breath waiting for the call. This will be a tough catch."

"Thanks for that vote of confidence," Ethan said. "Is there nothing you can offer in way of containing a Fallen One?"

Savin rubbed his jaw in thought. "The witch's dark magic should prove effective, and if you add a familiar into the mix that will only increase the power. But if she's bonded with the demon everything could blow up in your face. I'd suggest keeping her as far from the demon as possible. He could use her magic against you."

"As we've already seen," Tuesday said. "I won't give up on trying to help Ethan. The familiar is a good idea, though. Know of any familiars willing to risk their life for a long shot?"

"Actually—" Savin's generous grin poked dimples into his cheeks "—I do."

"How much does your organization pay a guy like Thorne to reckon demons?" Tuesday asked as they strolled down the sidewalk in a direction Ethan had pointed out.

The city rose around them in three- and four-story buildings, random trees sprouting in tiny courtyards here and there, and the constant car horns squawking at one another. Lights everywhere illuminated the dark streets and touristy areas like a carnival.

Ethan scrolled through the contacts on his phone, searching for the familiar's location. "I'm not sure. I requisition invoices to be paid directly to Savin. I'm not the money guy."

"Is that so? Are you telling me your promise to pay me for helping you was a lie?"

"No. You'll get what you deserve. But I won't be on the negotiating part of that. I don't like to be involved in the money."

"Aren't you going to put in a good word for me?" She turned and fluttered her lashes at him.

And Ethan was taken by that flirtatious move, even though he sensed it was more mocking than a flirt. "Are you worried about what Savin said about you going along with the demon to Daemonia?"

"Why should I be? I thought you said the reckoner would merely be used as a threat to get the demon to talk. Wait. Seriously? You're going to deport the demon with me attached to him? You ass!" She turned and marched onward, furred coat flying out in a rage.

Women! They changed moods like they changed their shoes.

Instead of chasing after her, Ethan sent her a mind message. *Tuesday, you're overreacting. I will never allow that to happen to you. I care about you.* He stopped, pausing to consider those thoughts. Did he really care about the witch?

Ahead of him, Tuesday stopped and turned around, arms swinging out at her sides. In his thoughts he heard her wonder, *Really?* Then her shoulders dropped and she shook her head, and spoke out loud. "Bad move, vampire. I'm not the kind of chick a guy should ever have a care for."

And she turned and strode onward, intent on putting distance between them. Was it because of the curse she wore? Did she believe love could never be hers? What if she did believe in it? Might she then have it?

His contacts list brought up Thomas the familiar's address, which was…in the opposite direction they were walking. Ethan tucked away the phone and ran up to catch Tuesday. She turned a corner down a narrow alley formed by the rough limestone bricks of a small church and a black wrought-iron fence that kept back the leaf-less branches from an overgrown shrub.

He grabbed her by the arm and spun her around, but didn't do the inconsiderate thing of pushing her against the wall and admonishing her for her silly emotional reaction.

"You don't get to tell me who I can care about," he said.

"Yeah? I thought you didn't like witches. If having sex a couple times is all it takes to turn your head I'd tell you to beware your female enemies, big-time."

"Tuesday, I know this is a wall you've created over the years—hell, the centuries—to make life easier to walk through."

"It's not a wall, asshole, it's a fucking curse."

"Right. The curse. But there's a wall, too. I know, because I do it, too. I love my walls. Keeps people at a distance, and makes it easy to ignore the fact that I do have feelings. So I've had a change of heart about a witch that I prejudged incorrectly. I like you. Get over it."

He leaned against the wrought-iron fence, crossing his arms over his chest. Yes, putting up that wall, like she had done. It was something he did by rote.

"What do you want from me, Ethan?"

"You know what I want from you."

She sighed and tilted her head against the wall, turning so her cheek faced him. "And I agreed to help you get what you want because I like to do shit that challenges me. Surprises me. Lures me out of the norm. Chasing a demon who could be my death? Sign me up."

"You think that if you find Gazariel you might get him to break the curse?"

She chuffed. "Only one way to make that happen, and I do like my heart exactly where it is." She turned to look at him and he maintained a cool gaze, arms still crossed defiantly. "This thing we accidentally created between us can only harm us both. You know that."

"Only if we have hope. And we've both lived long enough to know that hope is stupid and cheap."

"So you're saying you're just going with the feeling? That when it ends you can walk away? Wham, bam, thank you, witch?"

"Isn't that how you want it to go?"

She nodded. But he noticed the beginning of her wince before she smoothed away that regretful motion. She wanted more, he knew it. And he did, too. How could he get the demon to break that damn curse for her? She deserved love.

"Right." She lifted her chin. "In it for the ride, arms spread and head thrown back as we scream at the top of our lungs. Then let the chips fall where they may. I like you, too, vampire. There. I said it. You're right. I can do this. And when it's done? I can walk away."

She put out her hand to shake, as if they might seal the agreement to let their hearts stumble against one another, to fall into the experience of some kind of relationship, but knowing full well that it was only until they were both done using one another.

Ethan could get behind that. But not completely.

He gripped Tuesday's hand but then lunged forward to kiss her. She hadn't expected that, and she initially struggled. But he dropped her hand and cupped her head, keeping her mouth at his so he could deepen the kiss, dive in to her and taste her fears as they quickly wilted to allow in desire and want and the very same need he felt.

Her heartbeats entered his and at first they danced in a challenging standoff, but then quickly steadied and began to share the rhythm. She hiked up a leg against his thigh, drawing his hips to her body. Instant hard-on.

Which he crushed against her in a moaning plead for what he suddenly needed right now.

"Yeah?" she said as she tilted her head to catch his mouth at a new angle. "We are away from the crowds."

"Can you put up some kind of shield?"

"You mean my invisibility cloak?"

Ethan pulled from the kiss, meeting her eyes with wonder. "You have one?"

She laughed and then crushed a kiss to his mouth. "No, and who wants the confidence of a protection shield when the risk of being seen is much more fun?"

He unzipped and hissed when her cool fingers wrapped about his cock. The heavy fall of her coat shielded them from curious eyes, should anyone pause at the end of the alleyway and peer down at them. But she was right. The idea of being caught out only made his cock harder.

He slid down her leggings and hugged his erection against her mons. Directing him, she tapped the head of him against her clit. He could feel the tingling curls of sensation with each tap, taking everything she felt into his system and doubling it with his own. He would never regret the blood bond between them. Not even if he had to walk away from her when the demon had been captured and the code secured.

Maybe? He'd just been thinking the witch deserved love. What about him?

No time to think about it. Nuzzling his nose along her hair and down to her ear, he licked her lobe as she allowed him entrance into her hot, wet pussy. With a growl, he clapped a hand about her ass and rocked her onto him as he willed down his fangs and bit into her neck.

She swore and her fingernails clawed at his neck.

That exquisite pain heightened the pleasure, and as her blood spilled down his throat, Ethan spilled into her. He'd never tasted finer, nor had he felt uniquely connected to another.

A giggle from down the way clued him they'd found an audience. Ethan growled and retracted his fangs, but pulled Tuesday in closer, wanting to wrap her about his body until he felt nothing more than her heartbeats envelop his soul.

Chapter 17

Swinging out of the alleyway, Tuesday walked alongside Ethan this time. The man had a way of winning her when she most wanted to push him away. And it wasn't even the power of his cock and kiss. It was something innate. She was a part of him, and she had felt his truth and honesty as he'd kissed her roughly. The desperation in that kiss had made her understand her own desperation for acceptance. It was a long time coming.

But she wouldn't go all moon-eyed for the man and pledge her undying love to him. That way lay broken hearts and regret. Her heart broken. Men tended to wander off and never look back. Because love could never really fix in a man's heart for her. She and Ethan had agreed to go with whatever came their way, and she was good with that. Because life was meant to be lived in the moment, and no one reminded her of that more than Ethan Pierce.

"Is the familiar's place that way?" she asked, as he led her down the street. They passed a crepe hawker and she stopped. "I haven't eaten all day. You got some cash?"

With a smirk he tugged out his wallet and handed her a twenty-euro note.

"You want something? A coffee?"

"I just had a drink. And I'm not talking about the whiskey." His eyes glittered. It was a feeling that hit Tuesday in her very bones. And she couldn't prevent a return smile. "I'll wait over there. I want to check out the musician across the street." He thumbed a gesture over his shoulder, where Tuesday saw a guitarist performing, then wandered across the street.

The night was chilly but not too cold with her big coat to shield from the elements. The instant the hot creamy chocolate and bananas hit her belly, Tuesday groaned with pleasure. No one could tell her this much sugar was not good for her. This gastronomic nightmare spoke to her soul the way no kiss or sex could.

Standing at the curb, watching Ethan listen amongst the crowd as the guitarist performed a dazzling flamenco number, punctuated by frequent cries of *"olé!"* from the onlookers, Tuesday couldn't decide when she'd last been on a date with a man that hadn't seemed like a date. Of course, they were not on a date. They were tracking a crazy demon who was dating Ethan's ex-wife. But it felt date-ish. And certainly they had formed *some* kind of a relationship.

And then she realized she was laying claim to the man in a way that disturbed her. It was her reaction to the ex-wife all over again. What had become of the dark witch who preferred to fuck them and leave them? Who rarely trusted a man, and had been fine with her single no-commitments life over the centuries. Why was the idea of actually enjoying time spent with a man suddenly so alluring? Almost as if it was fulfilling a need she'd never thought to have.

A need she'd willingly sacrificed when at her lowest and near death.

It must be the Paris air. It was making her think. Too much. The City of Light was the city for lovers. So, yeah. Leave it at that, Tuesday. Just lovers.

Catching a drip of chocolate that ran down the side of her hand with her tongue, she traced her skin slowly, thinking to send the sensation across the street and to Ethan. She watched as he lifted his hand, shook it, then swung a glance over his shoulder, making direct eye contact with her.

She gave him a thumbs-up and a smiling wink.

He blew her an air kiss, then nodded that she cross over and join him as he wandered down the sidewalk. Hell, something crazy was going on between her and the man, but she didn't want to overanalyze it. She would take each moment for what it was, as he'd suggested.

"You didn't save me a taste?" he asked as she joined his side.

"I still have some on my fingers." She held out her forefinger and he leaned down to lick it, stopping long enough to suck it into his mouth and draw up a sigh from her. "And here I thought the crepe was awesome."

He winked at her and then clasped her other hand and led her onward. "The familiar lives near the Panthéon."

"Is that the big place with all the dead people in it?"

"It is. Alexandre Dumas is even interred there now.

He was moved a decade or so ago from another spot. Much against his wishes to be buried in his hometown."

"You knew the guy?"

"Of course! Though I never could inspire him to try his hand at writing about vampires. Always the musketeers."

"What's wrong with a sexy musketeer? I knew a few in my time."

"But dating a lawman? Wasn't it difficult for you in the earlier centuries? Seems like the witch hunts have always been a constant."

"I got smart after I got the sigil."

"I bet you did." He swung an arm across her shoulders and hugged her close as they strolled down a cobblestoned sidewalk, avoiding a crowd lingering outside the massive domed Panthéon building. "I never had much of a problem with witches until..."

"Until? Until what? Did one of them look at you the wrong way? Give you the evil eye?"

He grimaced, but they maintained their casual pace. "I had a lover in the early twentieth century."

"Oh, yeah? Someone other than your wife? And the nameless woman with the tragic blood transfusion?"

"I've had many lovers. As I know you have. But this woman was different. She swept me off my feet, you could say. But we were only together six months."

"Was she vampire?"

"Yes."

"And?" They walked a few more paces, Tuesday sensing Ethan's tension tightening the muscles in the arm across her shoulders. But he had brought up this thread of conversation. So... "Ethan?"

"She bit a witch when she was starving for blood.

And you know that's when the Great Protection Spell had rendered all witches' blood poisonous to vampires. I watched her die. It took less than five minutes for the blood to eat her up from the inside out."

Yeah, that had been the cool thing about being a witch before the spell had been broken early in the twenty-first century. A witch need not fear a vampire after centuries of persecution. The Great Protection Spell had been conjured to make all the blood in all the witches lethal to vampires. One bite and bye-bye vampire.

Tuesday had experienced a few occasions when a particularly vicious vampire had thought he was going to take what he wanted from her. No regrets whatsoever.

"She didn't know it was a witch she was biting?" she asked.

"No. And neither did I. We were out partying and she rushed ahead to feed. She was an innocent. And rationally, I know the witch was also innocent of the crime of murder. That witch had not asked to be bitten by a blood-hungry vampire. But at the time I didn't see it that way."

"You murdered the witch?"

He nodded. "I was in a rage. My old warring instincts emerged. I didn't kill her. I…couldn't."

"Of course not. If you would have made her bleed on you…"

"I'm not reckless with lives, Tuesday. You have to know that. But I did do some damage. Of which, I regret."

He must have been a force on the battlegrounds. How times had changed. Not always for the best, but the end of the Great Protection Spell had helped to ease tensions between vamps and witches.

"The past haunts us ever and always," she offered.

"That it does. But now you know about my witch thing."

"Yeah, but I'm not that witch, Ethan. And vampires have no reason to fear our species any longer. So for as much as I can sympathize with you losing someone you loved? You gotta get over it, vampire. Live in the moment, remember?"

"Thanks for reminding me." And then he smiled at her. "And I have gotten over it, apparently so much so that I've drunk from a witch twice within the last twenty-four hours."

Tuesday felt as if the something that had started between them had sunk deeply into her marrow. There would be no walking away from this man after they had dealt with the demon. And how to accept that her staying in his life, possibly allowing him to consider falling in love, could only mean their end?

"You can tell me about all your lovers sometime," she said. "If you want to. I'd like to hear about the women who captured your heart. Even if only for a day, week, month or year."

"Really? You didn't want to hear about Anyx."

"That was…" Not all that different. The man had lovers and a wife over the centuries. Wasn't as if she'd been celibate. Time to drop the jealousy. "We can share. But let's take it slow, yeah?"

"Agreed. Past lovers don't need to be doled out all at once. And they are the past."

"I can agree with that. Been there, don't need to look back."

"But you still owe me a couple lover stories. Which I will collect on later. Right now, I believe that is the familiar's building." Ethan stopped across the street from a nondescript four-story building fronted by stone mascarons and weather-stained pink granite. "I'm never sure how to go about approaching a familiar," he said. "Do I call out 'Here, kitty kitty'?"

"That would be obnoxious," a man's voice said from behind Tuesday and Ethan.

They both turned to find a short man with tousled brown-and-gold hair, green eyes and a confident stance lift a questioning eyebrow.

The familiar bowed to Tuesday, then took her hand and kissed the back of it. Tuesday was not impressed. She could recognize a charmer from a mile away.

"Ethan Pierce," the man said as he shook the vampire's hand. "It's been a few years, yes? How's bites?"

"The usual. I need your help, Thomas. Can we go up and talk?" He gestured toward the building.

"No." Thomas assessed Tuesday carefully, his green eyes narrowing, most likely reading her for powers or skills. Familiars had a thing with witches and could read them fairly well. "I'd prefer to stay outside. Was just heading out for a scamper anyway. Whatever you've got to offer me, make it quick."

Ethan said, "I need a familiar to help summon a demon."

"Nope." Thomas shook his head adamantly. "No can do. I don't do that kind of subservient shit. No witch is going to use me to channel a demon to this realm."

"The demon is already here. In Paris," Ethan explained. "We need to summon him into captivity."

Thomas quirked an eyebrow. "Why don't you go after him? Don't you head a troop of wild and crazy demon hunters?"

"We don't hunt demons. Exactly. Besides, we tried that."

"And failed? And why are you, the director of Acquisitions, asking me about this? Are you doing field-work now, Pierce?"

"I am. This is an important case. I don't want to cock it up."

Tuesday held back from mentioning that he'd already managed to do just that. She'd give the man a break. He was particularly cute, and she was still riding all the warm feelies after that quickie in the alley.

"You do have a partner that works with you, yes?" Ethan asked.

Thomas lifted his shoulders in affront. "Whether or not I do is none of your business. I won't do it. I do have my dignity. Good day to the two of you."

The familiar turned and strolled away, shoving his hands in the pockets of a summery white linen jacket.

Ethan called after him, "It pays!"

Thomas performed an agile turn—as graceful as a feline—and walked back up to them. "How much?"

Ethan shrugged. "How much do you charge?"

"A hundred thousand," Thomas said without pause.

Curious to see how the man who had explained to her that he didn't have a handle on the money would play this one, Tuesday listened avidly.

"Can't do that," Ethan said.

"Fifty grand."

Ethan winced.

"Oh, come on! What can you give me, man?"

"Ten," Ethan said.

Thomas turned and stalked away from them, but he flung out his arms and called without looking back, "Fine!"

"I'll need you after dark. Tomorrow!" Ethan called after him. "At headquarters. Ready to go."

Thomas delivered a thumbs-up over his shoulder and kept on walking.

"Ten grand?" Tuesday asked.

"His job isn't that complicated. Having sex until he's sated?" Ethan blew out a breath.

"Yeah, but it is dangerous. When the demon comes through, the familiar will shift to cat form and be left vulnerable. Not to mention whomever he works with will be in danger." Meaning, the person he'd be having sex with in order to become sated.

Familiars were conduits for demons to bridge into this realm. A witch could summon a demon via a familiar by invoking a spell at the point in which the familiar was sexually sated and open to receive that demon into this realm. Bridging a demon already in the same realm? Should be a piece of cake.

"You want me to invoke the spell?" Tuesday asked as she joined Ethan's side and they walked again. "I've conjured a demon or two in my day."

"Yes, and I've met one of them," he replied. "He almost brought down a four-story building on our heads. No, I'll have Certainly Jones do it. I don't want you anywhere near when the demon Gazariel is summoned."

"Don't you trust me?"

"Tuesday, I thought you said he'd rip out your heart if he saw you again. I'm trying to keep you safe."

"I appreciate that, but I think you'll need me to be

there. My sigil will focus CJ's and the familiar's magic and abbreviate the process. The familiar might not even have to go through all his...gyrations, to achieve bridging mode."

"You have something against watching a familiar have sex?"

"Do *you* want to watch? Kinky. The things I'm learning about you."

Ethan grabbed her and kissed her. Hard. Claiming. Just long enough to make her glad for his need to silence her in such a manner.

"I'd rather not watch, if truth be told," he offered. "Fine. I'll talk to CJ about the possibility of having you close. But I need you to be protected. If we can't ensure your safety, you're out."

"My, how your attitude toward me has altered in but a few days. Is it my dazzling personality? Or merely that you like fucking me?"

"Both." The wink was the killer move to seal Tuesday's crazy fall into something she wasn't about to name. No, never. "Now come on," he said. "We've a little over twenty-four hours until tomorrow night. I'm going to call CJ and get the ball rolling, then set up things to ensure the reckoner is on-site as well. After that, we'll have a little time to spare."

"I'm hungry."

"Again? You just ate a monstrous crepe stuffed with an entire banana and enough chocolate to feed a classroom."

"Are you judging my eating habits?"

He laughed. "Not at all. Let me make the phone calls, then I'll take you to a place on the island. I've always wanted to taste their food."

Chapter 18

The meal featured tiny jewels of savory-flavored gelatin and a salad that would have starved a baby bunny. Tuesday had been forced to order two desserts. When the waiter delivered the cherry cake laced with rum he winked at Ethan. But Ethan's attention remained on Tuesday as she teased her fork at the decadent, moist cake.

They'd talked about familiars and what a weird life that must be. To be able to shift to such a small animal, such as a cat, bird, insect, or snakes and worms, and then to transform back to a human shape. Had to fuck with the insides and internal organs, yeah? The paranormal realm was truly wondrous.

The first bite of the cake made up for the pitiful meal. Lush, rum-soaked cherries burst on Tuesday's tongue, and she moaned in appreciation, savoring the wicked dark flavor.

Ethan leaned forward, his interest suddenly intent. "That good, eh?"

"You want a taste?"

"I think I'd rather experience it through you."

"I don't think the mutual-sexual-vibes thing works with food. On the other hand..."

She forked in another bite and this time closed her eyes to really enjoy and experience the flavors. Sweet and tart, dense and creamy. Kind of how it felt when Ethan ran his tongue over her swollen, wet pussy. The man was always intent on her pleasure. Just thinking about it, combined with the cherries and cake, made her nipples tighten.

Ethan groaned.

She opened one eye to see the vampire silently pleading with her from across the table. She slid her hand over the table and clasped fingers with him. The touch shivered over her skin.

"I felt that," he said. "The way you felt it. Really? That good?"

"I'm using my imagination, and thinking about you...with your head between my legs." She dipped into the cherry syrup and touched the fork to her lips, licking it off with a slow draw of her tongue.

Ethan sucked in his lower lip and eased his free hand down to his lap. Tuesday felt the rub of his palm across his cock as a visceral hum in her loins. The man's sexual energy was focused and targeted to his core. Acknowledging it started an aching throb at her clitoris. She stabbed another syrupy cherry onto the fork and this time held it between her lips and slowly crushed it. Cherry juice ran down her chin.

"I'd crawl under the table right now if there weren't

people sitting but five feet from us. But can you feel this?" Ethan's hand under the table must have squeezed his erection because Tuesday reacted with a gasp.

"Sweet bloody cherries, yes. You're so hard, vampire."

A sudden throat clearing beside them darted Tuesday's attention to the side. The man sitting at a table by himself, a small cup of espresso steaming before him, gave her a snide look down his nose.

The voyeur did not approve?

Tuesday pulled up Ethan's hand to trace the cherry juice on her chin. He then dipped that finger into her mouth and she sucked it. With a tender bite to the tip of his finger and a lash of her tongue, she was gifted with the exact right pressure to her clit that set her off. A deep and concentrated orgasm clasped her for a few seconds. Enough to lift her gasp to a vocal cry of "Oh!"

For his part, Ethan pulled his hand from her mouth and muffled his groan behind a napkin.

Tuesday leaned forward, panting and squeezing her thighs together to milk one last shock of vibrant sensation from the orgasm. Yes, right there. She bowed her head and said in a tight whisper, "That was so fucking good."

"I am suddenly a fan of rum-soaked cherries." He clasped her hand and they stood to leave. Ethan gave the voyeur a smirk.

And Tuesday said as they passed him, "Let them eat cake."

Hand in hand, they walked to Acquisitions headquarters, and entered through a nondescript door in an alleyway. The same door that Tuesday had walked out of days earlier and then had been bound to Ethan. Now they were bound in a different manner, and because of the choices they'd made to do so.

A dark hallway led to an elevator, which rose four flights. It was near midnight so the building was mostly quiet, though Ethan mentioned that there were always people in some department doing something at all hours of the day.

A small reception area let in moonlight across the single desk and curved walls. Tuesday stepped behind Ethan as he waited before a steel platform and some kind of electronic reading device that resembled the scanner a person walks through at the airport. He waited for green LEDs to blink, then grabbed her and rushed across the platform.

"You don't have access," he said as he punched in a digital code on a massive wood door before them. "But that sneaky move worked better than I expected."

"You've never snuck a girlfriend into your office before?"

"You're the first," he said as he opened the door and she walked through.

Though she had been in here briefly before, she'd not taken the time to look around because she'd been seriously in need of a bathroom break and had also been focusing on the sigil burning through the shackle rope Certainly Jones had placed on her.

Eerily quiet, and barely lit by pale moonlight, the dark room smelled like cedar. Tuesday slipped off her coat and let it drop to the floor as she walked up to the desk. Dim lighting blinked on and highlighted the hexagon structure of the room. An excellent shape for creating magic. The walls were solid, dark-stained wood, and the windows had a view of the city lights, yet she wouldn't be able to pinpoint a monument or tourist attraction for the life of her.

"A vampire's retreat," she decided. "Cool, calm and dark."

"I spend a lot of time behind this desk. Might as well make it comfortable."

"Doesn't look very comfy to me." She swung around the desk and sat on his chair, which— "Oh, mercy, I change that statement. Is this the most comfortable chair on the planet?" She wiggled on what felt like a living material that conformed to her shape and curves and… was that a sudden warmth? "Is it one of those massage chairs? Tell me it is, because I am so in to that."

Ethan reached under the desk and the chair suddenly began to vibrate and undulate.

"Oh, fuck yeah." She closed her eyes and put up her feet on the edge of the desktop. "Don't mind me. I'll fly to seventh heaven while you're doing whatever it is you have to do."

Standing beside the chair, Ethan opened the laptop on the desk and began clacking away on the keys. "Just want to make sure the holding room is cleared for tomorrow night. And that no unnecessary personnel are on sight. I've decided we're going to summon the demon with the familiar directly here to headquarters. It will work if we make the proper preparations. Looks like CJ is the only one scheduled to be in the building, save the tech guys, but they're on the first floor. I'm bringing in Cinder on this one. He's IT. He'll grant us access and make sure all wards are down."

"Mmm…" Tuesday let her head drift off the back of the chair and twisted to sit sideways, catching a particularly deep kneading motion at the base of her spine. "This chair could probably fuck me if I found the right position."

Ethan laughed. "You're a lot easier than I'd initially thought."

"Oh, come on, don't tell me you've never gotten off on the vibrations from this fabulous thing?"

"Can't say that I have. Though, what is it with you women and vibrations?"

"Hit us in the right spot and we will sing, baby, sing. You don't feel it?"

He frowned then. "No, I actually don't." Was that worry in his eyes? "Huh. You think our bond is wearing thin?"

"It's possible. I would guess it will last so long as my blood served you. But we can always refresh it." She slid a hand up Ethan's leg, aiming for the front, where his dark jeans did not conceal the erection. "Maybe I can make you hum a little tune, eh?"

"I won't stop you from trying. I have to verify the security locks are activated in a few sectors for tomorrow night…"

She squeezed his erection through the rough fabric and then unzipped him. The man always went commando and his penis jutted out as the zipper teeth separated. She wrapped a firm hand around the stick shift and began to drive, even while his attention was focused on the laptop screen. But he did move his hips to give her better access, and soon enough he closed the laptop and leaned against the desk.

Sliding forward on the wheeled office chair, Tuesday licked up from the base of his thick rod, slowly, following the pulsing vein to the sensitive foreskin below the crown. She took her time, making sure every bit of him received her tongue. His fingers slipped through her hair, clasping greedily, and he groaned and rocked his hips slowly.

He was right. She didn't feel every slow, lazy lick reciprocating on her pussy as she would expect because of their blood bond. Their connection had depleted. But that didn't make this any less exciting.

"I'm going to make this better than cherry cake," she said.

Ethan bent forward, pressing his hand over her crotch and finding her aching pinnacle with a firm touch. "I'll help."

The pressure of his fingers over her clit prompted her to answer with a careful nibble to the side of his mighty shaft. With a growl that must have birthed in his core, he bent his head over hers and muttered, "Take me in your mouth, Tuesday. Please."

The desperation in his tone would not allow her to tease at him, nor would her own desire to take him past her lips and feel the press of him against the back of her mouth. Cupping his testicles with her other hand, she fed on him greedily, slicking and lashing and sucking.

He slid his hand inside her leggings and slipped a finger between her folds, curling into her and gliding in deeply. She pressed up her hips, hilting him within her pussy and her mouth. Having lost direct contact with the vibrating chair, she could still feel subtle movement from it, and that coaxed her body to the high from which she wished to fall.

Ethan's fingers in her hair gripped and squeezed and his body began to tremor. Control was impossible. Surrender unthinkable. Meeting at a mutual peak and then plunging together was the only option. He swore, and came in her mouth. She, in turn, came in bucking thrusts against his hand.

Dropping to his knees before her, Ethan buried his face in her hair, his fingers caressing over her pussy and maintaining a firmness that extended her orgasm.

"Witch, you own me."

She liked the idea of owning him. Sexually. But no other way. He was a fierce, powerful vampire. The only kneeling she required of him was to satisfy her sexual needs.

"I'll share myself with you, lover. But let's never take ownership. Agreed?"

He nodded, then kissed her hard and deep, showing her an exquisite glimpse of the control he masterfully claimed as his own.

A knock at the door paused them both. Ethan hastily stood and zipped with a wince and a curse. "Sit up," he muttered as he approached the door.

Fluffing her hair and tugging down her shirt, Tuesday sat up on the chair and grabbed a pen, assuming… well, she wasn't sure what she was trying to reflect but the fake-secretary-looking-busy act seemed like a good move.

Ethan opened the door. "Cinder. I didn't think you were coming up. I don't need you until tomorrow night. I thought I made that clear in the text. Is there a problem?"

The tall, dark-haired man entered the room and Tuesday saw his red, ashy aura. But also…hmm—he was something beyond vampire, but she couldn't quite make out what that *else* could be. He eyed her a few seconds, sniffed, then smirked. What was that about?

"No problem," Cinder said. "Just wanted to ask you about the outer wards on the building and your phone was on forward."

"Right." Ethan took out his phone and tapped a few keys.

"If you're trying to pull a demon in," Cinder said, "you need the building to be open. But I'm not cool with letting down all the wards. The Archives could go crazy. All the captive beasts on the premises suddenly set free?"

"It would be for a brief period," Ethan assured him. "Is it possible to let them down only around the holding cell and then be on standby for immediate reinstatement?"

Cinder blew out a breath. He didn't look like any kind of tech guy Tuesday had ever met. Broad-shouldered and built like a bruiser, but oh, so pretty. Her sigil warmed. And that alerted her.

"Angel?" she suddenly said.

Cinder turned to her. "What?"

"I, uh…what are you?"

Cinder chuckled and swung to face her, crossing his arms high on his chest. "What are you?"

"I'm a witch. Your boss had me kidnapped from Boston, and flew me across the ocean while under the influence of a nasty but powerful drug to help him track the demon. Didn't you get the memo?"

The tech guy swung a look to Ethan, who shook his head. Then he offered his hand toward Tuesday, so she got up from the chair to shake it. And then she knew.

"Demon," she said. "But…you've fallen."

"Labatiel, the Flaming One, Angel of Punishment," he explained. A bit of pride in his tone, though. Expected of demons. "Used to be trapped under Paris until a sinkhole released me and I came to ground."

"Cool. Maybe. But...you're also vamp?"

He nodded. "It's a long story."

"I bet it is." Angel of Punishment, eh? That could prove an interesting history. "You got any suggestions for how to handle the demon we're going after tomorrow night? I mean, you two do hail from the same place."

"I don't know who you're after. The boss didn't enlighten me."

"It's need-to-know. Or it was," Ethan said with a glance to Tuesday. Oops. She'd said too much. But Ethan relented. "Demon's name is Gazariel."

Cinder hitched a clicking sound out the side of his mouth. "The Beautiful One. A primping idiot. That's who you're after? Why are you finding this so difficult? Just hold up a mirror and catch him while he's preening."

Tuesday giggled. "Oh, you men. Always thinking there's an easy button for everything."

"He's proving an evasive catch," Ethan said. "And the witch I thought could lure him to us is actually repelling him."

She did not miss Ethan's admonishing glance. She'd take it in retaliation for spilling the intel beans.

Cinder's gaze took her in none too kindly. "Then why is she still around?"

"She's, uh..." Tuesday could sense Ethan's sudden discomfort yet he hid it with an authoritative lift of his jaw. "Can you do it or not, Cinder? You'll have a day to figure this out. I'll need you to be on call to drop the wards only around the holding cell and then set them back up."

"The building wards will need to be briefly shut down as well. It's not as easy as flicking a switch. Dropping them is. But resetting them?" He shook his head. "That'll require a witch."

Tuesday stepped forward. "I, myself, happen to be a witch."

"I will only work with a witch who works for and has been approved by the Council. I can't do it, man," Cinder said to Ethan.

"I'll send CJ to assist you. That will work, yes?"

"The dark witch." Cinder exhaled heavily. "Fine. I've got to get things started. This is going to be a bitch." The vampire strode out, leaving the door open behind him. "You owe me, man!"

Tuesday looked to Ethan and said, "Now *he's* a Richard."

Chapter 19

Back at his place, Ethan wandered into the living room after kissing a sleeping Tuesday on the cheek. She had muttered something about needing to catch a few winks, had hit the bed as soon as they'd gotten back, and two minutes later she was out. The woman had a talent for dropping into a dead sleep.

Tugging off his shirt, he tucked it behind his head and slumped down on the sofa into a comfortable position. Then he took out his phone and checked texts and emails. He'd gotten an email marked urgent from CJ with intel about Anyx. The dark witch had looked her up in the Archives' vampire room. He'd checked *The Vampire Codex, the* book on all vampires—similar to the witches' *Book of All Spells*—and this was what he'd found:

Anyx—no known surname following marriage to Ethan

Pierce in 1540 and subsequent divorce in 1600—has been observed to collect memento mori and death spells. 1720, she was stopped from using a plague hex on a village and was added to the Council's watch list. One incident in 1878 with a volatile organic poison resulted in the Archives seizing her eclectic collection from home in London, but other residences were not checked.

The vampire has remained under the radar but must always be kept on the watch list for occult fascination with bringing pain, suffering and death, or even possible experiments that could lead to mass genocide.

Known residences in Tampa, Florida, and Paris, France. Known former love affairs with Wolfgang Amadeus Mozart, Rasputin and Henri Telluir, a geophysicist of little renown. Current relationships unknown.

Ethan slapped the phone against his chest and muttered, "Anyx, what the hell have you gotten in to over the centuries?"

And had the book on vampires been updated recently? He'd thought it was a living book, always updating and rewriting the vampire history. Yet if Anyx was involved with Gazariel, the book had missed that. Unless Gazariel had lied to them about their relationship?

No, Ethan had seen the two in the restaurant. There was something going on between them.

As he'd told Tuesday, he'd witnessed Anyx's strange fascination for death early on and had extricated himself from a relationship that had no longer felt comfortable or safe for him. He and Anyx had lived as husband and wife for sixty years! And for the most part, they had loved and enjoyed one another's company. But they had spent a lot of time apart as Ethan served his tribe elders and fought in the Blood Wars. And Anyx, well, she'd traveled and tended her collection and kept it away from him until that one night he'd stumbled upon it.

Perhaps Gazariel was doing much the same after learning what a morbid and wicked vampiress he'd gotten involved with. Surely, for a demon who thrived on love and adoration, Anyx would present a challenge to his vanity.

It saddened him now to know that his ex-wife was so…strange. So dark and apparently evil. Was there a way to appeal to her? If she had been gifted the book with the Final Days code by The Beautiful One was there a chance Ethan could talk her into handing it over to him?

Judging from the report he doubted that would happen. She didn't seem mentally stable. So he had to set aside any lingering compassion he may have for the vampiress in order to help the greater good. And he could do that. He just…didn't want to know her reason why she had such a morbid fascination. He really didn't.

He texted CJ back with a request to recheck *The Vampire Codex* for updates, and for Anyx's Paris address. The report did not list it, but it should be entered in to a database somewhere in the Council's vast system. He'd send out a team to bring her in, but he didn't expect to find her. Something in his gut told him she had already received the gift. And that she may very well be trying to crack the code right now.

Heart sinking, Ethan clicked off his phone. He should be out there, looking for Anyx and Gazariel. But he had a solid plan for tomorrow, and it would work. He had to be patient.

There was one thing he could do. He paged through the dossier on the mission file on his phone and landed on the name of the muse who had created the book of names and sigils.

"Cassandra Stephens."

Stephans' location was currently unknown, but she had formerly lived in London and Berlin. Generally, phone numbers remained the same if the move was not a long distance. It was late, but he'd give it a try.

He dialed up the muse and as the phone rang he thought how odd it must be to know, as a muse, you were a human female—not immortal—who had been born to this realm and were connected to a specific fallen angel. And that angel's only goal was to find his muse and impregnate her in hopes of birthing a nephilim. Nephilim were monsters, and one had actually been born years ago. Cassandra Stephens and her Fallen One had helped to destroy the monstrosity. It was a long story, but Ethan could be thankful the woman was obviously kick-ass and determined not to let a label stop her from rising above her terrible fate.

After five rings, a sleepy voice answered. Ethan apologized for the late time. He told her who he was and who he worked for. "I don't know where you are, and I won't ask. But I need some information about the book of angel names and sigils you created."

"I…" A yawn was abruptly cut off. "Sorry about that. Uh, the book. It's been a while since I've had my hands on it. I thought it was with Raphael?"

"It's been stolen."

"Ah, shit. You need my help?"

"No, we've got things under control. But you wrote

the book. Can you tell me how you created the code to enact the Final Days or even give me the code?"

"I'm sorry, Mister Pierce. I didn't think I was creating any such thing while writing the book. The code sort of magically formed and became the awful thing it is now. You know how this weird paranormal stuff works. Add in angelic magic and you've got some mysterious ineffable shit going on."

"So, not a clue what the code is?"

"I'm really sorry."

And if she hadn't created the code she certainly wouldn't have an idea if there was a way to stop it or call the whole thing off.

"I had to check."

"I understand," she said with another yawn. "Are you sure you don't need help? I can hop a flight and be… heh. I don't even know where you are."

"I'm in Paris, and I'm not sure what you could do to help. I've got a crew ready to take down the demon who has the book."

"I wish you much luck. But if the demon is no longer an angel, then you won't be able to attract him with his muse."

"I don't think he ever had a muse. He fell directly to Beneath."

"Then no, he wouldn't have a muse. If you've got a Sinistari blade lying around that could prove useful as a threat against the guy."

"Good to know. We may have one of those. Thanks, Cassandra."

Ethan hung up, and texted CJ to check the demon room for a Sinistari blade. He recalled Bron Everhart, the same retriever who had brought Tuesday to Paris and had taken such a blade in hand a few years ago on a mission to obtain the Purgatory Heart. Such a blade was formed from the halo of the fallen angel. Those specific angels fell beyond earth and to Beneath where they became Sinistari demons, those who hunted the Fallen Ones. An angel blade was supposed to be the only thing that could kill an angel, besides a halo. It might not have the same effect on Gazariel, but it could provide another good threat besides the reckoner. It wouldn't hurt to go in fully armed.

Prepping for tonight's adventure involved warding herself with the obsidian and a smoky quartz, both on leather cords hung around her neck. Tuesday had found a pair of spangled black leggings at the thrift shop the day she and Ethan had gone shopping. Perfect. On top, she wore a plain black T-shirt. Because when combined with her spangled fur coat, she certainly didn't want to overdo the sparkle.

On the other hand, some sparkly black eyeshadow was necessary. And she loved the matte violet lipstick. So did Ethan. It drew his hungry gaze, and that was all good.

She rarely drew wards on her skin, and wasn't going to put any on until she got to the headquarters and talked with Certainly Jones. If they were going to cast a spell together, they'd need to sync wards.

Blowing herself a kiss in the mirror, she checked for the alicorn, which she'd tucked at her right hip in the waistband of her leggings. And the athame she would carry in her coat pocket. Ritual weapons, not things she expected to use in defense. Maybe? She could poke an eye out with the alicorn, if necessary.

She strolled out by the bed and paused. Ethan paced before the window, back and forth from there to the record player. He didn't notice her, and his brow was furrowed. Of course, the man must have a million things going on in his brain right now. But he seemed different than his usual stoic, controlling boss-man self.

Padding over to him and waiting until he noticed her, when he did, she tilted her head. "Tell me why you chose this particular mission to step back into field-work," she asked. "Was it because the bait was so sexy and you couldn't resist spending time with her?"

His smirk softened his tension and his shoulders dropped. He reached out a hand and she clasped it, but he didn't tug her into an embrace. Instead, he turned to look out the window. They stood there, side by side, hand in hand, unable to pick out a star in the night sky, as the evening, while dark, was illuminated by millions of neon lights and streetlights.

"I needed to prove to myself that I wasn't washed up," he said quietly.

The confession surprised her. Coming from such a confident and strong man? He had it all together. Except when he was winging it without a plan. Okay, so he might need some practice to get back to where he once was with the fieldwork. But washed up?

"That's crazy. You've impressed me at every turn on this mission," she said.

"I missed capturing the demon. Twice," he said. "And I can't seem to quit fucking the bait. Does that sound like a professional retriever to you?"

She shrugged. "Not sure the qualifications for a retriever. I assume hexing the help isn't one of them, but it doesn't seem to be dragging you down."

He squeezed her hand. "I've become lax in my methods. My targeting and reconnaissance. I don't follow protocol—I make up my own. And—"

"And it's been a while, so give yourself a break, will you?"

"Any breaks I take may result in the world being smothered by myriad angel wings."

He did have a point there.

"You've got me by your side. That's got to count for something."

"It does. It really does."

"Then we're good to go? All confidence levels are high and alpha-charged?"

He turned, and with a sweep, lifted her by the legs and tossed her over his shoulder. Heading toward the doorway, he said, "Alpha-charged and ready to go."

Watching Ethan organize the players in this demon-hunting mission was like watching a commander order his troops. He exuded a control and knowledge that impressed Tuesday. And everyone knew exactly what their roles were.

Far from washed up. But that he'd told her as much meant he trusted her with such knowledge. And that was something she'd treasure. His confidence.

The familiar was already on the other side of the steel door in the clean room, inside the cage with his partner, having sex. Thomas had said he'd need half an hour to accomplish the task of getting sated, then the witch could go in and invoke the spell to capture Gazariel. And Cinder, the tech guy, would then take down the building wards to facilitate it all.

Certainly Jones, the witch who would perform the invoking, paced the hallway outside the main room, head down and arms crossed over his chest. Long dark hair spilled forward and covered half his face. A particularly bold tattoo right over his carotid clued Tuesday it was a ward against vampire bites. Smart witch.

Unless of course, the witch enjoyed a bite now and then.

She should have had Ethan bite her before they'd set out for this adventure. Might have come in handy to reinforce their blood bond. As it was, she decided it was a temporary thing that only lasted about twenty-four hours. It was fun while it had lasted.

The dark witch's pacing moved him past her.

"You don't think you should be in there so you know when the time is right?" Tuesday asked him.

He tapped his ear, and she noticed an earbud. "I've got audio. And trust me, that's as close as I need to be right now. That is one noisy woman the familiar brought along with him."

"Well, if you need any help?"

"You stay back and keep the wards on you. If we need your assistance, we'll ask."

She nodded and strolled back to the steel door to lean against it. Certainly had warded her to the nines against angels, demons, light magic and dark, as well. She felt as if a suit of armor sat on her shoulders. And it was only slim protection against Gazariel's influence should he breech the cage wards.

She'd felt those wards. They were strong. They should subdue the demon. With hope.

Glancing over her shoulder, she eyed Ethan. He was speaking to the reckoner, Savin Thorne, who had just arrived. The big man wore a bowler hat over his messy hair. A loose-fitting coat that looked cobbled from different fabrics, something a gypsy might wear, barely hung to his hips. And as he nodded and gestured with his hands while talking to Ethan, she noted the sigils, or possibly wards, drawn on the back of each of his hands. They hadn't been there when she'd met him yesterday. She hoped he wouldn't have to resort to actually sending the demon to Daemonia. Because without the curse lifted from her, that meant she would have to tag along.

No witch could survive in Daemonia for long. It would be a fate worse than any torture a vindictive witch hunter could mete out. She should have made it clear to Ethan that she was out if it came to that. But not like she could protest now. Such refusal would shut down the whole demon-summoning operation. Her presence was needed and it was not. Be here to sync all the magic and connect with the demon, yet don't get so close that she scared off the demon, or got sucked into his vortex of wicked magic.

This unexpected trip to Paris had become quite the adventure. Kidnapping aside, she was glad to be here. It gave her purpose. And often, when living for so long, there were days she wondered what good she was doing the world. And since her magic was dark, it was rare she felt she *did* serve the world goodness.

Once, she'd been a healer and had educated women. Why had she ever stopped? Oh, right. Lack of love did tend to change a person as the years grew long.

It had never mattered to her before, but lately she wanted to do good. To change. To rise up from the darkness she had caressed and made her own over the centuries and become someone worthy of giving and receiving goodness.

And love.

The thought startled her so much that she didn't hear Ethan call her name. Only when he gripped her wrist and bent to meet her eyes did she slip back into the present moment.

"You okay?" His gray irises were clear and focused. He may have felt washed up, but he was far from that. "I called your name twice and you're standing right here."

"Sorry. My mind was wandering. Yeah, I'm good." Or at least, she was trying to be. "What if the demon won't tell us where he put the book? Do we have a plan for bringing in the vampiress?"

"I have a containment crew on call to bring her in, but we're having a time locating her address in the database. I have hope, though."

"I hope your hope is effective. Because I thought you were using the reckoner as a threat."

"CJ has some magical thumbscrews to twist if Gazariel doesn't want to give us the information. We've done this before."

"The Beautiful One is not going to give up anything without a sacrifice from me."

"You don't know that."

"Yeah, I kind of do. He's an asshole."

"A Richard?"

"The number-one Richard of all Richards. He'll ask for my heart in exchange for the book, I know it."

"But that doesn't make sense. If he takes your heart, it'll return the curse to him."

"Maybe, maybe not. Maybe he can simply tug out my heart and crush it and the curse along with it. But better he suffers and I die, than I live and he suffers."

"Let's not think like that. I'm going to protect you, Tuesday."

"I can take care of myself. I've some powerful magic. Probably more effective against the blood demon than your dark witch pacing over there like he's headed to his own funeral."

"The man has a wife and children. I'm asking a lot from him."

Yes, she recalled the feeling of overwhelming and true love she had gotten from CJ when she'd done a soul gaze on him. She wanted that kind of love. She really did.

"I still can't allow you to work the summons," Ethan said. "Gazariel will use your magic against us all."

"Not if the wards on the cage hold up. Let me go at him first. Break him down."

Ethan shook his head. "We're doing this my way. And besides, what if he's already given the book to Anyx? We're going to need him intact. And no magic you can throw at him will ever convince him to talk. You know that."

Tuesday nodded reluctantly. He was right.

"I expect to have a location on Anyx soon," he said. "I've got everything under control. This is what I do, Tuesday. Trust me."

"I do trust you. Completely."

"Thank you. Now, you stay back and out of the way. You've got all the wards on?"

"I'm loaded with them. You wouldn't be able to bite me if you wanted to."

"I can feel that repulsion. Which is why I haven't kissed you."

"And here I thought you were against PDAs."

"You can actually think that after our tryst in the alleyway? Or almost getting caught by Cinder in my office? What about in the restaurant?"

"I stand corrected. I see you're warded as well. The reckoner do that?" She tapped his throat.

"Yes." He stroked the lines drawn on his throat with a black felt-tip marker. She interpreted them as protective and closing, perhaps to keep him from speaking things the demon might try to trick out of him. "He suggested some additional protections to the ones I already have."

"Tell me one thing about the vampire chick you said you loved? The one who died by biting the witch."

"Huh?" Ethan glanced around to see if the other men were listening. They were not. "I don't understand."

"Did you promise to protect her always?"

"I, uh… Tuesday, you think I'm going to let you down?"

"No. I want to know if you let her down."

"That's cruel."

"It might be but… I need your truth, Ethan."

Ethan glanced to the men lingering in the hallway. None met his gaze. He lowered his voice and spoke near her ear. "I feel as though I let her down. But no, she chose that witch on the fly. I'm not sure I would have known he was a witch before she bit him, either. But I would have given my life to change it. To have been the one who took the bite and not her."

"You loved her that much?" Tuesday slid her hand along Ethan's cheek. Her heartbeats thudded. "More than your wife of sixty years? What about the chick who died from the blood transfusion?"

"Tuesday." He shook his head. "As I've told you, I've loved many."

Yes, and he'd loved a woman so much he would have died for her. And after knowing her but six months. Tuesday imagined such deep and abiding love happened only once in a man's life. Or a woman's. Yet he'd gone on to love others. And to experience heartbreak. And through it all, he survived. Perhaps Ethan's heart was capable of giving love to yet another?

She daren't dream. He would only be hurt if he fell in love with her. And he had been hurt by love more than enough times.

"You're a good man, Ethan." She kissed him quickly, then they turned as CJ spoke.

"The familiar is on target," the dark witch said. "Sated and open to bridge the demon. Ethan, notify Cinder to let down the wards. I'm going in. Everyone else follow, but stay back."

As Ethan called Cinder, they entered the clean room. The cage bars did not glow and the door was wide open. A naked woman gathered her clothing while a very naked Thomas lay sprawled on the center of the cage floor.

CJ approached the cage door. Standing aside to let the woman flee, he then gripped a bar in each hand and began to chant.

Tuesday helped the woman pull on her dress over her head. She nodded a quiet thanks, then looked to Ethan.

"You remember the way out?" he asked.

She shook her head.

"Thomas will be out shortly. Stand outside the door and wait for him. Thank you."

He held the door open and closed it behind her. Stepping up to stand beside the reckoner, Ethan crossed his arms and observed. Tuesday, back to the wall, kept a keen eye on the familiar in the cage, but also listened carefully to the Latin incantation CJ spoke. It was a standard demon-summoning spell with an adjustment to focus the reach within this realm. He battened it with protective sigils he drew in the air using a crystal wand. A white light trail followed in the wake of his movements. He traced a few of the spell tattoos on his left hand and then thrust his palm downward, facing it toward the familiar.

Thomas's body jerked and convulsed. Naked and sweating, he was open to allow a demon entity to inhabit his body only briefly before it apported into corporeal form. A spume of red smoke spiraled up from the familiar's pores, forming a tornado above him. The familiar opened his eyes, saw the red cloud and scrambled toward the cage door. As he fled, his body shifted, contorting and growing fur. A calico cat meowed and slipped out just as the cloud began to take human form.

Ethan rushed over and slammed the cage door shut, slipping a heavy bolt through a lock and activating the electronic security system with a few taps on the digital keyboard. The cage bars briefly glowed green then blinked out.

And within the cage formed the demon Gazariel, The Beautiful One. Long black hair spilled down his shoulders and to his elbows. Bare feet were marked with faint blue sigils. On his open palms glowed more blue markings.

He lifted his head, his red eyes glowing as he took in the cage and those standing around watching. On his cheek, Tuesday saw three long scratch marks. They bled black.

And when Gazariel's gaze met Tuesday's, he said, "You will suffer for this, my witch."

Chapter 20

The demon inside the cage stood tall, fists out at his sides. He wore black leather pants and no shirt. His abdomen was carved as if from stone and his muscles were many, forming him lean and imposing. Long streams of wavy coal hair hung over his broad shoulders and his red eyes glinted like rubies.

Slowly, the scratches on his cheek closed up, leaving but a spill of black blood trickling down his jaw.

With a hiss he released his wings, which spread to the cage bars without touching them. Black feathered wings that flashed like mirrors with each movement and seemed made of silk and sewn with silver threads. They were iridescent with all colors, much as a raven's wings.

Tuesday knew that angels rarely wore feathered wings, but demons often did. Had this angel's wings taken on a different form when he had fallen to Beneath and become demon? No matter. They were beautiful. He was beautiful.

And her sigil burned as if pleading with her to rush forth and touch those wings. To make contact with something that could both harm her and equally embrace her. The invitation felt so real.

She squeezed her hands, fingernails digging in to her palms to stop the urge.

The demon let out a guttural yell, retracting his wings when they touched the electrified bars. He swung about, his wings sending a rush of icy wind across the observers, lifting their hair and stirring up a bone-deep shiver that made Tuesday gasp.

Stomping a foot, Gazariel tested the steel cage floor. Thrusting out his hands, he sent demonic magic hurtling toward them, only to have it deflected by the wards. He took the brunt of that repulsed magic with a stagger backward and a screaming trill of swear words. He ended his tirade with a flip of his middle finger toward Tuesday, and a simple "Bitch."

Tuesday met CJ's eyes. The dark witch who had summoned the demon stepped back to stand beside her. "We'll leave him to the boss," he said quietly. "But stand on guard."

Always. Holding the alicorn in one hand and her athame in the other, she was prepared to fling some wicked magic toward the demon. Tuesday watched as Ethan questioned the captive.

"You'll get nothing from me that you could not get before," Gazariel announced. "How dare you steal me away from my very life?"

Tuesday had felt much the same upon waking inside this cage. But she would not sympathize with the demon. And yet, the compulsion to step forward and embrace him only grew stronger. This time a snap of the rubber band around her wrist was necessary.

The cat meowed and slunk toward the door. Tuesday leaned over to open it and the feline scrambled out.

"If you would have given me what I wanted during our first encounter I wouldn't have had to resort to such tactics." Ethan stood stoic before the cage, shoulders back and head lifted. A commander protecting his troops and interrogating the enemy. He wore wards drawn on the backs of his hands, beneath his chin and down his throat. But his true strength came from within; his courage and integrity. "You need only hand over the book, written by the muse Cassandra Stephens, which contains the code for the Final Days and I will release you. Simple as that."

Gazariel swiped a hand over his cheek, studied the black blood on his fingers, then gestured dismissively. "I don't have it."

"You are lying."

"I had it," the demon said with a sly red glance to Tuesday. "But now I do not."

"Then where is it?"

"In a safe place."

"Tell me where it is, and once I've retrieved it, you are free to go," Ethan stated. "Did you give it to Anyx?"

That caught the demon's attention. He gripped the cage bars, but released them as quickly with a hiss and a string of vile oaths that never would have been allowed Above. "I knew someone was watching us! Did you follow me, vampire? Why didn't you take me in hand that day when we were dining?"

"Did you give it to the vampiress?" Ethan repeated.

"Maybe." The demon rubbed his cheek again.

"You two had a lover's spat," Tuesday said, realizing now where the claw marks had come from. "Did she take the book from you and run?"

Gazariel flipped her off again. "Not worth my breath to converse with you lot of miscreants. I need something in exchange."

"How about your life?" Ethan offered. "You do know that if the Final Days is activated we will all die?"

Gazariel shrugged. "Assuming you remain in this realm. I, on the other hand, have made preparations to be located elsewhere."

"He doesn't have leave of this realm!" Tuesday blurted out. "He's as much a captive of the mortal realm as we all are."

Ethan cast her a castigating glare, which she took with a huff. She did not need a reprimand for providing him the facts.

"You know nothing about me, my witch," Gazariel growled through a tight jaw. He curled his wings forward, tucking them until the points crossed before his feet.

"I know everything about you, as you know everything about me," she said, and once again got *the look* from Ethan. She was supposed to stand back and keep quiet? She could not. Thrusting out an arm, she pointed the alicorn at the demon. "You are a vain and insignificant reject from Above, and then you were also rejected in Beneath and cast out to live in this realm. You, who couldn't bear to carry the curse of a loveless life so you put it on a helpless, dying woman. Some demon you are!"

Gazariel gripped the cage bars, and the action transferred mighty amounts of voltage through his system. He managed to hold on for much longer than Tuesday imagined any normal creature could, and as he did so, his eyes flashed brilliant crimson. Was he feeding off the electricity?

Ethan kicked a control button at the base of the cage, and the demon was propelled backward to collide with the bars at the back of the cage. Those bars hissed with smoke and sent the demon stumbling forward, so he almost landed on his knees, but he caught himself. Bent over, huffing, his wings slowly curled about him, enclosing him in a cocoon.

"Is she right?" Ethan asked. "Are you but a feeble reject from both Above and Beneath? Is it that your lover took off with the book, leaving you a simpering reject in her wake?"

"I don't have it. Not anymore. I was going to give it to her to—"

Tuesday filled in the words he probably couldn't bring himself to say—*to win her love.* Was the vampiress the one creature from whom Gazariel could not be loved?

"No." The demon stomped a foot. "I'm not going to utter a single word about that...bitch of a vampire." Gazariel lifted his head from the glinting cove of wings. His jaw was tight. He'd felt that pain from the cage bars, Tuesday knew. "Serve me your worst, Ethan Pierce."

"Very well." Ethan stepped back and gestured for Savin Thorne to step forward. The man tossed his hat aside, and shrugged up his shoulders, as if preparing to step into a boxing ring.

"Who is this mortal you've put before me?" Gazariel asked. "He may look imposing but I can feel no power within him."

The reckoner chuckled and rubbed his palms together before his face. When he spread his hands to face toward the cage, the wards on his palms took to flame. "I am Savin Thorne," he said to the demon. "I'm here to reckon you to Daemonia."

Ethan stepped aside to give the reckoner room to work. Tuesday stood just behind him. He could sense her in him. Because she was in him. And he didn't feel fear in her, but rather, indifference and a righteous anger. She hated this demon and wanted him gone. But he also knew they could not send him off to Daemonia until they'd gotten the information they needed from him. Nor could he actually send him away without also sending Tuesday along with him.

Thorne knew that as well.

The reckoner clapped his hands together over his head and began to chant something that sounded like a Polynesian tribal rite. It had a beat and a low, bellowing caw that sent chills up Ethan's spine.

Inside the cage the demon narrowed his gaze on the reckoner. With a shrewd sneer, he folded back his wings. He wasn't standing so tall and proud anymore. And it wasn't curiosity that bent him forward to better hear the reckoner's deep and loud voice. It had to be a nervous fear.

To Ethan's right stood CJ. The dark witch had crossed himself and touched some of the tattoos on his hand the moment the reckoner had started to chant. Ethan wasn't aware of any protections he needed against a reckoner. He'd worked with Savin twice before and had witnessed the man send a demon off to Daemonia in a cloud of black smoke. It had taken but ten minutes of chanting.

And they were nearing that mark now.

"All right!" the demon suddenly shouted, yet the reckoner kept up his wicked chant. "Make him cease and I will tell you where it is."

"Savin," Ethan said.

The reckoner silenced, closed his eyes and thrust his hands above his head again, but this time only touching together his forefingers, as if to pause something he could then continue when required. With a nod, he stepped back beside CJ.

Ethan stepped up to the cage. "Tell me."

Gazariel peered past him to Tuesday. "I will only tell my witch."

"That's not going to happen. She's not involved in this interrogation."

"I won't do anything to her. These damn wards have drained me already. And that bloody chanting. Ugh. I could almost see the gates to Daemonia. She knows she'll be safe. Yes?"

Behind him, Ethan felt Tuesday's nod more than saw it. He'd promised to protect her, and he did trust the efficacy of the wards in the room. And she was warded fully as well. He turned to look at her and without so much as a flinch, her confident posture conveyed to him that she was ready.

The woman was brave and strong. Of course she could handle this. Ethan nodded once, and Tuesday stepped forward.

Chapter 21

The leering look of satisfaction on Gazariel's face was slightly challenged by the fact that he was subdued, unable to reach through the bars and grab for Tuesday, as she knew he wished to do. So she walked up and stood but inches from those bars, and he did the same. She could feel him inside her. Feel his haughty vanity and his complex anger at the imprisonment.

And she well understood his pride in knowing that he had control over her, no matter the safeguards and wards. Because she would never have freedom so long as she wore his sigil.

And a larger part of her than she was comfortable with…wanted him. Close to her. Inside her. A part of her, as the sigil's burning caress promised.

"Where is it?" she asked, curling her fingers about

the alicorn and athame. "Come on, it's late and I need to go home and wash my hair."

"Snark does not suit you, witch. I prefer those times when you are raging in your dark beauty, calling down the rains to chase away the dust storms, or sending out an army of gargoyles to defeat a band of marauders. Or what about that time you burned out a lecher's tongue for harming a child? You think I haven't watched you over the centuries?"

Behind her, Ethan cleared his throat. He wanted her to get on with it, but she couldn't force the demon when grandstanding was obviously his thing.

"I've never sensed your presence," she offered honestly. A creepy discomfort kept her from prompting for the details.

"I'm sure the sigil did. But you were focused. Honed to a precise and elegant weapon. And now look at you. Being led on a leash by an insignificant vampire and his band of not-so-merry men."

"The reckoner fucked with your sense of safety," she observed. "If sent to Daemonia you wouldn't last a day. And how long is a day in that place? Decades? Oh, the fun they'd have with such a pretty, spoiled Fallen brat such as you."

The demon reached to grab at her but recoiled when his fingers connected with the electrical field. "Bitch."

"Actually, it's witch. Get it right."

Gazariel chuckled. "I like your moxie, my witch. Despite your reliance on that silly plaything. An alicorn? Really? It's been tainted by vampire blood. It will no longer serve you in any significant manner."

She looked at the pearlescent twist of horn. It did seem a bit duller than when she'd first claimed it. But she wouldn't set it aside. That's what the demon wanted her to do.

Gazariel bowed his head toward her. "We might have made an interesting pair."

"Seriously? Nope. I prefer my men with balls."

The demon gripped his crotch defiantly, gnashing his teeth as he did so. "Words—"

"*Do* seem to bother you. But now let's get this done with, shall we? The sooner you tell me where the book is, the faster me and the band of merry men will let you go."

"You don't actually think they'll release me, do you? The reckoner stands greedily waiting. I can see the lust for revenge in his eyes."

"Revenge? You've done nothing to him."

"It is revenge for all of our kind. A secret he holds so tightly it keeps him from his true powers." The demon's eyes glinted as he met gazes with the reckoner.

"I was promised you would be released as soon as the book with the code is handed over," Tuesday said, not wanting to get into whatever issues the reckoner had with demons right now. "I won't allow them to go back on their word to me. I do have your word, yes, Ethan Pierce?" she said loudly.

"You do," Ethan said. "He gives us the location of the book. We retrieve it, verify it's intact. We let him go. Simple as that."

Gazariel considered it for a moment, his eyes flicking from red to the brilliant azure that must have lured thousands of women to their knees before him. So damn pretty.

But also a Richard.

And it was only with that thought Tuesday was able

to keep it together and not attempt to reach for his chiseled abs.

"As the mean vampire guessed, I gave it to my girlfriend," he said quietly. Tuesday suspected none could hear but her, though the vampire should be able to with his heightened senses.

"She didn't love you," Tuesday said, trying out her earlier suspicion. "You thought by giving her the book you could win her love."

Gazariel lifted his chin imperiously.

"There was actually one creature in this realm who did not fall on her knees in adoration before you," she declared. "Must have been tough for a poseur like you."

"Enough!"

"Apparently, you were not enough for Anyx."

"I care little about that somber, death-obsessed vampiress. Besides, we broke up recently."

"Let me guess. Just before you were whisked away to this cage? I saw the claw marks," Tuesday said. "And you bleed black blood. No angel left in you, Beautiful One."

Gazariel's upper lip flinched.

"Why that book and that particular vampiress?"

"I had no idea, when first we met, that she had a disturbingly dark obsession."

"So I've been told." Tuesday kept herself from glancing Ethan's way. The vampiress did not sound like the sort any man could love. She must have some serious skills when it came to pleasuring them. "So you gave her a book with a code that could end the world as a sort of…love token?"

"I gave it to her days ago. She thanked me, but…she didn't say she loved me. Can you believe that?"

"Shocking," Tuesday said with all the snark exploding in that one utterance.

"I thought she would merely add it to her collection," Gazariel explained. "She collects death. Remnants from the *Titanic*. The leather straps from an electric chair that ended the lives of so many. A charm to give the bearer instant necrosis. Et cetera. So a code that could enact the end of the world? She was excited. It was the most powerful item she'd ever heard of. She was thrilled to have it. Little did I know she was using me to get what she wanted." He looked aside, and for a moment Tuesday almost saw regret cross his perfectly symmetrical face. "She's a bigger bitch than you are. Good riddance, I say."

"Along with the means to end the world? Gazariel, please."

He closed his eyes and sucked in a breath through his nose. "I do love it when you speak my name. It shivers through me like a teasing yet unrequited orgasm. Always promising yet never fulfilling."

Now she was ready to poke him in the eye with the alicorn, but Tuesday knew the wards worked on both sides of the cage bars.

"If you two are on the outs, then why the hell won't you give her up to us?" she asked. "Why not get the ultimate revenge against the one person who doesn't love you by sending us after her to claim the book?"

"Do *you* love me, Tuesday Knightsbridge?"

Pressing her lips together, Tuesday prevented an oath, but oh, did it tangle with her tongue for release. She needed to play nice with the demon, or they would never get anywhere with him. She pressed a palm over the sigil and said what she knew to be partially true, and what she hoped wasn't deeply true. "I do love you, Gazariel. You are beautiful. I adore you."

"Of course you do." Another deep inhale of satisfaction and he opened his eyes to beam a soft blue gaze upon her. She almost thought to see compassion in his irises. "I gave you freedom from death. And from love."

"Yeah, well... I would like to know love," she admitted.

"It is exquisite. I have it all the time. You are missing so much."

She tilted her head and couldn't stop the truth from spilling out. "I don't think what you believe to be love is really quite the thing. You are adored and worshipped. But that's not love. Love is...something different. It comes from the soul. It connects two people not out of desperation, or a worshipful lusting desire, but here." She beat her chest with a fist. "Deeply and to the bone. It is blood, bone and spirit."

The demon sniffed. "You think to know so much?"

"I know a lot, but certainly not everything. What I do know is that the manner in which I love you is not abiding or deep. It is only surface. You will only ever have surface love, Gazariel. And that makes you a sad, pitiful, impotent demon."

This time Gazariel's hand plunged through the cage bars, and even as he screamed at the pain of the wards burning his skin, he managed to grasp her throat.

Tuesday's body was pulled away from the weak attack, and she turned to shove Ethan away. "I'm fine. Just let me do this. I've got him. I do."

Ethan nodded. "You do. But I'm close."

Stepping back up to the bars, Tuesday waited for the demon to stop groaning and look up from his burned hand. The angry red skin smoldered, but they both watched as it healed, forming new, pale flesh and re-shaping his broken fingers into long, elegant append-ages.

"Admit you did a bad thing," she said to him. "Your ex-girlfriend has something that no one should be al-lowed to touch. And really? If she does manage to ac-tivate the code and brings down all the angels from Above, they'll smother you, too."

Shaking out his newly healed hand, Gazariel lifted his chin with a haughty thrust. "Assuming I remain on this mortal realm."

Tuesday crossed her arms, and stated flatly, "You can't go back to Beneath. Or even Above. You're stuck here." It was a guess, but she figured it was a good one.

Yet Gazariel looked down his nose at her. "It is as simple as going belowground. The angels won't fall through the earth. Not too far, anyway. Their wings will burn up the surface and the bodies of all those walking this earth. But Paris is a virtual maze of passages and tunnels beneath the manmade clutter."

Tuesday glanced to Ethan, who was hearing all of this. He didn't make a move or give her a sign that he understood what the demon was talking about.

"You think you'll be safe when your bitch of a girl-friend releases Above's angels as long as you're under-ground?"

"The catacombs are where Anyx said she intended to be when she set off the spell." Gazariel hung his head. "I thought she'd put it on the shelf next to her other collectibles."

"No, you didn't. You're not that much of an idiot."

The man sucked in his lower lip. The move reduced

him to such a human thing. Truly, an impotent loveless creature. She was right; he had not known true, soul-deep love. And she knew that because she was exactly the same as him.

"Maybe you are an idiot," she said quietly. "Love dumb?"

"If you wish me to continue speaking to you so openly you should try a little kindness, my witch. I happen to know you and that vampire are currently engaged in a frenzied affair. Does he know the *other* way to break your curse? The one that doesn't involve my ripping out your heart?"

Tuesday closed her eyes and sensed that Ethan was listening, carefully. He didn't say anything. And she could not allow him to learn the truth.

"It's not something that's ever going to come to fruition," she said quietly. "And if I could rip out my heart and give it to you without dying, believe me, I would."

"I do tire of so much love some days."

"You've never been lovable a day in your pitiful life."

"I am an extremely lovable demon. Adored. Worshipped. Ugh. It can get tiresome, let me tell you."

"I wouldn't know."

"No, you would not." The demon glanced to Ethan. "But...you could."

Enough of the sly entendres about her love life.

"Come on. Where is Anyx and what sort of booby traps do we have to wend through to get to her?"

"She intends to enact the code under the full moon."

"That's tonight."

"I believe so. At the stroke of midnight." Gazariel rubbed his knuckles against his bare chest and blew on them. Casual. Just playing for time, now that he realized he might have the upper hand.

"Thorne," Ethan said from behind them.

The reckoner clapped his hands loudly and again set into his chant.

"Guess your time is up," Tuesday said, as calmly as she could manage. But really? She wasn't in any mood to get transported to Daemonia with this vain angel-turned-demon-turned-love-sick idiot.

"What do you want from me!" Gazariel shouted.

"Where is she?" Ethan demanded.

The reckoner's voice rose. The cage bars began to shudder.

"Fine! She's beneath the Temple of Reason."

Tuesday turned to face the men behind her, and as one they said, "Notre Dame."

Chapter 22

Outside in the hallway the crew gathered to discuss their next move. They needed to find Anyx STAT. Since she'd only had the book a few days, Ethan wondered if the vampiress had figured out the code. Gazariel hadn't known. They convened outside the clean room, leaving Gazariel inside the cage after he'd given them Anyx's address.

"Now what?" Savin asked.

"I'm routing the containment team to the address I just got for Anyx, but I suspect we won't find her there," Ethan said. "The demon is telling the truth. We need to go below Notre Dame."

CJ whistled. "Beneath holy ground?"

"This adventure gets more fun by the minute," Tuesday said with little sincerity.

"Isn't it old Roman remains below the church?" Savin asked.

"That's the public level," CJ explained. "There are tunnels beneath the church that snake down much deeper, perhaps five or six stories. We might have to do some spelunking."

"I know a guy who'll grant us access through the church. Want me to call him?" Savin asked.

"If you can get him here immediately," Ethan said.

Savin tugged out a cell phone. "I'll go along, but only if you need me. Or do you want me to hang around here? Babysit the demon?"

"We need to take Gazariel along," Tuesday said.

"No." Ethan shook his head. "We can't risk it."

"With a little blood magic the demon will lead us straight to her," she said.

"Like drawing a compass on his chest?"

"More complicated than that, but very doable. And CJ and I can shackle him and make him utterly incapable to do anything but walk and breathe."

Ethan looked to CJ. The dark witch nodded. "It's possible. If he's had sex with Anyx recently—and she drew his blood—we could work the spell. Remnants of her DNA would still be on or in him. But we'd have to combine our magics," he said to Tuesday.

"Not a problem. And if we bring along the reckoner he remains a threat to the demon to stay on his best behavior. But you're not going to send him to Daemonia as long as I'm wearing his sigil."

"Of course not," Savin offered.

"Tuesday, can I talk to you over here?" Ethan nodded down the hallway. "CJ, you and Savin prepare for our adventure."

"Will do," CJ said. "But first I've to head up to tech

and make sure Cinder has the building wards back in place. Come on, Savin."

When the two men had left, Ethan took Tuesday by the arms and looked into her eyes for the longest time before he finally asked, "What's the other way to break the curse?"

"What?"

"I heard every word the two of you spoke. The demon said there was a way to break your curse without ripping out your heart."

She looked away from him, but he moved to the side and blocked her in by the wall, tipping up her chin and forcing her to meet the challenge in his eyes. "Tell me. You've known there was another way all along?"

"I've known since the moment the curse settled into me. He told me then. It's not something that will ever happen. And I will not tell you what it is, so to use one of your favorite lines, you don't get to tell me what I can and can't do." She shrugged out of his grasp and walked a few steps away. "You did promise to release Gazariel after we got the code. So the reckoner shouldn't even be an issue. I needn't worry about being tugged off to Daemonia. And I'm resigned to carry the curse within me for the rest of my days."

"Don't you want love, Tuesday? If there's a chance to break the curse in some other manner—"

"I said we will not discuss this anymore. Can you give me that?"

Ethan raked his fingers through his hair and gave her a nodding shrug. "I guess I have to. But will it interfere with the task we have before us?"

"Not at all. I swear it to you."

"Then you and CJ need to bespell the demon in whatever manner will help us, and we'll set him loose to lead us to Anyx. Do you have a means to stop the spell should she have already enacted it? Do you know how the code is activated?"

"I've not seen the book or the code. And I thought you were the man in charge. Don't you have information about how the code is activated?"

"It's a blood spell."

"How do you know?"

"That's what I was told."

"By who?"

"The one who ordered I retrieve the book," he said angrily.

"Who is?" Tuesday insisted.

Ethan looked away from her.

"Ethan? Who sent you on the quest for this book? Was it the Council? Because it doesn't feel right to me. You'd have more information if the Council—"

"It was a direct order from Raphael," he finally said.

"Raph— An actual—" Shivers traced Tuesday's nape. This was getting a bit too deep into angeldom and their mysterious ways for her comfort. "You got an order from an archangel?"

He squeezed the fingers of one hand before him and nodded. "Came to me a few days before you arrived with a demand we locate the thing."

"Why are you acting so weird about it? It's like you're embarrassed or—"

"I am not embarrassed. This is a need-to-know mission. And you don't—"

"Do not give me that excuse. I'm in this. Deep. And you couldn't have gotten this far without me. What's going on, Ethan? Do you often take orders from angels? How is Raphael involved?"

He gripped her by the shoulders as if to steady her, but he was actually finding his ground and forcing up calm when he wanted to walk away from her right now. His confession about not being up to snuff on fieldwork returned to his thoughts. Had he stepped into a mess too deep for even him to struggle out of?

"Raphael was keeping track of the book," Ethan said, "and...he misplaced it. That is confidential information. But you won't say anything, right?"

"Why would I? And to whom? I just think it's kind of weird that an angel allowed a demon to steal something so valuable from him." She tilted her head, and tried to read Ethan's gaze. "In fact, I find it nearly impossible that one so all-powerful could have had something taken from him without noticing. The only other option is that Raphael gave it up freely. And why would he do that?"

"I don't..." Ethan squeezed his eyelids shut. She was pressing him, guessing at scenarios that were turning out to be dreadfully true. And he'd never considered it, but had the archangel *purposefully* allowed Gazariel to steal the book?

"I think it's a test," Ethan finally said. "I don't know much, Tuesday. You have to believe that. I thought it was suspicious, too, after getting the command from Raphael to search for the book."

"But that could mean the angel might actually stand back and allow it all to happen. End-of-world stuff. Yeah?"

"I don't know about allowing things to go to completion," Ethan said. "I should hope not. But I don't know much about angels."

"Except that you take orders from any random angel that happens to request your services."

"He is an arch— Tuesday, we don't have time for this argument. Do you really want to do this now? Because it's not going to get us anywhere, and it will give Anyx more time to crack the code and enact the spell."

Frustration tightening her fists at her sides, Tuesday blew out a breath. Neither of them was helpless. They did have the power to stop this. Whatever *this* was.

"Fine. This whole adventure is fucked. Just like I knew it would be. But I'm with you. I promise. You got my back, I've got yours. Let's get to it. I can do blood magic, which is helpful if the code activation truly requires blood. And Gazariel is a blood demon. But I should go armed with supplies. Can I take a look around in the witch room and see what I can find?"

"I'll show you where it is." He held his hand out for her to take and she looked at it a moment. "I should have told you about Raphael from the start. But it wouldn't have changed things."

"I realize that. Maybe."

"I want things to be good between us, Tuesday. Don't block me out, please. We'll need to be strong and stand as one against whatever we next face. Can we do that?"

She slapped her hand into his firmly. "We can. And when this is over? I want to talk to that Richard of an archangel."

He pulled her to him. "When this is over we're going to talk about breaking your curse. For my sake."

"Why? Oh. Don't fall in love with me, Ethan. It won't end well for you."

And she strode off, but not before Ethan saw the tears forming at the corners of her eyes.

With CJ's permission, Ethan left Tuesday to ransack the Archives' witch room for whatever magical items she may need, then headed back to the clean room, where the demon was still caged.

He could not get the fact that Tuesday wasn't willing to tell him what could break her curse from his mind. Was it so much worse than having her heart ripped out? Nothing was worse than death.

The demon lifted his head as Ethan entered the room. Eying the base of the cage, Ethan verified that all the wards were lighting up the control panel. And he still wore the demonic wards on his hands. The wards on his throat would keep the demon from trying to trick useful information out of him.

The demon hooked his arms akimbo and inhaled deeply, expanding his chest. With a flip of hair over a shoulder, he asked, "You lied to her, didn't you?"

Ethan stepped up to meet the demon's blue gaze between the bars. "What do you think I lied about?"

"About releasing me."

"That wasn't a lie. Should we find the book, you're free to go. That is, if your girlfriend hasn't already tried to activate the code."

"My girlfriend? She was your wife first, vampire. You think I didn't know that? I could smell you on her. Wasn't sure what it was when I first fucked her, but since I've been in your presence?" The demon shuddered. "You are a part of her. Did you know about her weird and wicked obsession?"

"It's why she's no longer my wife. She's...troubled. And she needs to be contained."

Gazariel lifted an eyebrow. "Well then, it seems you've caged the wrong person. But isn't it like a man to want to imprison those females he can't understand?"

"You're a man, too."

"You think so? When I Fell I was neither one nor the other sex. Not much changed after becoming demon. And by giving Tuesday that hideous curse I found I could be either or. It's cute, the trick. Though I do prefer a dick to a clit. It's much more powerful, don't you think?"

"Apparently, you've never met Tuesday Knightsbridge. That's the most powerful clit I've ever met."

"Yes." Gazariel dragged his gaze up and down Ethan assessingly. "You love her. Poor fellow. You certainly won't survive through the night."

"You're an idiot. I've known her less than a week."

"Doesn't take more than a wink and a kiss to lose one's heart."

"You and I have chatted enough. The dark witches will be returning to bespell you. You'll lead us to Anyx."

The demon rolled his eyes. "I gave you her address."

"My team reports she's gone. The place was a shambles, as if she had no intention of returning."

"Bitch." The demon spat out a few words that Ethan assumed were demonic oaths. "She's really going to do it."

"Seems so."

"I need to get underground."

"We're all going underground in search of Anyx. But you have to do something for me."

"Something even more than being led around on

a leash for the shits and giggles of your merry men? What, pray tell, is that?"

"Promise me you'll take the curse from Tuesday. Give her the freedom to love that she deserves."

Gazariel lifted his hands and shrugged. "You really want me to rip out your girlfriend's heart? Okay, then."

"There's another way," Ethan insisted.

The demon approached the bars, and this time when he gripped them the electricity did not seem to bother him at all. Ethan again checked the steady LEDs to confirm the wards were activated.

"I've become conditioned to the pain," Gazariel said as he curled his fingers tightly about the bars and moved his face closer to Ethan's. His jaw was tense, but his expression remained calm. "You don't know what it is that will set my witch free from the curse, do you?"

"No."

"She wouldn't tell you? Because you did ask her about it. I know that much."

Much as he didn't want to admit his lacking trust with Tuesday to the demon, Ethan shook his head.

"It's not something I can give her, or even do for her," Gazariel said on a steady, deep tone. "You see, it's—"

"Ready to rock!" Savin and CJ wandered into the clean room. The reckoner punched a fight-ready fist into his palm. "Where's Tuesday?"

"I'm here!" The witch walked in and patted a leather bag she'd strapped across her chest. "Got all the accoutrements I'll need for a descent into the bowels of Paris to find a mad vampiress intent on destroying the world. And CJ has a bag of tricks as well." The dark witch patted his hip bag in proof. "Let's get the demon shackled and get on with this, yeah?"

Ethan glanced at Gazariel, who smirked at him as if to say "oh, well, now you'll never know the secret to freeing the witch from the curse."

"All right." Ethan stepped down from the platform. He'd learn the answer later, after they'd found Anyx. He would not set Gazariel free until he knew how to help Tuesday find love. "Can you bespell the demon without opening the cage doors and taking down the wards?"

"Of course." Certainly stepped forward, and with a hand held out for Tuesday, she clasped it and together the twosome began to work their magic.

Chapter 23

A witch generally avoided entering churches and cathedrals—for good reason—yet Tuesday was fascinated as she followed Ethan and CJ as they descended below Notre Dame two stories. Savin's contact had led them through the church basement, underground to a cold dark storage area, then had unlocked a vaulted door that had led into a cavernous blackness.

They'd quickly found a path. The walls were initially paneled with rotting wide boards, along which had been strung electrical cords—probably a good century old judging by the frayed cloth covering. As their footsteps tilted downward, the walls changed to limestone and the floors graduated from hard limestone to dirt.

Behind her, Savin and Gazariel brought up the tail. She didn't argue having the hulkingly handsome reckoner guarding her back. But the demon's presence tugged in her sigil.

By the seven sacred witches, why could she not simply tell Ethan how to break the curse? Revealing the truth wouldn't matter. It was not something he could do for her. And the way to break the curse was not something she could ever ask of another person. It simply wasn't done.

But giving him her truth suddenly felt important. If she told him, then she could move forward. Yeah?

"Bring Gazariel up front," Ethan called back.

As Savin shoved Gazariel past Tuesday, the demon waggled his tongue at her. The magic she and CJ had put on him kept him docile, and the blood compass they'd drawn on his chest would react to Anyx's presence. The demon didn't have to do a thing. They could read directions from the glowing diagram drawn in his own sticky black blood on his chest.

The crew waited, staring at Gazariel's chest, and were rewarded almost immediately with a flash of blue light.

"South," Ethan said, and he turned to lead them down a narrow aisle carved from limestone. Here and there an old section of wooden paneling and some ancient electrical wires were nailed to the wall. Chalk symbols marked by previous explorers were either signs of direction or made-up nonsense, maybe even cataphile gang symbols as Ethan suggested.

Parisian cataphiles were a fascinating subculture. Tuesday knew the crazy compulsion to explore the underside of Paris had existed for centuries. Actually, for as long as the city had existed. Daring cave spelunkers held underground parties and challenged themselves to find new, unexplored and extremely dangerous sections of the labyrinths. The catacombs spread all under Paris and in some areas as far down as seven stories.

When they'd been waiting for Savin's contact to find the right keys, Ethan had mentioned the legend of the vampiress who had been cursed by an angry lover in the eighteenth century. The lover had a witch bespell the vampiress frozen and put her in a glass coffin. She couldn't move her body, but she had remained conscious, always aware of what was going on around her. They placed the coffin somewhere in these very labyrinths. She had been found by a man who truly loved her decades ago. Needless to say, she'd gone mad during those centuries of suspended animation, and still struggled with sanity. It was a long and interesting story that Tuesday would have loved to hear more about.

While she wasn't much for spelunking, she wasn't afraid of the closed confines or the darkness. She had pulled on a white light upon entering and now vacillated whether or not to expend some magic to light up the ground with an illumination spell. There were patches of wet on the uneven limestone and dirt surface and she'd not worn shoes for hiking. Her boots had three-inch heels, and she could run in them, but forget navigating the bumpy surface with any skill. But she didn't know if they would find Anyx, and if so, how much magic she would require to stop the woman if she intended to activate the spell, so she holstered any nervous desire to use the magic for the time being and wobbled onward.

Gazariel walked ahead of them all, turning on occasion so Ethan could view the glowing map on his chest. The demon wasn't tied up, but CJ and Tuesday had put a heavy shackle on him. He was connected to her through the sigil, and much like the bonding spell CJ had cast on she and Ethan, Gazariel had to stay close, within the magic's range. And they'd wrangled as much of his demonic magic as possible. He was pouting, and every so often Tuesday felt the tug when she lollygagged behind.

If it wasn't a vampire leading her around Paris, it was a pouting demon tugging her deeper into the underground.

Gazariel actually deserved a good pout. Poor spoiled prince of vanity. Couldn't get the vampiress to love him so he had risked sacrificing the world to win that love?

Tuesday was able to stop herself from giving him a comforting hug, though.

They may need Gazariel to talk to Anyx. They may also have to use blood magic should the code already be activated. And that may require a lot of blood. From the same source. And they hadn't discussed exactly who that source would be.

By the blessed goddess, she prayed the vampiress had not the smarts to figure out the code from that book. A notebook in which some muse had scribbled down angel names and sigils? How irresponsible to put such to paper. On the other hand, that book had been in the care of an archangel. And now it was not. Superirresponsible. Didn't angels have their shit together enough to keep an eye on one very dangerous book?

Tuesday would give the asshole Raphael a piece of her mind. This whole experience was one big clusterfuck.

On the other hand, this adventure had introduced her to Ethan Pierce. And she wasn't going to begrudge that happy side effect.

The men leading their merry gang stopped walking.

Ethan turned and looked to her and Savin, cupping a hand around his ear as a signal that they listen.

Gazariel stretched out an arm to indicate they should continue walking. "What are we—?" Savin hushed him.

Ethan glanced at the glowing sigil on the demon's chest and then nodded toward the end of the pathway, where the faintest glimmer of golden light flickered. The scent of flame mingled with the dusty dry limestone.

"Is it her?" Tuesday asked the demon.

Gazariel listened, swore, then nodded. He strode away from the front of the line.

"Onward," Ethan announced and took up the pace.

When he reached a T-turn, he stopped without going around the corner toward the light. Tuesday walked up to him and he slipped his hand into hers. "Listen," he said. They both listened to what the vampiress was saying just around the corner.

Tuesday didn't have to eavesdrop for long, or even understand the meaning of the words. The vampiress's tone and cadence made her heart drop in her chest. "She's chanting an invocation. She's cracked the code, Ethan. She's begun the spell."

"We need to move now." Ethan pulled a stake from his thigh holster, surprising Tuesday that he would wield such a thing. He nodded to CJ, who confirmed the command to move. "Get the demon up here."

Savin shoved Gazariel up toward the turn.

"What the hell do you want me to do?" Gazariel said in a tight whisper. "Did you see the scratches on my face? I'm not her favorite person at the moment."

"Talk her down. Get her to stop speaking the spell," Ethan said. "Or she dies."

"With that?" The demon snapped a finger against the stake Ethan held. "That's not going to scare her. She's been staked once before. Survived."

Savin gaped. Tuesday knew it was possible for a vampire to survive a staking if he left the stake in and allowed it to slowly work its way out of the body while it healed. Not a fast process, or, she imagined, painless.

"Then we'll use magic," CJ offered. "Get in there now, Gazariel. She's speaking the spell. We can't let her advance to a final declaration to open the very heavens Above."

The demon stood firm.

So Ethan tugged out a blade from a holster at his back hip and flashed it before Gazariel's face.

"Is that…?" Gazariel swallowed. "A Sinistari blade? Are you kidding me?"

"Does it look like I'm kidding?" Ethan asked.

With a sigh of resignation, the demon led the way into a vast chamber that was lit with dozens of black candles. Flames flickered wild crimson flashes on the stone floor and walls. A dais toward the back of the limestone chamber revealed Anyx standing with her back to them, her arms spread wide. Silver jewelry glinted in her hair and at her wrists and waist. She wore a black sheath and no shoes. All around her a circle of candles flickered. And a dark liquid glinted in the pentacle drawn within that circle.

"Blood," Tuesday said as she recognized the ceremony. Where she'd gotten so much blood—the chick was a vampire. Stupid to even wonder.

Ethan joined Gazariel, who stood stymied by the scene. They didn't walk up to Anyx because a shallow trench about three feet wide and flowing with water dissected them from her.

Tuesday gestured to the flames flickering on the water. "A repulsion spell," she said to the men. "If you cross the water, even try to leap over it, you'll go up in flames."

"Defeat it," Ethan commanded her.

Not at all miffed that he'd sharply ordered her to do something, Tuesday spread her arms wide and chanted a suppression spell. There was no spell a vampiress could enact that she, a witch, could not counter.

Meanwhile Gazariel, nudged on by the threat of Ethan's blade, called, "Anyx! Come on, sweetie, let's not destroy the world today. I really like having humans around. Who's going to make my favorite filet mignon if they are all dead? And who's going to feed you, huh? Have you thought about that? You'll starve, bitch!"

The vampiress paused in her chanting, tilted her head, but did not turn to them. She was smart. If she paused the spell too long, it would dissipate.

A sweep of Tuesday's hand and the utterance *"Deflagro!"* snuffed the flames on the water. With an all-clear nod from her, Ethan jumped across, followed by Savin. Gazariel stayed put.

"So much power," Anyx called. "I must own it!" Now she turned, and with an elegant spread of her arms out from her sides and a curl of her fingers, she announced, *"Sarax conti expulsius!"*

The stone walls shuddered. Dust spumed from cracks, increasing the dry perfumed air. Ethan looked to Tuesday. She wasn't positive, but those could have been the final words to activate the spell. When the blood surrounding the vampiress began to bubble, then she was sure.

"That was it," she said.

"The code?" Ethan asked.

"Yeah, I'm not one-hundred-percent sure of the words, but I'm pretty sure they can be interpreted as 'open sesame, let the angels all fall down.' Get her out of that circle!" Tuesday turned and CJ already stood beside her. "We've got to penetrate her casting circle and strangle the spell."

Anyx shouted over her shoulder at Gazariel, "You were nothing more than a tool, you idiot demon!" And then she turned around completely. Elegant black hair, heavy like oil, spilled down her back. Eyes decorated with kohl glimmered with red. A visible red aura, much thicker than a vampire's usual aura, floated about her body. She was a part of the spell. It was her blood flowing in the water. Her scanning gaze stopped on the approaching vampire. "Ethan?"

Tuesday felt the intensity of the spell falter. The vampiress had to hold her focus to keep it going. If she was suddenly reunited with her ex? Fuck, she really didn't want to do this, but— "Go to her, Ethan!"

Stake held at the ready, Ethan approached the circle.

"It's really you? I've missed you, Ethan." Anyx took a step forward. Then, realizing she neared the edge of the circle, she stopped. Arms stretched out, she unfolded her fingers toward him. "Come to me. We can be together in the new world I am creating."

"Really?" Tuesday heard Gazariel mutter behind her.

"Anyx, you can't do this," Ethan said.

Tuesday and CJ quickly drew a circle on the limestone floor with black chalk before the flowing stream.

A channel cut through the rock from the stream to the dais, which was exactly what they needed. CJ flung out herbs and crushed troll hearts and recited a powerful cleansing spell.

Tuesday drew out the athame and looked at her wrist. Blood was needed.

"A whole freakin' lot of it," she muttered, feeling her heart fall to her gut. They needed as much blood as had already been spilled to counteract the spell.

This had become a no-return mission, and she was not happy about that. Because hey, she'd kind of thought that finding love would be a good thing. Like it was time to give it a go. And she'd found a man she wanted to risk that chance on.

Too late for regrets now. She wouldn't ask anyone else to do this. The magic in her veins was powerful and dark. Strong enough to subdue a spell a mere vampiress had cast.

Tuesday closed her eyes. "Fuck. Really?" The cut of the blade against her wrist did not yet pain her because she hadn't pressed deeply. If there was any other option, she wanted to hear it. Right now.

Five feet away from her, Anyx and Ethan had taken to arguing. He was trying to move her out of the casting circle but it continued to repulse him every time he tried to breach it with a stab of the wood stake.

"Gazariel!" Tuesday snapped her fingers. "Help him!"

With a heavy sigh, the demon leaped across the stream and started an argument with Anyx over her fickle ways. But when he mentioned her inability to come because she was a frigid bitch, she snarled and turned to face the dais again. One shout from the angered vampiress again ignited the flames in the stream.

CJ hissed, as he was nearly burned, and then jumped inside the circle with Tuesday.

"We ready?" he asked her.

"I'll provide the blood," she said.

He looked at her then, knowing what the sacrifice would mean. They'd not discussed who would do this. Because it wasn't something a witch on a suicide mission would discuss. They'd wait until the last minute and hope upon hope it wouldn't be necessary.

"You sure?" CJ asked. "Maybe we should give Ethan a moment to see if he can get her out of the circle."

"Not going to happen. And we're all out of moments. We have to do this now." And as if on cue, the stone walls rumbled and the stream spat up fire. Tuesday pressed the athame tight over her wrist. "It's going to take a while to bleed out."

"No!"

Tuesday ignored Ethan's sudden shout. Bits of limestone began to rain from the cavern ceiling. It was now or never.

Tuesday drew the blade over her skin, but it didn't cut deeply because Ethan grabbed her by the shoulder and shoved her out of the circle. The vampire caught the athame as she dropped it. Tuesday landed hard on the stone floor. And she looked up to see Ethan draw the blade across his carotid. Blood spurted and he bowed over the circle as CJ directed.

"No!" she cried.

It was too late. She had been pushed outside the circle and Ethan's blood had conjured up a seal. She couldn't enter it if she tried.

Her lover dropped to the floor and stretched out his

hand to her. She could not touch him. What the hell was he doing?

She crawled up to the circle. "I wish you hadn't done this. I won't let you bleed out. I can't. There's enough blood, yes, Certainly?"

The dark witch shook his head. "We need so much."

Tuesday bowed her head. She would lose the one person she had just realized she cared about most. It wasn't fair. Ethan was already growing weak from blood loss. His eyelids shuttered. The hand he held extended, dropped limply onto the stone floor.

"Help me!" CJ called as he began the chant that would shut off the Final Days spell.

Though her heart had just broken and shattered, Tuesday nodded and crawled forward. Compelled to stop an evil that could harm so many more, she spread out her palms, embracing the circle and sending energy through her being. She matched CJ's tone with her own rhythmic chants.

Out the corner of her eye she saw the vampiress dash toward the entrance. Gazariel called to the reckoner to go after her and Savin did so.

And from behind her Gazariel suddenly let out an ear-shattering cry that harkened to the angels, who spoke in myriad tongues to mimic all the beasts on the planet.

Tuesday's chest suddenly burned as if the fire had leaped from the nearby stream to singe her. She struggled to concentrate, to focus her vibrations toward the circle and her dying lover. Ethan now barely supported himself. His blood streamed toward the fire. When it touched the flames, they flashed brilliant white and danced up the channel toward the dais.

The fire in her chest was unbearable. Tuesday screamed. The magic she put out suddenly left her in one final gushing effort. In the circle, CJ managed to capture that magic and directed it toward the dais, where the magic ball splashed into violet flames.

The limestone walls ceased shuddering.

CJ dropped to his knees over Ethan.

And Tuesday fell backward, yet landed in Gazariel's arms.

Chapter 24

The demon bowed over Tuesday, inspected her face and smoothed the hair away from her eyes. "The vampire did it," he said in amazement. "He broke the curse."

"The Final Days?" she murmured weakly.

"Well, that, too. I think. We won't know until we go topside and see if all the tourists are flambéed, eh? But, Tuesday, the curse you've carried for centuries—it's gone. Didn't you feel it? I certainly did."

She slapped a palm to her chest, where the sigil had burned so viciously she'd felt as though her insides would sizzle. "But…"

"A true love willing to die for you." Gazariel spoke the means to breaking the spell. "He sacrificed for you, witch. And I am also clean now. That damn curse is completely erased!"

"But that means… Ethan!" She shoved out of Gazariel's arms and scrambled toward the circle, where CJ now stood over the fallen vampire. The dark witch stepped out and jumped across the stream to inspect the dais.

The vampire was lying on his back, arms splayed, eyes wide, his mouth open and the blood continuing to pour from his carotid. Tuesday slapped her palm to the open wound. Blood spurted. She summoned a healing incantation, but it sputtered and merely sprinkled over Ethan's neck. She'd depleted her magic to stop the Final Days.

"CJ, help me! I have to stop the bleeding or he'll die."

The dark witch returned to the circle, which was no longer necessary to keep closed, and kneeled beside her. "I think he's already dead."

"No!" She took the dark witch's hand and pressed it over the wound on Ethan's neck. "Recite the blessing for a vampire's everlasting life."

They did so together while the demon stalked around them, observing. Such a blessing was a powerful invocation that a witch could perform for a vampire, granting him immortality that even a stake or beheading would find difficult to overcome. It was rarely used. And only the most powerful witches could summon such a thing.

After minutes of desperate chanting CJ tugged his hand away from Ethan's neck. "It's not working. We've both depleted our magic. If anything might work—he needs blood. That's a vampire's best hope for survival."

"Then he'll have it." Tuesday searched for the athame and found it tucked under Ethan's leg. Without a second thought, she drew it across her wrist and pressed it to Ethan's mouth. "Come on, Ethan! Don't leave me now!"

He didn't move, so she had to press her wrist tight against his mouth. He didn't swallow.

"Sit him upright," CJ directed Gazariel. "Help me!"

"I'm rather of the mind to get the hell out of here," the demon said.

Tuesday hissed at the demon. "I saved you from being consigned to Daemonia. You will help. Now!"

Begrudgingly, Gazariel helped CJ set Ethan upright so the blood would flow down his throat. It took a while, but after a few minutes Tuesday saw his Adam's apple pulse. He had swallowed. And she was growing distinctly weaker. She'd expelled so much magic that even a little blood loss was not going to keep her upright for long.

Her eyelids fluttered.

"You can't do this," CJ said. "We need another donor."

"You," Gazariel said to the dark witch.

CJ tapped a tattoo on his neck. "Can't. I'm warded against vamps. If he drinks my blood it'll kill him for sure."

"He's warded against demons, too," Gazariel said with a nod toward Ethan's throat.

"We need the vampiress. Go get her!" Tuesday commanded the demon.

"Seriously?"

Tuesday wanted to argue with the obstinate demon, but it was all she could do to keep her eyelids open and her focus on Ethan. He was swallowing now, and that was a good sign.

But with a flutter of her eyelids, she passed out.

Tuesday came to and the first thing she saw was her vampire lover embracing his ex-wife. He held Anyx's slender body to his chest and gripped her head to hold it aside as he supped at her neck. His hand caressed her breast where the thin black sheath had slid aside to expose the nipple, and she moaned in ecstasy. And Ethan increased his efforts, drinking from her. Taking from her. Enjoying her. Rubbing her nipple to give her pleasure.

That was not a life-saving moment. It was a graphic display of sexual desire.

Backing away on the limestone floor, Tuesday's back hit a wall. Someone grasped her hand and helped her to stand. "You okay?"

"No," she said to CJ. And she wasn't. Her head felt as if someone was stirring her brains with a spatula. And her chest might explode if she did not— "I need air. I have to get out of here. Now."

Turning, she crept out of the chamber in the direction they had come. No one followed her blood-drained wobbling pace. CJ would stay behind and keep an eye on Ethan. She hadn't recalled seeing either Gazariel or Savin in the chamber. Only the two ex-lovers entwined in a disgustingly sensual embrace.

Vampires did not have to hold their donors so… intimately. Taking blood could be functional and discreet. They couldn't have been closer if they had climbed inside one another. She didn't want to think about it. She wanted to erase that image from her brain.

Stumbling blindly forth, Tuesday entered a dark tunnel and summoned a glow of light on her palm. It sputtered. She was weak. She needed rest and to heal. To restore after the tremendous expulsion of magic and blood. She'd given Ethan her blood to save him.

But what had she saved him for? A grand reunion with his former wife.

Noticing the strong coppery smell from the old electrical wires that had greeted her upon descent into the catacombs, she knew the surface must be close and raced forward. And there by the old wood door that led into the bowels of the church above, stood Gazariel.

"I need to get out of here." She pushed past the demon, but he gripped her wrists. She did not bleed anymore and stopping movement now brought the woozy dizziness up again. Standing still was impossible. Her world wobbled. Or did she?

"You're weak, witch. You need rest."

"I will. But I need air now!" She faltered.

Gazariel lifted her into his arms and carried her up and through the ancient church basement. It was well into the morning hours, so the church was closed to tourists and their exit was not observed.

Finally, fresh cold air smacked Tuesday's face. It was still dark, yet the moon beamed across her face. As if blinded by a desert sun, Tuesday closed her eyes.

"Where should I take you?"

"Away from here," she murmured, then passed out.

Ethan emerged from below Notre Dame and staggered across the street from the church to sit on the sidewalk before a closed souvenir shop. Behind him CJ filed out and stretched his arms. The book containing the Final Days code was tucked in his waistband. Savin was carrying up Anyx—whom CJ had bound with magic, though she was nearly drained of blood not only from him but from the spell. She may or may not survive. He didn't care.

Tuesday and Gazariel had not been below when Ethan had finally ceased drinking from Anyx. He'd pulled away from her neck, swallowed the last hot gulp and had felt himself again. He'd touched death while lying in the circle. Hell, he must have briefly died. But Tuesday's blood had lifted him from that abyss. He'd felt it trickle down his throat as if a cool, clean elixir. And yet, he'd held back from taking too much from her. He hadn't been willing to take her life to save his own. Better to die than to take Tuesday along with him. She'd done nothing to deserve death. It had been he who had forced her into this nightmare.

When someone had dropped an unconscious Anyx before him, he'd dove in, knowing he could take enough blood from her—and not caring for the outcome. He'd fed on her viciously, yet the blood lust had spurred his desires. He hated that feeling, yet it had saved his life.

A heavy sweep of wings preceded the sudden appearance of Gazariel by his side. The demon kneeled beside Ethan, and gazed skyward. "Morning soon."

"Where is she?" Ethan could only manage to whisper the question. He was exhausted. He needed rest to fully recover.

"She wanted to get away from you."

Why would she…? And then he remembered seeing Tuesday shuffle across the chamber floor. The look in her eyes had not been of horror, but rather…betrayal. She'd watched him drink from Anyx. But she couldn't have believed that meant anything to him beyond sustenance.

Of course she had. He had seen it plainly in her tearing blue gaze.

"I took her to the airport," Gazariel said. "My witch is free of the curse. You broke the spell."

"I—I did?"

Gazariel chuckled. "She never did tell you what would do it, did she?"

He shook his head.

"It's something she has known since the day I placed the curse in her. A true love had to be willing to sacrifice his life for her. And...her true love did." The demon winked.

"True love? But I thought..." Ethan blinked, sorting out the few details he'd learned about Tuesday's dark curse. "If she couldn't have love, then how...?"

"Oh, someone could fall in love with her. Just, the moment the guy realized it, or she did, then all goes to Beneath. Apparently, her true love realized how much he did love her only in that moment before it would have went to hell. You pulled through by the skin of your teeth. Good going, vampire."

Gazariel stood. With a sweep of wings, he misted into black smoke and was gone.

Ethan closed his eyes. He was thankful Tuesday had been freed of the curse. And because of love?

"Yes." He did love her. And perhaps he had only realized it that moment he'd dove to push her out of the circle so she would not die to stop the curse.

And now?

"I need to get to the airport."

Chapter 25

CJ directed Savin to bring the vampiress to head-quarters, where she would be contained. The Council would decide what to do with a vampiress who would see fit to bring an end to the world.

He told the reckoner he'd be close behind, but needed to do something first. Rather, he needed to follow the whisper that had not ceased since he'd stepped out of the church. It was a disembodied voice that he suspected only he could hear. And it was close.

Wandering across the street and toward the gated garden behind the grand church, CJ slipped through the thick shrubbery and into the quiet privacy of a small yet groomed garden that saw many tourists during the day. Now he was alone. The whisper lured him toward a bench that faced the back of the church, before a view of the flying buttresses and the massive iron cross that tipped the church.

CJ did not recognize the man who sat on the bench. He was tall, appeared slender and was dressed in a smart brown-and-black pinstriped suit. His palm was propped on the top of a straight black cane, which looked more accessory than necessity. He didn't look at CJ; his stare seemed fixed on the cross atop the church.

"Give me the book," the stranger said.

And hearing the voice, which sounded like a mix of all the accents of the world, yet was clear and precise, and so *ethereal*, CJ knew who the creature was on the bench. Ethan had mentioned who had sent him on this mission.

CJ tugged the book from his waistband and clutched it tightly to his chest. "You didn't do such a good job holding onto it the first time."

"Give it."

"No."

The book flew into the angel Raphael's hands. And now he met CJ's gaze with eyes that were all colors and glowed with a depth that CJ thought surely he could fall into and never land. And that wasn't a romantic notion; it was a deep and abiding fear that tightened the skin all over his body and closed up his throat.

"I was having a little fun," the angel admitted. "We do things like that every now and a thousand years or so. Ta."

And with a massive swoop of wings that lifted the hair around CJ's face, the angel disappeared.

And CJ dropped to his knees, utterly relieved, pissed, and thankful to be alive.

This time, Tuesday crossed through security without once looking back. Determination held her head high. Her flight left in forty-five minutes. As she waited for a little boy ahead of her to put on his tennis shoes, she grabbed her coat from the conveyor belt and pulled it on. Slipping into her ankle boots, she frowned at the dusty dried mud from the catacombs on them. It was time to get the hell out of Paris.

With a toss of her hair over a shoulder, she wandered forward. Her gate was to the left, and she— All of a sudden, she stopped at the junction of the turn and stood there, allowing the world to swish by her on all sides as if sped up on a security tape.

Time seemed to stop and voices were muffled. Clothing brushed past her. The stifling inner air ceased to bother. Her heartbeats thudded to recall what Gazariel had said to her.

True love had broken the curse.

But if so, then how had he been capable of holding his ex-wife like that? Was she wrong to think that moment in the catacombs had meant something to Ethan? His love for her *had to* be true to break the spell. Or had it dissolved as quickly as his ex-wife's blood had entered his system?

She'd been starting to have fun with Ethan Pierce. And yes, she may have even begun to love him. Or at least, leave a hopeful door open that she'd recognize it if it was love.

But all for nothing, apparently.

And yet… "I really did fall in love." Her throat tightened. Tears threatened.

So when someone turned her around and pulled her into an embrace to kiss her, Tuesday beat at the man's shoulder and kicked him on the shin in defense. When she saw it was Ethan, wincing as he bent up his injured leg, she gasped.

"Sorry," he said. "I shouldn't have surprised you like that. That was a Richard move. But I love you, Tuesday. You can't leave me. Not like this."

She slammed her arms across her chest and lifted her chin. "What about your wife?"

"You mean my ex-wife, who has been taken into custody to stand trial for reckless acts against humankind?"

"But I saw you." She squeezed a fist, hoping to staunch the tears, but they dropped down her cheeks. "You were holding her so tightly. Caressing her. I saw you stroke her..." She couldn't say it. It hurt too much to think of right now.

"I was taking her blood, Tuesday. And yes, I experienced a moment of sexual satisfaction. I'm a vampire. Drinking blood turns me on. But ultimately drinking Anyx's blood was a means to stay alive. Tuesday, please." He took her hands. "She means nothing to me."

"She's the one who saved your life."

"Not without your help. And your curse." He pressed his palm to her chest, right over her heart.

Tears spilled down Tuesday's cheeks as she struggled against throwing herself into his arms. "You've taken the curse from me. The sigil is gone."

"Gazariel said as much. It's true." He bowed his head to hers and tilted up her chin with a finger. "I love you, Tuesday. Truly. Deeply. Insanely. Not like the false, surface love you accused Gazariel of experiencing. I love you on a soul level. I can feel it in my blood, my bones and my spirit."

She gasped.

"And if you get on that plane and leave me I'm not sure what I'll do."

"You'd survive," she said simply. "We all do."

"But I don't want to survive without you. I know it's a lot to ask. And you have a home in Boston. But would you stay with me? Just a while longer? Please, Tuesday." His breath hushed against her ear. "I love you. I need you to believe me. I. Love. You."

The words felt true. They *were* true. Because if they were not, she would not recognize that right now. She'd still bear the curse and they might be standing in a desolate wasteland covered with the ashes of humans and angels alike.

The curse was gone. She could be loved. And…she was.

By the seven sacred witches, she really was.

"This is the second time I've come back to this airport intent on leaving."

"I don't think you're meant to leave." He smiled against her cheek then kissed it. "Not yet, anyway. Not until we've talked about us. You helped me to stop the Final Days. We've been through a lot. We've both literally walked through fire. Don't walk away from us now."

Us. Yeah, the word felt right. For now? For maybe a little longer. Together. Sharing their lives. She wanted to embrace that, to own it.

"I love you, too," she said. "I think I've known it for days."

She hugged him and tilted her head against his shoulder. She was tired and weak and, hell yes, she loved this man. Of course, he'd only been taking blood from Anyx to survive. And his honesty about how it had felt meant a lot to her.

"Take me home," she said to him. "Your home."

Epilogue

A year later...

Tuesday dusted a long rosewood shelf lined with sea-shells of all shapes, sizes and colors. She could hear the ocean echo out at her, and wasn't at all surprised when a tiny giggle sounded from within the spiral of a nautilus shell. With a bounce to her step, she moved on to the next shelf, where a triton fashioned of more shells and some kind of metal that gleamed green was kept under glass.

This was the mermaid room in the Archives, and she'd been assigned to tidy it up today. And tomorrow. And for however long it took to clean the small and crowded room.

Certainly Jones had offered her the job after she'd decided to stay in Paris with Ethan a year ago. They'd

gone back to his place from the airport, talked and…
had a lot of hex. Blood-bone-spirit sex. Soul-deep stuff.
They were really in love. And that was something neither of them had felt in a long time.

They'd wanted to ride that feeling and follow it wherever it would lead them, so she'd made a quick trip home
to Boston, had rented out her property for an indefinite
period of time and packed up her clothes and magical
accoutrements. Now Ethan's place was a bit more un-
tidy and he'd had to relegate three quarters of his closet
to her wardrobe. And Stuart now answered to her com-
mands, as well as Ethan's.

And every morning Ethan either woke her with croissants and orange juice, or left them on the counter because he'd gone in to work and hadn't wanted to wake
her. She'd never felt happier.

With the curse completely gone it was now easy to
recognize love. Small things, such as the sun shining on
this snowy February morning, had lifted her smile and
given her a bounce to her step as she walked to work.
She had a purpose now, and a fantastic lover.

Life was about as fabulous as it could get.

Bending to inspect a glass container filled with
some kind of sparkling jewels, Tuesday realized the
thin diamond-shaped items with one curved edge were
possibly mermaid scales. Cool. She'd never in her lifetime met a mermaid, and wasn't sure she wanted to.
They were supposed to be vicious.

When a man's hands suddenly covered her eyes from
behind, she sprang upright. She hadn't heard anyone
come in. And Certainly Jones, her boss, would never
do such a thing. So…

"Is it lunchtime already?" she asked with hope.

"I'm a little late." Ethan leaned in and kissed the side of her neck, sending a visceral shiver over her skin. "Had some business to deal with. Can we have a quickie?"

"Did you lock the door?"

"Always." His hand slipped around her waist and glided under her gray T-shirt that snarkily declared in block letters Don't Be A Richard.

Lunchtime sex had become a norm, and they were pretty sure no one was aware of their stolen liaisons. CJ would say something if he knew. That witch was a stickler about work ethic and protocol. So they were careful, but never quiet.

"I missed you," he said, turning her around to face him.

"It's been three hours since we drove here together from home."

"Three hours too long. I'm going to have to bite you again, and soon."

Their blood connection lasted about twenty-four to forty-eight hours. The shared sexual gratification that developed with a bite gave them the ability to hear one another's thoughts and to feel their emotions and sexual sensations. Love was a wondrous emotion that shimmered off Ethan like a warm summer sun. And yes, when they argued they could feel one another's anger, even fear, but that made the need to make up quicker. And they never quarreled much.

Tuesday tapped her neck. "Right here, big boy."

The vampire pierced her neck with his fangs, and while he did so, he slid down her leggings and she unzipped his fly. Behind her rose a nineteenth-century desk that he set her on as he licked at her blood.

Tuesday moaned as he slid his erection inside her and

pumped slowly yet deeply. She enjoyed when they went at it fast and furious, but even more so when he prolonged every move, seeming to luxuriate in the depths of her.

"I've got another job you might be interested in," he said.

"For Acquisitions?" She had helped him with one case regarding retrieving a grimoire from a crone a few months ago. All it had required was some sweet talk and a commitment to drinking the bitch under the table. Tuesday would never touch moss liqueur again. Oh, the hangover! "Does it involve another washed-up crone?"

"Faeries."

"Why me?"

He shrugged and licked her neck to seal the wound. He thrust inside her still. "It's a magic thing. Faeries are trafficking in humans, accept without the usual changeling to replace the stolen baby."

"And why, exactly, does Acquisitions need to get involved? What do you need to acquire, Monsieur Director? And would you tell me if an angel were using us as pawns in his stupid game of playing with the inhabitants of the mortal realm again?"

"I would tell you, and Raphael has not been seen or heard of since his selfish ploy. Did I tell you the book with the Final Days code suddenly appeared on a shelf in the angel room a few weeks after our adventure?"

She gripped his ass, pulling him deep into her. "You did not. But good to know. I hope it's chained, warded and bespelled to Kingdom Come. Mmm, lover, pull out and slip your cock over my clit. Yes. Like that." She bowed forward, putting her forehead to his shoulder.

"The faery thing will be fun for us," he said. "Maybe?"

She knew that tone. He was diving in to adventure once again. For a man who had worked a desk job for so long, he'd been taking on more jobs himself. And fieldwork suited him. As it did her.

"I do like trying new things," she said. Grinding her body against his erection, she mined the humming orgasm that whispered up to her core. "You think we'll ever get back to America?"

"Do you want to return?"

"It does carry memory of a lot of good times."

"Like witch hunts and torture?"

"Yes, Richard, just like that. You know me too well."

He hilted himself inside her, and that was all it took to fly. Tuesday's head fell back and she pulled her lover down to bite through her shirt at her breast. He didn't break skin. They'd save that for later.

"I'd like to keep the witch in Paris for a while," he said as he watched her face move through the joy and elation of orgasm. "Deal?"

She pulled herself back up to stare into his eyes. "You do have a lot to offer a witch who has been without love for centuries. Deal."

* * * * *

THE WITCH'S QUEST

This one is for my kids, Ashley and Jesse.
My two favourite examples of nice.

Chapter 1

The gnarled oak tree behind her looked...angry.

Valor Hearst straightened her shoulders and tried to avoid turning around to cast a glance at the disgruntled tree. Because the moment she started to look closer, things could become real. Especially in an enchanted forest such as the Darkwood.

She knelt on the forest floor, carefully plucking the *Amanita muscaria* mushrooms from a thick and curly frosting of moss. Normally, she would wear gloves to remove the poisonous red-capped shrooms, but having forgotten them, she instead used an entomologist's tweezers.

Dried yet still-glossy trails from snails streaked across a head-size fieldstone, which she scraped into a plastic baggie. The powder would serve as another fine ingredient for future spells. She'd decided that since she had risked coming here, she'd take a few minutes to gather spell ingredients before settling down to do the real work: enacting a spell that would, with hope, lure love her way.

Valor had never dared enter the Darkwood, but on this day she was feeling her confidence and was pretty sure that the warnings against witches venturing into the enchanted forest were nothing more than blather. Mortals and other paranormals visited the darkly mysterious woods all the time. She was no different from any of them. Save that her air magic packed a wallop when need be.

"So take that," she said, yet still couldn't avoid a suspicious glance over her shoulder.

Had the tree's bark curved downward in chunky folds to form a craggy frown? She narrowed her gaze, which was followed by her own frown. The bark hadn't been shaped that way when she first knelt down before the mushrooms.

Maybe?

"Quit spooking yourself," she muttered. "Crazy witch."

The Darkwood was off-limits to and unsafe for witches. That was what her friend and fellow earth witch Eryss Norling had said to her last night when they closed the Decadent Dames brewery together and wandered out to the parking lot under the half-moon.

Valor happened to be attracted to most things that were off-limits and unsafe. Whether they be events, challenges or even men. Most especially men.

She tucked the red-capped mushrooms into her fishing tackle box. It was painted in olive green camo and might have a fishhook or two in it, as well—ice fishing in the wintertime? Yes, please. But she mostly used it to collect herbs and spell ingredients. A tiny jade cricket that she had disturbed from sleeping under a mushroom leaped onto the edge of the tackle box.

"You're lucky you have a heartbeat," she said to the insect. "Otherwise, I'd pulverize your wings and use the dust in a spell."

The insect chirped and hopped off to a more private leaf.

And Valor pulled out a small mason jar half-filled with angel dust to use as a marker for the ritual sigil she now intended to create. A collection of rose petals she had gathered surreptitiously from a floral shop before heading out here today would also serve in the design.

No time to back out now. She'd come here with the intent of finally serving herself what she deserved. "Here's to love."

Cupping a handful of fine angel dust and funneling it through her curled fingers, she marked out on the thick moss the pattern that she'd studied in her great-grandma Hector's grimoire. Small, smoky quartz crystals were then placed at the compass points and rose quartz along the borders of the sigil. She kissed and blessed the flower petals, then placed them on the moss.

Leaning back to inspect her work, she decided the design looked much like a voodoo *veve*. But this sacred sigil, infused with her light magic, would wield so much more power.

She didn't notice the darkening sky as she laid a crow foot, a mouse rib and a dried rat heart at the center of the sigil. Red and pink candles were tucked into the moss, and with a snap of her fingers they ignited. So she had a little fire magic to her arsenal, as well. It was just for small tasks. A witch should never risk invoking more fire than she could handle.

Now the invocation—

Valor's hand slipped on the thick moss, and her leg suddenly slid out from under her kneeling position. She hadn't made such a move. Something tugged her ankle roughly.

She slapped the moss with both palms and yelped as her body slid backward across the forest floor, dragging her hands through angel dust, petals and crystals. Twisting at the waist, she searched in the dimming light. One of the tree roots had wrapped about her ankle, clasping the leather combat boot in a painful pinch.

"What in all the goddess's bad hair days?" She kicked at the root with her free foot.

And then the frowning bark opened wide and growled at her. The tree had a merciless hold on her. And the root only grew tighter about her ankle.

Valor had heard of faery trees. And this woods was a place where the *sidhe* mingled with those from the mortal realm. Another reason she'd been warned away. Faeries who did not live in the mortal realm generally didn't like witches.

She hadn't an enchanted sword to cut her way free. But she did have witchcraft.

"Loftus!"

Her air magic whisked over the ancient tree bark with the waning effect of a whisper. And the tree actually seemed to chuckle as its trunk heaved and the bark crinkled. The root about her ankle tugged again and her boot disappeared into the soft, loamy ground at the base of the tree.

She groped for the moss, on which the candles had extinguished and the angel dust sigil had been disturbed.

It was out of her reach. So was her tackle box, in which she'd stashed her cell phone.

This was bad. On a scale of one to ten for oh-my-mercy-this-is-bad, this probably rated a seventy.

"I'm fucked."

Valor had parked on a turnoff from the gravel road that wound about three hundred yards away from a highway. It was set near a gape in the forest and not easily seen or even known about. At the time, she'd been pleased that no one would see her car. And she'd entered the forest from the opposite end of the woods where Blade Saint-Pierre lived for the specific reason she hadn't wanted anyone to think she was trespassing. That vampire did not own the forest, but he acted as a sort of portal guardian, keeping others out of the forest.

For their own good.

Witches and the Darkwood? Not cool.

Valor tugged futilely at her pinned legs. Yes, now both were being sucked slowly down into the earth beneath the tree. She'd been here two hours for sure, and no matter how she tugged she remained pinned into the mossy ground by the oak roots. And that was exactly what had happened. She'd been *pinned* by a faery tree.

What she knew about such wicked magic was that eventually she'd be sucked completely into the earth and, perhaps, even into Faery. But she wouldn't make the journey alive. And judging by how far in she'd been drawn, she suspected the process generally took less than a day. She didn't even want to calculate how much time she had left.

She'd tried speaking a releasement spell. That had only bothered the crows perched in the crooked elm boughs overhead. They stared with beady black eyes at her like vultures waiting for carrion. She'd tried apologizing to the universe for stepping on sacred faery grounds. She'd felt the earth shudder then and had quietly lain there, palms clutching at the dried leaves and undergrowth, her cheek wet with tears.

All she'd wanted to do was invoke a spell. For her. For once in her long lifetime, she'd finally thought about herself and what she wanted.

Eyes closed now, she thought the loamy scent of moss and earth were too rich for such a fool as herself. The crisp promise of crystal clear water babbled from somewhere behind her. Even the bird chirps seemed to admonish her for being an idiot.

Would her friends think it was odd she did not show up for work tonight at the brewery? Of course Eryss would wonder. Give her a call. But Valor often did not answer her phone. Eryss would shrug and figure Valor had forgotten. It was a Thursday night. Never too busy. Instead of a staff of three, the Decadent Dames could easily manage the microbrewery with two.

They might not bother to drive by her loft at the edge of town in Tangle Lake until the next day when Valor didn't show up to help carry in a delivery of grains that was expected to arrive in the afternoon.

She'd be dead by then. Even now she sensed her energy waning, seeping from her. Bleeding her life into the ground.

"Stupid tree," she muttered. "A simple lash across the face would have served me well enough."

But she knew faeries—and their trees, for they were alive and sentient—never did anything half-assed. Be it mischief or unspeakable malice, it was either all-in or all-out.

Clasping the moonstone amulet she always wore strung from a leather cord about her neck, she bowed her head to the leaves on the forest floor before her. It was time to start thinking of leaving a message for her friends. Who may eventually find her decayed corpse still pinned to this earth, perhaps one clawing hand still sticking out from the ground, surrounded by the malevolent tree roots.

"Aggh!" She had to stop thinking of how dire her end would be. That wouldn't solve anything.

Valor grabbed a thin branch and decided the moss was so thick she could probably write in it. No. It would never work. The mason jar of angel dust sat two feet out of her reach. So blood was the next option. And her parchment? A wide maple leaf.

She broke the branch in two and was holding the serrated end poised to stab at her skin when the rapid beating of hooves alerted her. She glanced up and just had time to tuck her face against the leaves as the sleek doe beat a path toward her. The deer probably hadn't expected a nonanimal to be sitting in the forest, so the beast hadn't much time to correct her trajectory. Valor sensed the deer's surprise as her front hoof nearly stepped on her hand and she leaped high and over Valor's head.

Muttering a quiet oath and a quick blessing of thanks, Valor followed the deer's path. Then it occurred to her that something might have been after it. She swiftly turned and spied the man running toward her, a blur of gold and green. When he was but twenty feet away from her, he suddenly halted, appearing to put on the brakes as a runner in an animated cartoon would, heels skidding and body lagging behind as his speed dropped from swift to stop.

"Whoa!" Valor stretched up a hand to stop him. Which she realized was ridiculous because he'd already stopped.

Tall and lithe and not wearing a shirt, he gave a shrug of one shoulder that stretched his sleek, tight muscles up and down his abdomen. His arms twitched as he looked her over. His face was angular and cut with sharp cheekbones and a prominent slash of brow line. Short blond hair, blown wild and wavy by his racing speed, settled about his ears and forehead. Hip-hugging gray jeans revealed he was barefoot. And his abs were sculpted with more muscle than Valor could imagine what to do with. On those abs were traced violet sigils that she knew were faery in nature. And there, braceleting his wrists, were more faery sigils.

But she didn't fear him. She *knew* him.

"Valor?" And he knew her.

Kelyn Saint-Pierre padded up to her with a lanky ease that spoke more of a wild animal's gait than that of a human. Of course, he wasn't human; he was faery.

He swept a hand over his forehead, pushing the hair from his face. His violet eyes took her in from tangled brown-violet hair, moss-smudged cheek and faded green T-shirt to—her combat boots were well underground right now. It was too dark now for him to see into the shadows where all the horrible pinning action had occurred.

His expression switched from surprise to concern. "What's a witch doing in the Darkwood? Don't you know this forest is dangerous to your kind?"

So state the obvious.

Kelyn lived in the area, and she knew his sister and three brothers. Daisy Blu, a faery who had once been a werewolf, was married to Beck Severo. Valor had gone to Daisy's baby shower a month ago.

Blade was the brother who lived at the edge of this forest. That guy was a vampire but sported gothic wings that would give anyone a fright. And Stryke was a pack leader in a northern suburb.

Trouble, the eldest of the Saint-Pierre siblings, was a werewolf to the bone. And Valor and Trouble were drinking buddies who got together once in a while for Netflix and pizza. Guys like Trouble were meant for fishing trips and shooting the shit, never romance.

Summoning her pride, Valor tossed her long violet-streaked hair over a shoulder and lifted her chin. She was still able to lean on an elbow, but she knew she looked pitiful all the same. "I was just out for a walk."

Kelyn crossed his arms before his chest. His haughty posture and smirk spoke his assessment of her situation much louder than words could.

"You know," she continued casually. "Collecting some ingredients for spells. Communing with nature." She patted the moss. "Doing...witch stuff." It was difficult not to wince. Witch stuff? Ugh. She was never good at the lie. But, oh, so talented with getting herself into strange fixes.

Case in point: the witch pinned by the oak tree.

"I can see that." He made a show of peering over the ground. "Looks like a spell sigil to me. Witch stuff, eh?" Tucking his hands behind his back, Kelyn leaned forward in an admonishing teacher pose and said to her, "You know that witch stuff is the worst you could manage here in the Darkwood? The mortal realm powers you possess clash terribly with the faery energies that inhabit every inch of this woods."

"I'm not working magic at the moment. Just—" A glance to the angel-dust sigil and scattered ingredients proved her guilt. "What do you want, Kelyn? Don't you have a deer to chase?"

He righted himself and laughed. "We were racing. She won."

Right. The man was faery. And Valor knew he had wings. Trouble had told her they were big and silver and violet, and that Kelyn was ever proud of them. She also knew that of all four Saint-Pierre brothers, Kelyn was the strongest and most powerful. Or so Trouble had told her during a drunken game of truth or dare one night.

To judge by Kelyn's lean, lithe appearance, Valor had to wonder about such skills and strength. Sure, he looked riveted together with a factory gun and sculpted from solid marble, but Valor always tended toward the beefier, broader sorts. With dark hair. Always. A blond? Never had an interest.

On the other hand, why was she limiting her options when the reason she'd come to the Darkwood was to cast a spell for love?

Propping her chin in a hand and twisting at the hip to look more casual, she asked, "You go running through this forest often?"

Surely, he had noticed that her legs were sucked into the ground up to her knees, but she had a difficult time asking anyone for help. She was woman. Hear her roar!

She hated coming off as the weak one. The stupid witch who'd gone to the Darkwood without telling anyone.

"I do go for a run a few times a week. This woods is special to me." He smoothed a hand absently down his abs, which drew Valor's eye to the violet sigils. They looked like intricate mandalas, and she knew they were the source of his faery magic. "You talk to Trouble lately?"

"No," she answered defensively. Not sure why, though. She had no reason to be defensive. Kelyn must have known that she and Trouble were friends. "You?"

Stupid witch. Why was she making light conversation?

"Couple days ago. He never mentions you."

"Why should he?"

Kelyn shrugged a shoulder and cast his glance to the ground, his gaze stretching behind her. She shouldn't have said that. It was the truth, though. She considered him a friend. Just that.

"You look…stuck," he said. Suddenly, his gaze went fierce and he looked over her shoulder.

"What's—"

Before she could summon a stupid excuse, Valor heard the roar. A beastly, slobbery utterance accompanied by a foul, greasy odor that filled the air as if a stink bomb had been set off.

Kelyn leaped, and in midair his wings unfurled. The gorgeous violet-and-silver appendages lifted him with a flap or two and he met the creature that had jumped high to collide with him in a crush of growls and slapping body parts. The twosome landed on the ground ten feet before Valor, the heavy weight of Kelyn's opponent denting the moss and tearing up clods of sod.

Valor dug her fingers into the leaves and whispered a protection spell that drew a white light over her body and snapped against her form. The oak tree growled at the intrusion and she felt her knees get sucked deeper into the earth. The tree seemed to feed off her witch magic. And in the next instant, the protection shattered, like plastic crinkling over her skin, and it fell away.

Never had she felt so helpless. Pray to the goddess, Kelyn could defeat the aggressor, which was five times his size and built like a bear. It was a troll of some sort. Or so she guessed. She'd never seen one but knew they existed.

Kelyn punched the creature in its barrel gut. The troll yowled and kicked Kelyn off, sending the faery flying through the air where a flap of his wings stopped him from crashing into the tree canopy. Aiming for the troll, Kelyn arrowed down and landed a kick to the thing's blocky head.

Valor slapped her hands over her head in protection, but it didn't matter. Every moment that passed, she felt her body move minutely deeper into the cold, compressing earth.

With one final punch to its spine from Kelyn's fist, the troll went down, landing on the moss in a sprawl. It shuddered like a gelatinous gray glob of Thanksgiving Jell-O, and then, with an explosion of faery dust that decorated the air, it dissipated.

And behind the glittering shimmer stood Kelyn, wiping the dust from his arms and abs as if he had only tussled with a minor annoyance.

Valor couldn't stop looking around at the scatter of dust that glinted madly. More beautiful than she would imagine coming from such an atrocious creature. It almost put the angel dust to shame.

Kelyn approached. "What was it you were saying about muscled men rescuing you?"

"I didn't…" She'd not said anything about being rescued. But really? She might have to change her tune about the leaner versions.

"You didn't what? Ask for rescue? Looks like you might be in need of just that."

"I'm cool." Why had she said that? Why the need to act as though death were not dragging her down into the earth?

Kelyn squatted before her, arms resting on his thighs. "I can't win with you, can I, Valor?"

"What do you mean? Win?"

"You're a hard woman to please, is all."

"No, I'm not. All it takes is some good dark coffee to make me happy."

"Coffee served up with muscles. Like my brother Trouble has?"

"What? What is it with you and your concern about me and Trouble? We only ever—"

He put up a hand to stop her from saying more. "Don't need the details."

"There are no details."

Okay, well, there had been that one time. But she wasn't stupid enough to fill the brother in on the salacious stuff. Trouble had probably already done that.

"I really liked you," Kelyn said, looking aside now. He'd dropped his shoulders, and the sweat and troll dust glistening on his abs drew Valor's eye. "For a while there."

"What do you mean?" She met his lift of chin and then figured it out. "You mean…?"

He shrugged. "But then you tripped into my brother's arms and that's all she wrote. I always manage to lose the girl to him. What is it about him? He's a big lunk!"

Valor smiled at that assessment. Trouble did have some lunkish qualities. Okay, a lot of lunkish qualities.

But she had no idea Kelyn had…lusted after her? "Your brother and I are not in a relationship."

"Trouble is never *in* relationships," Kelyn said sharply.

Now he eyed her legs and squinted. He bent to study behind her, and there was nothing Valor could do to stop him, because she was stuck there.

"You've been pinned!" He gripped her by the shoulders. "What the hell? Why didn't you say something? I thought you were just lying around, digging up—whatever weird stuff it is you witches dig up in forests. Did you plan on staying here the rest of the night without saying anything?"

"I don't have much of a choice. I'm stuck! And my phone is in the spell box, which got crushed by the falling troll. I was prepared to die out here until you came along. And then your abs distracted me and I forgot to ask for help."

"Really?" He gave her the most unbelieving look ever and slapped a hand over his glittery abs. "*That's* your story?"

She nodded. "And I'm sticking to it."

"You're pinned, Valor! That only ever ends in death. How did this happen?"

"I was minding my own business, plucking some mushrooms—"

"Minding your own…? You were performing a spell!"

"Maybe."

"Valor! Even if you weren't, you've taken things." He gestured to the mangled tackle box. "Nothing should ever be taken out from the Darkwood. Especially not for magics that are not faery blessed."

"You wouldn't mind offering me a blessing or two right about now, would you?" she asked sheepishly.

Kelyn laughed softly. "I haven't such power."

"Stop laughing. It's not funny. I'm going to die here. I don't know how to get unpinned. My legs… They're getting sucked deeper and deeper. Kelyn…"

Now she surrendered to the worrying reality of imminent death. She gasped and heaved in breaths quickly. Was this what a panic attack felt like?

Kelyn gripped her by the shoulders and she had to crane her neck awkwardly to meet his delving gaze. In that moment, Valor wished she'd known about his affection toward her. He was a handsome man. And a kind one, from what she knew about him. Always volunteering around town, and he helped rehabilitate injured raptors from what she remembered Trouble telling her. The complete opposite of his boisterous and cocky older brother.

Curse her attraction to the bad boys.

"I can go for help," he said.

She grabbed his forearms, keeping him there before her. If he left her alone, she'd die. Already she had been consumed up to her thighs. "Get help from who? There's no one who can help me but a faery. You're a faery. Can't you do something? Your magic works in this forest."

He sighed heavily and shook his head. "I can fly and I've strength immeasurable and can even work some cool spells with my sigils, but I am mortal-realm-born. I've not half the power of those from Faery. And if you've been pinned by a faery tree, then you are in need of serious enchantment to get free. How long have you been here?"

"A couple hours? I came here around six."

"It's almost midnight, Valor."

"Shit. I'll be dead before morning."

"I won't let that happen."

He was sweet. But if he had no faery powers to defeat this pinning, she didn't know what he could do. She'd already insulted him once. She didn't intend to go to her maker having insulted him a second time. "Thanks. Maybe... Could you try my cell phone?"

"Where is it?"

"In my box."

Picking through the crushed plastic tackle box, he found the purple phone, but with a few taps at the cracked screen, he announced, "It's dead. Technology doesn't work here in the Darkwood. Hey, Blade's place is at the other end of the forest. I can run there and make a call—"

"No." She stretched out an arm, her fingers groping desperately. Kelyn's fingers threaded with hers. It was a natural clasp, something that felt hopeless yet bolstered her courage a little. "I don't want to be alone. Just stay with me, please?"

"Of course I will." He folded his legs and sat before her, not releasing her hand from his calming clasp. "We'll think about this. We'll come up with something."

"Actually, what I want you to do is listen to the things I need you to tell my friends."

Kelyn bracketed her face fiercely. "Don't talk like that. You will not die."

"Lying about my fate isn't going to change it. I did a stupid thing. The universe renders payment for stupidity."

"You were not stupid. Just...stubborn."

"So you've heard about me?" She tried a little laugh and it actually eased the tension between her shoulder blades. Valor blew out a breath.

And in that moment, when she knew death was her only option, she decided she couldn't walk out of this world without one last thing. "Kiss me," she said suddenly.

"What?"

"You want to, don't you? I mean, if you had a thing for me?"

"I did, but..."

"Please, Kelyn? I want the last thing I remember to be a kiss from a handsome man. I want to be held in strong arms. I want to know passion—"

And he kissed her. The sudden connection seared a delicious heat onto Valor's lips. Kelyn's arm wrapped across her back as he slid down onto the moss beside her and pulled her in tightly against his hard body. His other hand clutched at her hair. Hungrily she took from him, falling into his sweet taste, his open and easy manner. He felt like something she'd always wanted but had never known to ask for.

Why had she never noticed he'd been attracted to her?

Because she'd been too busy tagging along with the bad boys. Or those men who could only ever consider her one of the guys.

When he parted from her, their eyes lingered upon each other, as if to look away would end the kiss, their connection—her life. So they held gazes in the quiet darkness, dappled by a beam of moonlight that sifted through the latent troll dust in the air about them.

The squeezing pressure about her thighs moved higher, yet all Valor could do was whisper, "Wow."

Kelyn nodded. He touched her lips and held his fingers there for the longest time. She closed her eyes to fix this moment forever. She must. She would die with the taste of his kiss on her mouth.

"Best kiss I've ever had," he said.

She nodded and closed her eyes even tighter, fighting tears. Damn right it had been the best.

"Ah, shit."

That remark sent a frozen chill up her spine. Valor could feel Kelyn's sudden tension and she knew they were not alone. *Please don't be another troll*, she thought. Slowly she opened her eyes to see the pair of red irises that loomed over the two of them.

Chapter 2

Kelyn stepped before Valor, protecting her from the demon who had appeared in the forest. It was one of the Wicked; Kelyn knew that because the creature had red eyes. The Wicked were faeries who possessed demon heritage. Demons were looked down upon in Faery, and so the Wicked were condemned and ridiculed. This one must have been ousted from Faery. Not an uncommon thing.

Seeming to blend with the shadows that angled between the thin moonbeams, the demon topped Kelyn by a head, yet its narrow shoulders, clothed in frayed black, were deceptive in that most demons were strong and quite capable of standing up to any opponent.

"We mean you no harm," Kelyn said coolly, yet maintained a sharp edge. He set back his shoulders. He would not be defeated by a demon. "I've no prejudice against any of your kind. Move along."

"Prejudices," the demon said in a slippery tone. The dark-faced entity smirked, its black lips crimping. "You ascribe to prejudice simply by mentioning it. Unwanted one."

Kelyn did not flinch at the moniker. He'd never been allowed access to Faery. His mother was a faery and his father a werewolf. Because he'd been born in the mortal realm, Faery was not open to him. Though he'd always pined to go there. To learn about his true heritage.

The demon tilted a look toward the ground, taking in Valor, pinned to the forest floor by the elder oak. "Looks like she's in a pinch."

"Nothing we can't handle," Kelyn said. "Right, Valor?"

"Uh, yep. We're good!"

"A witch and a faery," the demon said. "Pretty." He narrowed his gaze at Kelyn's neck, where he always wore two talismans on leather cords. "Interesting. You've been to Faery?"

"No," Kelyn answered.

"But that talisman." The demon tapped his own neck.

"A gift. Now, enough of this. Begone with you!"

"Very well. But you'll never get her loose. She's been pinned through to Faery."

"How do you know? What does that mean?" Valor rushed out.

"It means you must be unpinned *from* Faery," the demon explained.

Sensing the demon wasn't so much being helpful as teasing at the dreadful future that awaited Valor, Kelyn did not relent in his stance before her and only wished he'd brought along his bow and arrows this evening. But he could take this dark creature. Easily.

The demon eyed Kelyn's clenched fist. "You said you meant me no harm."

"I'll do what I must to defend her."

"Touching. The dying witch has a faery champion."

"Leave!" Kelyn said. "Take your smirk into the shadows and let us figure this out alone."

"As you wish." The demon stepped back and spread his elongated hands out before him. "But, unlike you, I have access to Faery. I can get into Faery and unpin her. If you wish it."

Valor didn't say anything, and Kelyn was thankful she hadn't rushed to beg the demon for the help.

But really? If the Wicked could get Valor unpinned, he'd be willing to do anything. Even take a few spiteful punches, if necessary. Because Valor's life was at stake. And she hadn't much time remaining. Her hips were beginning to sink into the ground.

"You tell me true?" Kelyn asked.

The demon nodded. "I am not heartless. And…you have something I want." Again the demon's eyes glanced across Kelyn's chest where the talismans hung.

Of course such assistance would not be provided without recompense. Which was fair enough, Kelyn thought. He felt Valor's hopeful breaths taint the air. She needed rescue and he would not leave this forest without her in his arms. Alive.

"What might that be?" Kelyn asked the sly demon.

The demon smiled and walked before him, turning in a half circle before coming around to face them both and saying, "Your wings."

"No!" Valor yelled from behind Kelyn.

"That's the deal. Take it or leave it," the demon said.

"We don't—"

"Valor," Kelyn said to shush her. "Be still."

"You can't give him your wings. They are what make you…you! That's a terrible thing to ask in trade for—"

"For a life?" the demon interjected. "Seems more than fair to me. But if you're not keen on breathing, witch, then so be it."

The demon's eyes glimmered vivid pink. He was preparing to flash out of the forest as swiftly and quietly as he had appeared.

"Wait!" Kelyn reacted from his heart and soul, not his better senses. "You can have them."

The demon smiled.

"Absolutely not!" Valor punched the ground with an ineffectual fist.

Kelyn turned to face her, and the spill of tears down her cheeks startled him. Wasn't she the feisty tomboy of the group of witches who owned a local brewery? The one who hung around with Sunday and fixed cars and motorbikes, and never met a greasy engine she didn't want to take apart?

Or so he'd heard. He'd made it a point to listen when Valor was spoken about. Because he had lusted after her. Had wanted to ask her out. And almost did. Until… Trouble.

But with the lingering taste of her kiss still on his lips, he couldn't deny that those feelings had not grown any lesser.

"You are not going to sacrifice your wings for me," Valor said on a desperate pleading tone. "Just go! Get out of here!"

"And allow you to die? I am a better man than that. It's not my nature to walk away when I can help."

"Help? No! Just no! I couldn't live with myself if you gave up your wings to save me."

"Well, you're going to have to."

He tugged his ankle away from her grasping, pleading hands and turned to the demon. With an inhale that shivered through his system and tweaked at his back between his shoulder blades where his wings could unfurl, he grasped decisiveness. "We have a deal. But you will promise you'll go immediately to Faery and unpin Valor."

"With your wings in hand, my entrance to Faery will be secured. The moment you hand them over to me, I will leave and unpin your tragic lover."

Kelyn almost said "She's not my lover," but semantics were less important than getting this cruel task completed. Because to sacrifice his wings would be like handing over himself. He'd become lesser. Not even the faery he was now. He would lose...

Kelyn held out his hands. The violet sigils that circled his wrists were a match for those sigils on his chest. They were his magic. His strength. As were his wings.

But to walk away from a helpless woman when he had a means to save her?

"Do it," Kelyn said firmly.

The demon thrust out his arm, and in his blackened hand materialized a gleaming sword of violet light. "Kneel, faery."

Feeling the intense *sidhe* magic that emanated from the weapon shimmer in his veins, Kelyn dropped to his knees, his side facing the demon.

"No" gasped from Valor's lips.

Lips he'd kissed, and on which he'd tasted a sweet promise. But he must never taste that promise again. He couldn't bear it.

"Do it!" he yelled.

And his wings shivered as he unfurled them and stretched them out behind him into the fresh spring air. Moonlight glamorized the sheer violet appendages, glinting in the silver support structure that held a close resemblance to dragonfly wings.

The violet blade swept the night. Ice burned through Kelyn's body as blade met wing, bone, skin and muscle, and severed each of the four wings cleanly from his back. Overwhelmed by a searing agony, Kelyn choked back the urge to scream and dropped forward onto his elbows. His fingers dug deep into the cool moss. He gritted his jaw, biting the edges of his tongue.

Behind him, Valor screamed.

He wasn't aware as the demon gripped his severed wings and, in a shimmer of malevolence, flashed out of the Darkwood.

Bile curdled up Kelyn's throat. His stomach clenched. His wingless back muscles pulsed in search of flight. Clear ichor, speckled with his innate faery dust, spilled over his shoulders and dribbled down his arms to the backs of his hands. The violet sigils about his wrists glowed and then…flashed away, leaving his skin faintly scarred where the magical markings had been since birth.

The witch muttered some sort of incantation that felt like a desperate blessing wrapped in black silk and tied too tightly for Kelyn to access.

He wanted to scream. To die. To curse the witch. To curse his own stupidity.

But what he instead did was nod and suck back the urge to vomit. The task had been done.

He would not look back.

Suddenly Valor's body lunged forward, her hands landing on his bare feet. The tree roots had spat her up, purging her from the earth. She scrambled over them alongside him. The demon had kept his word, unpinning her from the Faery side.

Good, then. His sacrifice had been worth it.

"Oh, my goddess. Your wings." Valor gasped. "I… Kelyn?"

"Go," he said tightly.

"What?"

"Leave me, witch! Get out of this forest and never return. This is not a place for you. Be thankful for your life."

"Yes, but—I'm thankful for what you've—"

"We will never speak of this again," he said forcefully. Still, he crouched over the mossy ground, unwilling and unable to twist his head and face the witch. "Please, Valor," he said softly. "Go."

If she did not leave, he would never rise. He didn't want her to see him wingless and broken. Hobbled by his necessity for kindness, to not abandon a condemned woman.

"You need someone to look after those wounds," she said. "I might be able to find a proper healing spell if you'll walk out of here with me."

"I need you to leave," he insisted sharply. "I will walk out of the Darkwood on my own. When I am able. Do you understand?"

He sensed she nodded. The witch's footsteps backed away from him. She uttered a sound, as if she would again protest, and then the soft *cush* of her boots crushing moss moved her away from him.

And Kelyn let out his breath and collapsed onto the forest floor.

Chapter 3

Two months later

Valor walked down the street, her destination was the gas station on the corner. She had a craving for something sweet and icy that at least resembled food and that would probably give her a stomachache. It was what she deserved.

When she spied the classic black Firebird cruise by, she picked up her pace and then halted on the sidewalk but a dash from the parking lot where the car had pulled in to stop before a hardware store. That was Kelyn Saint-Pierre's car. His brother Blade had fixed up the 1970s' vehicle with spare parts and a wicked talent for auto body reconstruction. She knew it was Kelyn's car because she'd been trying to speak to him for months. Ever since their harrowing encounter in the Darkwood.

When he had sacrificed his wings for her.

She wanted him to know she had not taken that sacrifice lightly. That it meant something to her. But she didn't have a clue how to tell him that. To not make it sound like a simple yet dismissive "Hey, thanks." And she'd been racking her brain for ways to repay him. But how did one offer something equal to the wings that were once his very identity?

She'd researched faeries and their wings. Wings were integral to their existence; when faeries lost them, they lost so much more. Like their innate strength and power. And sometimes even the ability to shift to small size, as the majority of faeries could do. And Kelyn could never again fly.

The man had to be devastated. And now, as she watched him get out of his car and stride toward the hardware store, Valor couldn't push herself to rush after him. But she had to. She owed him.

A tight grip about her upper arm stalled her from taking another step toward apologizing to Kelyn. Valor turned and shrugged out of Trouble Saint-Pierre's pinching hold. Built like an MMA fighter, the man exuded a wily menace that also disturbed her need to give him a hug. They had once been friends.

Had been.

"What?" She rubbed her arm. He hadn't been gentle.

"You looking to talk to my brother?"

"Yes," she said defensively.

Bravery sluiced out of her heart and trickled down to puddle in her combat boots. Trouble was the sort of man who could be imposing even when asleep. The two of them had once been drinking buddies. Now he avoided her as much as Kelyn did.

"I have to—"

"No, you don't," he interrupted with that gruff but commanding tone that warned he meant business. "You stay the hell away from my brother. You've done him enough damage."

"But I want to apologize. I know I've hurt him. Trouble!"

He shoved her aside and strode toward his brother's car, but as he stalked away, he turned and thrust an admonishing finger at her. And Valor flinched as if he'd released magic from that accusing fingertip.

She would not give up. There had to be a way to get Kelyn's wings back for him. And she wouldn't rest until she did.

Two months later

It had now been four months since that fateful night in the forest, and Kelyn had survived the loss with his head held high and his dignity intact. He could no longer shift to small size, nor could he fly. The faery sigils had disappeared from his wrists and chest, rendering his magic ineffective. But he still had his dust and—well, that was about it. His strength? Gone. When once he could beat Trouble at arm wrestling in but a blink, now his brother did his best not to win, even though Kelyn knew he was faking.

And he'd lost his connection to nature, which had once been as if his very heartbeat. Senses attuned to the world, he'd navigated his surroundings by ley lines and had listened to the wind for direction and tasted water in the stream for clues to weather and more. As a result of losing his wings, he now always felt lost.

But he wouldn't bemoan his situation or complain or

even suggest to others what a terrible life he now had. Because he was thankful for life. Such as it was.

Sitting in the corner of the local coffee shop, nursing a chai latte, he scanned the local job advertisements in the free paper he'd grabbed before walking inside. Much as the Saint-Pierre children had never needed to work, thanks to their parents' forethought to invest for each of the five of them when they were born, he now needed... something. He hadn't volunteered at The Raptor Center since losing his wings. It felt wrong to stand in the presence of such awesome nature and feel so lacking. And with the proper care, those birds could heal and then fly away. Something he could never hope to do again.

So, what could a faery who wasn't really a faery anymore do with himself? His utter uselessness weighed heavily on his shoulders. He needed to do something. To move forward, occupy his thoughts and forget about what haunted him every second of every minute of every day.

Lately, he wasn't even interested in women. Because though he never revealed he was faery to the mortal women he had dated, he still felt different. Set apart. And he couldn't get excited about going to a bar or dancing or even a hookup when that missing part of him ached.

It did ache. His back, where his wings had been severed, put out a constant dull throb. Always reminding him of the wings he once had.

Closing his eyes and tilting his head back against the café wall, he zoned out the nearby conversations and set the paper on the table. He needed a new start. But he wasn't sure what that implied or how to go about it. Two of his brothers were werewolves involved with their packs. No faeries allowed. And while his interests had tended toward the martial arts and archery, he didn't feel inspired.

When a rustle at his table alerted him, he didn't open his eyes. It was probably the barista refilling his chai. She did it at least twice on the afternoons he parked himself here in the sunny corner away from the restrooms and bustle of the order line.

But when he didn't smell the sweet spices of fresh chai infusing the air, he opened one eyelid. And sat up abruptly, gripping his empty paper cup and looking for an escape route.

"Kelyn, please, give me two minutes. Then I'll leave. Promise."

Valor Hearst sat across the small round table from him, her palms flat on a half piece of blue paper that hadn't been there before. Every hair on Kelyn's body prickled in anger and then disgust. And then…that deep part of him that had compelled him to protect her in the forest emerged and he relaxed his shoulders, allowing in a modicum of calm. And desire.

He nodded but didn't speak.

"Trust me," she said, "I've been wanting to speak to you ever since…" She looked aside, as did he. No one in the town knew what paranormal secrets the two possessed. "But I was scared. And so freaked. And then your brother told me to stay away from you. But I was determined. And now I have it."

She patted the blue paper. "I know how to get your wings back."

"First…" Valor shifted on the metal café seat, uncomfortable and nervous. The blond faery eyed her with a mix of what she guessed was anger and revulsion. Well deserved. "I'm sorry."

"Don't—" he tensed his jaw for a moment, then finished "—say that."

"But I am. Kelyn, I'm sorry for what happened in the forest. It was my fault. I am so grateful to you. And you shouldn't have done it. You should have let me die. I'm just…so, so sorry."

"It was a choice I made. You did not influence me or have a part in that decision one way or another. So stop saying sorry."

"Fine. I'll stop with the *s* word. But listen to me."

"You have approximately thirty seconds remaining of the requested two minutes."

So he was going to be a stickler? Again, his annoyance was well deserved.

"I can help you get back your wings," she said. "I found a spell to open a portal to Faery. It merely requires collecting a few necessary ingredients, and then, voilà! We're in!"

"*We're* in?" He calmly pushed aside the paper cup and leaned forward so they could speak in confidence. Valor smelled his fresh grassy scent and wondered if it was a faery thing or just innately him. Never had a man smelled so appealing to her. And generally a little auto grease or exhaust fumes was all it took for her. She was glad he hadn't stormed out of the café yet. Which he had every right to do. "Do you think I have the desire to trust you?" he asked. "To work alongside you in a fruitless quest? To…to breathe your air?"

She had expected him to hate her. So his harsh words didn't hurt. That much. Yes, they hurt. But they could never harm her as much as she had hurt him.

"I think you should do everything in your power to bring me down," she offered to his question regarding why he should care. "To expose me to humans, if that's your thing. Whatever you do, you have every right to hurt me in return."

"I don't hurt women. I don't take vengeance against one who has not moved to harm me in the first place. I don't…want to believe your silly magic can do as you say."

"My magic is not silly."

"It got you pinned in the Darkwood."

"Yes, well, state the obvious. That was my constant need to prove how stubborn I can be, not my magic. I know now to stay away from that place. By all that is sacred and the great Doctor Gregory House, I have learned my lesson." She tapped the blue paper on the table and leaned in again to speak in quieter tones. "But this spell…it's ancient. I know its source. It will work, Kelyn. Please, give me a chance to help you get back what was taken from you. I want to help you."

"I don't need your restitution, witch." He stood and grabbed the cup. Turning, with a toss, he landed it in the wastebasket eight feet away near the counter display of half-price cookies.

Valor jumped up to stand before Kelyn, blocking his exit. Yet she stood as a mere blade of grass before his powerful build and height. "That kiss you gave me when I thought I was going to die?"

He tilted his head, his eyes—violet, the color of faeries—showing no emotion.

"It changed me," Valor confessed. "I can't say how. It won't matter to you. But it did. And I haven't stopped trying to find the answer for you since then." She pressed the paper to his chest, but he didn't take it, so she tucked it lower, in the waistband of his hip-hugging gray jeans. "Read it. It's a list of ingredients required to conjure the portal spell. When you're ready to give it a try, you know where to find me."

And she turned and walked out, forcing herself not to look back. To call out to him to please make life easier for her by allowing her to try and make his life what it once was. She hadn't told him that she hadn't gone a single night without reliving that kiss before exhaustion silenced those wistful dreams. And that she wished everything had been different, that she'd never entered the Darkwood on her own personal yet fruitless quest. A quest that hadn't been accomplished, and one she'd not dared to attempt since.

When the universe spoke, she listened.

Kelyn Saint-Pierre was a remarkable man. And she might have blown her chances of ever having him trust her. So she crossed her fingers and whispered a plea to the goddess that he might want to give the spell a try. For his sake.

And, okay, for her peace of mind, as well.

The witch left a trail of sweet honey perfume in her wake. Kelyn had heard she was a beekeeper and had, more than a few times, almost gotten up the courage to visit her and ask about beekeeping. Before, that was.

Before was the only way to define his relationship with Valor now. Before he'd lost his wings, and before she'd hooked up with Trouble. Before was when he'd crushed on her and had wanted to ask her out. *Now* was, well, now everything was After. Which was a ridiculous way to go through life.

Why couldn't he put the witch out of his brain and move forward?

He knew the answer to that. And it was probably scrawled on the piece of paper that she'd tucked in his jeans. He tugged it out and crumpled it into a ball. Raising his arm to make a toss toward the wastebasket, he suddenly curled his fingers about the crunchy paper.

The answer as to why he couldn't move forward was that he wasn't done with her yet. They'd been thrown together in the Darkwood by forces beyond their control. And ever since that day, he hadn't been able to *not* think about her. He thought about that desperate kiss. A lot. It had been different from any other kiss he'd taken or had been given by a woman. Weirdly claiming. And achingly right.

He'd never felt that way about a kiss before. Of course, that was Before. Now, if he couldn't accept himself, how could he possibly accept another person into his life, no matter if it was to help him find something lost or for something so simple as another kiss?

He wanted to be brave like his brothers. To be looked up to and admired by women, also like his brothers. He wanted to know his place in this world and walk it with confidence. While all his life he'd found himself standing to the side watching his brothers, until his wings had been stripped away, he'd never felt this heavy weakness and lack that he now did.

Stryke and Trouble were strong, virile werewolves. His brother Blade was a vampire who had a touch of faery in him. Blade even had a set of dark wings. But he hadn't brought them out in Kelyn's presence since he'd lost his wings. Even his sister, Daisy Blu, possessed a strength he admired.

What was he without wings? Self-acceptance was impossible without those very necessary parts of him. They were limbs. And a man who lost a limb truly did lose a part of himself.

Walking outside the café, he uncrumpled the blue paper ball and spread it open. On the top was written in red ink *To Invoke a Portal Sidhe* and below that an ingredient list. Werewolf's claw, water from an unruly lake, a kiss from a mermaid, occipital dust from the Skull of Sidon and true love's first teardrop.

Sounded like a whole lot of bullshit to him. What, exactly, was an unruly lake? But he knew witch magic was weird and steeped in millennia of practice and tradition. And while faeries in the know could access their homeland by opening a portal in a manner to which Kelyn was not privy, there probably did exist a spell to open a portal by other means. And his mother, while she had been born in Faery, had come to this realm decades earlier and could not return, so he hadn't bothered to ask her help. No need to worry her uselessly.

But what, then? Just wander into Faery and collect his wings from the Wicked One to whom he'd freely given them? He'd made a deal: his wings for unpinning Valor. He wouldn't renege on a deal.

As he'd said to Valor, it wasn't her fault. He'd made the choice to make such a sacrifice all by himself.

Eyeing the steel mesh garbage can that stood before the café on the sidewalk, Kelyn held a corner of the blue paper. A soft wind fluttered it like…a wing.

Gulping down a swallow, he shoved the paper in a back pocket and strode toward his car.

A week later

Kelyn still hadn't contacted her. Valor set aside the tin smoking can and leaned against the cinder block wall that edged the rooftop where she kept three stacked beehives. The smoke kept the bees docile so she could check that the queens were healthy and laying eggs. This fall she would have to separate the hives because they had expanded. She'd end up with five hives, which was awesome. And while bees that lived in the city tended to create a diverse and delicious honey, she was rapidly running out of space. She needed a country home, like her beekeeping mentor, Lars Gunderson, where she could manage a larger quantity of bees.

The sun was bright and she needed to cool off, so she left the smoker on the roof and skipped down the iron stairs to her loft. It was set on the third floor of an old factory building. The lower two levels were currently being refurbished and remodeled into apartments. When she'd moved in years earlier, the place was private and vast. But with neighbors soon to occupy the lower floors and the whole neighborhood turning yuppie, her desire to start looking at country real estate increased.

Tugging the heavy corrugated steel door, which was set on a rolling track like a barn door, she shut it behind her. She pulled off the white button-up shirt she'd pulled on over her fitted gray T-shirt. Dark colors attracted bees and angered them, so she always wore white to the roof.

She whistled. Mooshi popped his head up from behind the couch, moving ever so slowly on his adventure through the wild. Cats. So independent sometimes she had to wonder who owned who.

Running her fingers through her hair, she vacillated between bending over the spell books she had to search for a possible coercion spell and calling Sunday to see if she wanted help today with modifying the '67 Corvette Stingray engine. Valor was on a two-week vacation from the brewery, which she appreciated but also always found hard to comply with.

How to get Kelyn to pay attention to her and at least give her a chance at the spell? And why couldn't she simply let this go?

"Restitution," she muttered. The word he'd used so cruelly against her.

Yes, she wanted to pay him back for the horrible thing that had happened *because of her*. No matter what kind of spin he put on it, if she had not been in that position in the Darkwood, he would never have been faced with having to sacrifice his wings.

"What should I do, Mooshi?"

A rap at her door decided for her. "That's what I'll do." She would answer the door.

Maybe it was Sunday. Her best friend, a cat shifter, had promised to stop by one day this week with some red velvet Bundt cakes from the new café in town and a whole lot of car chatter. Sunday was one of her few female friends. Most often Valor got along with men because… she was just one of the guys.

She slapped a hand to her chest. No, she wasn't going to recall that awful thing that had been said to her. The words that had sent her into the Darkwood on a desperate mission.

She was over that now. For good or for ill.

"Definitely not good," she muttered, and tugged open the sliding door.

Kelyn stood before the threshold holding the blue half sheet of paper on which she'd scrawled the spell ingredients. He raked his fingers through his messy hair and met her gaze with his piercing violet eyes. "Let's do this."

Chapter 4

Kelyn followed the witch into a familiar loft. She gestured for him to sit by the industrial steel kitchen counter that stretched a dozen feet and served as a divider between the cooking area and the rest of the vast, open space that made up half the upper floor of an old three-story business building. The businesses had vacated decades ago, and apartments were slowly taking over. Hipsters and yuppies and, apparently, witches, had moved in.

"This used to be my sister, Daisy Blu's, place," he remarked as he slid onto a wooden stool and crossed his arms. Looking over the loft, he recalled that Daisy's decorating sense had been nil, and Valor's wasn't much more evident. Though she did have a motorcycle sitting in the corner before the eight-foot-high windows that overlooked the street. A street bike. Its back fender sat beside it on the floor, and a black metal toolbox sprawled tools beside that.

"Yep. When Daisy moved in with Beck a couple years ago, I grabbed this place. Love it. And the freight elevator fits my bike."

"Nice. So you have no desire to live in Anoka, closer to the brewery?"

"Do you know that Anoka is infested with ghosts? And I have an affinity for seeing ghosts. So not cool. I prefer Tangle Lake. Just far enough away from the suburbs, but I can still get to work in half an hour."

"What is that noise?"

"I'm vacuuming. You should see it swing around soon. It's over behind the bed right now."

"One of those robotic things?"

"Yes. I am allergic to housework, so I have my cat do it."

"Uh-huh." He wasn't even sure where to start with that one, so decided to drop it for now. And a cat? Yeesh. Not his favorite domesticated animal.

Kelyn turned toward the counter to find Valor leaning on it with her elbows. If he were not mistaken, he should take that wide-eyed, dreamy gaze as somewhat smitten. But he probably was mistaken. Reading women was his forte. But reading witches? Not.

"So, this list." He shoved the wrinkled blue paper he'd kept toward her. "That's it?"

"And a few more essentials that are required for most spells. Herbs. Crystals. Rat skulls and angel dust. But I've got all that stuff."

"You have angel dust?" He knew that was a precious commodity and hard to come by.

"Sure. Got some from Zen, your brother's girlfriend. I used it for the spell in the—er...you want a beer?"

If he told the chick who worked at a brewery that beer—any kind of alcohol—wasn't to his taste, and he much preferred water, would that annoy her?

Why was he worried about annoying her? He had no stake in whether or not she liked or hated him. All that mattered was she had a plan to help him get back his wings.

"Just water, please."

She quirked a brow. Judging him. Whatever.

"Fine. I think we should collect the ingredients in the order I've written them for you." She filled a glass of water from the tap and handed it to him. "You know of any werewolves looking to donate a claw?"

"Not willingly. But Trouble does have a beef with a nasty bastard who keeps trying to mark my brother's territory as his own. I could ask him about it. And if you know Trouble..." And he knew she did.

"The guy likes a good fight."

"Always." And that was enough mention of his oldest brother. "So, once we get all these things and you invoke the spell, what, exactly, do we do in Faery?"

"Uh, find your wings?"

He stared at her for the few moments he thought it would take for her to rationalize that insane statement. But in the process, Kelyn got lost in a shimmery brown gleam. Her eyes twinkled like stars during twilight. It couldn't be real. He'd never seen such brilliant eyes before.

The witch snapped her fingers before his face, rudely bringing him up from what he realized was an open-mouthed gape. "Uh..."

"You don't want to find your wings?"

"I do, but Faery is immense. It's larger than…well, the world, I'm sure."

"It's another realm. I get that. But the reason I chose this spell over another that also opened a portal is that this one homes us in on the item we seek. If all goes well, we should walk in. See the wings. Grab them. And get the hell out of Dodge."

"Sounds too easy."

"Sounds like a fun ride on the wild side." She pulled open the fridge door and took out a beer, twisted off the cap and tossed that in a mason jar half-filled with bottle caps. The brown beer bottle sported the Decadent Dames label on the side. "So why don't you give Trouble a call?"

"Why don't you?" Kelyn asked.

Valor slammed the bottle on the counter. And he immediately regretted his accusing tone. "What do you think went on between your brother and me? Because if you think anything beyond friendship happened—"

"It doesn't matter." He cut her off because he didn't want to know. "You and I? We're just working together toward a common goal. What you do with your free time is not my business."

"You make it sound as if it bothers you. I can be friends with your family, Kelyn. I'm friends with Blade, too. And Daisy Blu. So get over yourself and don't get your wings in such a twist." She tilted back a swallow and then held the bottle to her chest. "Sorry. I shouldn't have said that."

"It's okay."

"No, it's not. You don't have any, uh…"

"Valor." Kelyn reached across the counter and

grasped her hand, which startled her so much she set down the beer. "We're good."

"How can you say that?"

"I just did. Two words. We're. Good. You don't owe me anything. You don't need to apologize. What happened was a result of a choice I made. And only I can live with that. You don't get to share that with me. And while it pretty much knocked the wind out of my sails, I'm still here. And I'm doing something about it now. So if you want to help me, then do your witchy thing and stop trying to take the credit for something you didn't do."

"I…" She exhaled heavily.

It had been difficult to say all that. Because really? Part of Kelyn did blame the witch. If she hadn't been in the Darkwood in the first place… But the wise, logical part of him knew that he'd had total control over what had happened in the forest that day four months earlier. And he was no man to put the blame on anyone else.

"Fine. I can do that. I mean, I want to do that," she said. "But please have patience with me because it's much easier to say than to do."

"I get that."

"I like you, Kelyn. You're a good guy. Faery. How are you without your wings? I need to know."

"I'm the same as ever. Except I can't fly, can't shift to small shape and I've the strength of a regular human man now. Otherwise? Peachy."

She began to frown, but he put up an admonishing finger. "Forward. For both of us. Okay?" He offered a hand for her to shake.

Valor shook it. "Deal. You call your brother. Let's go kick some werewolf ass."

"I'm cool with that—what?"

The rhythmic hum of the vacuum alerted Kelyn to the robotic disk that glided toward the kitchen. And on the back of the thing sat a plush gray cat. It cast a golden gaze up at Kelyn as it rode by, calm and regal upon its modern-day carriage.

Kelyn tugged up his leg in a protective move. "Seriously?"

"That's Mooshi," Valor said. "I told you the cat does the cleaning. He can ride that thing through the whole place. What's wrong? You don't like cats?"

"They're not my favorite critters." Kelyn again caught the cat's eye, but he read its expression as more of an I'm-bored-what-else-is-there-to-do? look than anything else. "Mooshi, master and commander of the hardwood seas. Who'da thought?"

Valor had suggested Kelyn first ask his brothers Trouble and Stryke if either wanted to donate a claw, but realized the error of her ways when the faery cast her a horrified gape. Right. That would be like cutting off a man's fingernail. But really? It *was* for a good cause. What was one fingernail when compared to a man's reason for existence?

So, instead, they decided to track down the werewolf Borse Magnuson, who was known as an all-around asshole and resident idiot. A few years ago he'd been involved in blood games, pitting starving vampires against one another in death matches. Creed Saint-Pierre, Kelyn's grandfather, had put an end to most of those illegal gaming dens. Now, lately, Borse had been trying to establish territory on Trouble's property to the north of Tangle Lake.

So their path led them to the oldest Saint-Pierre brother. And everything Valor read in Kelyn's body language as he neared his brother told her they were not right. She and Trouble, that was. Trouble told them to stop by the local gym and he met them as he was exiting the building. He wandered over to his monster Ford truck, painted in olive camo and sporting silver wolves on the mud flaps.

Valor went to bump fists with Trouble, but the man didn't oblige her. Right. Not speaking to her since Kelyn's wings had been taken. She caught Kelyn's tightened expression. What? Did the guy think she'd gotten it on with his brother? And why did that matter to him? *Oh.*

Assuming a casual stance, Valor grabbed her thick hair and, corralling it into a ponytail, swished it over her shoulder as a distraction from what she felt was a blush riding up her neck. Did Kelyn have some kind of thing for her? He'd mentioned as much in the Darkwood that dreadful night. He couldn't possibly. She was the witch who had changed his life for the worse.

And yet. There was something she had missed. And why hadn't she realized that until right now?

Bad attraction vibes, girl. So terrible at picking up on that one.

"You two are after Borse?" Trouble smacked a fist into his palm. "I want in."

"Trouble, this isn't a matter with which we need help. I just need some info on the guy. Weaknesses. Flaws. Favorite drinking holes."

"Wait, Kelyn." Much as she didn't want to pit brother against brother, Valor felt having a werewolf in the mix could help. And with Kelyn's strength waning? "Did you tell him *why* we're working together?"

Kelyn crossed his arms, lifting his chin defiantly.

When he went all serious, two frown lines appeared between his eyebrows.

No, he hadn't told his brother anything. And what kind of tension was she picking up on now? Yes, there was definitely something she had missed between herself and Kelyn.

"Can I tell him?" she asked carefully.

"Why the hell are you two even standing alongside each other?" Trouble asked. "I thought you never wanted to see her again."

"Those are words you put into my mouth, Trouble. I hold nothing against Valor."

"She was responsible for you losing your wings, man."

"It was my choice."

"I'm helping him to get his wings back." Valor rushed in before Trouble's bouncy stance turned into a one-two punch to the mean witch who had hurt his brother. The man had a tendency to react quickly and only ask the important questions after the pain had been delivered. "I have a spell that will open a portal into Faery. We need a few items for that spell. The first being a werewolf claw."

Kelyn's admonishing tilt of head was expected, but she couldn't worry about pissing off the faery any more than she already had done.

Trouble slammed his fists to his hips. "You trust her?"

"I do. And I suspect Borse will be perfectly fine with one less claw."

"You got that right. But you'll have to take it when he's shifted. He'll tear you apart, brother."

"Thanks for that vote of confidence."

"No, seriously, Kelyn. I know you are the toughest

and strongest of the Saint-Pierre boys. Or at least you were until…her."

Valor caught the werewolf's accusatory look, but she set back her shoulders and held her head high.

"You need help," Trouble said. "And if the witch can get back your wings, I'm all in for ripping Borse's claws out."

"We only need one," Valor reminded the guy, who, she had no doubt, would take off all ten of the werewolf's claws if given the opportunity. "Kelyn and I learned he's going out on the hunt tonight."

"Then we are, too," Trouble said. "But no witches allowed. This is a man's job."

"She's got magic," Kelyn said. "She's coming along."

They tracked Borse to the dive bar at the edge of Tangle Lake. It was a favorite watering hole for the Saint-Pierre brothers. The bartender knew Kelyn was always the designated driver and served him iced lemonade with a nod and a wink. Half a dozen humans lingered at the bar, a pair of them discussing the latest Twins game.

At the pool table, Borse commandeered a game to himself. He was drunk. And it generally took a lot of alcohol to get a werewolf drunk. The trio decided to wait and follow Borse out to his car before approaching him.

It felt wrong going after a drunkard. Even knowing what an asshole Borse was, Kelyn had problems using violence to get what he wanted. Completely the opposite of Trouble, who nursed a whiskey and eyed the dartboard. Kelyn had always won at darts against Trouble. He hadn't attempted a game since losing his wings. He didn't want to try now. He just didn't.

Beside him sat Valor, who'd passed on the lowbrow beer and instead had asked for a lemonade, as well. She wore a thigh strap with a blade in the holster. She'd said it was a ritual blade she used for her spells and would be best to remove the claw. She and Trouble hadn't spoken since they'd arranged to work together, and while Kelyn knew his brother had a stick up his butt about the witch after all that had happened, he was surprised he'd not picked up on any sort of weird sexual tension between the two.

Had Trouble lied about them getting it on? Valor had seemed defensive about just that, but Kelyn had cut her off, not wanting to listen to any excuses. The woman was an adult. She could have sex with whomever she wanted to.

The creaky bar door slammed and Trouble gave a short whistle to Kelyn. Borse had left, muttering something about vampires. The werewolf had parked down the street behind a chain-link fence and next to a rotting supply shed that sat at the edge of the city park. So they had the advantage of darkness and privacy.

"What the fuck?" Borse spun around at the approaching threesome. His stance wobbled, but he maintained an upright position. "Saint-Pierres, eh? That land isn't all yours, Trouble, and you know it."

Trouble punched a fist into his opposite palm and lunged for the man. The first smack of fist to jaw resounded through the park and scattered a flock of pigeons.

"Stay out of the way," Kelyn said, stepping before Valor, who had pulled out her *athame* in defense.

She didn't need to be told to avoid danger. But she didn't need to be protected, either. Especially not by the man who had once already—ah, yes. What was she thinking? Valor stepped back, giving Kelyn every bit of respect the man deserved. She had to be careful not to offend more than she already had done. A man's sense of pride was always a delicate thing.

It didn't take long for Borse and Trouble's scuffle to escalate, and as their antics moved them beneath a shadowed copse of willow, the men shifted. Shirts tore away, though they both had the sense to shift halfway. Keeping their lower halves in human shape ensured that they remained partially clothed. A necessity should an innocent wander onto the scene and a quick shift back to were form was required.

The two shifted wolves went at each other while Kelyn stalked close but did not step in to interrupt. Valor assumed they both knew what they were doing, so, holding her blade at the ready, she waited.

But would a little magic provide Trouble the advantage? Her air magic could make Trouble's punches move faster, his leaps more aggressive. If she could focus it to land only on him and not the other wolf...

"No," she admonished herself quietly. "Let the boys handle this one."

Grunts and growls accompanied the battle that seemed as if it would continue indefinitely. Valor cast Kelyn a questioning look. He returned a shrug and a nod. He got the hint.

Kelyn lunged for Borse and delivered a fist to his bloody jaw. Valor had heard the rumors about Kelyn. That one punch from him would put any man—or beast—down for the count.

Borse shook his head and smirked at Kelyn when he realized the faery was not as strong as rumor told. He grabbed Kelyn's arm even as Trouble swung a leg and took out Borse's stance. Both Borse and Kelyn went down.

And Valor clenched her fingers into her palms. She thrust out her arm, bending her fingers in preparation to release some air magic. Sucking in her lower lip, she bit, almost drawing blood. Cursing at the pain, she inhaled sharply when she saw the fighters roll to a stop. Kelyn landed on top of Borse, and Borse lay still. The thug wolf was out. But for how long?

Kelyn thrust out his hand, gesturing for her to hand the knife to him.

"Oh. Right." She rushed to him and slapped the hilt into his hand.

Trouble, in half his hulking furry glory, leaned over them. He smelled musky and hot. An animal riled. Valor didn't fear the man whose upper half resembled an über-muscled wolf, including a full wolf's head. The one she was concerned with now was Kelyn, and he—he had pressed the side of the blade to his forehead, as if in thought, and closed his eyes as he crouched over Borse.

"Kelyn," she said, "hurry! He could come to any second."

"I can't." He pushed himself up and stepped away from the fallen werewolf, walking a wide circle.

Trouble swiped a big, clawed paw for the knife, but Kelyn jerked it away from him. "Get out of here," he said to his brother. "I'm not going to do it. I can't."

"What? Do you need me to do it?" Valor asked. Her whole body shook. She was nervous and exhilarated and scared all at once.

"No, I mean I won't do this." He handed her the blade. "Who am I to harm another man for something I want? It's not a need, Valor. I *want* my wings back, but I'll survive without them. As deserving as he may be, I won't maim Borse just to make it so."

The werewolf on the ground stirred.

"Let's get out of here." Kelyn grabbed her by the upper arm and pushed her in the direction of the bar where they had parked his Firebird. "Trouble! Go!"

Trouble growled and snorted, but the werewolf took off in the opposite direction and loped through the park.

And while Valor was disappointed they'd not gotten what had been but a stroke of the blade away, she was even more impressed at Kelyn's sacrifice. Once again. And his honor.

He truly was a good man. And she was fortunate to know such a person.

They climbed into his car and watched through the chain-link fence for a while. To see if Borse would wander out in werewolf form, or perhaps man shape. And to make sure Trouble didn't return looking for the trouble he famously indulged in.

"I'm sorry," Valor said quietly.

Kelyn turned on her with a surprising rage in his eyes. "I am tired of your apologies. You did nothing wrong, witch!"

"Would you bring it down a notch? I was apologizing because I know you want your wings, and now getting them seems an impossibility. Would you let someone care about you? Seriously!" She gripped the door handle tightly. "You've more of a chip on your shoulder about letting someone in than about getting back your lost wings. What's your hang-up?"

"I don't have a hang-up, other than wondering why in Beneath I decided working with you would be a good idea."

"Because you trusted me."

"Trust had nothing to do with it. I'm here because you were my only hope."

"Sorr—" She cut off the apology. "Fine. I disappointed you."

"I was the one who refused to take the claw. It's all on me."

"Right. Do you thrive on the guilt, Kelyn?"

He cast her a condemning glare, which Valor felt at the back of her neck like an icy prickle over her skin. So maybe he wasn't as honorable as she'd surmised.

"Okay, not going to discuss that one," she said. "On to plan B. Do we have a plan B?"

"I do."

"Which is?"

Kelyn shifted into gear and the vehicle rolled over the tarmac. "There's a cabin about ten miles south from here. Belongs to a peller. My sister's husband, Beck, had a run-in with the owner a few years ago. The man...can time travel."

Valor shot him a glance, but it was too dark in the car to see his reaction to her sudden interest.

"I'm not so sure I believe in the time-travel stuff," he continued. "But he was also a wolf hunter. He hunts all sorts of species, actually. Anyway, the cabin is sometimes empty because he's gone. In another time."

"That sounds too cool, and at the same time, severely whacked."

"Yeah, but if the cabin is empty, I say we take a look around. If the guy hunts wolves, there could be...things."

"Like claws?"

She sensed Kelyn nodded. And Valor smiled. "You're in the driver's seat."

Chapter 5

Kelyn used the GPS on his phone to locate the farm-house he'd been to twice before. And that annoyed the crap out of him. Normally, he'd navigate ley lines to find his way or simply recall the directions and turns. The ability to do so had always been innately a part of him, aligned with the sigils he'd once worn on his body.

He did not want to think any more about the skills that giving away his wings had stolen from him.

"Denton Marx is a peller," he explained as he parked the Firebird on the gravel drive before the guy's place.

"A spell breaker," Valor confirmed. "They are generally good, bad or nasty. I'm guessing Marx was the nasty sort?"

Kelyn wobbled his hand back and forth. "Depends on whose story you listen to. He did some bad things for what he thought was a good reason. My sister, Daisy

Blu, suffered because of it. But her husband, Beck, who was under a curse that was killing him, gained back his life, so they both sort of won because of Marx. I'd call him situationally convenient." He peered out the window, eyes taking in the periphery. "Doesn't look like anyone is home."

The lot did appear abandoned. Massive willow trees hung over the unmown front yard that edged a gravel road. Tall grasses disguised the ditch and frothed along the narrow drive. The rambler-style house was dark, as was the garage. The forest grew thick right up to the back of the house, though Kelyn knew there was a shed beyond it.

He'd been here a few winters earlier with his brothers. Denton had sought Daisy Blu's werewolf soul to rescue his lost love who was trapped in another time, a witch who could time travel. And Denton also time traveled. Wonders never ceased. A soul had been a requirement to work a spell to breach time. The man had failed. Thankfully.

"I don't think he's around." Kelyn opened the door and thrust out a leg, sniffing at the air. Normally his senses were dialed up to ultra. But since losing his wings? Forget about it. "I don't scent any others beyond the wildlife and floras. Let's take a look out back."

Valor followed silently, which he appreciated. If anyone were on the premises, he didn't want to alert them that they had visitors.

Pressing his wrists together to invoke magic that would heighten his senses, Kelyn cursed under his breath and swung his arms away from each other. Even after four months, he still forgot about his missing sigils. And a twinge in the center of his back, between his shoulder blades, reminded him what a fool he had been. Could a man be too damned nice?

Obviously, he could.

The grass was dry and brown here behind the house, and his footsteps crunched even as he left the gravel drive. He hadn't come armed. He didn't want to call up any more bad mojo from the universe than his actions had already done.

He didn't consider this venture breaking and entering. Just…taking a look around. Surely Denton owed the Saint-Pierre family for the pain he'd put them through with Daisy Blu and Beck.

"How do you know this guy?" Valor asked quietly as she caught up and reached his side. They wandered over some old, rotted wood boards that had been placed on the ground as a sort of walkway leading to the shed.

"He almost killed my sister and her boyfriend. Of course, that was when Beck was cursed as the ghost wolf."

"I remember that! That was a couple years ago. There was an article in the local paper about a big white wolf roaming the area."

"Beck was cursed as that white wolf."

"Wow. And you're friends with this Denton guy?"

"Not officially." He stopped before the steel door to the shed, suspecting the security would be excellent for a man who might take frequent trips away—to completely different centuries. "But if anyone has a werewolf claw, it'll be this guy. Keep watch on the house, will you?"

"Larceny. Love it." Shoving her hands in her back pockets, Valor turned to face the house.

Satisfied there were no cameras attached to the outside of the building, nor any connected on the nearby yard lightpost, Kelyn jiggled the doorknob. It was a standard knob and lock. Nothing digital. He didn't have anything to pick the lock with, so…he stepped back and gave the door a fierce kick right beside the lock mechanism. It slammed inward with a loud bang and a plume of dust.

Valor turned and gaped at him.

He smiled at her and shrugged. "Some of my talents have less finesse than others."

"So it would seem." She walked in after him. "Nothing like making an entrance. I like it."

The shed was dark, but pale moonlight strained through a dirty glass window panel set into the roof. The paned glass stretched eight feet square. It was littered with fallen leaves, yet the center of the room was lit enough to make out the dirt floor and assorted items sitting about. A mounted full-bodied buck greeted them with eerie glass eyes, its ten-point rack gleaming like ivory.

"Yikes." Valor walked up to the taxidermied creature. It stood as high as she. She studied it from head to tail, then walked back up to look into its eyes. She stroked its nose, pausing with her palm flat on its fur. Bowing her head, she said, "I'm so sorry for you."

Her empathy hit Kelyn right in the heart. Any chick who cared for nature was all right by him. "You see? The guy is an asshole."

"Duly noted. This poor creature didn't deserve such an end. I hate trophy hunters. So let's take a look around. I'll look over here and you—" He'd already begun to explore the north wall. "Yep, you know what you're doing. So, are you prepared to leave the country?"

"What?" Kelyn brushed his fingertips over an assortment of knives and tools he assumed were taxidermy items. None were clean, which made him wonder about the man's methods. Trophies would be created and tended with care and clean instruments. Magical items, on the other hand, wouldn't require such surgical cleanliness. He called over his shoulder, "Why leave the country?"

"The next item on the list is in Western Australia. Lake Hillier. The pink lake."

"Pink?"

"Yeah, I think it's algae or something that colors it literally a bubble gum pink. We need water from that lake specifically."

"Right, the unruly lake. What is an unruly lake anyway?"

"Apparently, a pink one."

"Australia is a long flight."

"That it is. And...spendy."

He caught her anxious tone. "You mean you're not going to treat me to an adventure across the globe?"

"I can pay for my own ticket. I'm just hoping you'll pay for yours?"

"I can cover us both," he offered.

"No, I can take care of myself."

"Valor. Send me the flight details and an online link and I'll take care of it. Okay?"

She nodded and picked up an old, rusted spring-loaded trap that creaked as she turned it about. "This looks dangerous and it smells."

"Probably blood on it from whatever the man last trapped."

She dropped it with a groan.

Kelyn's hand landed on a dusty glass quart jar without a cover. He could feel the vibrations wavering out from within and he bowed his head over it, placing both hands on the glass. Thankful that his senses were not currently superreceptive, he could only imagine the pain he'd sense if they had been at normal capacity.

"What is it?" Valor walked up behind him and gasped at the sight of what he held. "That's a lot of claws. And big. Sure they're not bear claws?"

"No," Kelyn said with a swallow. "These are were-wolf." It pained him to think that his brothers had gone up against Denton. Yet they had survived. Thank the gods for that. "Take one," he said quickly.

Valor reached in and pulled out a black claw that was as thick as her finger and twice as long. Then she took another. "Two to be safe." And another. "And three—"

"No." He took one of the claws and tossed it back in the jar, wincing at the horrible vibrations of pain he felt with the quick connection. "We won't be greedy. Two is more than enough."

"Fine." She shoved the claws in her jacket pocket. "Let's you, me and Doogie Howser get the hell out of Dodge."

"Doogie Howser?"

She shrugged. "TV doctors. I got a thing for them."

"I don't understand."

"You don't need to. Let's skedaddle."

They strode toward the open door. When they were but four feet away, the door suddenly slammed shut in a cloud of dust. And the door edges began to glow orange.

"The peller has an inner protection spell activated," Valor said.

She spread her hands out before her, testing the vibrations that wavered out from the door. Turning and clasping the moonstone that hung around her neck, she sensed the spell stretching along the walls and the ceiling, enclosing them completely. She didn't judge it to be anything particularly dark, more just menacing.

Kelyn spread out his hands as if to read his surroundings as she had done. She wasn't sure how much faery magic he still possessed, if any. The sigils were missing from his wrists and in their place, silvery scars served as a cruel reminder. That had to suck.

"You got some magic to get us out of here?" he asked.

"Maybe."

"I do love a decisive woman."

"Aw, you love me?" Valor flicked him a flirty wink over her shoulder. "Find me something silver, will you?"

"Okay. There's gotta be silver in a werewolf hunter's cabin." Kelyn looked around.

The shuffling Valor suddenly heard, which should have been Kelyn pushing things around on the shelves, sounded—when she thought about it—more like... hooves.

She spun around to face the stuffed deer. Which was no longer inanimate. Its eyes glowed white and its obsidian hoof pawed the dirt floor.

"Kelyn!"

"Found something that looks like a silver arrowhead. Though it's corroded." He turned and saw the same thing she did. "No kidding?"

"Toss me the arrow. Or better yet. Can you—"

"Got it!" He lunged for the buck as the beast charged Valor. The faery leaped and landed on the deer's back, one arm wrapping about its wide, strong neck.

Valor dropped and rolled across the dirt floor, out of the animal's charging path. It didn't slow, bowing its head and aiming its magnificent rack at the closed door.

Kelyn stabbed at the beast, landing the arrowhead in its chest as its antlers collided with the door. The protection spell fizzled, bursting out brilliant orange flames from around the door. The steel door blew off the shed, and the deer raced through with Kelyn riding its back.

"Can't say I've seen anything like that before," Valor muttered as she stood and brushed the dirt off her jeans. "Cool."

She wandered through the door to find Kelyn standing before a stuffed deer. He tugged the arrowhead out of its chest. The magic that had reanimated the deer had ceased the moment it left the shed.

Valor marched over and smoothed a hand over the stuffed animal's nose. "No one will believe this."

"Welcome to my world." Kelyn tossed the arrowhead in the air and caught it smartly. "Let's get out of here. Can you fit the door back into the frame?"

"Seriously? After the mess we made in there, you think replacing the door...?"

He did have a way of challenging her right in the witchcraft with his castigating, yet also kinda sexy furrowed brow.

Summoning her air magic, Valor whispered a rising spell and the door lifted and slammed back into the frame. Not at all the gentle fit-back-into-the-door-frame action she had been going for, but... "It'll do. What are we going to do about that thing?"

He smoothed a palm over the deer's back. "I like to think Marx will have a hell of a time figuring this one out when he returns."

"I like your thinking."

They wandered back to the car at the end of the drive, and after getting in the car Valor tugged out her cell phone. She perused the Delta flight schedule while Kelyn drove out and headed back to Tangle Lake. He was using the GPS on his phone and she knew it drove him buggy. Faeries were natural navigators. Poor guy. But, much as she wanted to, she wouldn't bring it up or apologize.

A ten-minute cruise down the main highway brought the Firebird to the exit for Tangle Lake. It was late, and not a lot of cars were out and about. Valor didn't live far from the exit.

"There's a flight to Australia tomorrow afternoon," she said. "You know your credit card number?"

"I do. Book the tickets."

"Sounds like a plan. Flying over an entire ocean is not going to be as fun as tonight was."

"You're not much for flying?"

"That's putting it euphemistically. Okay, give me your number."

He relayed his number to her while parking before her building. The autoconfirm promised an email soon. When Valor opened the door and stuck out a leg, he grabbed her forearm, stopping her from leaving.

"Thanks for tonight," he said. "We work well together."

"That we do. Thanks for trusting me. This spell will work, Kelyn. I promise that."

He nodded. "I'll pick you up tomorrow a couple hours before the flight."

"See you then. Thanks!"

As the Firebird rolled away, Valor had to stop herself from giving a little wave in its wake. Like *hey, yeah, that* was *fun*. Just spending time with the guy had been fun. And watching him ride the deer? She had to tell her friends about that one.

With a sigh, she wandered toward her building. The feeling that she should have leaned over and kissed him in thanks for the adventure was strong. A missed opportunity. Generally, she was a take-life-by-the-horns-and-ride-it kind of chick.

She knew why she was skittish around Kelyn. Same reason she'd given up on ever finding love. Men didn't consider her a woman. She simply wasn't...

"A real girl," she said, and followed that with another heart-clenching sigh.

Had she been able to accomplish the spell that night in the Darkwood, would she be singing a different tune now?

Could Kelyn ever see her as a woman?

Because she wanted to kiss him again. No, she *needed* to.

Chapter 6

Valor sat up on the couch, blew the tangled hair from her face and…dropped back into a dead sleep, falling forward to land her face against the hardwood arm. That woke her up again. And this time she heard the pounding and insistent knock at her door.

"Valor?"

Sounded like Kelyn's voice. Why was he at her home…she glanced toward the windows…in the middle of the night?

Her eyelids fluttered and she dropped into sleep again, this time her head falling to the side and hitting the soft leather back of the couch.

A rude meow sounded and she shook out of sleep. "No. Need to sleep. Have…flight…in morning, Mooshi."

"Valor, are you ready to go?" Kelyn called from the other side of her front door.

"Go?" She glanced toward the kitchen, seeing beyond the row of beer bottles and that one empty vodka bottle— curse her weakness for the hard stuff—where the time flashed in bright green LEDs on the stove. "Marcus Welby! It's time!"

She dragged herself off the couch and scrambled to the door, opening it. Kelyn breezed in.

"We've got to go," he said. "The flight leaves in an hour and a half, and it takes forty-five minutes to get to the airport. What the—are you not ready to go?" He reached for her head, and though Valor dodged his touch, he managed to snag his fingers in her hair. And that was possible because of the tangles. "You're wearing the same clothes as yesterday. And…you smell like a brewery."

"Yeah? Well, I do work at a brewery, smart guy."

"Not yesterday."

"Fine! I couldn't sleep," she muttered, her tongue still heavy with sleep and the remnants of a good drunk. Hell, the drunk was still with her, bless the goddess. Because it was a necessity. "I hate flying, and I'm always nervous the night before. I haven't slept. And yet…I think I must have fallen asleep, like, half an hour ago. I am so wasted."

He caught her in his arms and held her upright. "You drink to relax?"

"Beer usually calms me. Vodka seemed to take off the edge."

"Couldn't you have cast a spell or something? Valor, we've got to go. You have your bags packed?"

She gestured toward the door, where one small carry-on backpack waited. She'd had the forethought to pack after Kelyn dropped her off last night when she wasn't so nervous. Now all she wanted to do was sleep.

"The flight is long. You can sleep when we get seated." He bent and suddenly Valor found herself flung over the man's broad and reassuringly strong shoulder.

A humiliating position, and yet… Nah, she could go with it. Especially since…

Kelyn chuckled at the witch's sudden snores. He grabbed her backpack and with a glance to the cat decided Valor had to have made arrangements for its care in her absence. Probably a neighbor would stop by. He slid the door closed behind him.

What a way to begin an adventure.

Kelyn accepted an offer of ice water from the stewardess and refused another white wine for his guest. They'd been in the air four hours, and Valor could snore with the best of them. She did not do sleep deprivation well. But if she had been nervous about flying, then it was good she was sleeping now. She'd managed to lift her head once while they were waiting to board, smiled at him and then her head had hit his shoulder.

And he was enjoying it. Because right now her head lay on his shoulder, and her hand had strayed to his chest. One finger touched his skin at the base of his neck. It was weirdly intimate, and yet not. She was just a friend. And he did mark her as a sort-of friend, not an enemy. They were working toward a common goal.

But he was seriously beginning to feel the old attraction to her again. Not that it had ever gone away. Losing his wings had honestly reduced his interest in her. But the chick was not like the rest of the women he had known or lusted after. She wasn't fussy or high maintenance. He couldn't imagine any woman he'd known allowing him to carry her into the airport, hair uncombed and T-shirt wrinkled, after a sleepless night on a bender.

Valor Hearst didn't do the makeup and hair thing. Her long straight hair had a deep violet tint to it. Had to be dyed. He wasn't sure if witches could have a natural color like that. His sister, Daisy Blu's, hair was pink, but that was natural from her faery heritage.

Valor dressed as if she was ready to hop on a Harley and ride off into the sunset. Everything about her was casual confidence and gotcha smirks. One of the guys.

But the thing that had sealed his attraction to her a few years ago? It had been one night around a bonfire when a bunch of friends had gathered at a city summer festival. Beer and s'mores had been in abundance, as well as lawn darts and cheap sparklers. Valor had been pointed out to him as one of the witches who owned a local brewery. He'd thought she was pretty in that one-of-the-guys kind of way. Because she had an ease around people and wasn't always fluffing her hair or checking her cell phone for texts from girlfriends. He hadn't given her too much eye time. Until she'd laughed. It had come out as an abrupt burst of sound and ended with a snort. Ignoring what anyone thought of her and proud to be herself.

Ever since, he'd spent more time looking at her. And wanting to ask her out so he could hear that crazy, obnoxious laugh again. And wondering how she'd be as a kisser. Damn good, now that he knew. But he wished it hadn't been because she'd thought she was dying that he'd gotten that kiss.

And now he still couldn't stop looking at her and allowing his fantasies to take hold.

Valor's lips were pale pink and plump. And they were so close to him. He wanted to touch them, but he held the water glass in one hand and his other arm was wedged beneath her sleeping body. So he'd take her in for as long as he could. And enjoy this quiet moment with a woman he wasn't sure was safe to lose anything more to. He'd given up his wings for her.

What more did he have left, besides his heart?

Valor woke without opening her eyes. Her body took a survey of her immediate surroundings—hard plastic seat and walls, tight confines, stale air, compressed sensation going on in her sinuses—and she determined she was on a plane. Not on the ground.

Mercy.

The thing about flying was that it was unnatural. Yes, even for a witch. Witches didn't fly on broomsticks or by their own power. Well, they could do both with the right kind of magic. Air magic. But she'd always avoided considering such study. And the cliché of the broomstick was just that. She preferred her feet to remain on the ground. And even though there had been no other option to get where they were going—a ship would have taken far too long—it was never easy to dispel her nerves.

Fortunately, the alcohol had worked for a while.

Now groggy but feeling rested, she came awake more fully and curled her fingers against the hard warmth beneath her hand. Mmm, that felt great. And her pillow was firm but smelled nice. Like a forest after the rain. Why was that? Weren't airplanes the least inviting and uncomfortable conveyances in existence?

"You rest well?"

The voice vibrated against her cheek and into her very

bones, and Valor realized what exactly was up. She was lying on Kelyn, her cheek pressed against his shoulder. And that warmth under her hand? It was his hard pec. The man had to work out. Seriously.

Such a surprising but welcome bit of reality proved beyond nice. And she didn't want it to end. But really? This accidental sharing and caring between the two of them was not cool. On a scale of not-coolness, from one to ten, her current position probably topped out at an eight.

Maybe if she didn't move, he'd think she'd fallen back to sleep?

The smell of roast beef suddenly wafted through the air and Valor realized she was more hungry than embarrassed. So she slowly pushed herself up and met Kelyn's smiling violet gaze. "Morning."

"Evening, actually. At least, according to Australian time. But don't get too excited. We've still got another six hours to go."

"Ah, Meredith Gray!"

"Is she a doctor?"

"Yes, *Gray's Anatomy.* She and McDreamy—oh, never mind." She averted her eyes to the leather cords around his neck. A long, thin white spiral dangled from one of them. Looked like a seashell. On the other was a black ring of stone. She tapped it. Six more hours? Could a witch get a break? "Maybe I should go back to sleep."

"I take it you wish you could sleep through the whole flight? Maybe one more beer would have done the trick?"

She groaned. "Please don't mention beer. It was the vodka that did it for me. The beer makes me want to…"

Pee a very long time. She wouldn't say that. She and he were not that tight as bros yet.

"Aren't you hungry?" he asked. "They're serving now. Might keep your thoughts from…dire things."

"Yeah, maybe." She leaned back and slowly took her hand from his chest. "Sorry about that. Lying on you and all."

"It's all right. And you didn't drool that much."

"I—" She wiped her mouth and hoped to catch his teasing laugh, but he merely shrugged. Perfect. Not. "Really sorry about that one."

"Valor, your apologies are always superfluous. Now tell the nice stewardess what you'll have to eat."

When Valor turned to the flight attendant, she only then realized the luxurious space she sat in. It was still the inside of a tin can, but much more roomy than she'd experienced that one other time she was inside an airplane. They were in first class? Mercy, but she could never afford this ticket. And she did intend to pay the guy back.

"I'll take the roast beef," she said to the attendant, who sported a perfect blond coif and a red scarf tied about her neck. Valor refused the offer of alcohol. She'd drunk a whole growler of beer last night. Or this morning. Or whenever. Plus the bottle of vodka. Those two alcohols should not be mixed. Stupid nerves. "And some ginger ale."

Kelyn asked for the vegetarian plate and more water.

Fifteen minutes later, and after a necessary trip to the bathroom, the meal had served to relax Valor and she settled back to watch Kelyn finish his dairy-free chocolate cake. It didn't sound appetizing, but it certainly looked lush and moist. He was a vegetarian? Must have been disgusted by her shoveling in the minimal bits of roast beef she'd dug out of the gravy. He'd not said anything, though.

"Why are you so nice?" she asked.

He paused, a forkload of cake suspended before his mouth. With a shrug, he offered, "It's a Minnesota thing."

"Sure, but that's surface. And I'm from Minnesota." She pointed to her chest. "Not so nice. Mostly. People are always nice to one another, but are they *kind* nice? *Nice* is doing so because you think it's expected of you. Or because your mommy always told you 'be nice.' *Kind nice* is an innate calling to understand others and be accepting of them. That's you."

"I get that. I'll cop to kind nice eighty percent of the time. But flattery will not get you a piece of this cake. I'm eating it all myself." He forked in an appealing bite of layered chocolate frosting and cake. "See? Not so nice now, am I?"

She pouted about that. She'd wolfed down her dry cinnamon crumble so fast she hadn't even tasted it. So she enjoyed a good meal. And this first-class stuff? Not too shabby, if sparse on the meat.

"I'm no nicer than the next guy, Valor. I'm just trying to walk through this life and world respectful of all those who have as many trials and tribulations as myself."

"Yeah? What's it take to piss off a guy like you?"

"Why do you want to piss me off?"

"I don't. I'm just wondering what it takes. You can't be nice all the time. Seriously. Be honest about the remaining twenty percent. If you had one day in Trouble's shoes and could punch whoever or whatever because your temper flared as easily as his, what would it take to set you off?"

Kelyn set down the fork beside the half-eaten cake and rubbed the heel of his palm across his brow. "I guess it would have to be someone who harms another for malicious reasons."

"Like a bully?"

"Maybe."

"A murderer?"

"For sure."

"So you'd take the law into your own hands, then?"

"That's not what you asked me."

"Right." She sighed and turned toward him, nudging her shoulder into the seat. She'd already gone too far by sprawling across him while she slept. Best to be more careful about his personal space now. "Tell me what's up between you and your brother and me."

"What do you mean?"

"I know you think something about the two of us. I can sense it every time his name comes up."

"Doesn't matter."

"It does. Because every time I mention Trouble, your fingers curl into fists. See? You just did it."

He sighed and relaxed his fingers.

"Do you think me and your brother got it on?"

He didn't answer and instead shoved in another bite of cake. The force with which he stabbed the helpless dessert said all she needed to know.

"We didn't, Kelyn. I don't know what Trouble has told you, but we are just friends. Always have been, always—well, the dude has been avoiding me since…you know."

"He's protective of me. Of all his siblings. If someone does us wrong, he's going to retaliate." His attention focused on her. His irises gleamed like gemstones. Faery eyes were gorgeous. She'd never seen anything so intense and precious. "So you're telling me nothing has ever happened between the two of you? Be honest, I know you two do the Netflix-and-chill thing."

"We never chill, Kelyn. It's either pizza, beer or both. But *never* sex. I might have kissed him once. A quickie, just to, you know, test the waters. But no sex. You have to believe me. And it makes me angry that Trouble made you believe otherwise. What a jerk."

Kelyn shrugged. "Trouble is like that. Boasts about things to make himself look good."

"So he did tell you we slept together. B. J. Hunnicutt, I will so kick his ass for that."

"Maybe keep your distance from him for now. He gets an idea about a person and he goes ballistic pretty fast."

The soft light from above shadowed his eyes and emphasized his sharp bone structure. Hair raked back off his face to further expose his exquisite features, the man was beautiful in, hmm, an alien manner. Unique.

"I did believe him when he said the two of you had hooked up. And it bothered me because I like you, Valor. I've explained that. Yet I don't ever want to go after one of my brother's conquests."

"I am so not a conquest."

"I believe it."

"Thank you. So…are we good?"

He bobbed his head. "I was stupid to buy into Trouble's bragging. He does it all the time. And I know half the time it's exaggerated blustering. Idiot wolf. Will you accept my apology?"

"For what? You've done nothing but be a good brother. And if anyone needs to apologize—"

"It's neither of us. We've been through this already. Onward and with a new perspective on each other?"

"For sure."

"Great. Then to seal the deal you can have the last piece." He forked up the final chunk of chocolate cake and offered it to her.

The guy didn't have to offer twice. Valor dived for the prize. It was especially sweet, considering they'd cleared the air about something she hadn't even been aware was a problem.

So Kelyn liked her?

She could work with that.

Chapter 7

Seven hours later their feet finally touched ground. Wandering through the airport, Kelyn slung Valor's backpack across one shoulder and carried his bag on the other side. He'd had to rip the thing out of her hand. The chick was tough, but come on, let a guy do the chivalrous thing once in a while.

Now he turned to see if she still followed him—she'd gotten over her sleep deprivation just in time for midnight in Australia. Ha! He'd stolen a few winks on the flight and didn't need to sleep all that much. Despite having watched six movies and debating the merits of chemical-free lawns as opposed to spraying with an across-the-aisle passenger, he was good to go.

Valor sped up and passed him.

"I think the taxi terminal is that way," he said as she headed in the opposite direction.

"Cool, but I see an all-night buffet up ahead. And I'm starving. That tiny meal on the plane only whetted my appetite. Come on!"

Food that had actually been prepared in a real kitchen and not freeze-dried and reheated? He was in.

Kelyn picked up his pace and didn't make it to the cash register in time before Valor had confirmed she'd paid for both of them. Without waiting for his argument, she charged into the restaurant and grabbed a plate, directing him to find a table.

Let no man stand in the way of a hungry woman. Who was too darned cute as she navigated the aisles of food with a gleeful look on her face. And she was yet to notice the sprig of hair sticking straight out from the top of her head.

Ten minutes later, Kelyn sat with a plate stacked with steamed and fresh veggies, fried potatoes of various types and something called Vegemite spread on a piece of toast. And Valor had almost cleaned her first plate.

"Where do you put it all?" he asked and sipped his hot coffee.

She flexed a biceps and tapped it. "Right here. All the protein keeps me in shape for lifting the grain bags at the brewery and hefting heavy auto parts around the shop."

"That's right, you're a tool monkey."

"I prefer to call it getting my grease on, but close enough. Yeah, Daisy Blu and Beck let me and Sunday use one of the stalls at their auto body shop. We are working on a '67 Corvette Stingray. It's sweet. You like cars, Kelyn?"

"They get a guy where he needs to go. I'm more of a motorcycle man, I guess."

"Cool. I ride an old street chopper I picked up from Raven Crosse for a killer price. Fixing it up right now. But your Firebird is a classic."

"Blade fixed it up for me as a birthday present a few years ago. It was a junker I found on Craigslist for a thousand bucks. Blade can work magic with bodywork, and Beck restored the engine."

"Nice."

Reaching across the table, he patted down the tangle of hair on her head. "That's better."

She shrugged. "I'm no glamour girl. Get used to it. So, you ever hop on your motorcycle and ride up along Lake Superior? It's gorgeous in the fall with the colorful leaves. I try to go camping in the Boundary Waters at least once a year."

"Sounds like fun. But I don't own a motorcycle. I just like them. And believe it or not, I haven't been Up North. Been stuck in the Twin Cities all my freakin' life. Is this your first trip out of the country?"

"Out of the state."

"I have been lucky enough to visit Paris once. I like flying. Er…in an airplane," he felt the need to correct, because if he thought about flying with his wings… Yeah, he needed to put that heart-crushing memory aside. "You should have told me this was your first flight. I thought you'd flown before because of the, er…"

"Drunken disaster I was this morning?"

"Yeah. Seems like you had a routine established for alleviating your flight anxiety that could only have come from much experimenting."

"I've flown north to Thief River Falls to visit friends on a much smaller plane. Dude, you don't even want to know about that disaster."

He smiled at her cringing expression. To him, flight was everything. But free flight, courtesy of wings, was the ultimate. *Stop thinking about it, man.* With luck, what he'd lost would soon be regained.

"Speaking of drunken disasters…" He offered a sheepish grin. "I wasn't sure what to do, so we…left the cat behind."

"Everything's cool. My neighbor checks in on Mooshi. I thought you didn't like cats."

"I don't, but that doesn't mean I can't care about an animal's safety."

"Why the dislike? Are you allergic to cats?"

"No. I actually think it's a faery thing. Cats don't care for me, either. I'm surprised your Mooshi was so calm around me. Usually they come at me with their claws bared or else run and hide."

"Wow. Well, you are a likable guy and Mooshi is chill." She shoved in a forkload of food and looked aside.

A likable guy, eh? She liked him. But he wouldn't tease her about it. Yet. It made Kelyn feel good to know that she did. Had he a real chance to score with her now that he no longer had to worry that she and his brother had had a thing?

He sipped the weak black coffee. "So, are we headed straight to the lake tonight?"

"I'm in. The moon is almost full. We should have good light to explore."

"Is the lake accessible?"

"Sure, but I don't think it's touristy. Maybe? I didn't do a lot of research on it, but I do know it's kind of, sort of out of the way. We can head there when we're finished eating." She stood and headed for plate number two.

"Never leave a man behind." Despite his usual habit of eating small meals often throughout the day, Kelyn followed her, thinking he couldn't let a girl eat him under the table.

By the time plate number three had been cleaned, he was feeling the burn in his gut. Maybe he should concede the win on this one.

"You're kind of competitive," Valor said as she licked the whipped cream off her spoon, then stabbed it into the mush of blueberry pie. "You know that?"

"Just hungry." He pushed his plate forward on the table, thinking dessert was out of the question. Oh, that Vegemite. He shouldn't have had the third slice of toast. "Very well. I concede. You win the buffet challenge."

"I always do." She sat back, spreading her hair out across one shoulder. It was long and glossy; he imagined what it might feel like spread across his chest, tickling like sensual silk.

"You want the last piece?" She tapped the plate, on which sat a small uneaten blob of pie coated with whipped cream.

Recognizing the significance of the offer, Kelyn set aside his revulsion at all the sugar—and his full-to-the-brim stomach—and leaned across the table. She forked the pie and placed it in his mouth. It wasn't like he'd consumed a whole piece, but it was definitely the straw that broke the camel's very full stomach. He sat back with a groan.

"Poor guy. Will you be able to make this evening's adventure?" she asked, not hiding a teasing tone. "Or do you want to go snuggle up in a hotel room and recover from the food deluge?"

Snuggle up? Was she suggesting? No, she had chosen the wrong word. Maybe? But as for crawling under the covers and surrendering? Could he? *Man up, faery.*

"I'm in. How far away is the lake?"

"Not sure." She tugged out her cell phone. "I might have to arrange transportation. This could take a bit."

Enough time to give his stomach a recovery period.

"You bring your swimsuit?" she asked as they grabbed their luggage and filed out of the booth.

"What for? Are we going to *swim* in the lake?"

"Heck, yeah. You think I'd fly across the world to visit a pink lake and *not* go in it?"

"I'm not much of a swimmer. Actually, I never learned how." And please don't ask him to start now.

She shrugged. "It's cool. I think I read something about people being extra buoyant in the water because of the massive salt content. Dude. This is going to rock!"

Chapter 8

Witchcraft could be a handy thing when it came to enchanting a helicopter pilot and convincing him to fly over Lake Hillier. What Valor had discovered was that the lake was on Middle Island and not accessible to visitors because it was surrounded by forest. Only pre-approved visits were allowed, and such permission could take weeks to obtain.

And, indeed, the lake, when seen from overhead, was a gorgeous shade of bubble gum pink, surrounded by a white stone beach. Moonlight glistening on the waves added enough glitz that Valor commented about it being blinged out.

Why the lake was pink was still a scientific mystery, according to the chatty pilot, though the concentration of salt and bacteria did contribute to the color. The pilot said visitors were cautioned to cover any skin that would touch the water with shea butter, which Valor had purchased before they'd taken off.

It was already three in the morning, so they needed to work swiftly. With a few more magical words, Valor convinced the pilot that this was, indeed, a preapproved dropoff. And that his passengers were actually scientists on a photojournalism venture approved by the Australian tourism board. He nodded and gave them a salute as they prepared to disembark.

Valor asked the pilot to return in an hour and then they rappelled down from the helicopter, military-style. He'd managed to drop them right on the white beach outside the fragrant forest of paperbark and eucalyptus trees that hugged beach and lake. The air was heavy with the scent of air freshener, or that was what it smelled like to Valor.

Kelyn shucked off his harness and then helped Valor off with hers. He carried their only backpack, which Valor had packed with the necessary supplies. Standing on the white beach, she took things in for a moment. An uninhabited island all to themselves in the middle of a moonlit evening? *Why* had she come here?

Oh, right. This was a business trip and nothing else.

Tugging off her shirt, she tossed that on top of the backpack, then toed off her boots and pulled off her pants to reveal the bikini she wore beneath. She'd had to buy one at the airport, and much to her chagrin there hadn't been any one-pieces in her size. She hadn't swum in a pool, lake or otherwise since she was a kid, and she did not do the sunbathing thing. That was best left for real women like one of the brewery co-owners, Geneva, who probably caught her rays on the deck of a multimillion-dollar yacht, lying under the appreciative eye of her latest billionaire boyfriend. Ha!

Collecting the glass vials from the backpack, she started toward the water.

"Wow" came softly from behind her.

Kelyn pulled off his shirt and it dangled from his fingers as he looked her up and down with an assessing appreciation that would have made any woman blush proudly.

Valor shrugged and turned back to the lake. "It's just a body."

"So it is. But a nice one, at that."

Seriously? She couldn't figure what he was thinking— or looking at, for that matter. Her body was long, lean and straight. Everywhere. Small boobs and no apparent waistline because her torso plunged right into her hips and down her thighs. Valor had never considered herself a real girl when compared to the hair-fluffing, mascara-fluttering, lipstick-pouting mannequins that most men seemed to find attractive. Another point tossed to her witchy friend Geneva. Give Valor a wrench and a greasy engine, and she was one happy camper.

Kelyn caught up to her where she'd waded out about ten feet. The swim trunks fit low on his hips. The abs on the guy were nothing less than insane. More than a six-pack, for sure. But she didn't count because Valor was trying to keep from glancing at them too often and giving herself away.

Just another body, she thought of his ripped physique. She might not be a real girl, but her brain was all woman. Lusting madly for some man flesh was natural. But it was probably wiser if she did it on the sly.

"We going to put the shea butter on?" Kelyn asked

as he joined her side. The water hit them both high on the thighs.

"It's a quick pop in the lake. We can rub it in afterward and get the same effect. It'll just prevent our skin from getting dry from all the salt. You want to stay here while I go for a swim?"

"Hell, no. If the water makes us buoyant, like you said, and then you factor in that I'm a natural lightweight, I shouldn't be able to drown even if I tried."

"Is that a faery thing?"

"It is. Our bones are light and sort of honeycomb in design. For flight."

"Cool." She clasped the moonstone hanging from the cord about her neck. Nah, it wouldn't get lost if she didn't do vigorous laps. She eyed Kelyn, who assessed the water with that furrowed brow of his. "What are those?" She pointed to the charms that hung from the leather strips about his neck. "That one looks like a tiny unicorn horn."

"Close. It's a mouse alicorn."

"Seriously?"

He nodded. "And this one—" he held up the black circle that looked like a thin tourmaline ring "—has some kind of funky vibrations, but I've never been able to actually use it magically. I got them both from Faery. Never been there myself, but I know a girl who brings me back prizes from there every so often."

"Is that so? She a girlfriend?"

"Nope. But I do love her."

So he was going to be evasive about his love life? Fair enough. For as much as he claimed to like her, Valor didn't expect he'd actually want to kiss her. Again. Oh, man, remembering that kiss in the forest made her nipples harden. And she was not dressed to hide the results of those lusty thoughts. So best to avoid the discussion.

"Come on!" She dived and splashed up cool droplets. The water did taste salty as she swam a few feet and then surfaced. Sputtering out the nasty-tasting water, she flipped back her hair and stood, now waist deep. It looked less bubble gummy from this angle, but still kind of, sort of pink when it caught glimmers of moonlight. "Isn't this amazing?"

"It is a wonder." Kelyn hadn't dived, and still stood where she'd left him. The water swayed his body back and forth. "Go ahead for a swim. I can wait."

"I will. Maybe. The water tastes nasty. Let's get what we need first."

"You got something to put the water in?"

"Right here." Tugging the vials from the side of her hip where she'd tucked them in her bikini bottoms, she waved them before him. When he tried to snatch one from her, she flinched away.

"Four of them?" he challenged.

"Yep. This one is for what we need." She scooped in water and corked the vial. She tucked it back at her hip. "This one is for backup. This one is for just in case. And this one is for whatever is going to get fucked up. Because plans always get fucked. I swear it by Dana Scully."

"Valor." He closed both hands over the vials she hadn't dipped yet but didn't try to take them away from her. "We mustn't be greedy."

"Seriously? These vials will hold a few drops out of this massive lake. Hey, I only took two werewolf claws, so give me some credit for restraint. What happens if one of these breaks during our travel?"

She fluttered her lashes at him and he took the bait with a big smile and a reluctant head-bobbing yet agreeing nod.

"Fine." He crossed his arms and watched as she filled the next two vials and handed them to him. He waggled the first vial and held it up so the moon gleamed through it. "Still looks pink. This is freaky."

"You should be able to float in this lake," she offered, "for all the salt."

"Oh, yeah?" Kelyn leaned back and spread out his arms, floating away from her. "Oh, man, this is cool!"

"And look, you haven't drowned!"

"Yet!"

Filling the last vial, she tucked it at her hip alongside the other. Then, flopping backward with a splash, she joined Kelyn. It was easy to float in this water. And much better than taking another dive and tasting the horrible stuff. Her body felt as if it were floating higher than usual. Her head hadn't even gone under when she fell backward. *Cool.*

A tug at her fingertips turned her in the water and she spun in a half circle, her head floating close to Kelyn's head. He held her at arm's length. "My brothers will never believe I actually had fun in a lake."

"You're having fun?"

"Hell, yes. I've flown across the world. Jumped out of a freakin' helicopter. And now I'm floating in a pink lake. As far as life experiences go, this one tops the list."

"Seems like a faery should have had a lot of cool experiences."

"I'm like everyone else, Valor."

"Except for the wings part. But I suppose flying is like walking to you, eh?" She bumped her head against his shoulder, which set her body on a curving trajectory alongside his.

"It was," he said, and she felt his longing for what he'd once had.

Damn, she shouldn't have brought that up.

"We'll get them back for you," she encouraged. "I promise you that."

"I don't need your promise. Just the fact that you're willing to help is enough for me. So I wonder about the color of this lake. It must be algae that makes it pink."

"Probably. And just think. That algae is all over us. Getting in places we'd rather it not be."

"Sounds not so fun."

She laughed then, which always managed to come out as a chortle and a snort.

Kelyn stood abruptly and whipped his head back to disperse the water from his hair. Droplets trickled down his face. As she stood upright Valor slapped a hand over the two vials, spellbound by the moonlight that glinted in his eyes. The cool white illumination gliding along his sharp bone structure and violet eyes made them unnaturally beautiful. A true faery.

But he was staring at her with such a silly smile. And she had to wonder if she had something on her face. "What? Is it the algae? Is it pink?"

"I adore your laugh," he said.

"Ha! You're crazy. I laugh like a pig on acid."

"Maybe hallucinogenic pigs are my thing?"

"Yep, you are definitely too nice. Hand me those vials. Think we should get out and dry off before the helicopter returns?" she asked, while thinking she'd just said the stupidest thing on the planet.

Leave now, when they'd only gotten in the water and

it was like they stood on some kind of fantasy stage? She was alone with the guy. Who had expressed interest in her. Why not take advantage of it?

"Sure. But let's spend a few more minutes in the water to remember this place. And how we feel. You know… the moonlight is dancing in your eyes."

Valor felt a blush rise and looked down and away from his mesmerizing gaze.

"The water shimmers like jewels in your hair," he continued. "And there's this."

With a sweep of his hand between them, he dispersed his natural dust into the air. It glittered and hung suspended about them like millions of tiny stars fallen to earth.

Wow. Talk about instant romance. And yes, she was a woman who could appreciate a little romance when it presented itself. Which rarely happened, so…when life offered a challenge…

"You know I'm an air witch. But I can use the subtle surface winds to make this happen."

A sweep of her hand above the surface lifted up water that ascended around them in dotted columns as if caging them in. The droplets caught Kelyn's dust, and combined with the moonlight, they stood on a rock star's stage, highlighted for all to see.

"And how about this?"

Spreading out one arm and snapping her fingers shot up a spurt of water about twenty feet away. Followed by another spurt, and another, until they had become a fountain spilling diamonds beside them.

"Stunning. You win the magic portion of this evening. But now it's my turn. And I can't think of anything I'd rather do than this."

Thinking he was going to show her some of his faery magic, Valor lost all power of reasoning when he did not.

Instead, Kelyn bent and kissed her. His hand slid across her back and he coaxed her up against his chest. Her feet left the sand because the water truly was magical in making her weightless. Or maybe it was the kiss. It made her soar.

Yeah, it was the kiss.

She spread her hand up, walking her fingers over Kelyn's hard pecs as he opened her mouth and dashed his tongue with hers. Valor moaned into him, and the vibrations of her pleasure tickled in her chest. She gripped the wet ends of his hair, anchoring herself, while her knees bent and she was completely supported by his arm.

If the moon never set and the sun never rose, she would take this moment, standing in a pink lake on an unpopulated island, surrounded by faery dust and a glimmering pink water fountain, and remember it forever. Her heartbeat raced with the excitement gleaned from his touch, his taste, his intense focus on the kiss.

The last time she kissed this man, she'd thought she was going to die. Now she thought for sure she could live forever in his arms. Safe and desired. A real girl? Probably not. But she wasn't going to spoil the fantasy by thinking about it one moment longer.

Mmm, what a delicious kiss. Every part of her tingled with the giddiness. She leaned into him, hugging her hard nipples against his chest. The man moaned appreciatively. And that utterance increased her want tenfold. She dug in her nails at his shoulder, which didn't make him flinch. So much man. And all hers. For now.

And now was all that mattered.

When he pulled away, Valor whispered, "That was awesome."

"I'll say. We should kiss again—ah. Here it comes."

"What?" Something was coming? Could it be her, pretty please?

"The helicopter is back early."

"Dana Scully."

"Exactly. We'd better return to shore and pack up quickly."

Grasping her hand, he led her out of the water. As she exited, her magic ceased and the fountain dissipated. Valor pulled out the sweatshirt she'd worn here and used it to wipe off her legs and arms. They shoved pants and boots on and Kelyn flashed the LED beacon that would mark their position to the pilot.

As they stood waiting for the ride, he clasped her hand and she squeezed it. "Why did you do that?" she asked in quiet wonder.

"Kiss you? I thought you said it was awesome."

"It was. But I…I don't know. I didn't think we'd have a chance."

"Really? You've always had a chance with me, Valor."

"Until your brother."

"Which we've solved. Do you purposely argue about issues you've already won just to be annoying?"

She released their grasp and punched him on the biceps. None too gently.

"Annoying it is," he said, and rushed over to grab the rappel rope and gear that had dropped down from the helicopter.

Chapter 9

For some reason, Kelyn had paid for two first-class tickets across the world, a helicopter, rappel gear rental and a private limo. But he'd only put out for one hotel room with a king-size bed.

Valor wasn't averse to sharing a bed with a male friend. She'd done it before. Well, she'd shared the couch with Trouble because they'd both fallen asleep full of pizza and watching Bruce Willis. Yippee-ki-yay!

Setting her backpack on the end of the bed, she reasoned with herself. Sex wasn't always on the table for situations like this. She was a grown-up and the men she hung with were grown-ups, as well. They could share a bed without getting all squicky about it.

Except.

She felt a little weird about sleeping next to the guy she was kind of, sort of, starting to have feelings for. But she didn't want to tell him that. And she didn't expect he felt the same way. Only, okay, he had confessed to liking her until he'd thought she and Trouble had gotten it on. Which they had not.

And he had kissed her. Like, *totally* kissed her in the pink lake. That had been one for the books.

And now? Kelyn walked around the room, stripping off his shirt and announcing he was going to take a shower first, if she didn't mind. Despite the sensation of dried algae having worked its way into strange places on her body, Valor eagerly nodded and gestured for him to go for it.

Now that the bathroom door was closed, she collapsed onto the chair and put her bare feet up on the end of the bed. Then she took them down. There was something on her big toe. Dried algae? Beach sand? Some kind of crustacean from the pink lake? She didn't want to know. She needed a shower and to crash. It had been a long day and night, and the flight from the United States and her anxiety had only compounded her exhaustion. She could almost allow herself to fall asleep right here on the chair—not in the same bed as Kelyn—but she'd noticed a distinct smell in her hair and knew she wouldn't rest until she was clean.

The four vials of lake water sat on the table, looking barely pink under the awful yellow lamplight.

On to the next ingredient. Which, according to the research Valor had done during the cab ride to this hotel, could only be located in Wales. And Kelyn probably wasn't going to like that adventure. She'd tell him about it when it was too late to back out. And if she had to, she'd seduce him with another kiss.

She could totally work the seduction when she put her mind to it.

Smiling to herself, she tilted her head back, but sat upright when the bathroom door opened and out strolled a steaming man with slicked-back hair and abs that glistened with water droplets.

Of all the television doctors' names she had ever spoken in oath, she could not remember a single name now.

"All yours," he said, one hand propped casually over the twist in the towel at his hip. The towel rode low, exposing the cut muscles that V'd toward—oh, so many fantasies visited Valor's lusty thoughts. Most of them involved licking the water droplets from Kelyn's skin and…

"Yep." Despite her waning energy, she hopped up and slipped past him to quickly close the bathroom door. Only when she stood alone in the steamy little room did she dare to let out a breath and shake her head. "Man, those abs. Whoever thought faeries were scrawny, delicate creatures?"

How she'd managed not to drag her fingers across those spectacular ridged abs was beyond her. Would she survive this trip if they continued to share a room? Because she wasn't beyond having sex with a friend for the sake of it. To feed a desire. To get off. To have some fun.

But, for some reason, it felt dangerous to consider having sex with Kelyn. Emotionally risky. And maybe even like a commitment.

Valor shook her head. "Don't be a fool."

She'd never been one for long-term relationships. Until recently.

Because now? She craved something more than the

flirtations or few short months she'd shared with men most of her life.

But she hadn't had that in her life because she simply wasn't the kind of woman men considered for relationships. She knew that for a fact. Someone had told her so. In the most abrupt and heart-wrenching manner possible.

And besides, Kelyn would never see her as a woman who could satisfy his lust for the sexy and sensual. That man needed a real woman and not one who could only fake it when at her best.

She drew a sigil in the steam on the mirror. It was the same one she'd drawn in the moss with the angel dust that night in the Darkwood.

"You missed your chance to be loved, witch."

Kelyn pulled on a pair of clean jeans and grimaced. He normally slept naked. But that wouldn't work with Valor lying on the bed next to him. Well, it could.

He considered it a few seconds, then shook his head and zipped up the fly. "Nope."

He wasn't sure where he stood with her, and he didn't want to freak her out or press any issue for which she might not be on board. Such as the two of them getting close and…yes, sex was definitely on the table for him. But she didn't feel the same way about him as he did her. She couldn't. Why had he confessed his infatuation to her? She must think him some kind of crazy after all they'd been through.

And yet he'd gone for it at the lake. That kiss had been some kind of all right. He'd thought it was a signal between them that he was okay to move forward with whatever might happen between the two of them. But she hadn't given him that same signal, so he would have to mark the kiss off as a one-time thing.

Two times, actually. He'd not forgotten the kiss in the forest. She'd been desperate that time, thinking death was near. The lake had been completely different. Yeah, he'd blame it on the unruly lake and the enchantment that had literally glittered in the air.

Until the helicopter had swooped low and destroyed the moment.

He flung himself onto the bed, propped up two pillows behind his head and closed his eyes. Man, it felt great to get the lake smell out of his hair. And he was bone weary. Which also felt great. He wasn't one to sleep a lot, but he sensed he'd get forty winks tonight. Which was almost morning. It had been a long day.

Now they had gained one more ingredient for the witch's spell that would, he hoped, open a portal to Faery.

Did he believe after the portal was open they could simply take a jaunt through and his wings would be waiting there for the taking? Not at all. But the hope of having that entry—a place to start—was enough to keep him going. He wanted his strength and power back.

And he wanted to set foot in Faery. It was something he'd dreamed about all his life. Like any child who had ever dreamed of going to Disneyland, Kelyn had dreamed of going to his homeland. His mother had told him tales of the azure skies and many moons that could be seen at any time, day or night. How so many different species thrived, loved, fought and existed in Faery. Sprites, dragons, unicorns and so many breeds of *sidhe* they were impossible to tally.

The bathroom door opened, and Kelyn made a point

of not opening his eyes. He didn't want the tease of a wet witch in a towel to stir his desires and have him trying to hide a hard-on. If he made it through this night, he'd wake with blue balls, for sure.

"You sleeping?" Valor asked softly.

He felt the bed move when she sat on the other side. "Almost."

"Thanks for everything, Kelyn. It's been a great trip. And while I know we both had business in mind with the lake, it was an adventure I'll never forget."

"It was awesome. I like trying new things. I've always considered myself an adventurous guy. Me, the one who's never even been Up North. But today? Rappelling down a rope from a helicopter? That rocked."

"You're telling me."

"You weren't nervous about the flight, either. That surprised me."

"Didn't have time to freak out. And I think because it was wide-open, and I wasn't stuffed into a tin can, I lost most of my fear. It was like…free-flying."

"Not even close. But I'll give you that one."

"Thanks." She lay down and he opened one eye. He could see her bare legs stretched over the folded-back coverlet. She smelled like the hotel's orange shampoo, and it made him hungry. But not for food.

She turned to her side, and he knew she faced him, so he tilted his head and met her gaze in the darkness. He could still see quite well in the dark, even without his wings.

"You know that kiss?" she asked. "Not the one at the lake but the one in the Darkwood."

"Uh…yeah?"

"In that moment, when the tree was sucking me into

the ground, I thought I was going to die. And…I haven't kissed another man since."

That had been four months ago. Really? She hadn't kissed another man? Kelyn mumbled a noise of assurance.

"I wanted you to know," she said. "I haven't felt like dating since then. I know I have no right, and I promise I'm over with the apologies, but I've sort of carried what happened as a heavy burden. But I think I'm ready to shuck it off my shoulders now."

By rights? She should have carried that burden. For a little while anyway. And that was his angry, pissed-off self thinking that. But it was a real emotion, and he owned it as it tensed his muscles and chased away any thought of touching her sweet-smelling, wet hair.

Now she rolled to her back. "I'm tired," she said. "Good night, Kelyn."

He nodded, knowing she couldn't hear that motion. He didn't know what to say or how to act around her. Because he wasn't sure what was happening between them. While he had every reason to hate the woman, every fiber of his being wanted to reach out and pull her to him and hold her close.

And while he stared at the back of her head and willed his arm to reach for her, no part of his body moved, save for his heart, sinking a little deeper into his chest.

Chapter 10

Valor woke to bright sunlight. She'd forgotten to pull the heavy curtains, and, man, did the sun look high in the sky! It must be noon. She'd slept not so long, though, because they'd gotten in early in the morning.

Wondering about room service, she pulled down the sheet to get out of bed and realized a man's arm was holding her against his body. A warm body. Rigid pectorals hugged her back. And a relaxed arm braceleted with a ring of silvery scars about his wrist hold her prisoner.

Hmm…

Attempting to move the arm would surely wake him. How had she gotten into such a position with her back against Kelyn's bare chest and him holding her as if they were lovers? His curled fingers rested below her breast on the bed, not touching her. But still…

Nice. The wish to turn back time so she could have

been awake to enjoy their closeness more thoroughly ended with a sigh. It was probably a natural movement he did in his sleep when lying next to a woman. Surely such a good-looking man as Kelyn Saint-Pierre had slept with many. She wasn't special. And they did not have an exclusive thing.

So. She'd have to do this like the proverbial Band-Aid. Rip it off and risk waking him to save her the embarrassment of simply lying there until he decided to wake up.

Not that anything could embarrass her. There was nothing wrong with snuggling with the guy. And he smelled great. The orange-shampoo scent they shared had dissipated and now all she smelled was him. The man oozed an alchemy of earth and air and something ineffable. Perhaps a masculine sort of surety. So she remained there a few minutes longer, enjoying the contact. Was it so wrong to steal the pleasure of an embrace even if the guy wasn't aware of it?

She didn't think so.

After five minutes she decided this was getting weird. Much as she enjoyed it, she also felt squicky about stealing the guy's empathy. Which was what it had felt like since they'd gotten together on this adventure. Like he was being nice to appease her. When, really, why didn't he yell at her? Accuse her? Get out the anger he had to have for what had happened?

Blowing out a decisive breath, Valor nudged carefully at Kelyn's arm and, as she did so, glided forward on the bed, which effectively lifted his arm and allowed her freedom. When his arm dropped and she sat up, he startled awake.

The guy eyeballed her, closed his eyes and smiled. "Morning."

"It is. Or maybe it's noon. Or possibly even later. Didn't mean to startle you, but we were, uh…not sure how I ended up snuggled against you like that."

"It was nice," he said. Pushing his hands back through his hair, he again opened his eyes. The bright sunshine found his violet irises and danced there. "You snuggled up to me."

"Uh, no. I don't think so. I'm sure it was you who wrapped an arm around me."

Valor slid to the edge of the bed, prepared to stand, when suddenly Kelyn grabbed her by the shoulder and pulled her down. Her head landed on the pillow, and the faery moved in for a kiss. A kiss! It was a quick one, as far as kisses being clocked went, but it was fun and landed on her lips just long enough for her to regret not snuggling with him longer.

"Okay, *I* wrapped an arm around you," he said. "The witch wins again. Now, get dressed. We need to forage for food. Then onward."

He got up and strode into the bathroom, while Valor could only lie there, touching her mouth. His kisses got better and better. Even the short and admonishing ones. And he took them whenever the moment seemed to strike him. She couldn't think of a reason to argue with such blatant thievery.

Had he actually kissed her silly?

"Yes, Marcus Welby, he did."

They managed to find another buffet restaurant, which seemed to be the witch's favorite eating style. Plate heaped with an assortment of meats, veggies, cheeses and something blue and jiggly even Kelyn couldn't identify, she was in heaven.

"I like a woman with a healthy appetite," he said while buttering the toast, preparing to smear the fried egg with the runny yoke over it. He was a vegetarian, but cheated with eggs and butter.

"I like a man who's not afraid to be weird," she said. "Eggs on toast?"

"You think this is weird?" He pointed to her blue concoction in challenging comparison.

"Hey, it's one of the food groups. Sugar. But first, veggies." She scraped up a forkload of peas and scooped it into her mouth. "Did you book a flight for us? Wales is our next destination."

"I will do that as soon as I'm done eating. Can a person fly into Wales or do we need to hit England first?"

"Not sure. Never been out of the States before, remember? And I will need to do some serious drinking before we get on another plane."

"Yes, because that worked so well for your flight here. Unless you don't mind me carrying you on as extra luggage?"

"Hey, if I could not be nervous I would. There's not a spell in my arsenal that'll chill me out, so you'll have to deal with a drunk witch."

"I have no problem with that. You're cute when you pass out and snore."

She rolled her eyes but didn't cease her eating.

"Do you think if the airplane had no sides, and all the seats were open to the elements, you'd be good? You were with the helicopter."

"I… No. We didn't go very high in the sky. Maybe it's that in the airplane you go so high and you can't see how high it is. Just…accept me as I am, okay?"

"I do. I appreciate everything you're doing for me,"

Kelyn said because he felt the need to soften that dig at her snores. "So, can you remind me of what's the next thing on the list?"

"Uh…" She sipped the black coffee then made a great show of stirring in more cream and tons of sugar and swirling it with the spoon. He couldn't quite make out what she said when she mumbled, "Mermaid's…'iss."

"A what? Something about mermaids. And I know they are not the nicest of all this realm's creatures to deal with."

"You need a mermaid's kiss," she said heatedly. "Did you hear that?"

Right. He had read that on the list. Hadn't thought much of it at the time, though. Kelyn sat back and set his fork aside, no longer hungry. From the tales his mother had told him as a kid, he knew mermaids were vicious and feral. No smart man, werewolf or even faery liked to go near them.

And then there was that other issue.

"I don't know how that's going to work," he said. "I mean, first you have to find one. Depths of the ocean? And me not being a swimmer?" He shrugged. "But even if we do manage success, how does a person store something like that?"

"Don't you worry about the storage process. All you have to do is get the kiss. I'll take care of the rest. There could be an issue with you not being a swimmer, though."

"You think?"

Lake Hillier had been shallow, at least, as far in as they'd waded. And he'd floated like a dream. But searching for a mermaid could mean greater depths, and diving, and actually knowing how to breathe underwater.

His brothers had always teased him about avoiding the waterfalls out in the back of their family land and that someday he'd surely want to know how to swim. It wasn't that water frightened him or he feared drowning. He *had* tried to swim on many occasions. But lighter-than-air bones did not make for an easy swim. He had always floated on the surface like deadwood.

No way could he manage a dive into the ocean. It would be comical, to say the least.

"We'll figure something out." She lifted a fork of the blue jiggly stuff before her. "Here's to mermaid kisses and keeping the faery all in one piece."

In one piece? Reluctant to toast to that, but ever up for a challenge, Kelyn lifted his egg-smeared toast and tapped it against Valor's fork. "And to one wily witch who intends to dangle the faery from the end of her hook."

She winked at him then, and he couldn't help laughing. The witch did have a way of sneaking in an irresistible challenge. Feminine wiles? Kind of. Sort of. Valor was a tomboy to the bone. But he had lain with his arm wrapped about her through the morning and he knew she was soft and sensual, and her hair had smelled like oranges. He wanted to touch more and more of her. And steal another kiss.

And maybe next time he wouldn't have to steal it.

It might be a good idea to up his seduction game before they got to the mermaids. Because that was one situation he wasn't sure he'd come out of alive.

Kelyn hauled the drunk witch over one shoulder and onto the plane. Once again, he'd procured first class, knowing they'd have more room and privacy for Valor

to revel in her drunken nervousness. He smiled and complimented all the stewardesses as he made his way to
their seats.

Depositing Valor on the seat next to the window startled her awake. She curled up her legs and tucked her
hands under her chin. He settled next to her, pulling
the blanket from its plastic bag and tucking it over her.
"You're doing good, witch. It won't be long now."

The flight was twenty hours and included a quick layover in Cardiff, but she didn't need to know that.

"You're so good to me." Her eyes fluttered open and
she smiled drunkenly. "I love you."

"I love you when you're love drunk," he stated, knowing it was the booze that had delivered such effusive
adoration.

"I haven't been able to stop thinking about us, what
we could have been, since the forest," she confessed.

"Me, as well." Kelyn tilted his head against hers and
pulled in his long legs to allow others to get by in the
narrow aisle. "I think it's time we make a go for what
could have been."

Valor sighed. "If you say so."

And then she passed out.

The layover in Cardiff was more like a sprint. They
had ten minutes to hop on the plane to Anglesey. Valor
had made the dash on her own, but, teasing the last ves-
tiges of intoxication for all she could manage, she had
grasped for sleep again as the plane departed. With Kelyn's hand clasping hers she'd survived the flight across
the ocean and Europe.

Now she thanked the stewardesses profusely as the
plane landed. She'd been awake for about twenty min-

utes, had washed her face with a warm hand towel—man, did she love first class!—snacked on some grapes and cheese, and listened to Kelyn snore softly beside her. Bless the guy for putting up with her crazy-ass phobia.

He was too good to be true. What guy put up with stuff like that, and after having sacrificed his wings for her? She didn't deserve any of his kindness, but she wanted to earn his respect. And had he said something about them making a go for it?

A go for what? She couldn't remember what they'd been discussing when she was tilting twenty sheets to the wind upon departing the Sydney Airport. Hawkeye Pierce, that seemed like something she should have remembered.

Kelyn startled awake and looked around. The rest of first class had disembarked; the seats were littered with magazines and plastic water bottles.

"We've landed and can get off anytime," she said, "but I wanted to let you sleep. Coach is deplaning right now. How do you feel? Did you get some good rest?"

He snarled at her—actually snarled—and stood to get his bag out of the overhead compartment. "Come on," he muttered, and wandered off.

O…kay.

"Guess it's someone else's turn to be grumpy," she muttered. And instead of teasing him about it, she decided he deserved to act however he wished.

Valor followed Kelyn through the airport, loving the British accents that buzzed about her. There was something about a foreign accent that made her happy. It was so out of her usual realm. The Australian accent had pleased her, as well.

A taxi took them into town and Valor directed the

driver to a hardware store, where she intended to pick up some supplies for this leg of their adventure. She'd thought about it on the plane and had come up with as short a list as possible, yet still the essentials.

Down aisle nine, she grabbed a coiled green nylon rope and handed it back to Grumpy Kelyn. Sunglasses in place and hair tousled messily, he'd followed her into the store without a word. If he'd had a cigarette hanging out the corner of his mouth, he might have looked silver-screen cool. As it was, he was just plain annoying.

He slung the rope over a shoulder and shadowed her quietly down the aisle. The guy had a right to let loose his inner grump—why, his downright anger—toward her. It had to have happened sooner or later. So she wouldn't make a fuss and she'd try to stay out of what was surely a laser-beam glare radiating from behind those sunglasses.

Though, it took all her composure not to suggest she had a spell for his pouty face. And she did. She could whisper a man into a smile with but a few words. And that wasn't even a love spell; it was simply a cheer spell. Such a thing came in handy at the brewery when she sensed a fight was on the verge of erupting.

Down another aisle she sized up the harnesses and assorted safety gear used for climbing roofs. Holding one up before Kelyn, she checked the size, nodded and handed him the find.

They hadn't been able to carry weapons on the plane, and while she hadn't thought to look for a weapons shop along the way, she did manage to find a nifty jackknife in the hunting aisle. There were no rifles in this store, mostly traps and some camo gear. Generally she wore a thigh strap. A girl should never leave home without a blade. This folding blade was so small she could tuck it in a front pocket. It would have to suffice. When she asked Kelyn if he wanted a weapon, he merely shook his head.

So the grump continued. Fine. He'd be cursing his bad mood later if and when he needed to defend himself.

With hope, no defense would be necessary. How dangerous could a slimy chick with a tail actually be? Valor crossed her fingers and whispered a prayer to Liban, the goddess of the Irish Sea, for an easy task ahead of them.

Heading for the checkouts, she eyed Kelyn from the corner of her vision as he grabbed bags of chips and jerky from an array of brightly colored impulse items. So the guy was hungry? By the time they hit the register, he'd amassed four bags of snacks and a six-pack of bottled water.

"Good plan," she commented. "We'll need the fuel."

"Did you want something to eat?" he asked.

Valor turned her head to gape at him. "You're not going to share? What happened to you over the airspace between Australia and the UK? Dude, try a freakin' smile."

She might have actually felt his laser glare this time.

With a frustrated sigh, she handed over her credit card to the cashier, noticing Kelyn didn't offer, as she expected he might. Instead, he grabbed the stuff and headed out to the cab, leaving her to wonder if she'd done something wrong. Had she muttered something in her sleep about him?

Generally her own snoring woke her up, but she'd never been known to be a sleep talker. Hmm…she had never thought of herself as a mean or nasty drunk, either.

Must be a faery thing. Yeah, she would go with that.

* * *

Rain beat the tarmac and the sides of the hotel building as if it had a vengeance wish against the world. Kelyn paced the hotel suite, which featured two queen beds, a coffee maker and microwave and a narrow—and cracked—hot tub. He'd dropped the bag of supplies inside the doorway and was relieved when Valor said she was heading down to check out the restaurant and would bring up some food.

Thankful for a few minutes alone, he paced before the window that overlooked the weed-overgrown parking lot. This tiny town twenty miles out from the city where they'd landed reminded him of the proverbial quaint foreign village where assorted characters always got into loads of trouble with the craziest yet most down-to-earth acts. A movie set if ever he'd seen one.

Thinking about acting crazy…he'd been acting like an asshole since the plane landed. But he couldn't help it. He massaged the back of his shoulder, wincing at the pain that pulsed from where his wings had once been. Mercy, it felt like electric currents zapping in rapid beats and radiating out across his back. It had begun the moment he woke on the airplane and had not ceased since.

He spread out his arms and raised them above his head in an attempt to stretch the muscles and alleviate some of the pain. What was causing the weird phantom pain? Ah, hell. The moon must be nearing fullness. He'd been feeling this pain monthly. He'd always known his body aligned with the moon's phases. A faery thing.

The pain usually lasted a day and he then forgot about it until the next month. Pissy time for it to happen now, when he didn't mean to be so awful to Valor. She didn't deserve his anger. And he most certainly had not needed all those unhealthy bags of chips and—had he really picked up beef jerky?

A knock at the door that sounded like it came from a boot toe hurried him over to open it. Valor carried a stack of tinfoil-wrapped foods that smelled delicious.

"They offered room service," she said, walking in and handing him half the goods. "But I love sitting in a restaurant listening to others' conversations. All those cool accents! And I had a drink at the bar. And...I know you wanted some time to yourself. You feeling any better?"

"I'll be fine. Thanks for this. I'm starving." He really was in a foul mood. "Are we going to head out today?"

"It's already evening, and I'm not much for mermaid hunting in the dark. Or a monsoon. The weather report says this rain will continue through the night. There's a casino attached to the hotel. Maybe we could hang around tonight, then head out bright and early in the morning?"

"Sounds like a plan."

He set the food on the table and peeled open the foil. Savory scents wafted into the room. One of the containers held a burger dripping with cheese. He shoved that across the table. The other offered steamed veggies and white rice. It would do.

The water he'd gotten in the hardware store served them both, and, along with a couple bags of chips, they had a meal.

"You like to gamble, Kelyn?"

"Uh..." He paused with the fork to his lips. Sounded like a trick question to him.

"In the casino," she added. "I'm not much for the tables, but I do like to play the penny machines. What do they call them here in the UK?"

"Not sure. Shillings? We're both out of our element here." He winced and she saw it, so he leaned over the rice and gave it his utmost attention.

"Tell me what's up with you, Kelyn."

"Why does something have to be up?"

"Because while I don't deserve your kindness, you've been nothing but a gentleman since we set off on this adventure. So today has been a little unsettling with you playing the silent and pissed act. Did you sleep with your neck twisted on the plane or something?"

He pushed the food container away from himself and hitched a foot up on the end of the bed, tilting his head back against the chair. The position alleviated some of the pain between his shoulder blades.

"It's a faery thing," he finally said.

"Really?" Valor wiped a smear of ketchup from the corner of her mouth and guzzled down the last of a bottle of water. "Instead of spreading love, cheer and faery dust, you have a sneer and retreat day? I don't get it."

"I can feel my wings," he said heatedly. Then he cautioned himself not to release his frustrations on her and softened his tone. "It's like phantom pain. And it hits me once a month right around when the moon is full. Makes me irritable."

"Are you seriously telling me you're having a faery period?"

He glared at her.

"Sorry, couldn't resist that one. Come on," she pleaded with a growing grin. "You know that was funny."

Yeah, so she was right. But his smirk didn't quite touch mirth.

"So you're in pain. Because of your missing wings?"

"Yes. I'm sorry for being a jerk to you, but I just…"

He eased a shoulder forward, cringing at the sting. "It'll be better tomorrow. Promise."

"Kelyn, I'm so sorry. What if I give you a back rub? Do you think that would help?"

"I...don't know." He'd not thought massage could help, but he hadn't tried it before. "You don't need to."

"Let me try. Seriously. I have some healing magic in these fingers, but not a lot. I think all the working with engines and heavy-duty lifting at the brewery counters most of the vital energy I would otherwise have to heal. But I can give it a go. It'll feel like a nice warm deep-tissue massage if I work it right. Lie down on the bed. Pretty please?"

No woman had ever said *pretty please* to him before and made it so sexually inviting. She probably hadn't intended it to sound that way, but Kelyn felt her innocent suggestion all the way to his cock. And that was not so much weird as something that cautioned him.

But, really? He wanted to feel her hands on him. And who knew? Maybe a massage would bring them closer together, if not help with the pain. He wasn't averse to a little witchy healing magic.

Chapter 11

Kelyn stood and pulled off his shirt, groaning as the stretch tweaked at his back muscles.

"That bad, huh?" Valor walked around behind him and he flinched when her fingers touched his spine. "I'll be careful. Just show me where it hurts the most. Here?"

She touched gently where his wings had once sprouted from his back. When they'd been severed, nothing had remained, not even a lump. A thin scar was the only reminder he'd ever had anything back there.

He nodded. "That's the spot."

"The scars are like those at your wrists and on your chest."

"The sigils were a living, magical part of me. Sort of like stripping out my veins when I lost those. But the pain was brief and I don't feel anything on those places now." Unfortunately.

He missed having the sigils. He'd once been able to conjure air magic that might have rivaled Valor's. And the sigils had aided his navigation and enhanced his senses. Having sex with an activated sigil? Mind-blowing. Or so he'd been told. He'd never brought out his wings or exposed his activated sigils to a human woman while having sex. Just not wise.

"Lie down," Valor said. "Let me get my crystals out of my pack. I never go anywhere without them!"

He crawled onto the bed and lay stomach down. Tucking the mouse alicorn and black ring to the side, he fisted a hand under his chin and listened to her rummage through her backpack. He liked crystals and felt an affinity to selenite and tourmaline. The two were protective and cleansing stones. He wasn't sure about the circle he wore at his neck, but he thought it could be black tourmaline.

The sound of rocks clacking preceded Valor's voice. "I've got quartz, amethyst and seraphinite. Not sure how the seraphinite will react to a faery. It's a stone of the angels, you know."

"Legend tells that we faeries descended from the angels. That we were the Fallen Ones who landed on a realm other than this mortal plane, and that's how Faery was created. My mother used to tell me faery tales when I was little."

"The creation of Faery originated from angels? I like that. It's been a long time since I've seen my parents. I'm going to lay these on your back and work a little magic, and when your muscles have relaxed, I'll try a gentle massage. You good with that?"

"Work your witchy magic, witch. I'll let you know if it hurts."

"I don't hurt guys."

He laid his cheek on the bed and closed his eyes. "You just tease them, eh?"

"A chick's gotta have a little fun, right?"

He smirked. The cool touch of the crystals to his back felt great. And he knew when she laid the seraphinite on his spine between his missing wings because he immediately felt the energy in subtle vibrations that shivered across his flesh and into his muscles. It might have even permeated into his bones. He moaned with satisfied relief.

"That feels good?" she asked.

"It definitely hits the spot."

"And that's the seraphinite. Cool. Then I'll let that one sit there a bit and do its thing."

"So, your parents," he said as he felt her arrange the crystals along his spine. "You haven't seen them in a long time? Where are they?"

"Not sure. I never really knew either of them. I was raised by my great-grandma Hector in the 1940s."

"Hector?"

"Yeah, it's short for Hectorine. She is a gorgeous woman."

"Is?"

"Yes, she's still alive and intends to be so for as long as she can manage. You know we witches can achieve immortality with a spell, right?"

"I've heard that. Are you immortal?"

"I am. Or, at least, until the spell wanes. It's something we have to reactivate every hundred years."

"And how is it activated?"

She leaned over him, and the sweep of her hair shivered across his bare skin. Kelyn closed his eyes and tried not to groan at the delicious sensation, and it took a lot of effort to remain silent. "You don't really want the details, do you?"

"I do." He nudged up his shoulder blade. "Right there. Is that the quartz? It can feel it vibrate in my muscle."

Valor chanted some words in a language he didn't recognize, and as they whispered into his subconscious his muscles relaxed even more.

"Good," she said softly. "The healing energies are beginning to seep into your being. So. The immortality spell that grants a witch a century of life. Not all witches do it, just those of us who are averse to growing old and want to spend as much time as we can living, discovering and learning. It involves a vampire and his, erm…heart."

"You have to seduce a vampire?"

"Seduction can be a boon to get the vampire to comply, but no. We have to consume a live, beating vampire heart to gain immortality and stop the aging process."

Kelyn pushed himself up on the bed to glance over his shoulder at her, but she avoided his gaze.

"I know. Gross," she confirmed. "Lie down."

He did, and she replaced the quartz that had tumbled off his shoulder. Should he remind her that one of his brothers was vampire?

"We all do what we gotta do and what aligns with our morals, am I right?" Valor asked.

Like sacrificing his wings because he'd wanted to save the girl? "I guess so. No judgment. But if I ever see you eating a rare steak, I promise I will have a moment of judging you."

"Isn't that something your brother Blade would do?"

"Would you ever go after Blade for his heart?"

"Absolutely not. I sought a vicious killer when I performed the spell for myself. He had harmed so many."

"So you played judge and jury?"

"You're getting judgy now."

Kelyn laid his head down again and closed his eyes. Who was he to judge what was right and wrong?

"Let's take the crystals off and I'll massage your back…"

Setting the crystals up by the pillow, she then straddled him, sitting on his hips. Kelyn's cock responded to the intimate connection of her thighs hugging his. As long as he was lying facedown, everything would be okay. The touch of her hands on his skin felt like cool water to his aching muscles. She didn't press hard, only glided back and forth where his wings had once been and down along his spine. His core shivered and he smiled.

"You've got great lats and delts," she commented.

He chuckled softly. "You've got a soothing yet stimulating touch. You should be careful. I might respond in ways you hadn't expected."

"I think that means you're feeling better. But is the massage helping the pain a bit?"

"It is. Thank you."

Her touch grew firmer and she focused on his shoulders for a while, then slowly moved down his back. Paying attention to each vertebra, she glided her thumbs progressively downward. If he could make himself relax, he might even forget about her thighs squeezing against his hips. But his erection was not of a mind to let him off so easily. Damn.

"I have a confession to make," she said.

So did he, but he sure as hell wasn't going first with this one. "Go for it."

"Hmm…" She sighed. "Should I?"

"Yes, witch, you should."

"Okay, fine. I suggested this massage so I could touch you."

Kelyn smiled at that. Score one for the wounded faery!

"You're so strong and fierce, Kelyn. Everything about you screams controlled sensuality. Your body moves like a precision instrument. And your smiles and the looks you give me sometimes. And the way your brow furrows when you're either judging me or challenging me." She sighed. "But to see you out of sorts because you're hurting? Makes my heart hurt. And I won't go there with the *s* word. Too many *sorrys* already. But I do want to go here."

The touch of her mouth to the center of his back, below his neck, startled Kelyn for a moment. Because she lingered, her warm lips caressing his skin reverently, the tiny puffs of breath from her nose sweeping his skin. And as she leaned forward, her breasts brushed his lower back.

"You're a beautiful man, Kelyn."

Being called beautiful was weird. He wasn't. And she was being kind. The sort of kind that a person felt was necessary to make another feel good. He was lacking now. He'd never be the same man without his wings. Could he ever measure up?

The next kiss landed right where his wings should have flinched because of her touch. And he felt Valor's energy seep into him in waves of heat and violet and—hmm, a twinge of warning?

Yes, that had been a strange zap that tightened his muscles painfully. His body must remember that *she* had been the reason he no longer wore wings. *Get her off*, it seemed to say.

And yet his brain could only process the intensity of his growing desire to turn over and kiss her fully and deeply. But when he pushed himself up to begin to turn, she pressed a palm against his shoulder.

"Wait," she said. "Let me do this."

The witch's hands worked more magic than she could probably imagine. Kelyn felt her touch deeply, in his muscles and through to his bones. It wasn't uncomfortable until she skated over the places where his wings had been severed. But those glancing touches remained brief. Overall, her touch buoyed him like no pink lake could.

The urge to turn over and pull her down on top of him so she could feel all of him was strong. He wasn't crass, though. Yet her touch did not warrant patience.

"Feeling better?" she asked.

"Much." He nudged the seraphinite on the pillow and glanced aside. "It's pouring out there. We're in for the night."

"I figured that. Want to watch a cheesy movie?"

"Truth?"

"Always."

"I want to make out." He turned over beneath her and looked up into Valor's not-so-surprised grinning face. "What do you think?"

"Sounds better than a movie." She swept her fingers down his chest. She hadn't quite sat down on his hips, which was a good thing. But when her strokes lowered to above the waistline of his jeans, Kelyn hissed through a tight jaw. "My magic helped to relax you. I could feel your muscles surrendering and growing lax. But parts of you are very…"

"Tense," he said with a wink. And, grabbing her wrist to stop her from venturing lower, he pulled her down until she was nose to nose with him. He inhaled her witchy scent of sage and cheeseburger and studied her gaze. "There's only one way to ease that tension."

"Yeah, I figured. Oh, what's this?" She studied her fingers, which now glinted with his innate dust.

"You are familiar with what happens to faeries when we get aroused?"

"Right. I thought that was only when they come. Like, from orgasm."

"Close. Some of us put out dust when we're feeling… you know."

"Really? So, whenever you're turned on? Hmm…" She rubbed her fingers together, then sniffed the dust. "I could use this stuff."

"Seriously, witch? I thought we were, uh…doing something here?"

"Sorry. It's just so useful. And hard to come by."

"My dust is not included on your ingredient list."

"But you never know—"

He pushed up her shirt and tugged it off over her head, startling her to abandon her absentminded wondering. She wore no bra and her breasts were small and—the word *adorable* came to mind, but he wasn't sure she'd like that assessment. Kelyn pulled her down to lick one nipple and she quickly forgot the sparkles on her fingers. She shouldn't worry about missing out on collecting some dust for her spells. If they had sex, she'd be covered with the stuff. It made having sex with mortal women difficult to explain, so he had often tried to pick up clubbers glittered up to the nines. Come morning? Neither could determine who wore more glitter than the other.

"Oh, that's good," she said as he laved his tongue around her tight nipple. "You've definitely recovered from your grumpiness."

"That I have."

With his tongue, he teased a trail across her heated skin to her other nipple, as if indulging in a tiny treat. He was fascinated by their tightness and the barely there swells of her breasts. Every lick seemed to produce a different tone of pleasure from her. He most certainly was no longer in a bad mood, even if subtle twinges of pain had already returned to his back.

Easing his hips against hers, he reveled in the pressure against his erection. Oh, yes, if she moved her hips like that…

"Wait." She sat up, moving out from under him, and put her hands over her breasts. "This isn't the right time."

"The right—what do you mean? Aren't you into me?"

"Yes, very much so." She studied her fingers again, frowning at the dust that glittered on the tips. "But something doesn't feel right. It's like we haven't earned this."

"That's…" The strangest excuse for trying to get out of sex he had heard. Not that he'd been given excuses before, but seriously? Man, had he read this woman wrong! Kelyn blew out a frustrated breath. "I get it. You're not into faeries."

He shoved himself up and strode over to the window, pressing a palm to the rain-streaked glass. He flexed his shoulders, pressing back toward the center of his back. The ache had returned. And his cock was hard as steel, which was why he wouldn't turn to face her. Talk about leaving him high and dry.

"So, what time are we heading out tomorrow?" he asked. "Do we know where we're going?"

"Not yet. And would you chill, Kelyn? You're acting like I slapped you or something."

He turned a look over his shoulder. "Didn't you?"

"I did not!"

"Well, it felt like it. I'm getting mixed signals from you, Valor. One minute you're kissing me and touching me in all the ways that you know turn a man on. And the next?" He turned and stretched out his arms in surrender. "This."

Her eyes strayed to his obvious erection, and she inhaled deeply and let her shoulders drop. Hands still over her bare breasts, she nodded. "You're right. It is me. But it's not because I don't like you or am not interested. You're the sexiest man to walk into my life. Ever."

"Then what's wrong, witch?"

She shuddered. "You know you said *witch* like a swear word?"

"Sorry. I'm just—" he flung up his hands in defeat "—off balance right now. The moon and my phantom pain. All this travel. And I'm having trouble with this whole *us* thing."

"I get that. And they are all legitimate excuses—"

"I'm not making excuses, Valor. This is me. I expected… Hell, I read you wrong."

"You didn't. But I read you wrong. I think you're still hung up on what I did to you. How could you possibly trust me or even desire me after—"

Kelyn silenced her foolish protest with a long, hard kiss that opened her mouth and branded her with his desires. He wanted her so desperately right now. And she had lured him close enough to taste that which he wanted.

But if she didn't think the time was right, he didn't want to press. He was no man to force a woman into anything.

Reluctantly, he broke the kiss. "After?" he said to her uncertainty. "What's done is done, Valor. Move forward. I'm trying to. But it's like walking up a down escalator with you. I don't ever seem to connect."

He grabbed his shirt. Tugging it on, he strode toward the door. "I'm going down to check out the casino. While I'm there I'll give Erte a call. Good friend of mine who is an elf. He may be able to point me toward someone who knows this area and the best place to find mermaids." He paused at the door and glanced to her, still sitting there with her hands over her bare breasts. "Whatever that chip is on your shoulder about how I should feel about you? Knock it off, will you?"

And he walked out, hating that he was leaving her alone, but also knowing he hadn't the patience for her self-deprecating bullshit anymore. She needed to get over it. Or else stop trying to tease and seduce him.

The witch couldn't have it both ways.

Valor called Eryss, her best witchy friend back in the United States and also the principle owner of the Decadent Dames brewery. Eryss was in the process of opening another brewery in Santa Cruz, California, because that was where her man, Dane, lived and they'd agreed to share two places. Eryss got winter in Minnesota. And Dane was mostly okay with that. The guy was a scientist surfer dude who also worked for a secret agency dedicated to protecting paranormals from human discovery, so it was all good. Except for the part where he'd almost killed Eryss when he was carrying an enchanted witch hunter's dagger. Long story.

"Wales?" Eryss asked on a yawn. Valor hadn't done the time-change math and wasn't about to. "That sounds exotic."

"Really? The hotel we're staying in has a cheesy casino, overcooked Juicy Lucys and I don't think it ever stops raining here. But apparently it's the best place to find a mermaid."

"That it is. You have someone in the know to help you do that finding?"

"That's Kelyn's job. He might be looking into that right now. He's...not here in the room. Went down to the casino to pout."

"A pouting faery? Why? Are you two fighting?"

"Maybe. No. Yes. I don't know. Eryss, I'm such a freak." She knelt on the bed, then fell backward, head to the pillow and free arm flung out to the side. "I really like Kelyn, and I know he likes me, but...oh! Dr. Robert Chase, I feel like a sixteen-year-old angsty girl saying that."

Eryss laughed. "I don't think we women ever get over lacking confidence around men we admire. But you and Kelyn do have a history. I can understand your trouble hashing out your feelings toward him. As well, you do have the bad breakup that I know is still bugging you."

"Yeah, well, I tried to do something to alleviate that pain, but apparently it's not to be. Good ol' Valor. Just one of the guys."

"You've got to stop calling yourself one of the guys, Valor. I need to say this, and you know it's true. You push men away."

"No, I don't. I'm one of them. I'm a part of their tribe!"

"Exactly. And by infiltrating their tribe you confuse them and push them away."

Valor sighed and slapped a hand over her forehead. *Tell it like it is much?* "You know too much about me."

"What's that phrase you always say? Bros before ohs?"

So Valor preferred friendships with men. Oftentimes that meant she went without the orgasm she could have had if they'd been more than merely friends.

"You need to reverse that thinking," Eryss said.

"I'm trying to. But I'm…unlovable."

"Nonsense. I love you."

"Whoopee."

"I heard that."

"Sorry. You know I get down on myself so well."

"You do, indeed."

"It's that I think I like Kelyn. The guy fascinates me. And he's like Mr. Kind of the World. Nothing ever seems to rattle him, unless it's his faery period."

"His faery period? Do I want to know?"

"It's phantom pain he's feeling from his wings. But beyond that tiny bit of grumpiness, he's like the perfect man. And when he kisses me…"

"He's kissed you? We're talking about a new kiss, not the one in the forest when you thought you were dying?"

"Right. New kisses. As in plural. He's given me a few. And, oh, mercy, they made my toes curl."

"Then what's the problem? How does he feel about… you know, everything?"

Yeah, Eryss was too nice to just come out with

"Does he hate you for being the reason he sacrificed his wings?"

"He says he's over it and it doesn't bother him."

"Then believe him, Valor. I know how stubborn you can be about things. Will you give him a chance to be your hero?"

Now Valor scoffed. "A hero? Please, Eryss, you know I don't need a freakin' hero to ride up on his white steed and whisk me off in rescue."

"Sounds like a cool fantasy, but I agree. We women don't always need that kind of hero. Sometimes, to be a hero, a man merely needs to see us for what we really are. He needs to see our truths."

Like wanting to be accepted by a man and being really loved instead of considered just another one of the guys? Valor sighed.

"That sigh tells me you agree. But you know what? Sometimes you have to actually step forward and tell the guy what you want him to see. Believe it or not, the males of our species are not mind readers. Nor are we women. Just as I've told Dane many a time. I will never understand his always thinking I should know what he wants for breakfast. I mean, come on."

Valor chuckled. "You have found yourself an amazing man. I never would have thought you'd hook up with a science geek who also hunts witches."

"He's not a witch hunter. I thought we'd cleared that up. It was that weird enchanted dagger that was making him think he wanted to kill witches."

"Yeah, but he killed you dozens of times through your various reincarnations."

"Right? Whew! So glad that's over."

"Speaking of you and Dane, how's the little one? Kicking a lot?"

"I seriously cannot wait to get this little guy out of my stomach and into the world. I think I've got an MMA fighter in there, for all the kicking he does. And always in the middle of the night!"

"Like right now? I'm sorry I called so late. But you've cheered me up. Or, at least, you've given me things to think about."

"Relationships are hard for a reason. They're not worth having if you don't put some effort into them. But it's just the beginning for you and Kelyn. You two are on a fabulous adventure together. Enjoy it. And no matter the outcome, you need to live in the now. And speak your truths. Yes?"

"Yes! We rappelled out of a helicopter over a pink lake."

"I don't even have words for that. I can't imagine."

"It rocked. Oh, I love you, Eryss. You always make me feel better."

"Me and my snoring husband send our love. Now, go find the guy and kiss him back and tell him what you really want from him."

"I…"

"Valor," she said warningly.

"I will. I mean, when he comes back to the room, I will. I don't want to be pushy."

Eryss's heavy sigh said too much. "That means you really do like this guy. Because you generally play the aggressor in the relationship."

"Calling Dr. Bombay, anyone?"

Eryss laughed. "I love that you've finally found someone to challenge your sense of how a relationship with a man can work. I hope he's strong enough to push back as much as you do."

"He is. Do you know he put up with drunk preflight me? Twice."

"Give that guy a medal. Okay, take it slow but steady. And let him kiss that mermaid."

"I will. Talk later, Eryss. Night."

"It's three in the morning, sweetie. I owe you one for this wake-up call. You'll be hauling grains for weeks when you get back to town."

"Who is doing it now?"

"Mireio talked Dane into helping her. I think she batted her lashes at him. She's a kook. But you know we could never convince Geneva to lift a forty-pound bag of barley. She might chip her nail polish."

Valor laughed. "Well, then, she could get one of her billionaires to buy her a new manicure."

"She's off the billionaires, didn't you know?"

"I didn't. That's… Really? That chick never dates any man whose worth is less than ten figures. What's up with that?"

"She wants to see what it's like to date rustic. Those were her exact words."

"Oh, that is so Geneva. I can't wait to get back to town and hug all you girls. Give everyone a hug and kiss for me. Good night!"

Valor hung up and pressed the phone against her lips. She'd needed that conversation. And the encouragement. Maybe she did need to view this adventure with new eyes. Live in the now and not worry about what could never happen.

But as for telling Kelyn that she needed him to see

her? That felt difficult. Like exposing herself to a crew of hungry hyenas. No, she couldn't go that far.

"Slow," she muttered. "That's how we're going to do this."

Chapter 12

Valor woke to find that Kelyn had not returned to the room. She glanced out the window. The sun shone and the parking lot was drying up after yesterday's rain. Could they get lucky enough to have sun for their mermaid hunt?

She couldn't find hope without knowing if Kelyn had returned last night while she was sleeping, or maybe he'd not come back at all. Had he been that angry with her? Maybe Eryss was right. She needed to talk to him straight out.

Or not.

"You gotta stop being a flake," she muttered as she wandered into the bathroom. "Be you. The tough chick who takes what she wants and gives as good as she gets. Yeah," she said to her reflection.

She'd put the whole guilt thing aside and give Kelyn

the respect he deserved. And maybe she could loosen up the tough act. Just a bit. Let the guy in? She didn't always have to be one of the guys.

"Maybe," she said on a whisper that ended in a wink at her reflection. She patted down a tangle of hair above her ear, then decided the gray T-shirt she'd slept in and the skinny black jeans were good to go.

Ten minutes later, she wandered through the casino, cautioning herself not to look down at the crazy carpeting that resembled Scottish tartan on crack. The pattern alone could mesmerize a person and set her off course to crash into a nearby slot machine.

Not many people were in the casino. In fact, she saw fewer than half a dozen sitting before the slots. It was early. Probably most were in the restaurant eating or enjoying their vacations by lingering in bed. She didn't have to go far to spy the blond faery slumped in a chair before an electronic slot machine that flashed neon-haired women with purple kitty ears and tails. His feet were propped up on another machine, and one arm hung down the side of the chair, his knuckles brushing the floor.

That man was going to have one hell of a neck ache when he woke. Of course, if it gave her a chance to exercise her massage skills again, this time she would not balk when he tried to take it further with kisses and bare skin. Because she wanted to put her hands on him again. His muscles were so hard, and it wasn't often she got to practice her healing magic, either.

Valor glanced to a passing attendant who was polishing the chrome-edged slot machines with a cloth and spray. The elderly woman wearing a pink apron and bright white high-tops offered her nod to Kelyn and a shrug. "Didn't want to wake him," she said quietly. "He yours?"

Valor shrugged. "I guess so."

If only!

Then again, there was a lot she didn't know about this man, and the fact that he'd rather spend the night camped out in a cheesy casino than up in a comfy bed beside her said so much. Had she hurt him that much with her flaky refusal to push the make-out session to the next level? Or was he one of those sensitive types whom a woman could never please no matter what she did?

Goddess, but she'd had enough of that type of man. Yet tops on her list of not-wants was the man who could never see beyond her as just another one of the guys. How to change that impression? She couldn't do frills and makeup. That was so out of her realm of talents.

Valor slid onto the vinyl seat next to Kelyn and clasped her fingers about his wrist. The silver scars where his sigils had once been were not raised, but she sensed some minute power within. It seemed to poke at her own magic as if trying to shrug her off. Interesting. Could he have a bit of magic left within that he wasn't able to consciously access?

Kelyn startled and then groaned. His body eased into a stretch, his long legs bending and his feet slipping off the slot machine with an ungraceful thud. That prompted another groan from him.

When he finally popped open one eye, he managed a smirk. "Morning."

"That it is. I'll reserve the *good*, though, until I can assess whether or not you're going to have a screaming neck ache."

"Sorry," he mumbled. He cracked his neck one way,

then the other. His wince told her he wasn't pain free. "Should have returned to the room. I thought I was going to close my eyes for a few minutes. Guess all this traveling has worn me out. What's up for today? You ready to go?"

"Uh, sure. But it's early. We've time to catch some breakfast. You know how I do love a buffet."

"That I do."

"Unless you want to hang in the casino a little longer. I didn't think you were the gambling type."

"I'm not. But a few plays were necessary. Just to see if I could get all the purple kitties." He smiled a ridiculously charming yet tired grin.

"Did you find someone who can take us to mermaids?" Valor asked.

"Never."

"Oh. Uh, do you want me to give it a try?"

"Guy's name is Never." Kelyn sat up, wincing, and stretched his arms above his head, which tugged the shirt across his hard pecs right at about Valor's eye level. The ridges of his abdomen pressed against the shirt, as well.

Yeah, she was over the guilt and the weird need to push the man away. She wanted this guy. To touch and kiss and…whatever came next. No strings or expectations attached. *If* he would give her another chance.

"Never is an Unseelie who left Faery years ago," Kelyn said. He stretched back an arm, then swung it forward, working at the tightness. And then he leaned in close to her. "Erte told me about him."

"I've heard that name before."

"He's my best friend. Elves in the mortal realm are rare. He lived in Faery ages ago, but he prefers our realm. Go figure."

"And by ages, do you mean centuries?"

"I do. But the guy didn't have to consume a vampire's heart to live as long as he has. Long life is natural for elves. I trust him, but he said we should not trust Never."

"Great. Untrustworthy faeries. And vicious mermaids. Just what we need to make this adventure unforgettable. You hungry?"

"Always. Should we head to the buffet?"

"Sure, but first…" She wrapped her fingers about his wrist again and paused to summon her courage. Eryss's words resounded, yet she wasn't quite ready to go all in. "This is the last time I'm going to say sorry to you, but you do deserve this one. I've been kind of flaky around you and it's going to stop."

"Valor, I understand—"

"You might think you do, but that doesn't mean I can't aspire to a different tactic and try to be…" A real girl. Someone with whom a man could see relationship potential. "I want us to be good."

"We are good."

"All righty. But maybe I want us to be better than good. Like, you know, good is for friends. Something a little beyond that kind of good?"

"Such aspirations are a fine thing to have," he said, standing. "Beyond good it is." He offered her his arm and Valor stood and hooked hers in his, pleased he'd agreed so easily to her not-so-definitive suggestion about their relationship. "Can I take you out on a breakfast date?"

"I'd like that. Oh, hey, look." Valor ripped the paper tag from the slot machine. "You won twenty pounds from the purple kitty chicks."

"Nice. We are definitely getting the plate-size upgrade."

"Whoo!"

"What's a thin place?" Valor asked Kelyn as, two hours later, he navigated to the village for which the faery Never had given him GPS coordinates. "I've heard it mentioned and suspect it's to do with Faery."

Kelyn possessed an ease driving the car, one wrist propped on the steering wheel and his eyes taking in the periphery, as if he were adventuring and searching for great sites. She found it sexy, so casual and sure of himself.

"You know Faery is everywhere?" he asked. "Though it's not as close in the more populated places, like big cities."

"It's another dimension, of sorts, that overlies or underlies the mortal realm."

"Right. But you can only get there through a portal and you must be *sidhe* or have another means, such as a spell." He winked at her.

Valor caught that wink as if he'd given her a hug. She smiled to herself and felt that, whatever happened between the two of them, it was going to work. It had to.

"A thin place is where Faery bleeds into the mortal realm. It's not Faery. It's not the mortal realm. It's sort of both."

"Can you get into Faery through a thin place?"

"Maybe. It's not a portal. It's a place where the *sidhe* exist without being seen by human eyes. Sort of like FaeryTown in Paris. And like the Darkwood. That's a thin place. You did know that about the forest before you went there, right?"

Now he didn't offer a wink but instead a sideways glance.

"Maybe? First time I've heard the definition for thin place was today. But I get it now. Faery exists on top of the mortal realm. And woe to those who try to exert their power there. Or borrow a few mushrooms."

"Borrow? What about invoking a dangerous spell?"

"Dangerous?" Arguing would open a can of worms she wasn't willing to shake. Valor could but offer a guilty shrug.

"I understand pretty much the entire shoreline of Wales is a thin place," Kelyn said, "though not the major ports. That must be the village ahead where those thin puffs of dark smoke are curling out of chimneys. Quaint. And *that* is what we are looking for."

Valor looked in the direction Kelyn pointed. A long, winding fieldstone fence hugged the road, looking ever so Old World. And atop it crouched a man with dark hair and wings.

"Seriously? He sits out in the open with his wings revealed?" Valor wondered.

"I suspect he's wearing a glamour against human eyes." Kelyn pulled the rental car over to the side of the road thirty feet away from the faery, who hadn't moved from his perch. "You ready for this?"

Valor shrugged. "Are you?"

"I am. And so you know, he requires payment for this venture. Which I'm perfectly willing to pay."

Kelyn got out and strode ahead. While Valor, gripping the door handle, wondered exactly what sort of payment a faery would ask of another for the map to a thin place.

Chapter 13

As they approached the faery crouched on the stone fence, Valor invoked a white light of protection over herself by grasping the moonstone amulet and drawing her other hand from her crown and gesturing downward to the ground until she felt the energy clasp about the bottoms of her boots.

The air was heavy with a promise of rain. The gray sky flashed with intermittent peeks of sunlight through clouds. Valor noticed the black markings on the faery's neck and the backs of his hands. Delicate tracings that resembled some kind of *mehndi* creation, but she knew they were sigils. Most faeries wore them and used them to conjure their own kind of magic.

Kelyn's sigils were gone. No amount of massage or restitution could erase her guilt over that. She'd only once seen him in all his wondrous faery magnificence, that night when he unfurled his wings and went after the troll in the Darkwood. Magnificent.

Damn, she hated herself sometimes.

"Never," Kelyn said as he arrived before the faery, who jumped down to clasp hands in greeting. "Erte sends his respects."

"I return them," Never said. Dressed in tight black leggings with tears in the knees and a ripped black T-shirt, he looked like a punk rocker abandoned by his crew after a night lost in the wild. The dark faery's violet gaze, outlined in thick kohl, moved to Valor. A breeze tickled through his spiky black hair. A smirk of challenge lifted the corner of his mouth. "And this is the witch?"

"Valor Hearst," Kelyn introduced her.

Never stepped forward with a limber bounce that was almost imperceptible and yet Valor thought perhaps his jerked moves indicated a few cels from the film strip had been removed. It was a faery thing, that rapid movement that seemed to jerk and alter space and time. Though she hadn't seen Kelyn move so quickly.

She offered her hand to shake, and Never bowed and kissed the back of it. His dark menace whispered over her skin like gray soot.

The faery released her hand quickly, stepping back. He winced. "You needn't ward against me, witch."

"Probably not," she offered. "But all the same, I'm more comfortable wearing one in new places."

"Of course." He acquiesced with a tight smirk. "So, mermaids." He turned to Kelyn. "It's not often I hear of a fellow *sidhe* with a hunger to make out with one of those scaly bitches."

"It's for a spell," Kelyn said. "My wings were… I gave

them freely to another and now I want to get them back. The mermaid's kiss is an ingredient in a spell that'll open a portal to Faery."

"I see." Never walked around Kelyn, his dark clothing and hair making him look like a gothic punk rocker plopped into the setting of old-world charm, green fields and even a few white sheep grazing in the distance. "Why would you give a part of you away so freely?"

"It's not your concern."

"Probably not. But that cipher you wear at your neck could be my concern. Why have you a cipher that only the Wicked can use?"

Kelyn touched the leather cords about his neck, his fingers glancing over the mouse alicorn before he pressed the black circle between his fingers. "This? I don't know what it is, actually. A friend gave it to me."

"A friend? One of the Wicked? Though why one of those terrible things would give up such a thing surprises me. You don't know what you have? That—" Never pointed to the tourmaline circle Kelyn still held "—is a cipher that can be activated by the Wicked. It's a navigational device used in Faery. It leads to dark and dangerous things, my friend. One such as you has no power to use it. Though—" Never tapped his jaw in thought "—it does connect you to something. I'm not sure what, exactly."

"A cipher." Kelyn shrugged. "Then I'll be sure not to hand it over to a Wicked One. If it has no power in this realm, it's but a trinket, isn't it?"

"I suppose so."

Kelyn stepped before the faery to stop his circling pace. "Are we going to do this or not?"

"Of course. The thin place is close," Never said. The

faery's eyes scanned the steel-and-rose horizon. The sun was falling in the sky, despite their early start. "But first I'll ask my payment, as you've promised."

"If this is going to cost a lot…" Valor started, but Kelyn's sudden chiding glance stopped her cold. *Step back, witch*, was the feeling she got from him. Let him handle this.

All righty, then. She put up placating hands and took an exaggerated step back. She'd leave the faery business to the experts. It was all a part of the new and untested not-so-aggressive Valor. A girl the guys could see as more than one of their tribe.

Whatever.

"It'll cost no more than a swoon and a smile," the faery Never said as he walked around behind Kelyn and toyed with the man's blond hair. He eyed Valor from over Kelyn's shoulder. "All I ask is ichor."

"Ichor?"

"This is not a problem," Kelyn said to Valor with that same chiding tone touching his voice. "He's half-vampire."

The faery winked, and now Valor noticed that within his violet pupils were red stars. So, a half-breed Unseelie escapee was going to help them find mermaids? For ichor? She didn't get it. And generally she was pretty quick on the uptake.

And then she did get it, when the faery opened his mouth to reveal fangs.

"Make it quick," Kelyn said to the faery hugging him from behind, but he maintained eye contact with Valor. "We haven't got all day."

Crossing her arms, Valor stepped back. She didn't want to watch this. But when the faery lunged toward

Kelyn's neck, she could suddenly imagine nothing more than watching. Pearly sharp fangs sank into flesh, and Kelyn winced at the intrusion. The faery gripped him up under the chin while he fed from his vein. Faery blood wasn't red, nor was it even blood, but instead, ichor. A clear substance that sparkled with the faery dust that coursed through their systems. Ichor could be extremely addictive to vamps. But to a half faery, half vamp? Valor couldn't fathom what Never got out of such a drink.

And then she could, as the faery moaned a long and sexually pleased tone. The hand that grasped Kelyn's chin seemed to stroke lovingly. Even Kelyn hummed out a satisfied sound, mined deep from his chest. It was as if Valor were watching something illicit.

And she could not look away.

When she placed a hand over her heart, the thuds startled her. And she realized her skin had warmed even though the breeze was cool. Was she…turned on by watching such a thing? No. That wasn't her style. Maybe?

Kelyn stepped backward, as if losing his balance. Never gripped him surely and licked at his vein. The red-eyed faery caught Valor's interest and smirked against Kelyn's neck. He enjoyed that she was watching.

When, finally, Never released his ichor donor, Kelyn stumbled and put out his arms to right himself. He tossed Valor a loopy grin and she knew he was in a swoon from the powerful bite. As was Never. The dark faery reeled around and caught his hands on the stone fence, laughing and then falling to his knees in a wicked spin of orgasm.

"Well." Valor stretched and twisted her neck uncomfortably. She announced, "That was inappropriate."

Both faeries chuckled as she strode back to the vehicle.

* * *

From the back seat of the Jeep, Never directed the two of them to a sparsely wooded area that fronted the Irish Sea. Sure the rains would begin soon, Valor hoped they could get this done before that happened.

Kelyn found a clearing of jagged rock scattered with boulders—one the size of a VW—and parked the vehicle.

Tall grasses hugging the olive trees dashed in painted streaks greener than emeralds. Skylarks soared overhead. And the air seemed kissed with a fragrance Valor could only call life and breath and vitality. Her hair blew in unnatural flutters about her as she stepped out to look around. Her air magic sensed the intensity of the vita about her and responded like an electric force.

"That's interesting," Never commented on her hair. "Air witch?"

She nodded. "So tell me this. Why ichor? If you're half-vamp."

"Human blood makes me sick," he offered. "Iron and all."

"Ah." Faeries and iron did not mix. "Got it. So, are you going to stick around for the fun?" She opened the back of the Jeep, where they'd stowed the rope and harness.

"Wouldn't think of it. Even if I did have access to Faery—which I do not—the last thing I want to do is return to Faery. Don't want to end up working for dear old Daddykins. But you…" Never walked up to Kelyn and stood so close Valor wondered if he might kiss him. The two had bonded in some weird way with that bite, but she didn't want to question it too much. Never placed his palm over Kelyn's heart. "You do know what will happen if you manage to retrieve your wings from Faery?"

Kelyn set back his shoulders proudly. "I'll be whole again."

"Not necessarily. If someone else is wearing them, those wings will be tainted by that creature's essence, be it good, evil or merely malicious."

"Merely?" Valor prompted.

The faery smirked. Of course, faeries were big on malice and menace. And, apparently, black eyeliner.

"Be wary," Never said, and stepped away from the two of them. "If you're ever eager to donate to the cause again…" He winked at Kelyn.

Spreading out his arms dramatically, Never then released his wings in a whoosh of gray, black and red. With but a jump backward, the faery took to air, transforming to small size within a blink and zipping off across the lush emerald countryside. He looked like a dragonfly darting off to Wonderland.

"Cool," Valor commented. "I guess he wasn't so bad."

"If you say so." Kelyn grabbed the rope from her and wandered toward the trees.

She probably shouldn't press regarding the bite, but…

"Wait up!" She grabbed the harness from the back of the Jeep, checked that the jackknife was tucked in her back pocket, then ran after Kelyn. "So, are you going to tell me about the bite?"

"What's there to tell? You saw the whole thing."

"I did, and it was…"

"Inappropriate?" He chuckled and winked at her. "You know what it's like when someone is bitten by a vampire."

"I do. Not from personal experience but from hearsay." It was supposed to be orgasmic for the vampire, and the victim was generally left in a swoon, as she'd witnessed with Kelyn. "It's got to be a bummer for a faery who needs to drink blood but can't. That's just weird."

"I'm not going to question too much. It was what he required for payment. It was something I was willing to offer."

"So, did you, you know...?"

He hefted the coiled rope over a shoulder. A waggle of his brow teased at her. "You know?"

"You're going to make me ask it?"

"I am."

"Fine! Did you get off?"

"I did." And with that he wandered ahead of her toward the granite cliff.

Valor followed with a muttered, "Exceedingly inappropriate."

Chapter 14

The inky green sea swirled before Kelyn as he stood at the edge of a granite ledge that hung over the water. The drop to the water's surface was two feet from the stone. Never had referred to finding the *tongue* of stone that licked over the waters as an excellent vantage point from which to locate mermaids.

The air was heavy with moisture and brewed the salty ocean scents to a heady elixir that even he, with his muted senses, smelled all over, as if his skin were the nose. The sun had disappeared behind clouds, though a weak half circle of muted gold glimpsed out once in a while. It would rain soon, so he hoped to get this done before the deluge.

He checked the blue nylon harness he wore, which strapped about him like a vest. Attached to it were a couple D-rings, through which he'd threaded the length of rope.

Turning, he followed the rope along the granite surface about thirty feet to where the two of them had wrapped the other end of the rope around a massive boulder that had only budged a little when Kelyn testingly shoved against it. Valor had knotted the rope expertly, commenting she'd learned sailor's knots when she dated a seaman in the middle of the last century. It should provide a good hold.

And beside the six-foot-high boulder stood Valor. When his gaze met hers she shrugged, and with a wave, she called to him, "What could possibly go wrong?"

The chick was damn cute when she was working the false hope.

Turning back to the sea, Kelyn sighed heavily and took stock of this crazy venture he was about to literally dive into. He could not swim. His light bones made a free dive difficult, if not impossible. He wasn't even sure how long he could hold his breath underwater. And he was now only as strong as a human man.

Another glance over his shoulder to wink at Valor felt necessary. The witch had a way of challenging him. And he loved it. But was it worth the risk to get back wings that could be tainted by an unknown evil, as Never had suggested?

"Yes," he murmured. "I want to be whole again."

"I want that for you, too."

Kelyn startled at Valor's voice beside him. He hadn't heard her approach, which proved he was out of sorts and not on his game. He'd better check that if he wanted to survive this next challenge.

"This will work," she said.

Standing up on her tiptoes, she kissed him. It was a long, lingering kiss that said so many things he wanted to hear but dared not put into thought. Hope and want and desire. Better to feel it than have it spoken. Yes?

Could he allow himself to want the girl? He'd stayed in the casino last night because he'd been miffed at her rejection, but he'd also felt he was pushing her too quickly into something she didn't want. He was supposed to protect the woman. But he knew she didn't need protection.

Part of him wished she could need him a little bit. How to win over a woman who was her own hero?

Ending the kiss, she asked, "You good?"

"Yes, of course. But, uh…" He swiped the back of his hand over his mouth. "Better wipe that one off so the mermaid kiss will stick. A shame, though. Your kisses are something a guy wants to keep for much longer."

"I promise you another one after you've secured the prize." A gentle punch to his shoulder sealed her word. With a wink, she tugged at the rope, making a show of checking the secure knots. She patted her gray-and-black-camo coat pocket. "Got the vial and sticking paper right here. Soon as you've been deflowered, I'm moving in. I think I should put a protection spell on you."

"Not a good idea. I want the mermaid to kiss me, not be repelled."

"Right. As soon as you get that kiss…"

"I'm getting another one from you." He winked at her and she almost punched him again, but withdrew and instead bowed her head, smiling.

Yeah, she liked him.

"You might want to stand by to tug me up in case the mermaid's kiss disorients me," he suggested. "Never been kissed by a mermaid before, but I suspect it's not as delicious as yours."

"There you go being a sweetie again. It's gotta taste like fish, right?"

"I hate fish."

"We'll dine on veggies and cake later to celebrate."

"Sounds like a plan." He clapped his hands together and nodded with decisiveness. No more stalling. Time to either sink or swim. "Let's do this!"

Kelyn knelt at the edge of the stone tongue and gave a look to Valor so she stepped back about ten feet, giving him space. Good call. Should the mermaid see her, the creature might be frightened away.

He lay on his stomach and reached down, but his fingers barely touched the surface so he shoved himself forward until he could cup the cool water in his palms. The granite he lay on smelled like old civilizations. The sea smelled rich and steeped with ages of secrets only dead sailors could tell. He wasn't sure how to call up a mermaid, and Valor had no clue, either. Probably something they should have researched before coming out here.

He'd wing it. Wingless as he was.

Searching the metallic green surface, Kelyn could not see far into the depths. Murky waters. That did not seem to bode well. What had Valor cracked about him getting this kiss? Deflowered? Yikes, this would be the first time he'd ever kissed a fish.

But he was approaching this the wrong way. He needed to remain positive. The kiss was another ingredient to check off the list. And then he'd be that much closer to getting back his wings.

Stirring his fingers in the waters, he closed his eyes

and focused on aligning himself with the sea and the creatures within. As faery he had an intimate connection to nature and all her inhabitants. He could tap into a hummingbird's heartbeat and direct it to the best source for food. He could race an elk through the forest and oftentimes win. He could count a bird's chirps and determine whether it was a warning or a greeting.

And he could call a mermaid to kiss him if he desired.

That was the key. He had to want it and believe it was possible.

Feeling the ancient memories of the waters bestill him and calm his heartbeat, Kelyn hummed from the base of his throat, tapping into the Celtic rhythms he had never known, but that had been imprinted on his soul through the ages as a collective message from the universe. He did believe in mermaids. He believed in every myth about which the humans liked to tell stories. They were all real.

He wasn't sure how long he lay there, humming, stirring the waters with his fingertips, but he forgot the witch standing nearby and didn't notice the sun glimmer on the horizon with a wink before a fine mist began to wet his hair and back.

A bubble rose and broke the water's surface. And then another, and another.

He stretched his fingers through the water, and when the cool, wet hand clasped his, Kelyn cursed quietly. In for the ride, he reminded himself. No matter the slimy scales that abraded his skin. He leaned forward more until his entire chest hung over the waters. He could feel the rope tug against the rock and felt secure, so he inched forward a bit more.

The mermaid's head rose, pale green hair spreading

across the surface and forming liquid arabesques about her. Within the seaweed-like hair, bubbles formed, and Kelyn saw a tiny fish bob up briefly within the strands. She emerged to her nose, which was flat and gilled on both sides instead of sporting human-like nostrils. At her cheeks gills also flapped. Otherwise, she looked quite human, save for the green hair.

"Hello, pretty," he offered as charmingly as possible.

Her head rose a little more and her mouth curled into a smile. It was a soft mouth, shaded green as her olive skin but with a tint of rose to it. She tilted her head, brushing it against his open palm like a cat seeking a nuzzle. Kelyn slipped a heavy ribbon of her hair over... well, she didn't have an ear that he could see, so he dropped the hair and offered her a smile.

He wasn't sure if she could speak his language, so he didn't think conversation would be important. Instead he softened his gaze on her and winked.

The mermaid chirred out a giggly sound and behind her, her caudal tail fin slapped the water in a bejeweled display of opalescent scales. Water splattered Kelyn's face, but he laughed as a means to calm his nervous jitters.

"Your tail is beautiful," he said. "As are you."

And then he leaned forward even more, daring to close his eyes and hope upon hope she would understand he wanted a kiss. For ages, mermaids had been known to seduce sailors into kissing them, and then they'd drag them to their deaths at the bottom of the sea.

He'd have to be cautious he didn't become another statistic to fortify the legend.

When a wetness touched his forehead, Kelyn realized she'd touched her forehead to his. Her flesh was soft and slimy, exactly like a fish. And then it happened. Her mouth landed on his in a cold, yet sweetly exotic touch that shivered through his system like nothing he'd felt before. It wasn't as intimately surprising as the faery vampire's bite had been, but it did sharpen his senses to the salty taste on her mouth. She slid her webbed hands over his shoulders, pulling him closer to her until his face was in the water, lips still kissing hers, and then…

He didn't so much drop into the water as get tugged from the granite ledge like a sack of valuable pearls the greedy bitch wanted for herself.

The harness squeezed his chest as the rope resisted. Kelyn felt the mermaid wrap her arms tightly about his shoulders as the murky water engulfed him. His feet kicked at something slippery. Her tail felt as though it had wrapped about his shins. And then the rope gave a little more.

And a little more.

And soon it was as if the rope might have snapped or come untied, for the mermaid swam swiftly downward, taking him along. The kiss broken, he struggled to shuck off her hold about his shoulders. A shout released his air. Water bubbled about him, and her tail lashed roughly at his legs, beating at them wickedly.

Suddenly he was jerked out of her grasp. Snapped upward by a force about his chest, he realized the rope was still secure. Kelyn stretched his arms, aiming for the fading glimmer of the surface. His fey weight buoyed him swiftly upward.

As he ascended, the mermaid circled him, swishing her tail at his face. The scaled fins cut his skin and he struggled to push away the menacing weapon. It was as if a jellyfish were stinging him. He cried out, releasing his last gasp of breath as he surfaced. Thank goodness for his lightweight faery bones!

Yet, from below, the mermaid pushed up on the soles of his boots, rocketing him out of the water to land on the rocky outcrop right beside the boulder that had apparently rolled to the edge.

Kelyn landed on his stomach, grunting at the incredible pain of his body colliding with the solid surface. He rolled to his back and splayed out his arms, gasping for redeeming air and sputtering up the foul water.

"Wait! Don't spit." Valor's voice sounded above him. "Remember the plan. Let me take care of this."

The plan. She'd devised a simple way to retrieve the kiss. Using a piece of rice paper that she now pressed to his mouth, she carefully peeled it away and held it up to study. Scales glinted on the transparent paper. "Got it!" She curled the paper and stuffed it in a glass vial, then stood. "I'm going to put this in the car so I don't lose hold of it. Be right back!"

"Sure." Kelyn sputtered more water. Man, the sea did *not* taste good. "You do that. Leave the half-drowned faery here to die!"

Then he laughed a wet and weary laugh. He'd survived that challenge. He wasn't going to die and end up buried in some rotting shell of a ship filled with hundreds of other unlucky souls. Davy Jones had lost this one. How's that for a guy who had never taken a swimming lesson?

Pushing the hair from his eyes, he winced as his fingers traced the cuts marking his forehead and cheeks. He would heal, but not as quickly as usual.

The crunching of stone and the sudden wobble of the boulder beside him alerted Kelyn. Accompanied by a rush of sudden wind and rains from above, the boulder wobbled…

Tilted forward…

And dropped into the water, breaking off the granite ledge as it did so.

The rock fell away from under Kelyn's legs. Frantically, he shuffled backward. Then he slapped a hand to the harness and the rope knotted so expertly by Valor.

"Shit."

Chapter 15

Pulled with great force into the depths by the heavy boulder, Kelyn focused his intent on the rope in hopes of severing it with sheer strength. Ah! He had no sigils to access his former strength. Water rushed into his mouth, nose and ears. The only way out of this was to swim to the boulder and shimmy the rope from around it.

And that would prove much harder than expected as the flap of a mermaid's tail brushed his cheek and his ichor spilled out into the water.

Valor ran from the Jeep toward the ledge. She'd heard the crushing sound of rock breaking. And the abruptly muffled yelp of one very soaked and defeated faery. She stopped where the granite had broken and crumbled into the sea, stepping back to avoid the loose shards. She should have untied Kelyn immediately. *Fool!*

Kneeling at the rough stone edge, she studied the green water. The surface was remarkably smooth and calm. He must be quite far down already. She wasn't sure if faeries could breathe underwater as vampires could. Would he be able to release himself from the harness? She slapped a hand to her pocket and palmed the blade. It would serve no good in her hand.

What could she do to help? She was no swimmer. And she did not practice water magic. Her expertise was air magic.

"Maybe…" Air *could* be used as a tool.

Standing, she planted her feet squarely and bowed her head to focus her energies. Spreading out her fingers, she slowly raised her arms as she chanted a powerful spell to summon the wind from within the nearby forest. And to harvest the misting rain with that wind. Focusing her vita out through her fingers, she channeled the air elements. Lifting her arms high, she dashed her hands in a swirl that plucked out a tail from the air, collected the rain and swirled it into a tornadic spin of energized magic.

The tornado spun above the water, faster and faster, until the force of it began to open up the waters as if drilling down into rock. And when a column of open water had formed within the sea, Valor sent the tornado down, spinning, spiraling, mining deep, until she felt it connect with the boulder. Like a suctioned tentacle, the end of the tornado grasped the boulder and she commanded it to rise.

Water splashed up over her body as the wind tunnel carried the rock high into the air. And in the next moment, Kelyn stepped onto the broken granite ledge beside her, dropping the frayed rope that tailed behind the boulder.

With a sweep of her hand, she sent the boulder off into the sea and dismissed the tornado. A heavy fall of water that had been corralled into her weapon now released and beat upon their heads. Kelyn's knees buckled. He collapsed and splayed onto the stone.

And then all grew calm. Even the sky seemed to suddenly brighten, thanks to a thread of lingering sunlight. Valor looked over Kelyn's body; ichor covered his face and had started to puddle below his head.

"Dr. Bombay, this is not good!"

She dropped to her knees beside him and pressed an ear to his chest. She didn't feel his chest rise. That couldn't be right. He'd stood next to her, had even smiled. He couldn't be dead. Closer inspection saw the cuts on his face, from which all his ichor flowed. Had he lost too much? The man must have battled with the mermaid within the depths.

Talk about a fickle kisser.

Frantic, Valor clutched her hands before her as she scanned Kelyn's inanimate body. The charms at his neck were still there, the mouse alicorn and the—whatever the thing was that only the Wicked could use. Did it connect him to something? She reached to touch the black circle, but then did not. Now was no time to get curious.

But how to help him? Her healing magic wasn't able to bring back life, not even lure life to remain in a dying body. She could fix boo-boos and even mend the occasional broken bone. But how to give a man back his breath?

"CPR," she muttered. "Yes, how did that go?"

Years ago Mireio had convinced Valor to attend a

CPR course with her. Said it would be a good skill to learn if it was ever needed at the brewery for a customer. Because they certainly couldn't whip out the healing magic with a crowd of humans observing.

Pressing her palms over Kelyn's chest, she pumped once. Then again. Then a few times more rapidly. Bowing over his head, she tilted it back and, clamping her fingers over his nose, breathed into his mouth. Once, twice. Listened for breath. She repeated the sequence over and over, crying out to all the television doctors she had a habit of invoking when life pissed her off or challenged her.

"By all the TV doctors and Dr. Bombay, I will save him. I can't lose him. Not this guy. He's the nicest man I know."

He was the only man who'd ever given her a chance when she least deserved one.

Placing a palm over her other hand, she compressed his chest a few pulses. And this time, when she breathed into his mouth, she invoked all her powers of air magic and infused his system with her vita, her life. Conjuring a violet essence of vitality, she breathed that into him, blessed air that had originated from the universe, representing centuries and millennia of existence. Everyone breathed and walked in the life-giving elixir.

Gasping, Valor pressed her hands to Kelyn's chest again. This time when she pumped, her wrists weakened and her palms slipped from his wet chest. She was growing weak. Had expended too much magic. And...

"No, gotta keep going." Another breath escaped from her exhausted lungs. Valor lingered at Kelyn's mouth, her lips brushing his. "Please..."

A seabird soared overhead, cawing out a mournful

cry. Rain spattered his eyelids, and Valor thought maybe she saw one of them wriggle…

Kelyn choked up water. His body jerked and pulsed upon the wet stone. He groaned and with a choking contortion, rolled and spat out more water to the side. "Oh… scales."

"Oh, yes, thank you!" Pulling him to lie on his back, Valor hugged him across the chest. His fingers grasped at her wet hair, but he didn't move much more than that. "You're alive. I'm so happy. I thought… No, I knew you'd survive. Blessed be!"

"Valor," he said as if in a prayer. "I'm not dead."

"No, you're not. You're lucky I remembered CPR. That came in handy more than I ever expected it would."

"You gave me your…breath."

She shrugged. "It was the least I could do. But know this. That is the last time I let you kiss a mermaid, buddy."

His chest bucked as he laughed and then the faery wrapped his arms across her back and hugged her tightly to him. "No more mermaids. Promise."

Eyes closed, Kelyn lay on the wet, cold stone for a long time. The misty rain continued, and he didn't care. He'd gone beyond soaked. So long as he was not strapped to a big rock and tossed in the ocean again? He was good.

Valor's heat snugged his side. She hadn't said a thing after he closed his eyes. She understood he needed to restore, get back his meager strength and process what had occurred. He'd been dragged to the depths—so close to death—yet he knew Valor's air magic was what had brought him to the surface.

As well, the air from her lungs had ensured he did not die. She had literally given him a kiss of life.

He also sensed that such rescue had fatigued her. Magic extracted a price each time it was used.

But they'd done it. And now elation surged through him as if it were an electric current. He clasped Valor's hand and kissed it.

"You're amazing," she said. They both lay on the granite outcrop, looking up at the gray sky streaked with silver clouds and stitched with the flight of a dark bird soaring beneath the clouds. The moon held reign above the tree line somewhere behind them. "You feeling any better?"

"I am." He rolled onto his stomach and peered into Valor's eyes. Her hair was wet and looked like violet silk. He felt like a soggy piece of seaweed, but that didn't lessen his attraction to the witch's soft, parted lips. "I feel revitalized, actually."

She nodded. "The whole elation-following-death thing?"

"That's a thing?"

"Apparently. Guy gets close enough to kiss death. He survives. He embraces life with gusto."

"If by embracing life you mean this…" He stroked his fingers down her neck to her breast above where the soaked fabric highlighted her tight nipple. "Then I'm in."

She tilted her head to eye him. Moonlight glinted in her big beautiful browns. "You think so?"

He leaned over to kiss the hollow curving at the base of her throat. She swallowed against his lips. Tasting of the sea and air, she felt warmer than fire. The need to devour her so that he could feed the energy that had been taken from him was strong.

"I want you," he said softly, and tugged at her shirt with his teeth.

"Yes. I want you, too. Right now. Here, at the edge of the world." The witch pulled him down for a kiss.

Kisses salted with their fear and a new dose of accomplishment, they greedily took from each other. Kelyn peeled off her wet T-shirt and unbuttoned his jeans. The denim was soaked, but he managed to shove them over his hips. Valor pushed his chest and he rolled to his back. She straddled him and bent to kiss his chest, nipping at his skin and nipples as she did so. The erotic sensation and the sudden rush to grasp pleasure rocketed all feeling to his cock. He sat up, and she slid her legs about his hips. His hands clutched at her hips, then at her breasts and then her hair as he frantically sought to touch all of her, know every part of her.

Then he decided now was not the time for a thorough and detailed exploration of her body. Right now he simply wanted.

"I want to be inside you," he said. "Can we do that?"

"Yes." She shuffled off her boots and pants, then knelt before him, naked. A wet witch had never looked more appealing. "Let's take life and crush it between us."

"Now, that sounds worth the dive."

So he dived for her, gently laying her down on the granite. His heavy erection landed in the soft nest of her curls and he groaned at the sweet, tickling sensation. She wrapped her thighs about his hips and ground her mons against him. He wasn't going to take his time. Already his body trembled in anticipation of release.

"Come inside me," she whispered urgently, reaching for his cock.

Ah, that firm grasp was what he needed right now.

Bowing his head to her breast, Kelyn licked at the tiny swell as, with her guidance, he glided between her legs and inside her tight, squeezing heat. She might have whispered a doctor's name; it might have been some other name entirely. Didn't matter. He felt much the same. This was bliss.

She wrapped about him, embraced him, consumed him. And he didn't ever want to rise from such a place. Pumping slowly within her, he drowned a second time, only this time he enjoyed every gasping breath of it.

Her fingernails dug into his back. The pain sweetened everything and he thrust faster, seeking oblivion.

"Yes," she gasped. "Do it. Fly us both into the stratosphere. Oh, I'm so close, Kelyn. Faster!"

Being told what to do by a woman had never felt more right. Kelyn crushed himself into her, against her, about her. They crushed life together. Let the mermaids wail in jealousy, he'd chosen the woman he desired. And with a few more thrusts, they came together on the granite ledge overlooking a dangerous sea that he had taken on and defeated.

The rain picked up, forcing them to seek a different, less exposed, place for their sexual antics. The granite ledge was fine, but it was growing slick and cold. Welsh summers were never tropical.

Tugging up his jeans so he could walk, Kelyn hoisted Valor over his shoulder and bent as she gathered their remaining soaked clothing into her hands. He raced back to the Jeep, confident they had this little cove by the sea to themselves, but not caring right now if anyone had spied their naked gyrations.

The Jeep was open, though it did have a roof. Still, the

rain had blown diagonally for a while and much of the vehicle was wet inside. He set her down and Valor began to sort through their clothes. Kelyn dipped his head to kiss her on the neck. She giggled, and that giggle ended in a snort.

"I love that laugh!" He picked her up and she wrapped her legs about his hips. Leaning her against the side of the vehicle, he bowed to lick her rain-slick ichor-bedazzled skin. "I also love the taste of a wet witch."

"Oh, yeah? I can take that so many ways."

"This is the way I meant it."

Opening the back door, he laid her inside on the seat, but kept hold of her legs to pull her to the edge of the seat before she could sit up. He stretched out a leg and didn't quite kneel on the ground to get a good position. Valor hiked up one foot onto the open door top, the other she put on his shoulder. Dashing his tongue along the inside of her thigh, he licked away the rain and ventured higher, seeking the treat he desired to taste.

She squirmed but didn't push him away. Instead she scrunched her fingers through his wet hair. Everything was wet. The car, the dirt squishing between his fingers, her skin and, mmm…right there.

"Oh, Kelyn, yes. Just a little lower. And to the left."

He smiled against her thigh and kissed her there quickly. He appreciated a woman who knew exactly what she wanted and wasn't afraid to tell him how to get her there. And since his navigation skills had been lacking of late…

He suckled her swollen nub, tasting it, luxuriating in the moans and rocking hips that resulted from his intense ministrations. And that was the thing that sent the witch reeling. Now, with both feet hooked at his shoulders, she used the leverage to tilt up her hips. He followed her demanding movements, tending that sensitive spot with as much focus as she deserved.

She muttered another doctor's name. Should he be jealous? No. The crazy witch.

And when she cried out a triumphant "Yes!" that was followed by a quick, gasping "Inside me now, faery!" he popped up his head and flashed her a wink.

As the witch wished.

Kelyn stood and shoved down his wet jeans. His hard-on stood at full mast, ready to please. Grabbing one of her legs to pull her closer, he guided himself inside the hot, groaning witch. The wicked tightness of her, and her heat—she was molten—lured him to the edge, where he met her in an orgasm that surely the mermaids would be jealous of for their shouts of ecstasy.

Chapter 16

The bed was blessedly dry. Well, mostly dry. And it... sparkled. As did Valor. She rubbed a palm over her glinting forearm. When Kelyn came he literally spumed dust from his pores. Way to score with the faery. This trip was turning out much better than she had expected.

She'd expected a tense relationship between the two of them, if any at all. But what had developed proved more than magical. It was actually kind of enchanting.

"What?"

Valor realized she'd been staring at the side view of Kelyn, who sat naked in a chair before the window, watching the rain pummel the tarmac outside. He had an erection, and his fingers rested about the base of it. He'd occasionally stroke it, but not with any determination, sort of a reassuring move.

It was ridiculously sexy to know that he'd forgotten

himself while she was in the room, and had kicked back, lost in his own thoughts. Or maybe he hadn't.

He turned a look over his shoulder at her and, with a flick of his wrist, waggled his cock. They'd had sex again after returning to the hotel room and showering. But they hadn't used towels to dry off. In fact, she was still moist. Everywhere. The bedsheets were wet, too, but she didn't care.

"You're sexy." She pushed herself up to sit against a pillow. Bowing forward, she wrapped her arms about her bent legs and rested her cheek on a knee.

"And you have purple hair." His brow furrowed, but with more of a seductive concern than consternation. It was the sexiest move she'd ever watched a man make.

"That I do."

"Is it natural?"

"No. It's a spell. I can streak it any color I like for months at a time. This color is my favorite. It reminds me of a '64 Chevy Impala that I owned a long time ago."

"If it was a '64, then it has been a long time. Did we ever establish your age?"

"We did not. And I don't think it's important, is it?"

He shrugged. "Nope." Another gentle stroke of his erection. It wasn't quite full staff. Relaxed, his body was a study in curved muscle and hard, angular bone structure. "You like cars and motorcycles and all things greasy, including fries and steaks."

"That I do."

"Want to know what I like?"

"Besides running races with deer in the forest and being a super nice guy to everyone you meet? Yes. What is it that Kelyn Saint-Pierre really, deeply, honestly likes?"

"I like a certain witch." He shot a wink over his shoulder. "With purple hair."

The urge to rush over and wrap her arms around him was strong. But Valor decided to simply sit there and take it in. How many times previously had a man complimented her so sweetly? It was a nice moment. One to cherish.

They had spent the early evening risking their lives—okay, so Kelyn had—and by facing death they'd fallen into incredible sex. That whole passionate *la petite mort* thing. So the man was probably on some kind of high right now.

As was she.

They'd lie around a bit longer and come down from the sex endorphins. And then they'd head back to business. Just friends.

Maybe?

"Come here," he said lazily. "Come sit on this."

"You think so?"

"We're not going anywhere until the rains stops. Well, we can, but I like sitting here watching it streak the window. The thunder is relaxing, too."

Valor wandered over to settle onto his lap, back to his chest, directing his now-hard-again erection between her legs to squeeze it tightly with her thighs. That eased up a deep-throated moan from him. She leaned her head against his shoulder and he cupped one of her breasts with his wide, powerful hand.

"Did you think you were going to die?" she asked quietly while tracing the silver remnants of his missing sigil. Outside, lightning streaked the sky in brilliant gold.

"Yes. No." He exhaled against her cheek, and that

ended with a chuffing laugh. "Yes. I regret never taking swimming lessons when I was a kid."

"Adults can take them."

"They can? I suppose. I'm thinking maybe avoiding mermaids is probably the thing to do from now on. And always wear a life jacket."

"Good call. I thought you had died, too. For a few minutes there…"

He pulled strands of half-dried hair away from her face and pressed his lips against her cheek. "I didn't die. And you didn't die when you were pinned in the Darkwood. We're both alive. The universe is not done with us yet."

"Do you believe the universe has a plan for everyone?"

"Yes," he said. "Or rather, that we made the plan before we ever came into our bodies. Our souls wanted to find each other."

"I believe that, too. But we didn't have a very auspicious beginning. And you never know, the ending could be pretty crazy, too."

"Then we'd better enjoy what we have while we can. Yes?"

She reached down to grip his penis. The man beneath her groaned and rocked his hips. Time to drive.

Valor packed her things and took inventory of the magic ingredients they'd collected so far. The mermaid's kiss was tightly capped and secure. The pink water…

"Trapper John! See? What did I tell you?" She waggled a broken vial at Kelyn as he picked up the room.

"Can't you bespell the glass not to break?"

"I could—well, uh…" Why hadn't she thought of

that? Valor bristled at his knowing chuckle. "Cocky faery."

With a few Latin words, Valor spelled the remaining three glass vials not to break. It was a *duh* moment that made her chuckle, as well.

And Kelyn's head rose from packing his things to home his bemused gaze on her like an arrow to the target.

"You really like the way I laugh?" she asked.

"It makes me horny."

"What?" That information made her laugh even more robustly.

And Kelyn dived for her on the bed, pinning her wrists down and kissing her hard against her neck. He licked under her jaw and gave her a gentle nip, which spurred on her laugh even more.

"Let's see if you're ticklish, eh?"

"Oh, no!" She was. And he learned that quickly.

The faery went at her relentlessly, finding all her sensitive spots—goddess, behind her knee!—until she was gasping and pleading for mercy.

"Very well," he said, and his tickles softened to kisses.

A soft touch landing on her breast made her sigh and clutch his hair. "That's so weird that laughter makes you horny."

"Not any laughter. Only your silly, snorting chuckles." He kissed her forehead. "They're amazing."

"No one has ever told me something like that before."

"What? That you're amazing? I can't believe that."

She shrugged. "Maybe it's the company I keep."

"Just one of the boys, eh?"

"Bros before ohs."

"What?"

"Eh, it's something I say. I like my guy friends, and I like that they accept me into their confidence as just another guy. Not a frilly girl that might threaten their man cave."

Except…when she wanted more and the man couldn't understand that.

"What's wrong with being frilly?" he asked. "I like a little frill once in a while."

She shrugged. "Too much work. Seriously, Kelyn, if frills are what you need—"

He kissed her deeply, dancing his tongue with hers. Stealing away her protest. And Valor took that as a hint to shut up and let the man like her.

She could do that.

Another flight was met with but one dirty martini and a firm clasp of Kelyn's hand through most of the quick jaunt across the English Channel to France.

He kissed her as they landed at Charles de Gaulle. "You're getting braver." Then he shook out his hand, the one she'd had a vise hold on through the flight. "And I may not have feeling in my fingers for a few hours."

A snorting laugh from Valor was rewarded with a kiss. It felt wrong that such an awful sound should be answered with a hot, lush kiss, but she'd get used to it. Hell, she already was. And she intended to laugh at every opportunity.

"The ingredients in this spell are so specific. Occipital dust from a skull?" Kelyn asked as, an hour after landing, the taxi navigated central Paris toward the Île Saint-Louis, as he'd directed.

"Better specific than vague. We want this to work, right?"

"Yes." He clasped her hand and kissed the back of it. "You smell great."

Valor smirked. "I smell clean, not like mermaid slime or a pink lake. Is that what you're getting at?"

"Probably." He tilted his head onto her shoulder and nuzzled his nose against her neck, which felt so deliciously exciting Valor had to keep from turning to kiss him. She was not one for PDAs. "You know people are attracted to one another by scent? We select our mates that way."

"Hmm… But how do you know you've the right-smelling person?"

"It's instinctual. We know when we know."

"I see. And what do you know right now?"

"I know that you smell gorgeous." He kissed her neck and licked her skin. A shiver traced her body and coalesced in her nipples, tightening them. He noticed and tweaked one with his fingers.

"Kelyn," she admonished, and gestured toward the front seat.

"He can't see."

"But he *knows*."

"How do *you* know he knows?"

"I just do."

"Fine. Hands off. But this is the hard part."

"Yeah? I thought *that* was the hard part," she said with a glance to his crotch.

"Do you purposely do that?"

She nodded, knowing he was now horny with no means to alleviate that condition. Because of her. "Probably."

"Did I mention we're heading to my aunt's place?"

"Uh, no. I thought we'd grab another hotel room."

"Nope. Kambriel is my dad's twin sister. She and her husband, Johnny Santiago, live on the island. They own a huge place. I'm sure they won't mind putting us up for a day or two."

"They don't know we're coming? Great."

"They're cool. They're both vamps, so you know. They both sing in a goth band and travel the world a lot."

"I like vamps. I look forward to meeting them. Your family is such an interesting mix. Your dad is a werewolf and your mom a faery. Yet your dad's sister is vampire?"

"Grandma and Grandpa are werewolf and vampire."

"Right, Blu and Creed Saint-Pierre. I've met Blu once or twice. She's awesome."

"Grandma rocks. And she won't let Grandpa forget that. As for the rest of our eclectic mix, I used to be the only faery in the family until Daisy Blu chose faery over being a werewolf. She was once full werewolf with only traces of faery in her. She was forced to choose between the two. It goes back to the Denton Marx thing."

"The time-traveling wolf hunter. Wow. I guess I wouldn't be able to pick if I had more than two breeds running through my veins. We witches are pretty solid. So you're full-blood faery? Not a bit of wolf from your dad?"

"I've never exhibited any werewolf-like behaviors, but Dad always says I've the wolf in my soul because I'm the strongest of all the Saint-Pierre boys. But don't tell Trouble that. He likes to think he's the toughest."

"The way I understand it from Trouble, he's fully aware of your strength and respects that."

Kelyn shrugged. "The faery is always the last one invited to the fight because my punches tend to knock a guy out cold. At least, they used to."

Valor kissed his forehead. "You'll get your strength back. Soon. I'll do everything in my power to make it happen."

"You've already done so much. Thank you, Valor."

The look he gave her went all melty and worshippy, and Valor, for not the first time, had to catch herself from laughing in disbelief. He was so different from all the other men she'd ever dated or chummed around with. How had she gotten so lucky? Oh, right. He'd committed a brave and noble act to save her life, and now she was trying to catch up with him and make it all right according to her logic.

She was almost there. Almost.

The cab pulled over and, after paying and locating the right building, Kelyn knocked on the door to his aunt's home. The vampire who opened the door was dressed in skintight black latex and a silver hip chain dotted with rubies. Long black hair coiled on her head in pseudo demon horns, and her black lipstick looked as seamless and smooth as the latex. She squealed at the sight of Kelyn and lunged to kiss his cheek.

"Sweetie! Come in, come in! I can't believe you're in Paris."

"Hey, Aunt Kam." Kelyn smeared the back of his hand over the black lip print on his jaw, but was successful in only removing half. "Sorry to surprise you like this, but Valor and I are in town for a day or two and I was hoping we could crash here?"

"Of course! And Valor, eh?" The gorgeous vampire with pin-sharp black fingernails eyed her from head to toe. And for once Valor felt her lack of glamour as a bone-deep affliction. "Sweet," the vampiress commented, lacking enthusiasm. "Oh, but Kelyn, you'll have the place all to yourself. Johnny and I were heading out the door to Brazil for another honeymoon."

"Another?"

"We celebrate one every year. Honey!"

A long, lanky man with coal-black hair shaved along the sides and above his ears, and wearing black leather pants low at his hips, swung around the corner. On his shoulders glided a green snake half the size of a healthy boa constrictor.

"Kelyn!"

"Uncle Johnny." Kelyn clasped Valor's hand. "Is that your dad's snake?"

"Yeah, Green Snake the Third. I borrowed him for a show we did last night. So, who is this?" Johnny smiled expectantly at Valor.

"This is my, er, friend, Valor. She's a witch."

Valor offered a little wave over Kelyn's shoulder. She wasn't too sure about getting close to that snake. With its pink forked tongue flicking in and out, it looked suspiciously dangerous.

"Kam said it would be okay for us to crash here, but I'm bummed you two are leaving."

"The cab will be here in half an hour," Johnny said. "And we need to stop by Dad's house and drop off Green Snake along the way."

"Ah! I need to do my lashes," Kambriel said. With another quick kiss to Kelyn's other cheek, she skittered off, down the marble hallway on six-inch heels. "Love you, sweetie! Next time call ahead and we'll plan to be here."

"Sweetie?" Kelyn looked to Johnny, who, surprisingly, blushed.

"She's been calling everyone sweetie and honey since she found out," Johnny said. "I think it's hormones."

"Found out?" Kelyn asked.

Valor offered, "She's pregnant. She absolutely glows."

"She is," Johnny said proudly. "We're going to have a tiny bloodsucker. And I will call him Stoker." He winked at them. "Just kidding. So, what are you in town for? Vacation? Love tryst?" he asked, pronouncing the word *love* with a roll of his tongue.

"We're hunting for spell ingredients," Kelyn offered. "We've determined what we need is in the Council Archives, which brought us to Paris. You have any contacts there?"

"Uh, yes?"

Valor and Kelyn exchanged glances at that unconvincing reply.

"You can try Certainly Jones, who is lord and master over the Archives," Johnny offered as he stroked the snake easing along his shoulder. "He won't be an easy one to convince to let you dabble with the cool old crap collected within the Archives. Which, I'm guessing, you'll want to do. Dabble and/or remove something?"

"Just borrow a little portion of something," Valor explained with a close pinch of her fingers.

"Right. Certainly is not going to approve that. So then I'd go with Tamatha Bellerose, who works with CJ. She does most of the filing and labeling of the items they receive for storage. I'll give you her number and—hell, I wish we had more time, Kelyn. You look great, man. But I heard about your, uh, situation."

Leave it to his mom, Rissa, who spent a lot of time on the phone with her sister-in-law Kambriel, to spill the beans all the way across the ocean. "That's what we're trying to rectify."

"Yeah? I heard it was a nasty witch who caused you to lose your wings."

Valor offered her hand to shake, and as Johnny took it, she said, "Nasty witch, right here."

He retreated from the shake with a wipe of his palm along his thigh. "I see." The vampire eyed her with a discerning quirk of eyebrow, then flashed a glance to Kelyn.

"We're good." Kelyn put an arm around Valor's shoulders. "Get me that number and then you two should head out. Promise we won't trash the place."

"The guest bedroom is down the hallway. It's the gray room," Johnny noted. "Stay out of our bedroom. Unless you want to see things you'd rather not see. You're my nephew, so, yeah, I'd say stay out of that room." He winked again, but Valor did catch his concerned look at her.

"How much time do I have?" Kam called out from down the hallway.

"Ten minutes, lover!" Johnny blushed again. "Oh, there's no food in the house. Vamps." He thumbed his chest. "So you two are on your own for that."

"Not a problem. Thanks, Johnny."

"I gotta go grab our bags. Hold Green Snake, will you?"

Kelyn allowed the snake to slither over his arm and across his shoulders. Johnny sprinted down the hallway and out of view.

When her lover turned to her with a big grin on his face and a snake tongue flickering not far from that grin, Valor stepped back until her shoulders hit the wall.

"Really?" Kelyn said with surprise. "Grease Girl is afraid of a little snake?"

She couldn't even find words because the snake kept flicking out its tongue and eyeballing her with those big gold eyes. Very suspicious.

"Wow. I guess I found your weakness. Don't worry. Green Snake is harmless. I think." He winked.

And Valor walked a wide curve around the guy and his snake, and headed toward the gray room.

Chapter 17

Valor spoke to Tamatha Bellerose on the phone as she and Kelyn walked down the tree-shaded Rue Henri to the eleventh arrondissement where the Council's headquarters was located. A division of the Council, the Archives was a collection of articles, spells, grimoires, objects of a magical nature, creatures of mysterious origins, and other nefarious and possibly deadly items an organization such as the Council should keep in hand and under lock and spellbound key. Some things had been collected by Retrievers, other stuff was donated.

The Council was an overseeing body that didn't so much govern the paranormal nations as watch and keep tabs.

Valor had heard the Archives had rooms designated for objects and history related to each species, and that the witches room was filled with every spell, grimoire and alchemical instrument a witch could ever dream to know. She was excited to look it over, but Tamatha had warned her she and Kelyn didn't have clearance to simply browse about and take what they wished. Tamatha would have to obtain the skull dust—and she would, because she was behind helping Kelyn after Valor had explained the situation about his wings. And any family member of Johnny Santiago was a friend to her.

The only problem? Certainly Jones headed the Archives and he kept a tight hand on the contents. Visitors simply weren't allowed access.

The good part of that problem? He wasn't due in until later in the evening. He'd pulled babysitting duty for his twins this afternoon while his wife was out on a cleanup job. So Tamatha had suggested Valor and Kelyn hurry over. *An infinitesimal amount of bone dust scraped from a skull? No one should miss that.*

The headquarters was located in an unassuming four-story building that they only found because Kelyn suddenly paused and put out his hands as if to stop the ground from rising up.

"What is it?" Valor asked.

"I can feel it."

"Feel what?"

"Everything." He met her gaze with a wondrous little-boy grin. "It's amazing."

"Cool. You getting some of your navigation skills back?"

"Maybe. Paris does have a lot of ley lines running through it. The earth's energies feel…welcoming."

"That's awesome. So…down that alley, you think?"

"Yes." He took the lead, angling down a dark alley-way paved with uneven cobblestones. "You know, since we're in Paris," he called back, "maybe we should check out FaeryTown? I didn't get a chance when I was here years ago for Johnny and Kam's wedding."

"Is that the place where Faery overlies the mortal realm? It's a thin place, right? Maybe you can get to Faery through FaeryTown?"

"Not sure. I don't think there are portals there. And if there are, you need to be in the know. You know?"

"Right, got it. This chick is so not in the know."

"FaeryTown is just a sad, sorry place where faeries exist in mortal space." Kelyn's long strides moved him so swiftly Valor had to double-time to keep up. "The inhabitants either left Faery or were born here. Lots of dust addicts there, too, or so I've heard. You know Johnny's dad, Vaillant, used to be addicted to ichor?"

"Yeah, vamps and faery dust. Not cool." Valor joined him at a metal door set into the brick wall, but neither of them knocked, as Tamatha had requested. "So, are you going to take me to an ichor den later and show me a good time?"

"How about we climb the Eiffel Tower and kiss at the top of the world?"

"I like that idea. How'd you get to be such a romantic?"

"It's easy around you, Valor." Leaning up against her, he blocked her in against the wall. His violet gaze enchanted her. "You challenge me, and yet you always accept, as well. Even when I'm doing the grumpy faery thing. Do you know how rare that is for a guy who's always had trouble dating?"

"Why the trouble?"

He swiped a trace of faery dust from her neck and showed her. "I'm so over dating club girls with glitter makeup in order to hide my dust."

"That must be difficult."

"Exactly."

"I'm not much for dating, myself," she lied. "Too complicated. So many expectations."

"Right?"

"I mean, who wants to fall in love and have to commit to the one person?" She did! She so wanted that.

"Commitment." Kelyn shook his head with disdain. "So, uh, we're not dating, right?"

She hadn't expected that one, but Valor shrugged and forced a nod. "'Course not."

"But we're lovers." He tucked a kiss at the base of her earlobe.

"So you're thinking more like friends with benefits?" *Please say no*, she thought.

"Honestly? I'm not cool with that."

His kiss melted her tensions and Valor relaxed against his hardness. She shouldn't have lied to him, but she didn't know how to put that intimate desire out there. To be mocked and disregarded.

"I want you as more than a friend," he said.

"I want the same thing."

She was ready to show him exactly how much she wanted him by sliding her hand down his jeans when the door creaked open and out popped a silver-haired witch. The twosome straightened and tugged at their clothing as if they'd been caught making out behind the pews by the Sunday school teacher.

Tamatha Bellerose resembled a retro rocker with her green wiggle skirt and white-and-black polka-dot blouse that revealed tattoos on her arms, fingers and neck. She wore her silver hair in victory rolls and had a lovely rose blush to her cheeks that drew attention to her bright green eyes.

"Valor Hearst?"

Valor shook her hand. "Indeed. Wow. You've got some power in that hand. More than air magic?"

Tamatha pointed out the sigil for the elements on each finger as she said, "Earth, air, water and, on occasion, fire. I can feel your vita, too. You've walked this soil almost as long as I have. Nice to meet you. And this is?" She turned an admiring gaze up to Kelyn, who thrust back his shoulders at the feminine attention.

"Kelyn Saint-Pierre." He shook her hand and she held it.

"Of the infamous Saint-Pierres? Wow. You all get around this planet, don't you? But you're not wolf. You're faery. Nice." She rubbed his hand with her palm. "I can feel what's missing from you. Oh, darling, you need to get back your wings before it's too late."

"Too late?" Valor hadn't thought there was a deadline.

"What do you mean?" Kelyn asked the witch.

Tamatha took his other hand and closed her eyes. Valor guessed she was reading his vita. Something she'd not thought to do. She could do that, but she wasn't expert at delving into past lives or anything beyond current events.

"You've been weak and unable to shift since it happened," Tamatha said, but the statement ended as a question.

Kelyn nodded.

"A faery's wings are his life. As strong as you are, you will only grow weaker. I'm sorry." She dropped his hands. "Sometimes I get feelings about people, and they're always accurate. Anyway…" She tugged a blue glass vial out from the waistband of her skirt and handed it to Valor. "The Skull of Sidon was discovered a few years ago by archaeologist Annja Creed."

"Why does that name sound familiar?" Kelyn asked.

"She used to have a TV show about history and archaeological stuff."

"Oh, right. *Chasing History's Monsters*," he said. "I loved that show. Used to watch it all the time when I was a kid."

"I watched a few reruns after we obtained the skull, for curiosity's sake," Tamatha said. "That woman can kick butt and she's smart. Anyway, the skull was rumored to have been destroyed after Creed found it, but of course, we stepped in and made sure that didn't happen. Gotta keep tabs on all the supernatural stuff floating about in this realm, ya know?" She tapped the vial. "I scraped that from inside the left occipital hollow. No one is ever going to know it's missing."

"Unless of course…"

All three turned at the deep male voice that echoed from down the alleyway.

Certainly Jones's tall, lithe figure flashed out of shadow as he straightened his shoulders. "That *no one* is me."

Chapter 18

Kelyn heard Tamatha swear under her breath. Turning, he lifted his chest defiantly, yet he knew they were the ones in the wrong. Still, he wouldn't allow Tamatha to take the blame.

"I recognize you," Certainly Jones said as he approached. The man was dark, as were his hair, his clothing and the tattoos that covered virtually every portion of exposed skin, save his face. Kelyn could feel the magic waver off from the man, and it wasn't a pleasant feeling. "Weren't you in town a few years back for..."

"A wedding." Kelyn offered his hand, and the witch shook it. Strong grip, yet Kelyn could feel the malice in his magic vibrating in the touch. "I'm Kelyn Saint-Pierre. Kambriel Saint-Pierre is my aunt. She married Johnny Santiago. I think we may have met at the wedding. Uh, my friend and I—this is Valor Hearst—we meant no harm, Monsieur Jones. You shouldn't blame Mademoiselle Bellerose for this."

Certainly tilted his head, eyeing all three of them in slow but judging perusal. "Did I hear correctly that what is in that vial was taken from the Skull of Sidon that is under protection by the Archives? Who's working a spell?"

"I am." Valor shook hands with Certainly, but Kelyn noticed she didn't offer to hand over the vial. Good girl. "It's a spell to open a portal to Faery. Kelyn needs to get his wings back. We have to go to Faery to find them."

Certainly again looked Kelyn over. He'd never felt a gaze so deeply. It was as if the witch could read things about him even he didn't know. "What happened to your wings?"

"It's a long story. Suffice it to say, we've been gathering ingredients for the spell. We should have asked you for the skull dust. I know that's wrong. But I'm also not willing to give it back. And I will stand strong if you insist."

Certainly smirked. "I could take it back with a flick of one finger." He waggled a tattooed finger before them. "A portal spell? What are the other ingredients?" he asked Valor.

"Uh, well, a werewolf claw. We got that. Mermaid's kiss. Just barely got that. Water from Lake Hillier, it's pink. Pretty cool—"

Certainly hissed. "What in all of Beneath kind of spell requires such water? Don't you know that stuff is volatile when mixed with the light sort of witchcraft?"

Valor exchanged gazes with Kelyn. He sensed her sudden anxiety. And also that she hadn't a clue what

Certainly was talking about. "Why would the spell require such an ingredient if it doesn't work?" he asked.

"Oh, it'll work. But in the hands of a light witch, it could produce a catastrophic effect, as well." Certainly opened the door and turned to them. "Let's check this out. I've the *Book of All Spells* inside. If you're going to steal from me, I want to make sure you don't end up blowing away half the population in the process of invoking the spell."

The storage room dedicated to witches was three stories beneath the surface of Paris, and it was a marvel. Valor followed Certainly into the room, and when he said she could look but not touch, she took that to heart and started down the first aisle, forgetting that she'd left Kelyn at the door. The air was dark and heavy with dust, and there were shelves upon shelves of books and compendiums and grimoires. It reminded her of some kind of fantasy library, in which anything on the shelves might get up and dance as soon as she turned out the lights and closed the door. Of course the lights were oil lamps. CJ had explained electric lighting was iffy with this much magic in storage.

"Don't go that far!" CJ called as Valor neared the dark end of the first aisle.

Ahead of her, the walls appeared black, and yet when Valor squinted she saw into the depths. The book spines were black and...*things* seemed to be moving. Vines? Or were those tentacles? Did she smell sulfur?

Compelled to take a step forward, she startled when someone gently grabbed her arm. Kelyn leaned in and said at her ear, "You should listen to the dark witch who can take us out with a flick of his tattooed fingers, yes?"

"Yeah, but look." She gestured toward what might have been pinpoint red eyes peeping out from between two books.

"This way." Kelyn tugged her back the way she'd come. "There's a wall of herbs and other nasty things like bones and rat skulls I'm sure you'll be interested in."

"Really?" She turned and passed him, veering toward a dully lit corner where the ceiling grew thick with ancient herbs, some hung and dried, others growing in *kokedama* Japanese moss balls or delicate hydroponic glass balls. Her witchy senses were drawn toward the scent of dragon's blood and she touched the long, narrow vial that glittered with violet substance.

"I said don't touch!"

She waggled her head at CJ's admonishment as Tamatha joined her side. The witch was glamorous, yet seemed more down-to-earth than even Valor's best friend Eryss, and Eryss was an earth witch.

"It's like being a kid in a candy store, isn't it?" Tamatha whispered.

"Oh, yeah. What's that?" Valor almost touched a vial in which something phosphorescent blue wiggled inside red liquid.

"Dragon parasite. Excellent for stanching fire spells. And did you see the gargoyle's eyes?"

Valor studied a jar of stone eyeballs that pulsed with red veins. "Nice."

"Oh, this is not good."

At Certainly's dire utterance, both women lifted their heads. Tamatha gestured for them to join the dark witch, and they walked over to stand beside him and Kelyn. The group perused the massive *Book of All Spells*, which was, when spread open, about six feet wide and four feet tall, and stuffed with tissue-thin pages. Yet the page it was open to seemed alive as the illustrations danced, and Valor even picked up cinnamon and some darker earthy scents from its content.

"Water from Lake Hillier reacts to light magic unless it is blessed by a dark witch," CJ recited as he read the page. "And you've got all five ingredients? The claw, water, kiss, skull dust and tear?"

"Heading home tomorrow to check on the tear," Valor confirmed. "I'm sure I have it in stock. But if the water merely needs to be blessed by a dark witch…?" She gave him a hopeful grin and exchanged nods with Kelyn, who stood at one corner of the book with his arms crossed.

"Where do you intend to perform this spell?" Certainly asked.

Valor shrugged. "Probably at home in my spell room. Why?"

"That's not what is required." He tapped the page. "Didn't you read it all the way through?"

Valor leaned over the book and scanned through the ingredient list and the basic incantation, both of which she was familiar with. And yet it went on to describe summoning location and conditions. And there was even a warning about the lake water that was new to her.

"That information wasn't in my grimoire," she said.

"You must have an abridged edition."

"No. It was once my great-grandmother Hector's grimoire. She passed it down to me. It's original. Sometimes I can even smell her perfume in the pages. Everything was handwritten."

"Not according to this." CJ tapped the page. "This book is the master book of all spells ever created. The moment a new spell is written, spoken and/or chanted, it is recorded here. Your great-grandmother must have removed some pages from her grimoire. It's the only explanation for your missing information."

"Now that you mention it, there are a few places where I've wondered if a page was torn out. Well, can I get a copy of the spell from this book?" Valor asked.

CJ stood straight and eyed her with the darkest jade eyes she had ever seen. No compassion in them, and yet she could feel a certain softness emanate from him, as if he wanted to be kind, to assist her. Surely if she told him about Kelyn's desire to get his wings back, the witch would sympathize.

"Please," Kelyn said. "We wouldn't ask unless it meant more than life itself."

And all in the room felt Kelyn's heartfelt desire to be whole once again. He didn't even have to explain.

"Of course," CJ said. "You've already stolen the skull dust." He shot a condemning look at Tamatha. "Not like we can actually put that back, is it? I'll have a copy of this spell made. Tamatha, can you get the handheld scanner?"

"You mean you can't magic a copy into her hand?" Kelyn asked.

"I am not a Xerox machine," Certainly commented, and followed with a heavy sigh. "As for performing the spell at your home, Valor, it'll never work. It has to be at the place in which you wish the portal to open. In a thin place."

"Like the Darkwood," Kelyn offered hopefully.

"Exactly," CJ agreed.

And Valor cringed to imagine returning to the forest where it had all begun. Was she even allowed back in?

Would the wicked trees pin her once again? It was too risky. And it would dredge up so many awful memories of her dreadful beginning with Kelyn. They'd only just engaged in something wonderful. Why ruin that with something bad?

She met her lover's gaze across the massive book. His violet eyes twinkled, yet he didn't quite smile. He was trying to read her and had probably seen her reluctance, so she pulled on a smile.

"Sure," she said. "The Darkwood it is."

"Great," CJ said. "You have the lake water that requires blessing on you?"

"It's at Kambriel's apartment on the island."

"Bring it to me and I will bless it. I was on my way home, actually, when I had a feeling there was a reason I needed to return to work." Again, he cast a condemning gaze at all three of them with the ease of dealing out cards.

"Tamatha said you were watching the kids?" Valor said.

"Vika got home from work early. Now, I'll give you my address, and you'll come to me if you want this done."

"Of course." She tugged out her cell phone, scrolled to Contacts and handed CJ the phone to enter his info.

Tamatha returned with a scanning wand, and in but a minute the spell had been scanned and digitally sent to Valor's phone. She verified she'd received the complete file, then shook CJ's hand. "I owe you for this."

"Of course you do. We'll meet again someday. And when you do get back your wings?" He turned to Kelyn. "Be cautious. If someone else has been wearing them, they will be tainted."

"So I've been told. I will be careful. Thank you, Monsieur Jones. We both appreciate everything you've done for us, and I am at your beckon, as well. Whenever you need it, let me know."

"I consider myself richer for the friendships I've gained today. Now, out with you." CJ gestured for them to leave and bent over the massive spell book. "I'll be home in a few hours."

Once outside and in the cobblestone alleyway, Kelyn pulled Valor into an embrace and kissed her there against the brick wall in the darkening midafternoon shadows. Their kisses had become so easy, yet never simple. Each time his mouth fit against hers, Valor felt it in a different place. This one seemed to focus on her nipples, teasing them hard, so she rubbed them against his chest. His moans always spoke so much more than words. The man could kiss her anywhere he wanted. She might even let him kiss her in the back of a cab next time.

"You sure about having the fifth ingredient at home?"

Valor nodded. "Ninety-five percent sure. Should we go grab the water and head over to the dark witch's home?"

"I'm curious to see a dark witch's place. Let's do it!"

The dark witch blew a haze of whiskey-tainted smoke over the opened vial of the Lake Hillier water. The vial briefly glowed pink before he capped it and handed it back to Valor.

"It's done. Blessed," Certainly said. "It shouldn't prove an issue to work with it now. Unless the dark blessing is warded between now and when you perform the spell. If you've wards up on your home you should remove them before entering. And most certainly do not enter the thin place warded. Got it?"

"Thanks, CJ." Valor handed Kelyn the vial, who tucked it in the backpack in which all their valuable finds were stored. "So, before we go, can I ask about the chandeliers?"

The dark witch sat back on the velvet sofa, stretching his arms over the back and tilting his head to take in the constellation of glass chandeliers that hung in the two-story open-space loft he and his lover, Vika, and their twin one-year-old sons, had commandeered in the seventh arrondissement of Paris. *There must be hundreds*, Valor thought. A few were actually lit, providing more than enough lighting.

"It's a long story," Certainly said. "But I once required prismatic light to keep away the demons that had infested my soul after a rather unwise venture into Daemonia. There are always consequences to using dark magic. But Vika still loves me."

Vika was Viktorie Saint-Charles, a light witch who lived with CJ and who operated a cleaner operation with her sister, Libertie. Cleaners were available to do just that—clean up dead paranormal bodies best not left lying out for the public to stumble over.

"It's beautiful," Kelyn commented, hooking an arm over Valor's shoulder and leaning in to nuzzle his nose at her hair.

The door opened and in breezed a red-haired witch wearing a long black Morticia gown and a bag of groceries.

"Vika, Queen of My Heart." CJ rose to kiss his lover. "We've friends for a little whiskey and magic." He glanced to Valor and Kelyn. "You two up for that?"

Kelyn exchanged looks with Valor, and his smile grew quickly. A challenge, if either of them had heard correctly.

"Oh, yeah," they said together.

Chapter 19

"Will your boyfriend do it?"

Vika, the light witch who was currently mixing drinks for what had become a party of many, gave Valor a curious wink. She'd asked if Kelyn would donate a bit of faery dust for the drinks. Because with a little magic and dust she could make an out-of-this-world drink.

"Faery dust will get you high, but you won't have a hangover," she added. "I've only had it once before. CJ would love it."

"He will if I ask him sweetly," Valor said, because this was a fun challenge. And while she wasn't into recreational drugs, what could a little faery dust hurt anyone? Wasn't as if she were a vampire who could become addicted to the stuff. "What do you have in those drinks?"

The mason jars Vika used for drinking glasses sparkled under the many chandeliers lined above the kitchen area of the vast loft. The whole place was open with only a few walls for semiprivacy, such as the ones sectioning off the bedrooms and the one backing up Vika and CJ's spell area. The twins had been tucked away in their cribs before Valor and Kelyn arrived, and Vika had checked on them briefly before gathering the drink supplies.

A boisterous redhead laughed over near the gray sofa where she and her boyfriend, a former angel/soul bringer, stood chatting with Kelyn. She was Vika's sister, Libby, and her boyfriend was Reichardt. They had stopped in on the way home from a day at the park, and when they saw the party starting they had jumped right in. Valor secretly wondered if Reichardt could still produce angel dust. She was running low on that particular ingredient, thanks to her failed attempt at—argh. No, she wasn't going to land on that depressing thought. Her love life was actually looking up. Dwelling on her flaws would never move her forward. *Onward!*

"Cherry juice, vodka, cardamom and salt," Vika said as she mixed a shaker full of said ingredients. "Ice, of course, and a touch of dragon's blood."

"For a fiery taste," Valor added.

"You know it. And now we need the secret ingredient." The witch glanced through elegant kohl-lined green eyes over to Kelyn, who was laughing along with the others over Libby's gyrations that detailed trying to actually fly a broomstick.

CJ's brother, Thoroughly Jones—also called TJ— had arrived with his wife, Star, a cat shifter. The man was CJ's twin, and together they put out some awesomely dark, sexy vibes that Valor hadn't realized could attract her until she saw them in double. What had become of her preference for the big, beefy bad boys?

The dark witches were bad personified. Some Lynyrd Skynyrd blasted, and one of the twin witches was currently drawing a chalk circle on the floor while explaining to the menfolk how to catch a war demon in three easy steps.

"Kelyn!" Valor gestured for him to come over. Nursing the whiskey CJ had poured him, he wandered toward them, barefoot. When had the man abandoned his footwear? Actually, all the men, save Reichardt, were barefoot.

She made a show of glancing at his feet, and Kelyn shrugged and offered, "The floor is heated. Can you feel it? It's awesome." He kissed her on the cheek. "What's up? You ladies making drinks?"

Valor glided her palm up his chest and kissed him. "We are, and I have a big favor to ask. Sort of a fun one, actually."

"Anything for you, lover."

Valor tapped his chest and worked her best pouty lips with lash flutter on him. She'd once practiced before a mirror.

"You got something stuck in your eye?" he asked with concern.

"Seriously? I work my one and only sexy move on you and you think I've got a condition?"

He laughed. "Just teasing. What's up?"

"Could we borrow a sprinkle of your dust? Vika says when added to the drinks it'll get us high."

"Is that so? And what about the faery in the room who doesn't want to drink his own dust?"

"I have an angel dust elixir for you," Vika said, pointing to the vial of iridescent liquid that sat next to a canning jar half-filled with a green drink.

"Angel dust, eh?" Kelyn shrugged. "I've never been much for alcohol." He waggled the whiskey glass that could only be minus a few sips. "But I've been doing a lot of new things lately. I'm intrigued. I'm in!" With a snap of his fingers, his dust sprinkled over the jars that Vika had been mixing, settling onto the surface with a glint.

Vika met Valor's wink with her own. "Dust Bombs for all!"

An hour later everyone was dancing around the chalk circle drawn on the hardwood, in which stood a war demon, who also nursed one of the Dust Bombs. Built like a block with obscene muscles, the visitor from Daemonia had black skin with a distinctive sheen. His horns glowed crimson, and he couldn't stop giggling.

TJ was currently arm wrestling with Kelyn, and Kelyn was holding his own simply because the dark witch, who had removed his shirt to expose tight muscles, was so high on the Dust Bombs he could barely see straight.

Libby was dancing with Valor, and every time she hip bumped her, Valor went flying into Star's arms. The women laughed and Valor's snorts always brought up Kelyn's head in search of her. The room sparkled with dust, and yet Kelyn hadn't imbibed any more of the whiskey. Vika had made him something special that contained pomegranate seeds and angel dust. His grin had grown unstoppable.

Certainly and Vika danced slowly before a window, and every so often he'd spin her and he'd put up his arms and shout, "Witch of My Heart!" Apparently the man had a thing for bestowing titles of affection upon his lover.

The arm wrestling match suddenly ended in a tie and the war demon challenged Kelyn with drunken taunts. "Come on, step inside the circle, my faery boy!"

As Kelyn wobbled toward the circle, CJ made a quick detour and shoved the faery away. Kelyn landed on the sofa, sprawled, his grin growing crooked. "Careful, faery. He'll take you to Daemonia."

"You're no fun!" The war demon pouted, then tilted back his jar, which was empty. He lashed out a long black tongue, mining the bottom of the glass, but couldn't get any more out. "Aggh! I want me some more faery dust!"

At that outburst, Kelyn shuddered and called out, "Leave the faery alone!" which then segued into drunken laughter.

This time a hip bump set Valor on a trajectory toward the sofa. Kelyn saw her coming and held out his arms to catch her—but she missed and landed on the opposite end. The faery hugged his empty arms across his chest. And Valor snorted out peals of laughter.

"I'd come after you and kiss you," Kelyn managed, "but I can't even see straight!"

"Ha!" Valor rolled off the couch and landed hard on the floor. Turning onto her back and gazing up into the constellation of chandeliers that blurred and turned into a massive cloud of muted light because of her inebriation, she decided that the witches in Paris knew how to party. Big time.

The music switched to something sensual, and CJ called out, "Lover, oh, Mistress of the Faery Dust Bomb!"

Vika popped her head up from the kitchen fridge, where she'd been looking for more ice. A snap of her fingers spun a flame into the air and it floated toward CJ, who caught the amber ball on his palm and then, with a sip from his glass, blew the alcohol through the flame, creating a magnificent burst of blue sparkly flames that alighted into the air.

"Don't burn the place down!" Vika called. "I don't have enough ice for that!"

Kelyn reached out to catch a falling blue flame, and as it lit onto his fingers it alchemized into liquid and glided along his skin, finding the silvery scars at his wrist and, for a moment, lighting up the sigils that had once been there. "Sweet. Whoever said dark witches were evil?"

Meow!

Valor lifted her head from the floor and spied the black cat with the white star on her chest chase the blue flames rolling across the floor as if they were marbles.

"CJ," Vika called admonishingly. She tried to look stern, but she wobbled drunkenly, too.

CJ called out a Latin word and all the flames fizzled.

"Aww…" The war demon pouted. "They were so pretty."

"Who's up for naked limbo?" someone shouted.

The airplane hadn't even left the tarmac at Charles de Gaulle, but both Kelyn and Valor sat in first class with heads bowed toward each other, snoring. Still on a high from the Dust Bombs, Valor had glided onto the plane, arms held out and making noises like a kid would were she playing at flying. She'd been hyped with exhilaration and when Kelyn had followed with a staggering gait—yet he'd managed a perfectly sober stride through customs—she hadn't felt an ounce of the usual nervous anxiety.

Once seated in the confining tin can, Valor had yawned and whispered a spell for sleep. It might have been the faery dust coursing through her system, or it could have been a lucky magical moment, but the spell actually worked.

It had been a long adventure, and but one ingredient remained. And then to Faery.

Nine hours later, Kelyn sat in the back of a cab with Valor, cruising from the Minneapolis airport to the northern suburb of Tangle Lake. Both were still a little drowsy, but whether it was jet lag or dust lag they couldn't be sure. They didn't need to talk now. Holding hands? That was some kind of awesome.

They'd come down from the high and he was thinking he should have gotten a drink recipe from Vika. Angel dust? That had been some good shit. He'd seen in a range of colors he'd not even imagined before. And while his senses had seemed to increase to what they had once been, it had all been a crazy rushed blur of dancing, laughing, avoiding the war demon's challenging taunts, chandeliers—and, yes, naked limbo.

Chandeliers? He still didn't get it, but he didn't care. They'd had a great night to say goodbye to Paris.

Now he could feel Valor's energy flowing into him and it didn't so much invigorate him as exude through his body with a reassurance that she was the right woman for him. He'd not felt this way with a person before. So trusting. Completely at ease. Relaxed.

Was he too relaxed? Should he be more cautious of her magic and the forthcoming spell? A spell that could change his life. Would she perform the spell right? What if it failed? He needed to get to Faery and find his wings.

But even more? He wanted to finally set foot in Faery. It was a home that had always called to him, a place where he belonged. Growing up, he'd felt as if he lived in the wrong world. Sure, his family and home felt right. And the forest surrounding his home, along with the Darkwood, were what he imagined freedom must feel like. But they could never be Faery. Right?

So when finally he did make it to Faery, and found his wings, would he then be able to turn away from all that it offered and return to the mortal realm?

Why would any man do such a thing if given the opportunity to stay?

Kelyn walked Valor up to her building door, but she noted he'd told the cab to wait for him. Back here in the United States it was midafternoon, and she was no longer tired or high, though she couldn't promise her aching bones she wouldn't crash the minute she saw the bed. Travel had whipped her good. And even though Vika had said there'd be no hangover from the Dust Bombs, she wasn't so sure the throbbing in her temple wasn't just that.

Yeah, a few winks of rest felt necessary. But she wanted to crash with Kelyn by her side. Didn't he want to come in and stay with her? They could make love until they fell asleep together from jet lag and adventure withdrawal.

She opened the door to the building, and Kelyn put a palm up on the door frame and leaned in to kiss her. She grasped at his shirt, pulling him closer, wanting to feel his body heat against her breasts, wanting to jump inside him. To make him stay. He couldn't leave her now.

How could he leave?

"I've got some things to check on," he said as he broke the kiss. "Call you soon?"

"Sure. Uh…"

He lifted a brow, waiting for her to say something.

"It's good," she decided. "Right. Uh, back to business. I'll talk to you soon and we'll make plans for stage two of the operation."

"Awesome." He kissed her again. It was too quick. Not even long enough for her to kiss him back. "Thank you, Valor. This adventure has meant a lot to me." He clasped her hand and kissed her knuckles. And with a squeeze of her hand, he strode down the sidewalk to the waiting cab.

As if he'd said goodbye for the last time.

Fingers clutching at the door pull, Valor stood in the doorway, watching the cab drive off down the street until it turned the corner at the end of the block.

Gone without a care? Her heart pulsed. It felt as if she'd received a blow to all the feels. She gasped as sudden tears spilled from her eyes.

She missed the man already. And it felt as though he'd taken a piece of her heart along with him. He hadn't looked at her as the cab rolled away. Not even a goodbye wave.

Why hadn't he looked at her?

Touching the tears on her cheeks, Valor had a sudden, devastating realization.

"Seriously? Oh, my goddess! By all the television doctors!"

She slammed the door shut and dashed up three flights. Once inside her loft, she aimed for her spell room and found an empty vial.

Chapter 20

Kelyn waited for his brother Trouble to open the front door, and before his oldest sibling could manage a grin, Kelyn swung up his fist and laid his brother out with a right uppercut.

Mostly.

Trouble wobbled, stepped backward, put out his arms to balance, then landed on the easy chair behind him with a grunt. "What the…?" He rubbed his jaw. "Dude, you really have lost your strength. That punch should have knocked me flat. Good try, though." He smirked.

Kelyn strode inside and closed the door. He had gotten that out of his system, but he still felt dissatisfied. As if his lady's honor required defending. So he bent before his brother. "That was for making me think you and Valor had something going on."

"Me and the witch? Of course we did. We used to get together for Netflix and chill all the time."

"You made me believe you'd slept with her."

Trouble shrugged. "A guy can't have too many notches, can he?"

"But you didn't earn a notch from her."

Another shrug. Yeah, so Trouble had a habit of boasting about his conquests. Real and, apparently, imagined. Kelyn had always figured his brother padded the number and the experiences with his own ideas on what that total should be. But Kelyn had always believed he and Valor had had sex. It was the very reason he'd not pursued her and had such a tough time initially trusting her.

"So what's the deal?" Trouble shoved Kelyn backward. "You and the witch getting it on now? She's the one who stole your wings, man!"

"For the last time, she did not steal my wings. And yes." Kelyn fiercely stabbed his brother's chest. "She. Is. Mine. Got that?"

Trouble put up placating hands. His smirk was a constant. But for once could the guy move beyond the childish teasing and boisterous grandstanding and attempt to show some understanding?

"She means something to me," Kelyn insisted, "so you stay the hell away from her."

"I have been walking a wide circle around that witch. As you should be. What happened on your trip that changed your mind about hating her?"

"I've never hated her. You know I don't hate on women. I sacrificed my wings for her, Trouble. She had nothing to do with that decision. It was all my doing."

"You sacrificed your wings because you are a good man and you could never let a woman suffer or die.

Which would have happened had you not made such a selfless sacrifice. But she meant nothing to you at the time. You meant nothing to her. She played you, man. You were a sucker!"

Another punch was due. This time Kelyn managed to clock Trouble up under the jaw, shifting his skull on his spine. That knocked him out.

"She's always meant something to me. It just took me a while to figure out what it was, exactly."

Standing over his silent brother, Kelyn heaved out a frustrated sigh. This was not his way. He didn't beat on his brothers. Not unless it was a friendly fight. And such scuffles had happened often growing up in the Saint-Pierre household.

Why now was he so defensive over what he had with Valor? He knew he didn't have to protect her from Trouble. To defend her honor. A simple *stay away* would have sufficed.

He rubbed his fist, coming down from the anger.

What an asshole to come here and do such a thing. He turned and opened the front door.

Behind him, Trouble roused and muttered, "My little brother is in love."

Fingers clenching the door frame, Kelyn tightened his jaw. Was that it? Was he in love?

Maybe he was.

Yet the witch gave no clue that she felt the same way. So what was he going to do about that?

An hour after Kelyn had left Valor alone at her loft, her door buzzer rang. Tossing aside the towel with which she'd been scrub-drying her hair after a long shower to erase the travel from her skin, she checked her reflec-

tion. The soft pink velvet sundress she'd slipped on because it had been conveniently hanging on the back of
the bathroom door hung to her thighs. She slept in it, but
it was a dress, so she could answer the door in it, as well.
Wasn't like she had abundant cleavage to worry about
flaunting. She was flat chested, but never too pissed over
that. Especially since lying on her stomach was the only
way to sleep. *Suck it, big-busted women.*

Dodging Mooshi, who was sprawled on the floor beside the sofa, belly up, she glided up and slid the massive rolling door open. Kelyn stepped over the threshold,
cupped her head with both hands and gave her the most
sudden and delicious kiss she'd ever gotten. It stole her
words. And it erased her anxiety over his earlier abrupt
departure.

Wrapping her legs about his hips, she tasted mint
on his tongue as it danced with hers. He clasped her
thighs, kicked the door shut and carried her in toward
the kitchen and beyond, not breaking the kiss.

"Watch out for the—"

Mooshi meowed angrily and scampered off while
Kelyn managed to double-step to avoid a stumble. And
then he resumed the kiss, which was so greedy and demanding it felt as though he was begging for her without words.

Just when she'd been bumming that he'd walked away
from her without wanting to stay, he returned. And without a word he was proving how much he wanted to be
here now.

Setting her on the big round table before the windows, which she generally used for cleaning auto parts,
Kelyn moved the kiss from her lips to her jaw. A few
hungry nibbles with his teeth and lashes with his tongue

had her cooing and squirming upon the table. He glided those teasing kisses up to her earlobe, which he suckled. Drawing his teeth along the shell curve, he tickled the top inner cove of her ear. That was a new erotic spot.

"Mmm, I was hoping to see you again. I didn't think it would be tonight."

"Need you," he muttered and pushed up her dress. "Right now. Wait—a dress?"

"Don't read too much into it."

"Not a problem." He unzipped and shuffled down his pants. Commando was his style and his cock sprang up at attention. "Yes?"

So he was a man of few words? Worked for her.

Bracketing his hips with her legs, she turned her feet inward, pushing him toward her with her toes. He bowed over her, one hand guiding his hard-on into her while the other gripped her wet hair as he kissed her breast none too gently. The hot, searing heat of his entrance granted Valor a rush of giddy pleasure. She gasped and pulled at his hair and then pushed up his T-shirt so their bodies could be skin on skin.

His intensity was off the scale. He thrust roughly inside her as if he were trying to pin her to the table. This pinning she could handle. Digging her fingers in at his shoulders, she moaned and whispered, "Yes."

A nip to her breast deepened her pleasure and then she muttered an actual swear word. He pinched her other breast, and the shock of it increased the high of this wild and wicked coupling.

When dust exuded from his skin, it put off a sweet, tantalizing scent. And maybe she got a little high from it, too. Not as high as she had been at the dark witch's home in Paris. But it added another element to their coupling that pushed all sensation high up the charts.

Licking his shoulder, Valor bit him, testing his reaction.

"Oh, yeah?" He bit her breast but kept his lips over his teeth, and then toyed with her nipple until she pumped her hips roughly against his, demanding, seeking, wanting.

And when his body began to tremor above hers, Valor reached down to tighten her fingers about the base of his cock. But he thrust too rapidly for her to keep a good hold, so she let him come inside her. His loud, short shout sounded like a yes mixed with a sigh.

He hilted himself within her, pushing up and lifting her derriere from the table, the fingers of one hand still at her breast as he tilted back his head and rode the orgasm. "Dr. House!"

Valor laughed and snorted, which sent him into a delicious growl. With a slip of his finger over her clitoris, and as she ground her mons up against Kelyn's torso, she, too, reached orgasm and shuddered beneath him, her elbows knocking the table. She almost slid off until he caught her and bowed over her, laying his head against her chest.

Somewhere in the loft a cat meowed, with judgment.

"Just needed to be inside you," he said. A jerk of his hips tightened his erection within her. He groaned and rocked his hips, the move further rubbing him against her clitoris, which prolonged the exquisite aching giddiness. "Feels right here."

Gasping and breathing heavily, she clasped her hands over his head, holding him there as they experienced a long and delicious gaze into each other's soul. Their sweat-sticky bodies melded skin against skin. So much in his violet eyes. Could it all be hers?

With a kiss to her breast, Kelyn collapsed on top of her and they lay there for long minutes in a silence that harmonized with their breaths and sighs.

Valor sat on Kelyn's lap, and he sat in the big wicker chair placed before one of the tall windows overlooking the street below. This end of town was mostly residential apartment complexes and some old factory buildings that housed hip restaurants and coffee shops as well as a quilting store and a couple art shops.

She licked the cherry Popsicle she had suggested they share to cool them down. She hadn't pulled up her dress, and her tiny breasts hugged his bare chest. With a bite of the Popsicle, Valor pulled away from Kelyn as she giggled and teased him with the red frozen treat.

He bit off a big chunk and let it melt in his mouth. Then, before the juice was completely swallowed, he kissed her, dashing his cherry-sweetened tongue with hers. She curled into him, and he cupped her ass to hold her tighter to him. He'd pulled off his pants, and his cock was hard. Valor's foot toyed with it absently, but when she noticed, she turned her attention to stroking the side of it with her toes.

"So we have all the ingredients, then?" he asked. "You got the fifth and final?"

"Yep. I had it in stock like I thought I would."

"So that was tears of love or something?"

"True love's first tears. Silly stuff."

"Right. And tell me why or how a witch keeps something like that in stock?"

"I had it right next to my frog's bellow and banshee's scream."

"Of course. How stupid of me not to know that is standard witch's gear. So, when are we going to do this?"

"We have one more thing we need." She hooked a thumb over her shoulder, pointing to the paper lying on the kitchen counter under a yellow highlighter. "I had a chance to read over the whole spell that Certainly copied for me, and it looks like I'll need a familiar."

"You mean like a cat shifter?"

"They come in all breeds, but yes, cat shifters are the most common familiars. My best friend Sunday is a familiar."

"Dean Maverick's wife?"

"Right. Dean was promoted to principal of the Northern pack because Ridge Addison has retired. But I'm not sure I should ask Sunday to do such a thing for me. The familiar needs to lead us through the portal into Faery. Could be risky. And I don't want to endanger Sunday."

"You don't have to. I think I have something better than a familiar."

"What's that?"

"Matilda."

"Should I ask?"

"Matilda is my kestrel falcon. Well, I don't own her, but she is my friend and we've been together since I was little. I don't keep her in a mews, though. She lives free in the Darkwood. Whenever I visit the woods she finds me. She can cross over to Faery."

"Really? Wow."

"She's gone into Faery many times. Likes to bring me back things. Like these." He held up the mouse alicorn and the tourmaline cipher. "She could guide us through the portal. And it would mean a lot to me to finally get to Faery accompanied by the one friend I've had for so long."

"I think that'll work. It's only nine. We could head there tonight, if you want to."

A huge red drip from the Popsicle splattered Kelyn's abs, and Valor bowed to clean it with a lash of her tongue.

"That," he said on a low growl. "Or we could have sex again?"

"I vote for the sex. The spell didn't specify a time of day, only during the waning moon, which it is, so I think we can do night or day. And if I have to return to that place, I'd prefer day."

"Are you okay with going back into the Darkwood?"

"Honestly?" She curled up against his chest and met his gaze. "I'm a little scared. Hell, I'm freaked. What if that tree comes after me again?"

"I'll protect you."

"You will. But you've nothing left to sacrifice this time."

"I would give everything I have for you, Valor."

"You already have." She caught a breath in her throat, feeling it tickle and threaten at tears. "We make a good team, yes?"

"That we do."

She kissed him and he made a grab for her breast while he was still holding the melting Popsicle. Valor jumped at the cold touch against her nipple. The soft treat crushed into her skin, and the stick fell to the floor. "You going to take care of this mess?" she asked her lover.

"I thought you'd never ask."

* * *

After sex, and a shower to wash off the faery dust and Popsicle juice, Kelyn suggested they head out on the town for a little celebration. He wanted to take Valor out, treat her special.

"You could wear the dress you had on before our wild table sex," he said. "Never thought I'd see you in a dress."

"I do dresses. When I feel like it." She was still naked and combing her fingers through her hair at the end of the bed. "But you know, I'm not actually a real girl, Kelyn. In case you hadn't noticed."

"What in the world does that mean?" He pulled up his pants but didn't zip and leaned over her to kiss the crown of her head. "You're real."

"Yeah, but not in the girlie sense. I don't do pink or ruffles or makeup. It's just not me. So if we go out…"

"You can wear whatever you like. It doesn't have to be a dress. And I think you're a girl no matter what you say. A girl who rocks combat boots."

She smirked, but he sensed her reluctance. So she was a tomboy. Didn't bother him. Valor was the first woman he actually felt comfortable around. No need to worry what the chick would think of him if getting on his horny exploded dust all over her skin. And, seriously, what man liked sorting through ruffles and tons of makeup to get to the real woman beneath?

"Where did you plan to take me?"

He figured someplace too upscale might freak her out. Much as he wanted to treat her and show her a good time, they could do that anywhere, really. Didn't have to be a four-star restaurant or a fancy ballroom. Of which Minneapolis didn't have a lot to offer.

"How about the Blue Room?"

"The nightclub in St. Paul?" She shrugged, indifferent. "That's cool. Maybe I could manage a little makeup for that place."

"The whole place is blue, including the lights. Makeup will make you look weird. Go natural, the way I like you."

She nodded. "Okay, but let me find something to wear. I can be ready in ten."

"I'm going to head down to the car and give Blade a call. Ask him about entering the Darkwood by his place tomorrow. I'll wait for you outside?"

"Yep."

Chapter 21

She was stunning. But Kelyn didn't tell her that. The first time he'd given her a compliment, she punched him in the biceps and sneered. So he kept it to himself as he admired Valor wandering to the bar to get a drink. She wore a silky number. Violet. It was cut high to expose one thigh. And her combat boots were like her trademark. He loved the look so much he wanted to shout it for everyone to hear. He loved the tomboy with the purple hair and an affinity for invoking television doctors' names when she was pissed—or well sexed—and who could kiss him so silly he forgot about his woes.

She tossed back a shot of vodka at the bar, then turned and gestured with a kink of her finger for him to join her on the dance floor. Some kind of erratic, bouncy tech music rocked the blue-lit bar. It shimmied through his veins. Always one for some let-loose dancing, Kelyn joined his lover in the middle of the dance floor.

Having a mom and dad who loved to dance to any music that was on the radio when he was growing up had encouraged Kelyn to dance right along. And he had some moves, if he did say so himself. Hands above his head, he bounced to the beat along with the dance floor crowd. This was freedom. This was also connection.

"I love that you love to dance!" Valor shouted above the music.

He pulled her against his body and licked the sparkling skin below her earlobe. "I could dance with you all night."

"Then let's do it!"

And so they did. Basked in the blue glow, their teeth and the whites of their eyes glowed under the black lights, revealing laughter, smiles and a sexy wink every now and then. They closed down the bar, dancing nearly every dance, save for a few drink breaks.

At two in the morning, the pair wandered down the tree-shaded sidewalk toward the parking lot, hands clasped and Valor's head tilted onto Kelyn's shoulder.

"I've never known a man who likes dancing so much," she said and hugged him tightly. "You rock in so many ways I can't even begin!"

"Makes me feel alive." He kissed the crown of her head as they arrived at the Firebird. "It's like flying."

"Oh." She sobered quickly, and only then did Kelyn realize what he'd said.

"Well, it is. I can't deny it." He leaned against the car door, crossing his arms. "So the wings made me… me. And I'm eager to get them back. Is that what you need to hear?"

"Yes. And we're going to make that happen tomorrow. Then you can fly all day and never touch down."

"I'll have to if I want a kiss from you. I could take you flying over the treetops."

"Would you? That would rock." She pumped a fist. "Is what I've heard about faeries and their wings and, uh…sex, for real?"

That when someone stroked a faery's wings it was a sexual touch and produced the same sensations as if more intimate parts of them were being touched? Hell, yes. And with sigils activated? Beyond words. But he'd not had an opportunity to experience such. He'd actually never slept with another faery. And wings out with a human woman? Wasn't going to happen.

"You'll have to wait to find out." He winked at her and she plunged into his arms and kissed him. "First thing I'm going to do after I get my wings is make love to you."

"That could be awkward if we're still in Faery and, I don't know, there's a defeated and pouting demon standing nearby."

"You have a point. I'll save it for when we get back home. I expect I may have to do some demon fighting to get back my wings. But I can take the guy. This time he won't have a helpless witch to hold over me."

"I'm so—"

He kissed her quickly so she couldn't apologize again. "Let's go to my place."

"Your place?"

"What?"

"I've never been there. Yes! I finally get to see my man's place."

"Nothing to get excited about. It's a place out in the country. Pretty simple."

* * *

It was simple, and gorgeously stark. Kelyn lived about five miles west of his parents' home in Forest Lake. The road to his home wound through thick spruce trees and white paper birch. Even when they'd arrived, Valor wasn't sure they had because she didn't see the house until they stood on the doorstep and he invited her in.

The small, one-level house sat over a stream. Yes, a narrow stream actually flowed beneath the framework and parallel to the footings. Inside, it was decorated with what Valor decided was a Japanese aesthetic. Simple rice paper walls slid noiselessly aside to reveal the tiny kitchen done in unvarnished blond pine. The living room offered low gray seating cushions set on a long bamboo mat. No other furniture beyond a small wood altar placed before a window that made up an entire wall.

She bowed to study the altar and found a piece of quartz, tourmaline, a raven's feather and a small copper bowl on it. Understated and, apparently, the man was not a collector of things. She could dig it.

"Please tell me you have a bed?"

His kiss to her neck sent shivers directly to her nipples, which tightened in anticipation. Clasping her hand, he tugged her toward another rice paper wall, which he pushed open to reveal a mattress set on a low pine base. The white sheets were pulled taut, making her want to jump on it and mess it up. Again, another wall was completely a window, and it revealed the dark woods outside.

"I'm in love," she said as she bowed and landed on the bed, stretching her arms across the sheets that smelled like cedar. "I wasn't sure what to expect of your place, but this is you. Simple and spare."

"Are you calling me simple?" He landed on the bed, on top of her, and nuzzled a snuffling kiss between her breasts.

"No!" She laughed and kicked her feet. "Kelyn! No tickling! Please?"

"Fine." He rolled off her and splayed out his arms. Tilting his head backward, he managed to reach a little remote at the head of the bed and push the button.

Faint white light illuminated the forest outside the window, and Valor turned in time to see a doe dart away. Another pair of eyes glowed from within a grassy crop at the base of a tree. "A possum! Wow, it's so beautiful out here. You must hate going into town."

"I do spend a lot of time out here by myself. I could spend all day flying through the trees."

She clasped his hand and kissed it, but it didn't feel right to bring up the wing thing again. Tomorrow was the day. "Is this woods a thin place?"

"Parts of it are, but it's not like the Darkwood. You are welcome in this forest whenever you wish to roam. And you can pick mushrooms to your heart's content and collect whatever it is you witches use in your spells."

"So why even go to the Darkwood?"

"Because it feels different there. I sense the connection to that place I want to touch."

"I get that. It's sacred to you."

"It is."

"Then why not live there?"

"No one lives in the Darkwood. Blade lives as close as any would dare."

"I was a fool to go in the Darkwood. I knew the warnings."

Valor sighed and felt the emotions that had preceded her stupid venture well up in her heart and threaten tears. She'd thought she'd gotten over that. But really? She was a woman who had needs. She'd never get over it.

"Why *did* you go in there?" he asked. "You said it was for a spell, but you never told me what spell you were casting. Was it as dark and dangerous as I've teased at?"

She rolled onto her stomach and he did, too, so they both looked toward the window. A squirrel crept close to the cabin, digging in the soil on a quest for nuts. Kelyn brushed the hair from the side of her face and kissed her cheek softly.

The idea of confessing to him both encouraged and frightened her. The weird gulping feeling in her throat, which could result in tears, cautioned her. And yet her heart leaped. She needed him to know her completely. For good or for ill.

"It was a personal spell," she said, eyes straight forward, peering through the window. Her heartbeat thundered and she tucked her fingers over the edge of the mattress to hide that they were shaking. "I had recently broken it off with a man I really thought I loved."

Kelyn rolled to his side and looked up at her. Yeah, so she had had a boyfriend and, believe it or not, that did sometimes happen in her world.

"Actually, he was the breaker upper. I didn't want to break it off. But it was the classic reason."

"The classic reason?"

"Yes. None of my boyfriends or lovers over the years ever said it so plainly as he did. But…he did."

She bowed her head against the sheet for a moment. Not crying, but trying to summon the courage to spill. The room was so still. She thought perhaps even the creatures outside had suddenly paused to listen to what she had to say.

"So, he told me," she said, lifting her head, "I wasn't the kind of girl men considered for marriage and having babies and happily-ever-afters. Because, you know, I *know* I'm not a real girl. And apparently all men do, too. But no one had ever said it to me like that. Just straight-out calling a fish a fish. He actually shrugged, kissed me on the head and said goodbye. Then he calmly stated that he'd been dating another woman at the same time and he intended to ask her to marry him. Can you believe that?"

Kelyn shook his head. "Asshole."

"Right? So, anyway, I think I'd finally had enough. I mean, I've lived a long time. I'm heading toward my eighth decade. And I've had a great life. I love my life. But you know? I felt like he could have been the one. That maybe we could have had something. Together."

"I'm sorry," Kelyn offered. "Breakups are tough. But what he said to you? It wasn't true."

Valor smirked. "Yes, it was. I know that. I like being one of the boys. Except when I don't want to be." She tilted her head to look into his violet irises, feeling as if he would never be so cruel to her. And she knew that with a certainty that made her smile.

"So, did you intend to cast a love spell in the Dark-wood that night? Bring your true love to you?"

"Love spells can be messy, and you've got to really want the intended one because you could be stuck with him for-freaking-ever. Actually, I was going to cast a spell on myself to make me more lovable."

"Valor, you are so lovable. Combat boots and all."

"Yeah, well, you're Mr. Nice Guy. You have to say stuff like that."

"I think the spell worked." He teased at the ends of her hair. "But not the spell you wanted to cast."

"What do you mean?"

He kissed her then and pulled her into a hug. "Just think about it for a while. I'm not going to point out the obvious. In fact, I have something more interesting in mind."

"Such as?"

"I've never had sex with a woman on this bed."

"What? I don't believe that."

"I've told you, I have to pick up club girls who are all sparkly and then go home with them. I wake in the mornings amid pink frills and so much freaking glitter it's like I landed in a fun house. The only advantage was that the woman was never the wiser that I put off faery dust while we were getting it on."

"That is…quite the problem to have. So…" She spread her hand across the white sheets. "Virgin sheets?"

He nodded. His grin teased at her like no tickle ever could.

"But first." She pressed a hand to his chest to stop his approach for a kiss. "Tell me what worked when I was supposed to speak the spell in the Darkwood. I don't get it."

"Valor." He tugged her against his chest and pushed the hair from her face, staring into her eyes as if to seek her soul. "I'm not telling!"

And with that, he landed a tickle right at her waist that had her flinching out of his grasp and squirming across the sheets.

"Cheater!" she managed. Snagging the end of his shirt, she pushed it up over his head and forced him back onto the bed, his head landing on the pillow. His hands and lower arms were still tangled in the shirt, so she had him in an effective pin. "My turn to tease you."

Kelyn tossed aside his shirt but then put his arms up above his head and clasped his hands together. "Okay." He rocked his hips under her. "Go for it."

Valor waggled her brows at him. Time to tease the faery.

Bowing to his chest, she kissed him at the base of his neck, then lashed out her tongue to taste his skin. He didn't have the salty taste she would expect, but rather something a person could not describe with taste words, so she settled on wild green forest freshness. It had become her favorite flavor.

Dragging her tongue down the defined indent between his rock-hard abs, she twirled it around his belly button, then ventured lower to explore the angled cut muscles that V'd into his jeans.

"You men are so interesting," she said. "What do you call these muscles here? I mean, they're like the sexiest thing ever."

"I'm not—oh, yeah." A nip of her teeth to the skin above his jeans' fly dissuaded any discussion.

She unbuttoned and unzipped him, being careful because the guy did not wear underwear. His soft blond curls sprang out behind the unzipped metal teeth and then his erection rose like the mighty totem it was, demanding worship.

"Dr. Who," Valor muttered in appreciation.

"I don't think he was an actual doctor."

She gripped his cock firmly. "You want to argue semantics or are you going to lie back and take it, faery?"

"I'm cool. I'm sure he was a doctor. Somehow. Maybe?" He pushed his palms over his face and as she touched the tip of his cock with her tongue, his groan bellowed out from his chest. "Oh, yes, a doctor for sure."

Bowing to the lush, bulging head of him, Valor took it in her mouth and sucked it like the Popsicle they'd shared earlier. While she stroked her curled fingers up and down the shaft, she used her tongue to tease, prod, circle and dance over the swollen smooth helmet until his hips were pumping in demand.

So she answered his unspoken plea by taking him deeply into her mouth, up and down, sucking and squeezing. Feeding his wanton moans. At his sides, his fingers clenched at the bedsheets. Beneath her breasts, his thighs tightened. And with one hand she cupped his testicles, which were tight and so hot. That touch set him off. His shivering muscles suddenly pulsed and he came into her, spilling down her throat. The faery shouted, "Yes!" and his hips bucked a few times before he relaxed with a heavy exhale.

Valor kissed his thigh and gave his softening erection a squeeze. Her fingers sparkled with faery dust, and she tasted a familiar sweetness that reminded her of the Dust Bombs she'd drunk in Paris.

The sheet glittered with fine dust. And a glance out the window spied a pair of curious glowing raccoon eyes. Valor's laughter echoed out into the night and was joined by her faery lover's laugh as he flipped her onto her back and made love to her until morning glinted on the horizon.

Chapter 22

Kelyn leaned over and kissed Valor, who sat in the passenger seat of his car. He'd parked on the loose gravel drive, which circled before his brother Blade's barn. The big red barn served as a garage slash home and also sat a hundred yards away from the Darkwood.

"You want to come in and meet my brother?"

"I met Blade once. I know his woman, Zen." She tucked her hands between her legs and shrugged. "Right now I'd rather sit here and concentrate on not being so nervous."

He knew she was crazy afraid to go back in the woods again. Witches and the Darkwood? Not cool. And she'd only gone there because she'd wanted to speak a spell to make her lovable. His heart had broken to hear that.

"You know I'll protect you, Valor."

"I know that. You go tell your brother what we're up

to. While I wait, I'll check through the spell stuff and make sure I've got the incantation down."

"Sounds like a plan."

He left her in the car because he didn't want to push, and he had felt her anxiety radiate out from her in a distinct quaver. He was nervous, too. But it was an opposite feeling to Valor's, which had her all pent up and closed off. While him? He felt like stretching his arms wide and opening himself to the universe.

Striding across the gravel that fronted the property, Kelyn ran a hand across his hair. The sun was high and his body jittered with anticipation. This could be it! If Valor's spell went as it should, a portal to Faery would be opened. And he could step through.

Yet his excitement tangled with dread. Kelyn had always dreamed of Faery. But no detail from his mother's tales had ever been enough to satiate his imagination or longing. And once finally there? Would he want to return to the family and friends who meant so much to him? To Valor?

"Hey, bro!"

Blade stepped up to the opening of the garage that spread across the entire lower area of the massive barn. He used it to work on cars and had a shop fully stocked with every tool imaginable toward the back. The upper level was where he lived with Zen, his girlfriend who had once been part faery, part angel *and* part demon, and yet was now merely faery. Long story.

Blade hooked a thumb at the hip of his black leather pants. His bare abs were as cut as Kelyn's, yet his shoulders were broader and his long, straight black hair dusted at his elbows. "Where's the witch?"

"She's waiting in the car." Kelyn thumbed a gesture over his shoulder. "A little nervous."

Kelyn stepped into the garage's cool shade. The scent of motor oil mixed with sawdust wafted in the air. His brother, who stood shoulder to shoulder with him, waved toward a half-assembled '57 Ford F-100. A pair of legs stuck out from under the low front end. Stryke rolled out on a creeper and winked at Kelyn, then stood and slapped his greasy hands together.

"You guys should have Beck over here helping you," Kelyn commented. Beck was their brother-in-law, who actually owned an auto body shop. Valor and Sunday worked there on occasion on their own projects, which was how Kelyn had originally heard about Valor.

"Beck and Daisy Blu are on vacation in Greece. Didn't you know that?" Stryke asked. Tall and brunette, he smiled and punched Kelyn's shoulder gently. Of all the brothers he was the calm, wise one whom everyone else went to with their problems. "Or you been too busy with your own woman to care?"

"Maybe." Kelyn set back his shoulders.

"So the witch is your woman?" Blade whistled. Kelyn did not miss his side-eye, a warning yet discerning look. Of course, none of them could ever avoid the family assessment of dates, lovers and otherwise. "Trouble said she's bad news."

"Trouble is a jerk-off who let me believe he fucked her when he had not. He's trying to steal the spotlight like he always does."

"Sounds like Trouble," Blade muttered, a common assessment oft issued by any and all family members.

"Valor is cool. And yes, she's my woman."

"Well, then." Stryke wiped his greasy hands across

the thighs of his jeans. "Best I meet her." And he strode off toward the Firebird.

Blade put a hand on Kelyn's shoulder when he turned to follow Stryke. "Witches can be bad news. You sure about her, bro?"

"Positive. She's a witch of the light. Doesn't work dark magic. And she saved my life. If it hadn't been for her air magic, I would have drowned in the ocean when we were in Wales. I trust her."

"Wales? And you? Going near large bodies of water? You have been on a trip. Is this spell going to work?"

"Hey, boys!"

"It will." Kelyn's eyes followed the stairway up to see Zen, clad in jean cutoffs and a white tank top, skipping down the steps from the upper loft. "Zen." He gave her a kiss on the cheek when she tilted up on her tiptoes to seek the acknowledgment. Her soft copper dreads batted his shoulder and she smelled like maple syrup.

The threesome watched as Stryke offered a handshake to Valor, who now stood outside by the hood of Kelyn's car. The twosome exchanged words.

"Valor is cool," Zen said. "Why didn't you bring her in?"

"She's nervous for today's adventure. I'll bring her around, official-like, when all this is done."

"So you're going to venture into the woods with a witch?" Zen mocked a shiver. "I know you go into that Faery woods all the time, Kelyn. It's like your second home. But with a witch? I mean, for as much as I like her, you know about witches and the Darkwood."

Stryke wandered back in while Valor remained by the car, arms crossed and her sight fixed on the forest.

"She's anxious," Stryke commented as he joined the

threesome. "But pretty. Who would have thought my little brother would hook up with a witch?"

"Right?" Blade put an arm around Zen and kissed her on the brow.

"Would you guys get off the witch thing?" Kelyn said. "She's no different from the rest of us, and we're all a bunch of misfits trying to fit into this crazy mortal realm. So back off."

"Officially backing off," Stryke said with a salute and a curt but mocking bow.

"I'm going in." Kelyn turned and backed toward the drive, pausing in the open entrance. "Shouldn't take us too long. But, uh…well, you know."

Blade nodded. Stryke gave him a thumbs-up.

Kelyn turned and strode off.

Arms akimbo, Zen stepped forward, her eyes tracking her brother-in-law. "You boys going to keep an eye on them?"

"Fuck, yeah." As Kelyn and Valor strode toward the forest edge, Blade released his wings in all their gothic glory. The black-and-silver appendages that resembled large bat wings flapped once and he folded them up against his shoulders.

At his side, Stryke shifted to four-legged wolf shape and stepped out of the pile of clothing that had dropped off during the transformation. The two brothers waited at the garage door opening, keenly aware of the risk Kelyn was stepping toward.

Kelyn and Valor paused before a maple tree that soared thirty feet high at the edge of the forest. It was massive and the red leaves shivered with the breeze.

It didn't appear menacing, but one never knew in this crazy woods.

He clasped Valor's hand and looked down at her. "I know you're worried." He hooked his other fingers in the quiver strapped over his left shoulder. It contained his arrows; the bow he held at his side. He'd claimed them from the trunk before walking out here.

"It's cool," she said.

"No, it's not. You're scared, and I get that. We can go elsewhere. Find another thin place."

"No. I had a good think before your brother came out to say hi to me. This trip back to where it all started is kind of full circle for me. And you. Us." She squeezed his hand. "Besides, Matilda is here and I want you to be comfortable with everything."

"I'm as nervous as you are, lover."

He felt her relax against his arm. With a brave inhale, Valor nodded decisively. "Then let's rally all that nervous energy and do this."

The rambling forest floor was carpeted with moss, tree roots, branches and mushrooms, flowers, seedlings, anything and everything. The trees grew thick in some spots, almost as if hugging together in a family photo. Scents of life, both plant and animal, perfumed the air with a sweet summer fragrance that made Valor smile.

Kelyn had said he knew of a clearing that he would take them to, and he assumed the lead, bow held in one hand, eyes taking in all surroundings as he deftly navigated the uneven ground with sure steps. He must know the forest well enough that he needn't rely on his wonky ley line navigational skills. No matter. The man exuded a virile confidence and sex appeal that hit her right in the heart. He'd said he was nervous too? He certainly did not show it. And that went a long way in alleviating some of her anxiety.

Valor hadn't put a protection ward over herself before entering the dusky emerald woods because she needed to be clean to pass through the portal, and CJ had said it was a necessity to maintain the dark blessing on the lake water.

She kept an eye peeled about her periphery. And she walked as far from tree roots as she could manage. Though that was virtually impossible, for in some spots the roots crissed and crossed like a loomed rug. She had to be prepared for any surprise attacks. Of course, calmness was key. Kelyn's fate relied on her performing the spell accurately and without fail.

"Where's Matilda?" she asked as they strode deeper into the woods where the shadows deepened and the air thickened with humid soil and pollen. A dragonfly flittered close, then darted off with a silent flutter of wings.

"She'll find me. How you feeling?" Kelyn clasped her hand. Concern beamed from his violet eyes.

Valor nudged up beside him and they walked a little slower, shoulders hugging. "When I'm with you I don't fear a thing."

"You should never fear when I'm with you, Valor. I'd do anything to protect you."

"I know that." Which was the reason they were here, wasn't it? He'd sacrificed so much. Could she ever repay him? Today, she would.

"Can I tell you something?" he asked.

"Always."

His eyes glittered, even in the darkening shadows.

Somehow, the thin strands of moonlight squeezing through the treetops managed to land right in his irises.

"I've dreamed about Faery all my life and have longed to go there. I've always felt it was missing from my very soul. So now? *Excited* is putting my feelings lightly. But I'm also worried."

"Why? You're going to finally visit Faery."

"Yeah. *Visit*."

They tromped over a fallen log coated with moss and lichen, and he tugged her to a stop, gesturing for her to sit on the log beside him. She first checked the nearby roots—they seemed thin and weren't close to the base of any wicked-looking trees—so she sat. He nuzzled his cheek against hers and kissed the edge of her jaw. She could sense his tension despite his seeming eagerness for everything to happen.

"What if, when I get to Faery, I don't want to leave?" he asked.

Valor's heart dropped in her chest to consider she might never see him again after today, but she coached her face to remain neutral, to not wince and show him how such information devastated her. "But your family is here in the mortal realm."

"Right. But…Faery," he said in such an awe-filled tone Valor felt his awe shiver over her skin as if falling faery dust. "It could be the place where I belong."

"Do you feel like you don't belong here?"

"Sometimes. Don't get me wrong, I love my family. They are everything to me. But with three older brothers, two who've worked the alpha-wolf thing all my life and the other a vamp with wings even bigger than mine, I've tended to stand to the side, never confident of my place in *this* world." He glanced at her, his eyes dancing between hers. Pulling her hand up to kiss, he offered a wink. "Though lately, I've felt more settled. This might sound forward, but…I can't imagine leaving you, Valor."

"Then don't," she said too quickly. It took all her inner strength to fight tears. Because only real girls cried, and she would use her tomboy for all it was worth right now. "But, I mean, if you want to take a look around while you're there…"

He bowed his forehead to her hand. To have won his respect and know how he felt about her went a long way in kicking the door shut on that silly witch who'd once thought she wasn't lovable. But he struggled with a choice that hadn't even been presented to him yet. And that worried her.

"You wouldn't *not* come back, would you, Kelyn?"

"I honestly can't say."

"Oh."

"I'm sorry, Valor."

"Don't be. It's your right." She tilted her head against his, and this time the shiver was impossible to staunch. Her heart hurt. After her confession to him last night, she'd actually begun to feel lovable. If he left her, it would devastate her and prove, once and for all, that Valor Hearst would always be one of the guys. "If you feel such a strong calling to Faery, then you should stay there. Or maybe visit and then come back here to see me? I…I don't want you to stay."

He wrapped an arm around her shoulder and hugged her close. "I needed to hear that from you. I don't *intend* to stay, but when I'm there, I'm not sure how I'll feel, so I wanted to tell you. To warn you, I guess."

"Duly warned. Just, uh… Kelyn?"

"Yeah?"

She should do it. Tell him she loved him right now. But that wasn't going to change things. And—

"Ah!" He stood and pointed high. "There's Matilda."

A piercing cry from the kestrel sounded overhead. Kelyn rushed ahead into the clearing.

"Right," Valor muttered as she followed him. "The silly girl stuff can wait for later."

The bird landed on Kelyn's shoulder. He pulled something out of his pocket and fed it to her. She was beautiful. Wings of brown, gray-blue and black folded over her back as she perched on her owner's—make that faery friend's—shoulder. She was small, but her big black eyes seemed soul filled and she looked at Valor as if she were assessing her. With a tilt of her head, she rubbed it against Kelyn's jaw.

Wow. Now, that was trust.

"Matilda, this is Valor. She's my friend," Kelyn said. "Matilda and I have been together since I was a teenager. I guess that makes her my longest and most trusted girlfriend, eh, sweetie?"

"I'm honored to meet you, Matilda," Valor said. "You hang with a very esteemed kind."

The bird actually bobbed her head, as if in a bow. Then she bent forward and plucked at the leather straps around Kelyn's neck, briefly lifting the one that held the cipher Never had explained could only be used by the Wicked.

"She likes that one," he said. "It's our bond."

"Cool. She brought you that from Faery?"

"Yep. Matilda is always bringing me presents. She's my girl."

"I'm a little jealous of a bird, and not afraid to admit

it." She winked at him. "So, is this the place you want to work the spell in?"

"Yes."

The clearing they'd wandered into was deceptively beautiful. It was similar to the clearing Valor had found when *that thing* happened. Looking about, she felt the hairs at the back of her neck prickle. Sunlight beamed through the leaf canopy, lighting the mossy clearing like a stage. Scattered branches and a massive fallen oak were frosted in green moss and tiny yellow wildflowers. Yet beneath the beauty lay a sense of unease and rot. Valor felt it as a shiver over her arms.

But they were here. And she had a job to do. The oak log would make a perfect altar to set up the spell, yet the exposed roots were thick and gnarled and seemed to creep toward her.

Valor took a step back. "Nope."

She scanned about and spied another fallen log, also coated in moss. It was not still attached to roots. Probably it had fallen decades earlier. It would serve for an altar. Setting her leather spell bag down, Valor began to sort through the items while Kelyn chattered with the bird.

"She'll guide us through the portal," he said after a round of chitters shared by both of them.

"You speak falcon?"

"Yes. Don't you?"

Valor smirked. He could probably speak to all the animals. "Well, if a tree comes after me, would you have a few words with it, please?"

"Will do. You need my help?"

"No. I'm going to draw a casting circle and I should be the one in it. You and Matilda stand over there by the

maple sapling. I'll focus the direction for the portal..."
She turned and faced two parallel birch trees sporting
peeling white paper bark. "There. Between those trees.
Sound good?"

"Better than good."

"All right. Stand back. I'm going to sprinkle some
ash for the circle." She tugged out the bag of ash taken
from a fallen rowan tree.

"Kiss me first," Kelyn said.

Dropping the supplies at her feet, Valor rushed to
Kelyn and plunged into his arms. She lost all fear of
crazy trees as Matilda flew up from his shoulder and
cawed.

The kiss dazzled her senses. Dragonflies fluttered
in her heart. Kelyn's arms were kind tree roots that
wrapped about her body and comforted her soul. And her
core tingled with the promise of intense sexual energy
between the two of them. She could rip away his clothing right now and take him on the mossy forest floor.

Maybe she should? If there was the chance he'd not
return from Faery?

Tickling the tip of her tongue with his, Kelyn ended
the kiss and gave a quick kiss to one of her eyelids and
then the other. He bracketed her head between his hands
and bowed to meet her gaze.

"Let's do this," he said. "For good or for ill, I've got
your back."

She bumped fists with him. "Here's to you getting
your wings back, and...the two of us having wild faery-
wing sex later tonight."

Chapter 23

The witch knelt in the center of an ash circle before the altar placed on a mossy oak log. Matilda perched on Kelyn's shoulder, her head cocked forward, wings back, fiercely intent on the witch's actions and her mesmerizing intonations that echoed up from the circle and bewitched the forest into a humble calm.

Sunlight melted over Valor's violet hair, gilding her a Wicked enchantress who moved her hands slowly, ritualistically, as she took up the first item and held it before her to bless it. The werewolf claw stolen from a time traveler. It glinted once, betaken by her magic. She placed it on the moss and swept her fingers over it as she spoke words in a language that must have been created and brewed by witches throughout the centuries.

Second, the vial of unruly lake water the shade of chewed bubble gum that the dark witch had blessed.

Valor had specifically put up no protection spell of her own because of that ingredient.

Kelyn glanced high toward the tree canopy. He knew others watched. They would not interfere unless necessary. And he trusted them.

She poured the water over the claw and it emitted a pink smoke reminiscent of the lake's color that lingered before her. The mermaid's kiss she held above the smoke so it infused the paper and then seemed to peel the kiss off so it dropped onto the claw. Valor's fingers curled and her shoulders swayed as her intonations grew more rhythmic, like a song that only monks could chant. She sprinkled the skull dust stolen from an eclectic archive over the concoction on the moss. A sudden flare ignited the claw and burned blue in thin flame.

And, finally, the last ingredient. True love's first teardrop. How did a person come by such a thing? Sure, witchy spell stuff was all odd and rare and mysterious, but...

It struck Kelyn at that moment that it might, indeed, have been something she stocked for her witchy trade, or, on the other hand... Had she obtained it recently? Because it was...hers?

The realization made him crouch and bow his head. He touched his heart, sending out all that he felt for her toward the witch. Respect, admiration and love. And in that instant she lifted her head and turned to look at him. Matilda cawed. Kelyn nodded, confirming something neither had dared speak out loud to each other. She loved him?

And he had fallen in love with her. Wow. This was immense. He wanted to pull her into his arms and kiss her silly, then—

A banshee's cry erupted in the sky, startling Kelyn upright. He gripped an arrow from his sheath and notched it on the bow. Matilda veered, aiming at the dryad that stalked toward Valor. And as the arrow missed the vile creature, another winged being swooped down and delivered a shoulder punch at the dryad's chest, sending it off course and reeling in the air.

"Thanks, Blade!" Another arrow notched onto the bow, Kelyn tracked the dryad who had come from a nearby oak while shouting to Valor, "Don't stop!"

Valor spread out her arms. With a few more incantation words, the blue flame, emitting pink smoke, rose above her and soared toward the birch trees she had designated as a portal.

Kelyn followed the returning dryad. His brother, who had unfurled his black-and-silver wings, followed it, but the creature was small and swift, and blended with the tree bark, so one moment it was visible, the next, not. Just as it tracked overhead, and Kelyn's arrow once again missed the target—curse his lacking faery skills!—the dryad dodged low and was met by Stryke's wolf, who snatched it by the throat with his powerful maw.

"It's ready!" Valor announced. She gestured to Kelyn. "Where's Matilda?"

Kelyn searched the sky but didn't sight the kestrel falcon. He caught Valor's hand with his and now he saw the portal that gleamed before them. An oblong oval centered between the two birch trees like a liquid skein of ocean water. He hoped there weren't mermaids on the other side.

"Are those your brothers?" Valor asked as they rushed toward the portal.

"Yes, they'll keep the dryad at bay."

"You ready for this?"

"All my life! Matilda!"

The kestrel dived from the tree canopy and swooped over their heads. She glided toward the portal and, with a flap of wings, broke the skein into myriad glitters of wavering sky.

"Now!" Kelyn pulled Valor after him. They both leaped through the portal and landed...

...in thick emerald grass dotted with red mushrooms. Their bodies rolled and they sprawled amid a dusting of blue-and-violet flower pollen.

Kelyn stood and brushed the violet pollen from his forearms. He helped Valor to stand and before he could hug her, she pointed behind him and shouted in surprise. He swung around quickly, but when reaching for his bow, realized he'd left it behind in the mortal realm.

He didn't see anything wild or vicious headed toward them. "What is it?"

"The sky is freaking azure and that tree bark is actually yellow."

He chuckled at her marvel. And then took a moment to look about. Indeed, the deep blue sky bejeweled the air. The yellow tree resembled most trees, only the bark was golden and the leaves were also a shiny yellow gold. The grass at their feet was green. Looked like normal grass. And the mushrooms dotted about also looked normal.

And there in the sky, far yet large, loomed a green moon, and beside it hung a pearl moon.

"Is that for real?" Valor asked as she noted the same thing.

"Most definitely."

Kelyn rubbed his fingers together and sniffed at the violet pollen. "Whew! That's potent." Like the lushest flower he'd ever smelled. And yet a darkness permeated that scent and he wanted to get it off his fingers. But rubbing frantically against his thigh did nothing more than further imbue it into the whorls.

Insect sounds chirped, buzzed and chirred about them. Nothing too unfamiliar, but the noise seemed to rise and fall in sync, almost like a symphony. Cool.

They stood in a field that edged an extremely dark forest. Kelyn couldn't see past the tightly spaced trees any farther than about ten feet. He highly expected to see eyes flashing at them from within.

"I wonder if these are the same as in the mortal realm." Valor squatted to inspect the mushrooms.

"Uh, sweetie?"

She looked up at him in inquiry, her violet hair spilling over the grass tips.

"Remember what happened last time you tried to take something from Faery?"

She quickly dropped the mushroom and stood. "Right. Just here for your wings. So, where do you think we should go? I vote no on the creepy forest."

"Two votes against the forest. So maybe…" Kelyn swung in the opposite direction. Gray boulders serrated by glistening violet crystals sat on a low hill and were frilled with trimmed shrubbery.

That was odd. Who trimmed the shrubs way out here? Or *were* they way out anywhere? They could have landed in someone's backyard for all Kelyn knew.

Much as he'd like to wander about and admire the scenery and take in the scents that at first smelled familiar, but then changed to something slightly sinister, he had come here with a job to do. Get in, get out.

In theory.

After he had his wings, could he not spend some time wandering about as he wished?

"I think that's them!" Valor rushed across the grassy field toward the forest.

"I thought we voted against that way." But when Kelyn saw what she headed toward, he took off, as well.

The *them* she'd shouted about was what looked like his wings. And two of them were not attached to a body, because the demon who had taken them was cutting them off his back at the edge of the forest.

As they neared, the demon snapped upright, one wing in hand, the place where it had been severed leaking thick black blood. The other wings, tattered and almost beyond Kelyn's recognition, lay on the ground in a pool of demon blood.

"Ah! So you've come for your wings, eh?"

"Looks like they are not serving you well."

The demon clutched the severed wing to his chest and gave them both an imperious lift of chin. "They're mine. You gave them to me." Then he eyeballed Kelyn, at right about neck level. His eyes glowed brightly.

Kelyn touched the cipher hanging from his neck. "Do you see something you'd rather have much more than my useless wings?"

The demon's lower lip quivered.

"I can make a trade. Of course, this is merely a trinket. And those…"

"These are worthless!" The demon thrust one wing at Kelyn and he caught it. "You can have them for the cipher. Awful bit of goodness and nice. I should have taken the cipher from the start. I knew I could use it, but I'd always wanted wings."

The wing in Kelyn's grasp shivered. He clasped it to his chest, feeling as if a part of him had been returned, and yet that part was now tainted and worn. "What have you done to them?"

"Not a bloody thing. I've worn them since you gave them to me. Thought they'd get me entrance back into the Unseelie court's good graces, me being Wicked and all. Those unspeakably *pleasant* things!" He kicked at the wings on the ground. "I cannot raise my fist at an attacker to save my life! Awful bit of niceness and honor running through those ugly wings. Do you know I helped a crippled sprite across a stream? What was that about?"

Valor cast Kelyn a knowing grin. So his kindness had paid off. But how, exactly? Sticky demon blood smeared across Kelyn's arm and wrist. It smelled rotten, while the sheer fabric of his precious wing had tears in it and the edges were frayed.

"Give me the cipher!"

Kelyn tugged the leather cord from around his neck but clasped the circle tightly. The demon made a gimme gesture with his hand. As Valor bent to touch one of the severed wings, the demon slapped a foot onto it and *tched* at her. "Not until he hands over the cipher."

Kelyn rubbed his thumb around the cool, hard surface of the thing. He'd never known what it was, beyond that it had sort of sealed his friendship with Matilda because it was the first gift she'd brought him from Faery. He swallowed and searched the sky. Matilda flew overhead. It was a nervous flight in a tight circle that made him second-guess giving the thing away. "I'm not sure."

"Kelyn, your wings?" Valor nudged.

Matilda cawed once. The stark cry pleaded with him. But it wasn't the same plea Valor had made. The bird had issued a confirmation of alliance. He could feel her heartbeat in his chest. The flap of her wings beat the air, holding her aloft. She didn't want him to hand over the cipher?

But he'd come all this way. He held his reason for being in hand.

"I'm waiting, faery." The demon stepped forward, crushing one of the wings under his foot. "It's a bit of stone that'll allow me to navigate to my people. You know they hide us here in Faery. Cast us out to a place at the edge where no others can be bothered by us, the half-breeds who are so hideous."

"You're not hideous," Kelyn said. And he meant it. The demon had helped him and Valor when they were desperate. And he had chosen freely how to pay the demon for such help. "But I'm not sure…"

He looked to Valor, who shrugged. She could never understand all the complicated consequences that ran through his brain right now. If he handed over the cipher, would Matilda…? What would become of his and Matilda's bond?

And yet with his other hand he clutched the tattered wing against his chest. He could not survive with but the one wing. He needed all four. And his soul screamed for him to fit those missing pieces back into his life.

"Very well." Kelyn thrust the cipher forward. It dangled from the leather cord. "It's yours." He flipped his hand, and the necklace soared toward the black-skinned demon, who caught it with a gnash of his fangs.

"And these are yours." The dark thing kicked the remaining wings across the grass toward them.

Overhead, Matilda keeled out a warning caw. It was so piercing Kelyn winced.

"I'm out of here." The demon stepped backward into the forest and became one with the blackness, red eyes flashing twice in blinks before dissolving to nothing.

Valor picked up a wing and inspected it. She turned a beaming smile at him. "That was easy. Who'da thought, eh?"

Right. But what had he sacrificed in turn this time?

"Never look gift wings in the mouth. You did say the spell would take us directly to my wings." Kelyn traced the serrated end that yet bled black demon blood. "Good job, witch."

"You don't look happy. I know this looks bad, but they'll clean up."

"They're tattered," he said on a breath that caught at the back of his throat. "Used and damaged."

"It was the demon that made them this way. Once you have them back on, they'll be good as new. I'm sure of it."

"Sure." His eyes searched the azure sky. No Matilda anywhere. Had the moons darkened?

Valor stepped up to him. "Let's put them back on, yes?"

He nodded and with one last search of the sky, bowed his head and fell to his knees before her. With a reluctance that felt as heavy as grief, Kelyn pulled off his shirt and then handed her the wing he'd held.

"How do I do this?" she asked.

"Just put them where they belong. Right over the scars. They should heal to me. I hope. Valor."

She paused before walking around behind him.

"Thank you," he said. "For everything. I know how you got the final ingredient."

"Y-you do? Right. I told you, I had it in stock."

"Valor." On his knees before her felt right because she stood a goddess before him, and he her lucky consort. "You are a real, exquisitely lovable woman. I love you."

"Oh. I, uh… Jeez. Are we going to do this right now?" She sniffled and a teardrop spilled down her cheek.

He hadn't expected that reaction. And he wasn't sure what to do now. Miss Tomboy was going all tears on him?

"Yeah, so maybe I did get that last ingredient right after you left me at home the other day. I was hoping you might have stayed the night with me. But you walked away. And I, uh…you know."

She couldn't say it. But he didn't need her to say it. He felt the love emanate from her.

"Sorry I left you hanging like that. I had to go to my brother's house and straighten something out between us."

"Oh. And did you?"

"Yes. Trouble and I are good now."

"I'm glad. I sure hope he can be good with me, too. I hate having lost him as a friend."

"Give him some time. I have a feeling he misses pizza night with you."

Valor shrugged. "It's fun, but if I'm going to share my pizza with anyone now, I'd prefer it be you."

"No pepperoni?"

"How about veggies on half?"

"Deal."

The moment demanded a fist bump, but Kelyn instead pressed his cheek to her stomach and hugged her. The witch was his. He was no longer threatened by her friendship with his brother. And his wings had been found. And even as the insect song seemed to rise in warning about them, he could only be thankful.

Rocking back onto his toes and looking up to her, he winked. The witch actually blushed. Yep, he loved her.

"So," he said with a splay of a hand, "you going to stand there with my wings or will you put them on and let me see if I can get them to work again?"

"Yes, of course!" She scampered around beside him, and then she backtracked and leaned down to kiss him. "I love you, too. Thank you, for not giving up and for letting me help you get to this moment."

"I couldn't have done it with anyone else. Now..." He shrugged, feeling itchy to return to normal. Tugging off his T-shirt, he tossed that aside. "Let's do this!"

"All right!" She went around behind him and he thought he heard her brushing something across the grass.

"What are you doing?"

"I'm trying to get as much of the demon blood off as I can."

"Good call." Kelyn leaned forward, catching his hands in the thick grass.

A sprite buzzed nearby. The creature was no larger than a bumblebee, but she was as perfectly formed as most humans, with wings, and wore tiny pink petals as a dress. She buzzed back and forth before his nose until he had to swat at her to make her stop. But he did so carefully.

"Do you notice the insect buzzing is getting louder?" Valor asked.

"Maybe they're upset about us being in their territory." He shrugged again. "Do it now, please?"

At first touch of the wet, sticky base of a wing to his back, Kelyn felt the sensation vibrate through his being as a weird electric current that touched all nerve endings beneath his skin. He flinched, but Valor held the wing in place. And when she immediately placed another wing on his back, heat rushed through at the point of connection. The last two she set against his skin at the same time, doubling the strange jolt of vita that at once hurt, but then seemed to cool and glow all over his skin.

At his wrists another cool burn revitalized the violet sigils. He felt the same icy cut as they drew in curves and mandalas into his chest.

He gasped and his body seized up, his back arching. The wings were fusing to him and it was more painful than the phantom pains he'd experienced. Yet he smiled through it all. They were back. And soon he would be the man he once was.

"Whoa!" Valor stumbled and fell into the grass beside him.

"What happened?"

"I think some of your faery vita repulsed me. It's powerful stuff. Yikes!" She shook her hand. Kelyn noticed a pale blue vine shooting up from the grass that attempted to twine about her wrist, but she managed to unloose it. And when she stood, she gasped with awe. "Wow, your wings are… Oh, Kelyn, can you feel them?"

"Yes, they're almost completely restored. How do they look?"

He tried flapping them and was able to move each independently and then all four in tandem. The sweep of air against his face from the movement felt great. Familiar.

"Oh..." Valor's utterance felt unfinished. Like it should have ended with the invocation of a TV doctor's name.

"What? Valor, tell me. Did something go wrong? It doesn't hurt anymore. I think I should give flight a try."

"Oh, Kelyn."

He stood, feeling his old and familiar strength surge through his system like blood rushing back to an unused limb. Mighty and renewed, he spread out his arms and looked to Valor, who sat on the ground, hands supporting her and mouth open in a horrified gape.

"What?" he asked.

"Your wings," she said. "They're black."

Chapter 24

Her gorgeous lover, the man with whom she had fallen desperately in love, stood before her renewed and strong. His fists were tight and veined, wrapped with fierce power. His abs and chest, ornamented with the violet sigil markings, were like steel. Broad shoulders stretched proudly back. And behind him, his wings gleamed... black.

When once his wings had been violet and silver, shimmery with life and boldness, now they swept out behind him, tattered and the blackest black. More so than his brother Blade's gothic wings. Yet Kelyn wielded them as if he knew nothing else and they hadn't changed.

Perhaps they had not changed? Was it merely the demon's blood that had altered their appearance but not their original goodness?

"Black?" Kelyn looked over a shoulder and preened one wing forward with a hand. "Huh. Yep. They're black. I'll survive."

"You'll…" He was being obnoxiously dismissive about what she felt had to be a horrible change. Maybe the wings needed a little time to readjust to Kelyn's body and reacclimate? "Right. You will survive. We should probably get the heck out of here while the getting is good. Where's Matilda?"

"There!" He pointed overhead and Valor spied the kestrel soaring toward the silver portal. "Run!" he shouted. "We haven't much time!"

Valor took off after the kestrel, combat boots crushing the long grasses, and stirring up the blue-violet pollen in her wake. The insect chirring sounded like a tornado engine. That couldn't be good.

Everything would be all right. They'd return to the mortal realm and Kelyn's wings would return to violet and silver. He'd be as he once had been. Life would move forward. Together.

Pumping her arms, Valor was thankful her boots were worn and comfortable. She wasn't much for running, but when survival was at stake? She could manage.

The portal loomed close ahead. Matilda banked to the left, aiming for the gateway—

The insect noises had ceased. The only thing Valor heard was her own huffing breaths and the blood pounding through her veins. A split second of wondering if she should stop and look around surfaced. Dread surged to Valor's throat as she realized the world had gone so still. And she slowed but didn't stop.

Something hissed, like a massive snake.

Turning, even as she kept moving across the grass,

she caught a glimpse of the threat. The creature rose from the long grasses in a slithering, sinuous glide. Narrow, pointed wings flapped, pulling it off from the ground. Blue and violet scales covered it from its long head, all down its snaking length, to the tail. A freaking snake with wings? Oh, man, she did not like Faery one bit.

"Dr. Doug Ross!"

The creature cawed like an entire unkindness of ravens, then violet flames whipped out of its fanged mouth and snapped up toward Matilda. The flames lashed at the bird's tail feathers as she banked in the azure sky. But she could not avoid the attack. The kestrel screeched and went down like a cannonball, landing in the grass before the undulating portal.

Valor screamed and the sound alerted the creature. A monster snake? She turned completely and picked up her speed toward the portal, seeing a smoking mist rising from Matilda. Behind her the flapping wings drew closer. The thump of something beating the ground intermittently made her decide it must be hitting the ground with its tail. And the smell of smoke rose as she realized a new sound filled the air.

That of flames.

With one glance over her shoulder to see the trail of flame following her in the grass, Valor used her last burst of energy to leap and dive for Matilda. She landed over the bird on all fours, pressing her body down but not completely touching the bird, enough so that she could protect her as a wild path of flame ate through the grass and...

Valor closed her eyes, muttering a witchy prayer for safety and wishing like hell she had water magic to put out the flames. When finally she lifted her head, the world had again quieted. And…she wasn't on fire. Yet.

Still huddling over Matilda, she looked around behind her. The flames had fizzled to smoke. And the only reason they hadn't gone after her was that she was lying in the cool shadow of the liquid portal. Burned grass smoked all around the oval on which she lay. The shadow had saved her from a burned ass. And death.

"Blessings," she whispered.

Glancing about, she didn't spy the snake creature. It was gone. Maybe. She'd keep an eye out. It couldn't have hidden in the grass. It had been so large.

A snake. A freakin' snake, of all things!

Setting her repulsion aside, Valor turned back to the ground. Nestled in the grass lay Matilda. She wasn't dead, but a few tail feathers smoked from the fire attack that had knocked her out of the sky. Valor wasn't sure how to handle a bird without causing it further harm. Kelyn could do it. He had an affinity with all animals.

She scanned the meadow. Where was Kelyn? Hadn't he been behind her? He must have taken off after the snake thing. She called out to him. He'd been right there behind her, telling her to run for it—

Her heart dropped to her gut. Realization cut her to the bone.

"John Carter," she swore. "He's staying. He knew exactly what he was doing by telling me to run. He knew if I ran through the portal without him… Oh, Kelyn."

She bowed her head over Matilda, and the tears rushed up so quickly she couldn't think to fight them or consider that girls like her didn't cry. Because she was a real girl. Kelyn had made her realize that. And yet. He'd sent her away. Without him.

Had he been lying to her all this time? Had he never seen her as she'd only dreamed he could? Had her stupid hopes for a hero been quashed by the man's blind desires to return to his homeland?

It hurt to know she'd been used. Had he done that to her? She didn't want to believe it, but all the past hurts and rejections now came rushing back to plunder her soul. No man would ever have a care for her beyond what she could do for him. Like gaining him access to Faery.

"I've been such a fool!" She beat her thighs, kneeling there beside the inanimate bird. "Why do I let men treat me like this?"

A chitter of insects stirred nearby. She didn't care who heard her rant. She needed to shout and scream and...

Why couldn't she keep a man interested in her? Did she have to do the skirts-and-heels thing? Kelyn hadn't seemed concerned about the way she dressed. Maybe it was her stupid, idiotic laugh? But that had seemed to actually turn him on.

Was it that she was too alpha, always trying to be the one in charge? She had let him take the lead. Hadn't she?

Catching her forehead in her palms, she growled in frustration. And yet the portal behind her reminded that she hadn't the leisure for this ridiculous pouting. Her time to escape this horrid realm could be coming to an end.

"Right. Suck it up, witch."

Something she'd said to herself many times before. And the last time she tried to suck it up, she'd wandered into the Darkwood, to devastating results.

"Not going to be a fool anymore." She turned on her

knees and looked up at the portal. "I will get out of here. Leave him behind. And never look back."

Because Kelyn was doing his own thing now. In… Faery. Exploring. Or whatever it was he felt he had to do in a place he'd always longed to go to. Hell, he'd tossed over the cipher, knowing it somehow connected him and Matilda. Was that why the bird had been struck down? She'd been weakened when Kelyn severed their bond? The man *should* run off. He had no right to claim friendship with such a majestic creature.

Valor hoped he flew off forever. With wings that had been tainted by evil.

"No," she whispered in protest to her foolish anger.

Were the tainted wings the reason he'd pushed her away so easily? Given up on Matilda, as well? She wanted to cling to that, but a new resolve tugged her away from the stupid reaction. The man wasn't interested in her anymore.

Time to move on.

The portal undulated, a liquid, silvery oval. Valor had no idea how long it would remain there; it was her escape to the mortal realm. Yet she needed a guide through, and that was Matilda.

She stroked the bird's wing and cooed softly. Injured, but how so? Spreading out her hands over the bird, Valor focused her vita downward and whispered a healing charm that would transfer her life force into the bird. She'd never tried it on an animal before, only bees, and even then her healing powers had been minimal. Yet with a touch of vita, a bee could flutter back to the hive to restore its energy on the honey.

She could heal a boo-boo, ease Kelyn's aches and

pains, but beyond that? "I won't let you die, Matilda. I've got to try this."

Something swooped overhead. Still holding her palms to infuse Matilda with her vita, Valor glanced upward. It wasn't a faery man with black wings. Nor was it the snake creature. Just a bird? Nerves rose to prickle her skin with a fear she hadn't wanted to acknowledge.

She did not like being abandoned in a foreign land. How could he have been so cruel?

"It's the wings," she muttered, and pulled back her hands to her hips. "They've changed him." Just as Never and CJ had warned would happen.

But that didn't mean she wasn't walking away from him when she got the chance. He'd made his choice. Now she had to make hers.

She inspected Matilda. Eyes closed, the bird seemed to be sleeping, so Valor would allow her to rest and let her magic do what healing work it could.

Standing, she pressed a hand against her forehead to shield her eyes from the brilliance, even though she saw only the two moons. The vibrant sky had grown almost white. It seemed to reflect up from the emerald grass, making her wish she had a pair of sunglasses.

How to track Kelyn? Did she want to find him? She'd decided to walk away from him. He could do what he wanted now.

"Unless he was attacked by the snake thing before it went after Matilda?"

Much as she knew he had not been, a small part of her still wanted to make sure the man was, at the very least, safe. He could stay. That was what he wanted. But she couldn't leave until she saw him alive.

Yeah, that was her story, and she was sticking to it.

She could use her air magic to summon creatures of air and wing, but that might bring back the thing that had attacked Matilda. The other option was to go on a search, which would involve entering the dark forest. And she wasn't keen on entering any forest in Faery.

"Summoning spell it is."

She clapped her hands decisively and stepped away from Matilda to plant her feet squarely yet still remained within the portal shadow. No telling what the smoking grass might do if she touched that. It could have vicious monster spume in it that would melt her boots. Focusing her energies to her fourth chakra—the air chakra— she spread wide her arms to open her diaphragm. She wasn't sure her mortal-realm magic would work here in Faery—in proof, Matilda had not remarkably come to from her healing magic—but she had no other option than to try.

Chanting an invocation to bring forth the creatures of air, she kept one eye peeled for the snake and was prepared to halt the chant if she spied it. Her body hummed as her chant grew faster and deeper and seemed to birth from her lungs and permeate her chest in vibrations that imbued the universe with her will. Forming mudras with forefingers touching her thumbs, she focused the energies to draw what she could toward her.

And when something landed beside her, and she sensed it was another person—not a snake—Valor opened her eyes to look upon a man who was not Kelyn.

Tall and lithe, his dark hair listed in the breeze. Silver-eyed, he wore rich, bejeweled clothing that reminded her of something from the nineteenth-century Bohemian times. A violet frock coat hemmed in jewel-glittered lace served as a backdrop for the sparkling rings on his long fingers. A matching glitter twinkled in his eyes. Behind him, magnificent silver wings folded down neatly as he assumed a haughty pose.

"Who are you?" she asked.

He quirked an annoyed brow above his silver gaze, as if she was an idiot for not knowing the answer to that one. Propping a hand on a crystal staff that suddenly appeared at his side, he announced, "I am Malrick. King of the Unseelies."

Kelyn had raced into the dark woods after sending Valor off toward the portal. It had been a cruel trick, but he knew she wouldn't have left without him.

And now that he was here in Faery, he didn't want to leave. Nor would he. This was his homeland. He belonged here.

Whistling a few times did not summon Matilda to his side. The kestrel must have led Valor through the portal and could not hear him from the mortal realm. Just as well.

Maybe. Kelyn brushed his shoulder, wishing his sidekick were there, along with him. Matilda was his connection to…not home. This place was his real home. It had to be. He felt the call of its earth, sky and vital beings in his wings.

And he could taste the awesome adventure waiting him on the air.

Marching forward, he ventured deeper into the woods but found the brambles tugged at his ankles, so he lifted up a few feet to fly slowly between the trees. Man, it felt great to fly again! Black or otherwise, his wings were back. Sprites and birds littered the dark confines of the woods, and creatures with eyes of violet, gold and blue watched him from the inky shadows.

Scents of musty rot, fruiting lushness and a liquid crispness combined in a heady perfume. His sensory skills had returned to their usual übersensitivity. Thank the gods for that. Now he could find his way with his eyes closed, or smell when predators approached before they got too near. He could even draw in Valor's innate womanly perfume and get lost in it...

No, he'd sent her away for her own good. She didn't belong in Faery. And as much as he'd enjoyed her company these past days, she would only hold him back now. Because a witch *in* Faery? That couldn't be good for the witch.

He winced as his thoughts settled. She could never hold him back. But he didn't want to acknowledge how much he'd like to have her along with him on this venture. He couldn't. What had been done was done.

Compelled, Kelyn followed a curiously exotic scent that curled into him and softened his determination. It coaxed with a hint of juicy citrus and led him onward with a hearty splash of warmth and suede. Spices he could not name alchemized with the earthy scents below his feet. He wanted to know the source of the perfume so desperately that his heartbeat sped up, as did his wings. He glided forward, deeper into the black woods.

The sprites darting in and out of his path seemed to screech at him, but he couldn't understand what they were trying to convey. If they were warning him back, he didn't need a tiny creature telling him what to do. With a snap of his fingers, he sent one of the diminutive things reeling into the shadows.

A crimson haze wove betwixt and between the obsidian tree trunks. Kelyn inhaled the mist like a dark witch's drugged cocktail. And he landed on his feet in a clearing lighted by thousands of fluttering lampbugs. There, before him, loomed a void in the darkness in a form about as high as he was and no wider. Reaching forward, he touched the void. It was cold, and it actually flinched as his fingers barely skimmed the fabric. It was something...

A woman spun about and he stepped back with a gasp. Adorned in floaty red fabric that barely covered her breasts and mons, her pale violet skin glinted. Her violet eyes beamed brightly, and her lavender lips curled into a wet, sensuous entreaty.

Kelyn drew her in and sighed at her utter loveliness. He could taste her already and wanted to feel the skim of her bright skin over his.

"You desire me, visitor?"

Her voice slipped over his skin as if slickened with exotic oil and followed by what he imagined were greedy kisses.

Entranced, Kelyn nodded. "I do."

The red fabric or dress—whatever it was she wore— seemed more a part of the misty haze and moved over her, caressing and always barely concealing. And that weird mist wove within her hair, which was so black it truly did appear a void set against the backdrop of dark trees.

She opened her lush mouth and Kelyn saw the fangs, which glinted like diamonds. With a lift of her chin and a lowering of her lashes, she sniffed once and said, "You've the stink of witch on you, my faery warrior."

He liked being called such and took a step closer. Shaking his head, he couldn't find words to argue or defend. All he desired was to be closer to her, to feel her, to be inside her...

"She doesn't love you." Red sparkles dazzled the air as she spoke, seeming to form words in puffs before her. "She is a witch. Most wicked and vile."

Kelyn smiled drunkenly as the sparkles floated onto his face and tickled his eyelashes.

"She uses her wiles as magic. A magic that destroyed you once and will do so again."

He followed the seductress's hand, which swept gracefully before her, stirring the bewitching dust that had emanated with her words. One finger crooked and her coo of welcome splashed against him with roses and earth and all the scents of desire.

With a purse of her lips, she teased him to kiss her. And he wanted to taste that luscious mouth.

Stepping closer, he found himself surrounded by the curling ruby mist. It embraced and caressed, and everywhere it touched him he felt her lips on his bare skin. A man could close his eyes and get lost, never desiring to return.

She hummed what sounded like an angel's song, yet it was tinted with something deep and longing. Something illicit.

Kelyn leaned closer, his feet planted on the ground and his wings fluttering to hold his body at an extreme forward angle. Tendrils of the woman's hair wrapped across his shoulders, luring him into her sweet yet slippery seduction. He closed his eyes, ready to fall into the kiss...

"Kelyn!"

Snapped out of the enchantment, he hitched a look

over his shoulder in the direction from which he'd heard Valor's scream. She was still in Faery?

The seductress grasped him by the neck, her thumb squeezing his windpipe and a long, sharp nail cutting his skin. "You are mine!"

He felt his tongue rising, stretching as if she were trying to pull it out through his teeth. His jawbone cracked. Kelyn kicked at the woman, but his foot only plunged through red mist.

Grasping at his back, he cursed that he'd left his bow and arrows in the mortal realm. A swing of his hand forward cut through the red mist, yet landed on no solid body. Briefly, he felt the thumb release from his neck, but as he gasped in a breath the squeeze of her fingers resumed.

Again, his name carried through the dark woods, perhaps on a whisper of Valor's air magic. It sounded sweeter than this bitch's seductive mist. How had he managed to walk right up to her and not be suspicious?

Grasping at the arm and hand that held him, his feet now off the ground, Kelyn dug in his fingers, but she didn't flinch. The woman's mouth snarled, and her fangs grew longer, stretching below her chin.

"I will eat your tongue, wrong one," she said on a growl.

And he expected it to go down that way if he didn't get out of this horrible vise clench quickly. In his periphery he saw the flashing illumination of hundreds of sprites buzzing about their struggle. Choking from the tug on his tongue, Kelyn swung out a hand and grasped madly. The burn of sprite fire pierced his fingers and palm, yet he clutched a few of the creatures. Not having a plan, and acting purely on instinct, Kelyn crammed the sprites into the seductress's mouth as she lunged for him.

Sprites squealed, and the bitch's mouth sparked as if she'd swallowed fireworks. The red haze whipped about Kelyn's body, squeezing his arms tight against his sides. But his tongue had been released and he was able to yell as the pain of having his organs compressed could not be squelched.

And then, with a sudden hiss, the haze slipped away from him like a dead snake falling to the ground. The red mist spumed in a great mushroom cloud before him, covering the black void. Kelyn stumbled backward, his heel hooking on a tree root.

When the mist dissipated it revealed the tree trunks and a few sprite corpses sprawled on the dense forest floor. No more red seductress.

"Kelyn!"

"Valor." Energized by the call for help, Kelyn turned to sprint out of the forest, taking to the air with a flap of his wings and a surge of determination.

Chapter 25

Kelyn swooped down to land in the tall field grass before the violet-haired witch. He folded down his wings and rubbed his throat where ichor had dried from the cuts. He made a quick summation of the scene around him.

The portal had not been breached. It still undulated, set within the sky and riding low over the meadow. Why hadn't Valor left Faery? But more important, who was the faery standing beside her now? Didn't the man know Valor was *his* woman? And no faery seductress would make him believe otherwise. He'd been close to dying in that seductress's hands. Or, at the least, losing his tongue. *Fool!*

But he wouldn't stand powerless now.

Kelyn grabbed the man by the throat and lifted him from the ground. In reaction, his captive repulsed Kelyn with but a nod of his head, lifting him from the ground and sending him backward to land against the portal's base. Kelyn felt the weird liquid vibrations surround him, but he would not be sucked through. A familiar was necessary...

He noted the kestrel falcon lying on the ground. Still. Dead? Had the witch done something to her?

"What is going on?" Kelyn demanded. "What did you do to Matilda?"

"Me?" Valor stabbed her chest in question. "You're the one that severed your connection with her. You hurt her!"

The mysterious man stepped up beside Valor. "This fool is the one you are so worried about missing?" the silver-eyed faery commented snidely. "He stinks of the Wicked."

"I am not. I sent the demon off after he left me with tattered wings!"

"Yes, you gave him a cipher." The stranger clucked his tongue accusingly. "Poor move. You and the bird were connected through that talisman. She'll not listen to you again unless you get it back. But the stink that clings to you is very much demon. You've been kissing a Wicked One in the Wilds."

The faery served Valor a side glance and she, in turn, crossing her arms tightly, cast an accusing glare at Kelyn.

Kelyn stood with a proud thrust of his shoulders and flapped his wings once, drawing them tight together and straight out behind him in warning. "I am Kelyn Saint-Pierre, and I am faery."

"Saint-Pierre?" The man narrowed his gaze on Kelyn. Adorned in clothing that looked as if it had been stolen from a museum featuring aristocratic court costumes, the pompous bit of pouf and jewelry had the audacity to challenge him with his sneering smirk. Who *was* he? "Do you know Rissa?"

Startled to hear that name from the stranger, Kelyn could but speak the truth. "She's my mother. And who are you?"

"He's King of the Unseelies," Valor interrupted. "Where were you? Is he telling the truth? Were you kissing another woman? I thought we were going back to the mortal realm together. And Matilda! Some snake creature shot flames at her and took her out."

"A wyvern," the Unseelie king said. "Malicious bits of fire and scale, but they are not carnivores. I sense the falcon is still alive, if wounded. Let me hold her. I'll give her back the vita she has lost. Not that it'll help your return journey home."

Kelyn stepped before the fallen bird. "No, she's mine. And I don't care what you're king of, you can step away from Valor right now. She's mine."

Valor bristled at that announcement.

"You certainly claim a lot while standing in a land that isn't your own," Malrick said.

"Faery *is* my home."

"Not at all," Malrick proclaimed. "You, boy, belong where you were born. There is a reason we are come into this world in the realm in which we are placed. No one is misplaced. Ever." The king twisted his beringed fingers about the crystal staff. "Rissa's son, eh? A sylph with soft pink curls and a ruby-rose mouth? I loved her once."

Kelyn gaped at the man. His mother had never told him about an Unseelie king. Or had she mentioned him in her faery tales? He couldn't believe him—Malrick.

Didn't want to. It didn't matter anyway. He would not allow the man to dissuade him from his explorations.

"That was a long time ago," Malrick added.

"My mother was born in Faery. Are you telling me she was not misplaced to the mortal realm and should still be here?"

"No. She was called to the mortal realm, as some are. She belongs there now, but she is always welcome in her homeland. And in my…well…" Malrick let that one hang.

And rightfully so. The creep.

"Ah." Malrick walked around before Kelyn. "Your wings are tainted with blood from the Wicked. That's what's making you so obstinate. They can be cleansed and you'll be in your right mind again. He's changed, yes?" He turned a look to Valor. "Not who he once was?"

"You're telling me. The Kelyn I know would never have left me to return to the mortal realm alone. Though he did warn me before we came here that very thing might happen."

"Exactly," Kelyn snapped at her. "So get yourself back to where you belong and leave me here where I belong. Let the Unseelie heal Matilda, and then she can guide you back." He picked up the bird and handed her over to the king, who carefully took the bird, but also gripped Kelyn's wrist. The sigils burned brightly on Kelyn's skin, searing painfully, and it took all his strength to rip away from the grasp. "What in Beneath?"

"Not Beneath, boy. This is Faery. And it is not your home. Nor will it ever be. You seek to find your roots? They are buried deep and sure within your family, which resides in the mortal realm."

"I'll be the judge of that. You spout nonsense to confuse me."

Malrick gently caressed the bird at his chest. "I never speak nonsense. And I would never lie to Rissa's son."

The king bowed his head over Matilda and kissed her soft, feathered crown. Whispering words Kelyn did not recognize, but that he felt in his veins, the man tended the bird carefully. Silver static sparkled over Matilda's body, flashing in reds, violets and gold.

Kelyn glanced to Valor. She wouldn't meet his gaze. Instead, she shoved her hands in her back pockets and toed the grass with a boot. He'd almost kissed the Wicked red seductress. Almost. But obviously Valor believed otherwise.

Every moment he stood defiant before the Unseelie king and the witch, he betrayed the woman he loved. But…he was home. And it felt right. Maybe?

He didn't belong? Then where *did* he belong?

Malrick released Matilda, who flew up into the sky with a joyful peal and began to circle their trio, waiting for her cue to lead them back through the portal.

But Kelyn wasn't about to leave. And nothing could make him. Not a Faery king. Not even a guilty conscience.

Lifting his palm, he touched a sigil on his chest and repulsed the king with a blast of focused faery energy.

Malrick stumbled backward, and only by stabbing his staff into the ground did he prevent himself from falling.

Valor cast him an accusing glare. Why hadn't she left when he'd been determined to stay? He didn't want to hurt her, but he didn't want her around him now. Because, indeed, he'd been tainted by the demon's blood coursing through his wings. And yet that taint felt powerful and he could use it to survive in this land so unknown to him.

It was for Valor's sake that he must be cruel to be kind.

Malrick approached and Kelyn unfurled his wings to their full expansion, displaying them in all their glory. "You stay back. This is what I choose. The witch can leave. She'll be much better off without me."

"No, Kelyn, I won't be," Valor said. She sniffed back tears.

Really? Again with the tears? Since when had Valor become such an emotional, pouty...woman? Well, he wasn't going to let the ridiculous display affect him. And the tug of remorse in his chest was a fluke. The result of testing his newly returned magic.

"I love you!" Valor suddenly shouted.

Malrick lifted a brow, silently imploring with a *don't you want that?*

"You love me, too," Valor insisted. "I know you do. So does your family. You've no family here in Faery."

"I belong here!"

"You do not," Malrick insisted.

With a splay of his hands, Kelyn announced, "Then I belong nowhere."

"You belong here." Valor thumped her chest, right over her heart. "Don't stay, Kelyn. You have nothing here! You won't even have the cooperation of the Unseelie king. That's got to warn you."

Malrick shrugged and with a flick of his beringed fingers, he offered, "I can be what the mortals deem an asshole at times."

"Yeah? Well, so can I."

Kelyn charged the king, slamming into his chest. Intense magic clashed with his own. He felt it in every pore, vein and bone. Shoving off from the ground, the twosome soared through the faded azure sky. Flapping their wings, they traveled higher, struggling with both fists and wings. The king was more powerful; Kelyn knew that. But he wasn't about to give up so easily.

"How could I even return now?" he asked as he deflected a kick from Malrick. "If what you said about my connection to Matilda being severed is true."

"She trusted you once. But you gave away that trust. It will have to be re-earned."

"I had no idea the cipher bonded us!"

"Oh, yes, you did!"

Malrick swung up his staff, catching Kelyn in the gut. Intense electricity shot through him. His wings ceased flapping and he dropped. As he fell, he saw Matilda fly low, aiming for the portal. The time to enter must be drawing to a close. The kestrel could sense it; he knew that. He needed Valor to go through.

Suddenly Malrick twisted in the air and, from behind, he clasped Kelyn across the chest. He tried to beat his wings, but the Unseelie king held tight. The king chanted foreign words that felt ancient and sacred. Faery language? They seeped into Kelyn's thoughts, softening and…oh, the ache for acceptance. Then, all of a sudden, Malrick released him with a push that sent Kelyn soaring toward the portal.

Malrick called from the sky, "You may return for a visit, son of Rissa! That is all you are welcome to do here in Faery. Be kind to the kestrel. But be patient. She does not trust you now. Begone, the both of you!"

Try as he could to flap his wings, Kelyn couldn't halt his trajectory. Below him Valor raced toward the portal.

Matilda pierced the skein and flew through, followed by the witch, and—it was as if he were being sucked into a vortex.

Kelyn yelled as he was forced from Faery.

Chapter 26

He had to be alive.

After all they had been through, Valor was not going to let it come down to Kelyn dying after he'd finally gotten back the one thing that meant more to him than even her.

Palms pressed to his chest, she couldn't feel it rise and fall. He lay sprawled across the loamy forest floor. Tree roots cradled him on either side. Matilda circled above. Valor sensed the bird's nervous energy. Matilda knew something was wrong with her friend. Or was she still Kelyn's friend? The things Malrick had said about the bird no longer trusting Kelyn were horrible. A simple talisman had bonded the two of them?

Since walking into Faery, Kelyn had betrayed both of their trusts.

Glancing at the wings spread across the ground, Valor

couldn't find excitement for the fact that the darkness had left them. Now violet and silver, they'd returned to their original condition and were no longer tattered. Malrick had done that for Kelyn. The Unseelie king had also been responsible for forcing Kelyn back into this realm.

But to his detriment?

"You are not dead," she stated as a confirmation to the universe. "I will not allow it! You survived nearly drowning. You can survive this! Come back to me, Kelyn."

She laid her ear on his chest and listened and…she heard a heartbeat. Faint and slow, yet it seemed to increase by the second. Spreading her fingers over his bare chest, she closed her eyes and focused her vita toward him. Her palms heated over the violet sigils that tickled at her touch and then they grabbed her and held her there as if by force.

It didn't frighten her. In fact, Valor felt as though Kelyn were drawing on her energy through his sigils. If he could heal himself through her, then more power to him.

Matilda cawed and swooped low, brushing Valor's hair with a wing tip. It hadn't been a warning, but rather a touch of reassurance, so she persisted. Kelyn drew from her in increasing intensity. Her vita flowed out in vibrant violet energy gleaming with iridescent sparkles, and it flowed in through Kelyn's pores, brightening his skin and causing his sigils to glow.

Fingers growing stiff above her lover's chest, Valor's breaths segued to gasps. A moan preceded her dropping beside him onto the forest floor.

Eyes closed, Kelyn came to, knowing that, once again, Valor had brought him back to life. Perhaps this time he wouldn't have died. He'd been knocked unconscious by the shove through the portal and landing on some particularly hard tree roots.

He'd been shoved. Back to a realm…that he could no longer deny was his home.

He'd acted terribly toward Valor in Faery! Tricking her into running off without him. Sacrificing his bond to Matilda. But it had been the wings. They'd been tainted by the demon's blood. A Wicked One. And the seductress. She had been another Wicked One according to Malrick.

He'd had the audacity to defy the Unseelie king. And now he felt regret for all of it. He had been out of his mind, acting like someone else. So he'd deserved that shove. And he was thankful for it now.

But could Valor forgive him? And Matilda? Where was the kestrel? And the witch? He'd drawn on Valor's vita, the rich, warm energy of her being, to surface to consciousness.

Kelyn pushed himself up and away from the tree root. Looking to the side, he found Valor collapsed next to him. He carefully tugged the hair away from her face and bent to press his mouth to her forehead. She was warm and he felt her pulse at her temple. Alive, but weakened by him?

He gently shook her shoulder. "Valor!"

"Huh?"

"Blessed Herne." He bowed his forehead to hers. "I think I took too much from you. I'm sorry."

"No problem." She shook her head, weak, but alive. "You can always take what you need from me. Whew! That did take a lot out of me, though. Might need to sit here a bit and catch my breath." She looked him over, from his face to his chest to his wrists.

All his sigils glowed brightly, at his chest and about his wrists. His wings even sparkled, and he pulled one forward to stroke it and see that the ichor flowed through his veins circulating through the shimmery fabric.

"They're good as new," he offered. "The Unseelie king did this for me. And that would have never happened without you."

She smiled up at him. "You mean so much to me. I know you wanted to stay in Faery, but so many people need you here in this realm."

Kelyn nodded and whispered, "I know that, lover."

"But you were forced back here. You're not here because you want to be."

"I'm going to be okay," he said, hugging her as tightly as she hugged him. "That was the tainted wings talking when we were in Faery. I promise that I want to be here. With you. No one else but you." He tilted down his head to kiss her forehead. "I'm sorry for how I treated you in Faery, Valor. It was…"

"The wings. They were blackened with evil magic. We both know that. But, uh, what's up with kissing some Wicked chick?"

"I chanced across her in the Wilds. I didn't kiss her. I mean, I wanted to. I think she was working some kind of enchantment on me."

Valor shrugged. "It's cool."

"No, it's not. And I didn't kiss her. In fact, she tried to rip out my tongue."

"Probably what I would have done if you had kissed her," she offered nonchalantly.

"I'll never kiss another."

"Really?"

He knelt before her and kissed her, there beneath a beam of perfect moonlight that highlighted them upon the stage of lush moss and loam. Curling his fingers into her hair, Kelyn pulled her closer, wanting to never lose grasp of her again. Or to even think he could survive in a world where she did not exist.

Not only had she helped restore his wings, she had given him back that wild crush for the woman who had fascinated from afar. And now he had her. No woman had ever felt so right in his arms. Or at his mouth. Her soft, lush lips were meant for his. Her breaths bled life into him, and her heartbeat kept his racing.

"Mmm…" She broke the kiss, bowing her forehead to his. "I'd love to continue this, maybe even have sex with you. Right here. Right now."

"Sounds like a plan to me," he said. "We did have plans, if you remember."

"I do. But besides feeling like I've run a marathon, there's the thing about me—a witch—being in this forest."

"Forgot about that."

"I will never forget." She glanced aside to the massive tree trunk, which appeared firmly rooted into the ground, but one never knew. "I think I should skedaddle while the skedaddling is good. But where's Matilda?"

"I…I don't know. I think I've lost her." Kelyn pressed a hand over his chest where it ached to even consider the friendship he had so callously handed over in a greedy grab for his wings.

"You didn't know the cipher connected the two of you like that. Did you?"

"I knew it was a bond between us. It was the first

thing she ever brought me from Faery. I shouldn't have
been so stupid."

"You would never have gotten back your wings."

He bowed his head.

"You'll have to earn back her trust. Give it time.
You are a kind man, Kelyn. Matilda knows that. And
I have to believe you had no other choice to get back
your wings."

"Maybe," he whispered.

He felt Valor shiver mightily and remembered her
urgent need to get out of the Darkwood.

"Right. Matilda, I honor you!" he called out. "And I
will do everything in my power to win back your trust.
Good friend, I thank you for your guidance into Faery.
Please feel my love!"

Somewhere, high above, Matilda cawed. And Kelyn
smiled. She wasn't swooping down for a greeting, but
she had replied. It was a start.

"We'd better leave," he said.

"Sure. But you might have to help me walk out of
here."

"Say no more." Kelyn stood and, still holding her
about the waist, flapped his wings. "You ready for this?"

She laughed and hugged him. "Oh, yeah!"

They soared through the forest and up through a
clearing in the leafy canopy. Clutched against Kelyn's
body, Valor couldn't be afraid of this flight. Instead, she
spread out her arms and laughed with joy as they crested
the treetops and took to the open air. His wings carried
them swiftly through the sky. She'd never once considered flight in anything other than a dreadful airplane.

Why had she waited so long?

"This. Is. Awesome!" she yelled.

Kelyn joined in her joyous laughter and swooped low over the treetops so she could touch the leaves as they passed over. The air brushed her skin and left behind a wondrous shiver, and she left all her worries behind in the Darkwood below.

"Can we do this more often?" she asked as her lover veered toward the big barn in the distance.

"As often as you like. You're the first woman I've ever taken on a flight. You're the only one I've trusted. I love you, Valor."

"I love you!" she shouted.

Clasping her firmly, he rolled them so Valor felt the leaves brush her hips and shoulders, and then they spun upright again, taking the air like birds. Or faeries.

Matilda whisked by them, teasing with a caw that she was faster, and Kelyn laughed and shouted thanks to his friend.

"I'm going to have to start incorporating flight into my air magic," Valor said. "This is amazing!"

"Hold on! We're heading in for a landing."

Banking to the left, Kelyn descended lower and swept down toward the gravel drive. They landed before Blade's barn. The brothers, in their human forms, stood waiting to greet them. They were thrilled to see Kelyn had gotten his wings back.

"That didn't take long at all," Blade commented as Kelyn tucked down his wings. "Less than an hour."

"Less than an hour?" Valor shook her head. "It was more like half a day."

"Faery time," Kelyn said. "You gotta love it. Hey, do either of you guys know anything about Mom and the Unseelie king?"

Stryke whistled and searched the ground as if something near his boots suddenly fascinated him. Blade crossed his arms high over his chest and shrugged.

"You both know something. That's crazy." Kelyn shook his head. "I met him. If he and Mom had a thing…" He didn't want to think about it now. And besides, that had been *before* their dad met Rissa. He hoped.

Valor yawned and Kelyn got the hint. Much as he'd love to tell his brothers about the short but wondrous time he'd had in Faery, he could save it for another day.

"We should go," he said, putting an arm around Valor's shoulders. "We have things to, uh…"

"No explanation necessary," Blade said quickly.

"Yep." Stryke kicked at the stones on the gravel drive. "See you two another day."

Furling his wings back and tucking them away, Kelyn grabbed Valor's hand and they strode to the car.

Chapter 27

Kelyn strolled through the forest behind his house. Valor skipped ahead, dazzled by the moonbeams that seemed to light her path. She didn't even notice the hand-size night moths that flittered by or that the underbrush harbored curious hares, ferrets and smaller animals.

Everything he had lost was now back! He took in the world like a blind and deaf man who had regained those missing senses. He could read the air and earth as he had done since he could remember. It would rain tomorrow, for the humidity combined with the color of the sky told him so. The oak tree to his right had lived for seventy-five years and had many more years ahead. And he knew the elk family that often lingered outside his home was grazing about a quarter mile away, closer to his father's land. The earth seemed to rise beneath him and welcome his every footstep, marking each step he took as familiar.

As well, he felt the ley-line energy. Two such lines crossed ahead at the clearing. Ancient and ever sending out vibrations, the lines hummed in the sigils at his wrists, veering him slightly to the right until he stood directly on top.

Tapping a fingertip against the violet sigil below his left pec, he turned his finger around the circle design, testing his magic. Ahead, the fallen branch that blocked Valor's path lifted into the air and landed in a crop of thick brush.

Valor glanced back at him. He gave her a thumbs-up. Yeah, he had his magic back, too.

The witch turned and raced toward the clearing he'd told her about. No witches disallowed here in this woods; she was as welcome as she was in Kelyn's heart. And, actually, this forest was his heart. Why had he believed that Faery would welcome him with open arms and that he actually belonged there?

Here was home. Standing alongside the most amazing woman he had ever known.

With her long brown-and-violet hair streaming behind her, Valor shouted in awe as the mossy clearing opened before her as if stage curtains were being pulled back to reveal the glorious set. She bent to tug off her boots and tossed them aside, then wandered across the moss as if testing new carpeting.

An emerald hummingbird buzzed up to Kelyn. He nodded. "She's cool. Just excited." The bird fluttered off. He'd sensed its uncertainty, but as quickly as it had left, it returned and hovered around Valor as she stood in the center of the clearing and gazed up toward the tree canopy. Moonlight sparkled on her face, hands and bare feet.

"This rocks," she said as he gained her side. "That bird is so cute! I never see hummingbirds. Wow."

Orbiting her a few times, the bird then zipped away toward the tree canopy, its wings flashing in emerald winks.

Each footstep across the moss released fresh and verdant perfume. Combined with the dry oak and pine resin, and the subtle sage that wisped in Valor's hair, the night smelled abundant and welcoming. Kelyn bracketed his lover's face. Excitement lived in her deep brown irises. And trust. Yes, he was thankful that the Unseelie king had forced him back here to the mortal realm. How he would have missed staring into her eyes had he remained in Faery.

"You are so beautiful, Valor. Breathtaking," he said. "I'm glad I gave my wings away for you. And I'm glad I trusted you enough to work with you to get the spell ingredients. And I'm glad that you fell in love with me. I love you."

He kissed her, deeply, abidingly. Every sigh, laugh and tear she put out he wanted to be there to receive it, enjoy it, wrap his arms around her and be the man she needed him to be. A man who did, indeed, see her as a real woman, not one of the guys.

Her fingers glided down his bare chest to his waistband. She unbuttoned his jeans, which alleviated the pressure on his erection. They both knew the reason for coming out here tonight. There was nothing more either wanted right now than to make love. Faery-style.

He pulled off her T-shirt and bent to kiss each breast. How her body undulated to meet his kisses, to show him how good his touches felt to her. And her moans spoke a language of passion.

"This moss is cushy and thick," she said. "Almost like a bed, if you get my hint. Oh, don't stop that. I like it when you do that."

He put an arm behind her back and pulled her close as he sucked in her nipple through tight lips. She squirmed sweetly. Using his free hand, he pushed down her leggings and she wiggled them off. She attempted to push down his jeans, but his hard-on prevented it from being a smooth action, so he stopped what he was doing and shoved them down.

"Wait!" Valor said as he aimed for her breasts again.

He stepped back, spreading out his hands in question. How the moonlight danced over her pale skin! It was almost as if she were coated with faery dust, it was so soft and magical.

"Wings out, lover boy. I came here for the big reveal."

"This isn't big enough for you?" He shook his hips to waggle his cock.

"Oh, it is. I'm talking wings, faery."

"You've already seen them."

"Oh." She crossed her arms over those delicious breasts. "Fine. I guess you don't want me to touch them. You don't want me to run my tongue all over them, either? Suit yourself."

The witch didn't actually think she could stand there, naked, and expect him to pass on such an intriguing challenge?

"I'll bring them out for a kiss," he coaxed, wanting to play the teasing moment out longer.

She shrugged. "Seems like me touching your wings

is an advantage for you. So I should be the one getting something for that. Yes?"

Her logic was…almost there. And the little quirk of smile at the end of her statement made him wish it had ended with her snorting laughter. Man, he loved her laugh. He'd get it out of her before the night was through.

Bending and falling to his knees on the soft moss, Kelyn kissed her belly and glided his fingers over her skin. Up, toward her breasts, where he lightly brushed her nipples and stirred a wanting gasp from her. Her long hair swung over his knuckles and he swept it purposely across her breast.

Then he kissed her mons, tickling his tongue within the soft nest that topped her sex. She wobbled a bit, but he caught her hip with a sure hand.

"You want to stand for this?" he asked and gave her hip a little shove with two fingers.

She toppled backward, and as her feet gave out, he tapped the sigil at his hip, which activated his air magic. A sweep of wind caught Valor and gently cradled her to lay her on the moss.

"You trying to show me up?" she asked.

"Admit it. That was impressive."

"Eh."

He blew out a mock-frustrated breath. "You are one hard woman to please. Guess I'll have to go deeper."

He bowed over her and moved his tongue along her sage-scented folds, and with his fingers traced her salty wetness. She spread her legs, inviting him in. With a leisurely sigh, she splayed her arms up over her head and wiggled her hips. Settling in.

He knew she loved it when he tongued her clit quickly, so this time he worked slowly, tasting all of her in long sweeps, then using more abbreviated yet intense pressure, memorizing her tiny whimpers and noting each specific tilt of hip or tense of thigh muscle as his tongue mastered her breaths.

If all he had to do for the rest of his life was make Valor happy, sign him up for the long haul. He'd never tire of her moans, her giggles and that awful yet strangely sexy snorting laughter.

"I love you," he said. A kiss to her thigh and then a deep tongue kiss to her clit. Pushing two fingers inside her, he curled them forward.

"Oh, yes," she growled.

A good clue she was ready to come. He made all his touches more focused, intense and so slow...

With a shout and a clutch at the moss by her hip, Valor orgasmed, her mons thrusting against his hand until she shivered and settled into the wild carpet with a gasp and a sigh.

Overhead the hummingbird flittered. And a family of chipmunks watched from within a fallen log. Kelyn smirked at that. They had an audience.

"Again?" he asked and licked her swollen clit.

"Give me a few minutes to catch my breath. And quit stalling! Let out your wings, lover. I want to see them." She sat up, tugging up his head by his hair as she did so. "Time for me to show you how much I love you."

He was good with that. "You ready for this?"

She nodded, her grin curling into a wickedly gleeful giggle.

Kelyn stood, pulling her up with him. He stepped back and tilted his head to catch the moonlight on his eyelids, cheeks and mouth. He could feel *la luna*'s cool presence shimmer in his veins. And his sigils hummed with recognition of the immense power he gained standing there. Spreading out his arms, he took a moment to honor the moon and this forest and his home. This was the only place he'd ever existed and held in his heart.

And now his heart had made room for the witch.

As he willed his wings out, they materialized in a sparkle of dust and unfurled behind him. He extended them as if stretching his arms, and it felt so good. The air whispered across the satiny-sheer wing fabric, and the bone-like cartilage that stretched along the tops of the four sections tightened until the wings were taut and at their full spread.

Valor whispered a soft, "Wow. I like those much better when they are not black. They fit you so well. You are like a regal forest prince. Goddess, you're my hero."

The admiration that seemed to surprise her rippled over his skin like a warm tongue teasing up his pleasure. He held out a hand to her and she took it, but didn't step before him. Instead, she dropped his hand and walked around behind him. He had never allowed a woman to touch his wings. Never had had the reason or chance to reveal himself so completely until now. So he was as curious and excited as Valor seemed to be.

"I wish you could see how the moonlight looks on them," she said. "It's like liquid stardust. I think I can even see the ichor moving through the veins. So cool!"

She hadn't touched them yet, and Kelyn shrugged. He never felt his wings at his back, just as a man did not feel his arms on his body. They were appendages that worked without needing command and were as airy and light as his very bones.

He would allow Valor her curious fascination. He trusted her completely. With her, all his secrets were safe. And even the not-so-secret stuff he wanted to share with her. Always.

The first touch of her finger to the top of one of his uppermost wings sent a shiver through that wing and tingled at the point where it met his back. Kind of like wind brushing his nipples. She trailed her palm along the top of it, drawing it to the curved end, which was at least five or six feet long. Between both hands she pressed the end of his wing, and then he felt her lips against the sheer, delicate fabric.

Kelyn shivered. Now, that felt amazing. Almost as if she had touched her mouth to his cock. Wow! He'd never anticipated that such a simple touch could make him feel that sensation. As he felt her fingers move inward toward his spine, he curled back his wings, for he could move them much like arms, and touched the ends of them over her hair and arms and legs. His wings were so sensitive he could determine where and what on her he touched. Even a flutter of her eyelashes!

"That tickles a little," she whispered, then blew on one of his lower wings. "How do you like that?"

"Oh, yeah." That breath moved over all his skin and landed right at his core. And with each breath that followed, he moved closer to the edge. His toes dug into the moss. His hands, he didn't know what to do with, so he put them at his hips, then, no—that didn't feel right, so he... Ah, hell. He stretched out his arms, grasping nothing but air. This was awesome.

He wasn't sure what she was doing, but now it seemed as if more of her body touched his wings. So he curled them back and wrapped them about her waist and chest, and she moaned as he knew that sensation was her nipples gliding across the sheerness.

But when she turned and pressed a palm against the base where his four wings met his body, perhaps to steady herself, Kelyn lost it. The pressure building in his cock released and he came. Just like that. Body shuddering, and muscles tensing and relaxing, he grasped at the air and hissed a sweet cry. Dust sprinkled out from his pores, falling gently to the moss.

Valor twisted under his wings and walked around before him. Her eyelids glittered with dust and some glinted on her lips. She kissed him even as he gasped in elation. Crushing his body against hers, he drew his wings forward and around his shoulders to wrap her tightly against him. She wrapped her legs about his hips. And the kiss did not end, nor did the second orgasm that swiftly followed.

And not wanting her to miss out on all the fun, he found her wet clitoris with his fingers, gently easing over the sensitive flesh. But a few dashes coaxed her to surrender.

There beneath the moonlight, the two of them had wing sex. The night air coruscated with dust. And all the creatures hidden in the shadows chirped or cawed or even bellowed in an approving chorus. And Valor and Kelyn would never again be the same.

Later, they both lay on the moss, bodies panting and skin glinting. Kelyn spied the shadow fly overhead and followed it as Matilda circled.

"See?" he asked quietly, and sensed Valor stir from what had been a reverie.

"Matilda. Oh, she dropped something—I caught it!" Valor lifted her hand, which held a leather strap, and turned to her side to show Kelyn.

It was the cipher that had bonded them. Matilda had

dropped it to land specifically on Valor's hand. Had she returned to Faery to steal it back from the demon?

"It's yours," she said, offering it to him.

"No, you keep it for now. She wanted you to have it. She approves of you. I want to deserve her trust. And I will. String it next to the moonstone so every time I see you I'll know Matilda is not far away."

Valor kissed him and tucked her head against his shoulder.

When they returned to Kelyn's cabin, Valor suggested they drive to her place. She wanted to shower, change clothes and check on Mooshi. Twenty minutes later, he joined her in the shower at her place. Mooshi sat on the closed toilet seat waiting for them to come out.

"That cat doesn't like me very much," Kelyn said as he dried himself off.

"He is cautiously optimistic of you."

Kelyn lifted a brow at that one. "Sure. Whatever you say." He glanced at the cat, who eyed him and revealed a fang with a lift of its furry lip. So much judgment in that tiny movement. "It's still early," he said, leaving the bathroom as quickly as he could to avoid a possible cat attack. "Only eleven. You want to do something?"

"Like what?" Valor teased at his nipple with her fingernail. "More sex?"

"I actually don't want to do anything that will make Mooshi uncomfortable. I was thinking…dancing."

"Yeah?" She kissed him quickly. "Yes! Let's do it."

"There's this place I want to take you to." He raked his fingers through his hair. "It's a faery nightclub Up North."

"Really? Cool. But Up North? That's like a three- or

four-hour drive. The place will be closed by the time we get there."

He waggled his brows. "Not if we fly."

She thought about it a few seconds, then thrust a victorious fist above her head. "Let's go dance our booties off! But I can't wear that." She glanced to the piled heap of clothes that she'd worn to venture into Faery.

"Find something that makes you happy. I'm good with jeans and a shirt."

Valor sorted through her clothes rack with the glee of a girl who had gotten invited to the prom by her secret crush. Only it wasn't a secret anymore. And the guy had told her he loved her. And he meant it. She knew that he meant it because he loved her stupid laugh and he'd showed her himself with his wings out and had allowed her to touch them. Never had she felt more like a woman in those moments when they made love on the moss beneath the moonlight.

Kelyn saw her for the woman she was. The man was her hero.

She pulled out a particularly bright blue spangled minidress that she had borrowed from Mireio years ago and hugged it to her chest. She could do the sexy when she wanted to. And her man deserved it. But would it look as good during flight?

She thought about soaring over the treetops for miles, hundreds of miles, in the spangled dress. "Yeah, it'll rock."

Five minutes later she wobbled into the kitchen and Kelyn turned with a big smile on his face. The guy looked amazing, his hair always tousled and emphasizing his gorgeous bone structure. He wore the same T-shirt he'd worn into the forest, but it was still clean and the dark jeans hung low on his hips. Sex personified.

"You look…" His eyes dropped to her feet, and she turned out one foot in display. "Uncomfortable. Amazing. But…not right."

"Ah, come on. I actually like this dress. Makes me feel sexy."

"The dress is dazzling. I love it on you. Goes with the faery dust sparkling in your hair. And these are the best of both of us." He tapped the moonstone and cipher that dangled before her breasts. "But the shoes?"

"I'm trying to do the sexy."

"And you do it well. But five-inch heels are not *my* kind of sexy. I prefer the combat boots."

"You do?" Her heart thudded in relief as she clasped her hands before her and spread her legs to manage her balance. "You're saying that because you don't want me to fall and break my neck in these things."

"There is that." He glided his hand up along her neck, sending delicious shivers over her skin. "I like the boots. Valor, you were right. You're not a real girl."

She wasn't sure where he was headed with that statement, but her giddy heartbeat took pause.

"You are a strong, confident, gorgeous, real—" he kissed her "—woman. And you're mine."

"You mean it?"

"That you're a woman or that you're mine? Both. Now get rid of the stupid shoes and put on some dancing gear."

The flight Up North was a dream. The night was warm and the sky fluffed with clouds, which they flew well below. They remained as close to the treetops as possible to avoid a late-night driver picking out the large unknown flying object in the sky.

Valor kept her arms spread out most of the journey, eyes to the moon and cheeks kissed by the brisk sky. Kelyn held her firmly against his chest, but when at one point he grasped only her hand and flew out at her side, she couldn't believe it was actually happening. She was flying! With the man she loved.

It took less than an hour of flight to land before the secret club plopped in the center of a dense forest. Pine sap and cicada song filled the night. Kelyn said it was another thin place, but not specifically Faery—it also served Daemonia—so she would be welcome there, as were any and all. So long as they were not human.

The three-story gray brick mansion sported black-tiled turrets at two corners. Light from inside flashed out from the high turrets, turning them into neon light-houses. Entry was gained with a fist bump from Kelyn to the slender bouncer with long pink hair, green eyes and six arms. Fortunately, she only lifted one fist so Kelyn didn't have to figure which to meet with his knuckles.

Valor followed eagerly, taking in the bright walls, which seemed to undulate and glow in neon. The floor beneath her boots was lit in squares of pink and violet, and littered with faery dust, confetti and spills of iri-descent drinks. Scents of alcohol, candy, earth and the ocean filled the gigantic ballroom. Splashed in neon and dazzled with faery dust, the people undulating, bounc-ing and dancing were stunning.

The faeries were an easy call for Valor. Most had vio-let eyes, wild hair colors and clothing that barely covered their skin. Their multishaded—and colored—skin glit-tered with dust. Demons sported red eyes and dressed a little darker, though not all of them. A horned woman with an undulating spotted tail had a reason to show off her steel abs and high breasts. Valor had never seen blue areolae on a woman before. Fascinating.

A few sets of eyes glowed as Kelyn led her through the melee and toward the center of the dance floor. A sniff of faery dust signaled to Valor that she'd probably get high from this experience. Awesome!

Her lover danced away from her, but not too far, finding the beat in his bones and swaying his hips in time with another dancer who Valor wasn't sure was male, or female, or perhaps both. Chrome scales moist with perspiration grew along the dancer's hairline, and down its neck and most of the exposed skin that was covered by a simple black sheath.

It was a different crowd from the folks the Decadent Dames served. And standing amid the crazy wildness made Valor shout in joy and end with snorting laughter.

"This rocks so hard!" she shouted over the noise.

Kelyn's wings swayed in time with the beat as he bounced up to her and, taking her by the fingers, twirled her like a ballet dancer. He spun her up to him and grasped her tightly across the back, bowing to kiss her even as he dipped her beneath a fall of iridescent faery dust.

"I love you, witch!"

"I love you, wings and all!"

Wings, witchery…and combat boots. It would keep them together for a long and wondrous time.

* * * * *

LET'S TALK
Romance

For exclusive extracts, competitions
and special offers, find us online:

f MillsandBoon

𝕏 @MillsandBoon

⊙ @MillsandBoonUK

♪ @MillsandBoonUK

Get in touch on 01413 063 232

MILLS & BOON

THE HEART OF ROMANCE

A ROMANCE FOR EVERY READER

MODERN
Prepare to be swept off your feet by sophisticated, sexy and seductive heroes, in some of the world's most glamourous and romantic locations, where power and passion collide.

HISTORICAL
Escape with historical heroes from time gone by. Whether your passion is for wicked Regency Rakes, muscled Vikings or rugged Highlanders, awaken the romance of the past.

MEDICAL
Set your pulse racing with dedicated, delectable doctors in the high-pressure world of medicine, where emotions run high and passion, comfort and love are the best medicine.

True Love
Celebrate true love with tender stories of heartfelt romance, from the rush of falling in love to the joy a new baby can bring, and a focus on the emotional heart of a relationship.

Desire
Indulge in secrets and scandal, intense drama and sizzling hot action with heroes who have it all: wealth, status, good looks…everything but the right woman.

HEROES
The excitement of a gripping thriller, with intense romance at its heart. Resourceful, true-to-life women and strong, fearless men face danger and desire - a killer combination!

To see which titles are coming soon, please visit

millsandboon.co.uk/nextmonth